ASSASSIN'S
HEART

SARAH AHIERS

HARPERTEEN
an imprint of HarperCollinsPublishers

HarperTeen is an imprint of HarperCollins Publishers.

Assassin's Heart
Copyright © 2016 by Sarah Ahiers
www.epicreads.com

Library of Congress Control Number: 2015943574
ISBN 978-0-06-236378-7

Typography by Kate Engbring
15 16 17 18 19 RRDH 10 9 8 7 6 5 4 3 2 1
❖
First Edition

For Anne

Who pushed me, even when I pushed back

one

†

I SQUATTED QUIETLY ON THE SLOPED, TILE ROOF OF A bordello, cloak pulled around my body for warmth, bone mask secured against my face. Below me, a man stumbled across the flagstone street like a drunkard. It had taken him long enough to finish his overpriced dinner.

The man bumped into a water barrel. He removed his expensive leather hat with its elegant stitches and dunked his head into the barrel. The rainwater darkened his silk collar. I scowled beneath my mask. He shouldn't treat his silk so poorly. The man shook his hair like a shaggy dog, the water flashing in the light of the sweet-smelling oil lanterns outside the bordello.

Below, passersby took a single look at the man and veered away, pretending not to see him or his altered state. Good. My job was always easier when everyone followed the unspoken rules of the night.

Behind me, the light from the full moon dimmed. Even though it lasted less than a second, hardly noticeable to most people, my life could depend on noticing the details of my surroundings.

Someone was trying to get close to me. It was all the warning I needed.

Beneath my cloak, I freed a dagger small enough to be concealed in my palm and sleeve. I needed to be steady and calm. Panic was for amateurs and led to injury or death.

I inhaled deeply, shifting my weight from heels to toes. My fingers tightened around my knife.

A single second could be the difference between life and death. I knew better than to hesitate. I sprang backward and twisted toward the creeping figure.

I took in everything I could with my first glimpse of the attacker: a man, tall, dark cloak, dark leathers, bone mask blank of features except for eyeholes.

He dodged left, his cloak flaring wide with his movement, defensively camouflaging his shape. A trick that would work better if he'd been faster. I'd already seen his torso, his limbs, his head. The cloak wouldn't distract me.

I slid a foot behind his ankle, hooking his leg. My fists met his chest and I shoved.

He fell to the roof. Only my quick grasp of his cloak prevented him from thumping against the tiles. A fight it may've been, but neither of us wanted to draw attention. That would've been unprofessional.

His hazel eyes watched me, expression unreadable beneath

his mask. The right half was the white ivory of the bone, the left decorated with dyed red squares in a checkered pattern.

I held the knife to his throat, the sharp edge pressed against the rough hairs on his skin. Someone needed to shave.

There was a moment of quiet stillness as he thought over his next move. The excitement of the fight coursed through my veins. I smiled beneath my mask. I'd already won.

"I yield, Lea." He held up his hands in defeat, his voice muffled behind the mask.

I slipped my knife into a pocket on my sleeve and offered Val my hand. It took all my weight to pull him to his feet.

"How do you always know?" He brushed dust off his legs and flicked a leaf from his cloak.

"You blocked out the moon again."

He pushed his hood off his head and the moonlight turned his short blond hair silver. I tried not to stare, even though his leathers wrapped tightly around him, straps clinging to his arms, buckles firmly gripping his chest and body, highlighting his muscles, which I knew, like mine, came from working hard almost every night.

Of course, it wasn't just the leathers that made him look good. No one could say Valentino Da Via was not attractive as hells.

"You should know better than to try to sneak up on me," I said.

"One of these days I'll surprise you."

His face was covered by his mask, but I could picture the smirk on his lips, the playful challenge in his raised brow.

I laughed. "One of these days I may let you."

I returned to my surveillance of my mark. The man had moved only a few steps from the barrel, arm against a wall as he caught his breath.

Val took a casual seat beside me, left leg tucked beneath him, the other bent at the knee against his chest. Unprepared and lazy.

I nudged him with my shoulder but said nothing. He hated it when I corrected him.

I could smell the oil he'd used to clean his leathers. His body heat pressed against mine, and warmth, with a thrill of something like lightning, spread through my chest.

"Have an early night?" I asked. A robed woman emerged from the door beneath us and shouted at the man before she returned inside. He had to know he was a spectacle if a prostitute took time to scold him.

Val shrugged. "No night, really. My mark didn't show. Either got wind someone put a contract on him, or he got lucky."

"Luck doesn't last forever," I quoted the familiar assassin motto.

Val grunted. "I'll get him tomorrow night, or the next. I'm patient."

It was easy being patient when he didn't need the money a completed kill would bring. But it wasn't Val's fault he was rich, or that my Family wasn't anymore.

Val leaned closer to me, his thigh pressed against mine. A moment later his hand followed, fingers resting on the leather-clad skin of my leg. And though I couldn't feel the circles his fingers traced, I still shivered beneath his touch.

I pulled away, every bit of me protesting.

"I'm working," I whispered, but it sounded weak even to me. "And someone could see us." That sounded even weaker. Our relationship was a secret, and the thrill of keeping ourselves hidden was half the fun.

Val chuckled. My chest tingled again, but he kept his hands to himself.

I took a slow, quiet breath.

The man below took a step, another, and then he stumbled again. I watched him closely. I was responsible for him now. He belonged to me. He wavered again, before steadying himself against the wall.

"That your mark?" Val asked.

I nodded and reached to the back of my belt for my small water skin.

"He doesn't look like much. Did he anger someone?"

"No. Personal request. Has an illness or something and wants our help to lead him to Safraella a little early." I pressed the warm metal nozzle against my lips.

Val nodded. Sometimes people paid clippers to help them commit suicide. These were always the simplest jobs. But even with a suicide request, I remained professional. It kept my skills honed if I treated every mark like they might flee or fight.

"How long are you going to watch him before you make a move?"

I swallowed the water and returned the skin to my belt. "I already did. He just doesn't realize it yet."

The man staggered a few steps into the street. I held my breath. He collapsed. Easy. Not that they always were. I cleared my throat. But it was a god's work I performed, and no one ever said Her favor came easily.

Val shook his head. "You and your poisons. When did you get him?"

"After his dinner. He always buys a wineskin from the same vendor. Wasn't hard to make sure he got one laced with something extra."

"Nice. Though I'd choose a knife in the back any day."

I nudged him again. "Be careful what you wish for in the dark, no?"

A stranger approached my mark, stared at him, then glanced around before walking away. Good man.

I stood. Val silently dropped off the roof and into a darkened alley to wait for me while I finished. No need for anyone to start a rumor about the Da Vias and Saldanas working together.

I climbed down and approached my mark. The streetlights spilled over my dark cloak. No one would bother me when I was about my work. No one would dare. Not if they valued their lives.

I hummed a song under my breath, a nursery rhyme my nursemaid used to sing to me when I was young. It was a silly little thing about falling asleep and feeling safe and warm. I'd hummed it once when I was marking my first solo kill, and the habit had stuck. It seemed right. Maybe someone would sing to me at the end of my life.

I checked the man's pulse. Quiet and still. The poison I'd used was painless. Hopefully he'd soon stand before our goddess Safraella, and She would quickly grant him a brand-new life where he'd feel safe and warm once more.

Behind me, the door to the bordello opened, pouring more light onto the street. "You there," a woman shouted. "Boy, get away from that man."

I glanced over my shoulder.

"Didn't you hear me?" The woman stepped from the doorway, her colorful skirts reflecting brightly against the lights. Her face was bare, her feather half-mask put aside now that her nightly duties were done. "Shoo! Go on before you get yourself in real trouble."

I stood and faced her.

She took one look at my mask, the right half bone white, the left half decorated in black flowers, and her painted face lost all color. She took a step away. "Clipper!" She clasped her hands together and held them to her face as she bowed her head. "I'm sorry, Mistress Saldana, I'm sorry." She backed away. "I didn't recognize you. I thought you a child trying to rob the dead."

A boy. I wasn't tall, even at seventeen, but I was certainly bigger than a child. And no child would run around wearing a dark cloak at night, unless they wanted to impersonate a clipper, and that was illegal. And a death sentence if a member of the Families caught them.

No harm done, though. I dismissed the woman with a flick of my wrist. She bowed in gratitude and slid inside. The door closed with a click.

I returned to my mark.

The street seemed to heave below me.

It lasted barely a breath. Maybe just a bit of dizziness from turning too quickly, or the colorful lights of the brothel confusing my eyes. And if I were any other person, any other clipper even, I would've shrugged it off.

But I wasn't.

I brought my fingers to my throat and felt my pulse, counting the beats. A touch fast.

I closed my eyes, quieting my thoughts, trying to listen to the messages of my body. Maybe I was being too paranoid.

My stomach rolled violently, like a snake coiling around its own tail. I shoved my mask to the top of my head and barely managed to stumble to the alley before I vomited.

My skin burned. This wasn't a normal sickness. No, this was something much worse. I quickly recalled my evening. The water skin. Which meant it was fast acting. Vomiting followed immediately by pain.

Could be three possibilities.

"Lea?" Val dashed over.

I sat on the ground, my spine pressed against a building, and tried to catch my breath. Wait—breathlessness left only two possibilities.

"What is it?" Val dropped, ignoring the puddle soaking his knees as he knelt before me. He reached out, then paused, his hands floating over my arms, unsure what to do. His wide eyes appeared white behind his mask.

My cloak bunched around me. I struggled against it, my hands shaking to reach a pouch on my belt. Limb weakness. That ruled out all but one. No time left.

I batted the cloak. Val sprang to action, jerking the cloak away from my hands and body. My stomach rolled again.

"Poison." I gasped at the pain blazing across my skin and through my flesh. "I've been poisoned."

two

'GODS, LEA!' VAL PUSHED HIS MASK TO THE TOP OF HIS head. Worry and panic etched lines across his face.

Free of the cloak, I unbuttoned a pouch on my belt. It held nearly a dozen vials, each tightly stoppered with a scored cork. I ran my trembling fingers across the symbols known only to me, searching for the right one. My heart raced faster and faster.

My finger traced a loop with a line through it. The antidote. I yanked it from the pouch. My hand shook. The vial tumbled from my grip. The glass clinked against the stone street before it rolled away into the shadows.

Tears squeezed from my eyes. I didn't want to die like this.

The poison raced through my organs. It would attack my stomach, my heart, my brain. Once the full seizures started, no antidote would save me.

I groaned, reaching into the darkness. The poison turned my body against me. My arms jerked like a wounded seabird.

Val pushed me aside, his hands struggling against mine. The scrape of the vial as he snatched it from the street was the most beautiful sound I'd ever heard. He jerked the stopper out with his teeth and pulled out a dagger with his free hand.

"In your mouth or in your veins?" He clutched the open glass and the dagger in his gloved fingers, waiting for my answer. My voice emerged as a groan.

"Lea!" he shouted. "Which one?"

The poison rushed through my body. My head slammed the brick wall behind me. I opened my mouth as wide as I could, hoping he'd understand.

Val brought the vial to my lips, his other hand restraining my head. The liquid poured into my mouth, tepid and sharp. It tasted terrible, like soap soaked in urine.

Val clutched my hands, keeping them still. He took deep breaths and watched me closely, his eyes wide, his mouth tight, lines of worry creased in his forehead as he waited to see if I would die.

My breaths came easier and my heart slowed its racing pace. The pain in my stomach faded. I took a deep breath and Val sagged in relief.

"Gods." He looked at the street before he reached for his mask. His fingers trembled as he pulled it down. He'd hidden his fear, and any other emotion he didn't want me to see. These were the things I loved about him, knowing he cared so much that he couldn't hide it from his face, that he needed the mask to hide it for him. That he'd been scared, yes, but had reacted calmly. He had kept himself under control when I'd needed him.

"It's fine." I exhaled. "She knew I had the antidote."

"She?" He stood. "Your *mother* did this?"

I waved a shaky hand at him. "She's been testing me on poisons again. I should have expected this."

When I was seven, I told my mother I hated poisons. Poisons meant distilling herbs in darkness, meant mixing things but not making a mess. Poisons meant death.

My oldest brother, Rafeo, said poisons were an important skill and that I should be proud I had such an affinity for them, because many did not.

He was only trying to make peace, but I didn't feel pride over poisons. I was proud of the feathered mask I'd sewn for Susten Day and how I'd only pricked my finger on the needle once. And that the wooden horse I'd carved had a flowing mane.

Mother had not been happy. My attitude was more proof I wasn't the daughter she wanted, that I wasn't the proud Saldana girl-child she felt she deserved.

Mother took the mask away.

After that, I stopped playing with embroidery needles, costumes, and childish toys, and instead focused on things that made *her* proud: knives and poisons and masks crafted from bone.

I unhooked my water skin and poured the tainted liquid onto the street. I'd be filling my own water from here on. Lesson learned, Mother. Again.

My hands wobbled as I restrung my water skin. Maybe next time she'd pick something less violent. Or maybe I could convince her now that I didn't need a next time. I could find an antidote under pressure. Even if I'd almost died this time, and would have without Val.

"That's crazy," Val said. "Your Family is crazy."

"It's not any crazier than yours. It's her way of making me a better clipper. Also, in the future, you shouldn't open vials with your teeth. You could accidentally poison yourself."

He stared at me, expression unreadable behind his mask. "That's what you got out of this? That I could have poisoned myself while saving your life?"

His bravado would've been worthless if he'd died. "I'm just looking out for you."

He exhaled, the air hissing against his mask. "Fine. Is there anything else I can do for you?"

His anger rolled off him like steam, but I'd learned long ago the best way to disarm Val's anger was to ignore it.

"Yes, actually." I slowly shifted my seat and pulled a gold coin from another pocket. I handed it to him, my entire arm still shaking from the remnants of the poison. "Mark my kill for me, please."

The coin had been stamped with the crest of the Saldana Family. Murder was illegal in Lovero, unless one was a member of a Family. As disciples of Safraella, pledged to Her dark work, all clippers were exempt and could accept assassination contracts.

"You know Estella doesn't want us marking kills," Val said.

It had always been a tradition for the Families to mark their kills. But two years ago my aunt and uncle, our Family priest, and Rafeo's wife had died in a plague outbreak. Only by Safraella's grace had we all not caught the contagion.

The head of Val's Family died in the plague, too, along with other Da Vias, and afterward Estella Da Via had taken over and told the Da Vias to stop marking kills. She thought it was an antiquated way of worship and that the murder was enough.

My mother thought Estella was just a miser and wanted to keep the gold in their Family. Luckily, even though the Da Vias had the most money and members, no one wanted to see them as the first Family. The Saldanas tried to keep the entirety of the nine Families in mind when making decisions. The Da Vias cared only about themselves.

"I'm not asking you to mark *your* kill. I'm asking you to mark mine." I paused to catch my breath. "For me. Surely your Family head won't begrudge you that."

"My aunt makes her own rules for the Family."

"You asked if you could help. Never mind. I'll do it." I pushed against the wall, trying to get to my feet. My legs wobbled, and only my grip on the stonework kept me upright.

"Lea, don't." Val gripped my arm. I clutched his shoulders and slid my fingers down his biceps as he lowered me back to the ground. "I'll do it. Just don't hurt yourself."

I nodded, and he walked to the body in the street. Val knelt over him, then opened the man's mouth and slipped the coin onto his tongue. The coin would act as a balm and prevent the man from becoming an angry ghost, because it signaled that the person deserved a quick rebirth. Instead of wandering the dead plains, Safraella, goddess of death, murder, and resurrection, patron of Lovero, would see the offering and grant him a faster return to a new life. A better life.

Val returned to the alley. He pulled me to my feet and I remained still, making sure I'd fully regained my balance.

"You should mark your own kills." I tested my weight on one foot. "It's close to blasphemy that you don't, and my father plans to bring down an order that all nine Families must mark their kills." The Saldanas as the first Family held the most power over the nine Families. Rank was decided by wealth, numbers, territory, and other factors that contributed to status. Once the Saldanas had been more numerous and rich, but ever since the plague, Father worried the other Families would force a vote for a new first Family. If enough of the Families voted against us, we could lose our position.

"I do whatever Estella tells us to do," Val said. "You have a choice in how you relate to your father as the head of your Family, because even if he didn't love you, he can't afford to lose you. I'm pretty sure Estella hates everyone except the face she sees in the mirror."

"Still, it's not right, Val."

"A lot of things aren't right since the plague, Lea. A lot of things." He looked away from me.

Val's parents had both succumbed to the plague. It was

what had brought us together, sharing grief over our dead. After that, he'd courted me, in secret of course, because no one could know about us, that rivals were involved romantically. And I let him.

I often wondered what Val missed more, his mother and father, even though they surely had been granted happy, new lives, or the way things had been for the Da Vias before Estella took charge.

"I can't break away from the Family in this, Lea." Val lowered his voice. "I can't break from the Family in anything."

I didn't respond. We were clippers. We all served Safraella faithfully. But this wasn't the first time I was reminded that Val and I lived in different worlds.

Yes, my mother had tried to kill me again tonight. But she'd done it to make me a better clipper. In her own, twisted way she was protecting me by making me stronger. If Val's Family ever tried to kill him, they'd make sure he wouldn't have an antidote.

three

"ARE YOU DONE FOR THE NIGHT?" VAL ASKED. "ARE YOU hungry?"

We headed deeper into the alley, leaving the body in the street for the cleaners to remove. When they saw the coin in his mouth, they could record which Family had been responsible and notify relatives if the body was identified.

"After a job? Always. And I'm going to need some food to help fight off the remains of the poison."

"Get changed and I'll meet you outside Fabricio's."

I sighed. "Again?"

"We could go to Luca instead."

"Why can't we go someplace your Family doesn't own? It's so risky."

No one knew about us. No one *could* know about us. Not his Family. Not mine. And not any of the other Families, either, though the city of Ravenna belonged to the Da Vias and the Saldanas and none of the others would dare trespass without permission.

He shrugged. "Any restaurant would be a risk, Lea. At least at Fabricio's or Luca we eat for free and we know the staff keep their mouths shut."

I rolled my eyes but didn't push the point. The staff *did* keep quiet.

I tugged my cloak into place. "Fifteen minutes?"

He stretched his arms. "Ten."

I laughed. So damn competitive. Of course, I couldn't stop my muscles twitching at the challenge, even if they were still sore.

He turned, but I snagged his hand at the last second. "Val. Thank you for being here, when I needed you."

His eyes softened behind his mask. He nodded and squeezed my fingers before releasing me.

"Wait, one last thing."

He groaned and faced me again.

I handed him a push dagger, a small knife that fit between the knuckles. "I think this is yours."

He stared at the dagger, and then his eyes drifted up to mine. "When the hells did you lift that from me?"

I shrugged. "When you were helping me to the ground."

"After you'd almost died from being poisoned?"

"Yes."

He blinked a few more times, a sure sign he was organizing his thoughts. Val and I had an ongoing competition of lifting objects from each other, unnoticed. He was much better at it than me, so when opportunities came to catch him off guard, I took them, even if it was a little unfair using my poisoning to my advantage.

Val shook his head and laughed. "All right. You're one up on me."

I snatched his hand and pulled him against me, his body strong and solid. I tapped his mask where his lips would be. "Never underestimate me."

He grabbed my shoulders and pulled me against him even tighter. We were so close I could almost feel his heart beating through his leathers as they creaked, could almost smell his skin. His warmth leaked into me, and I clutched his arms to remain steady.

"I never do." He released me and sprinted away.

The race was on.

I climbed to the roof of the bordello. If Val beat me to Fabricio's, he'd lord it over me the whole dinner.

I raced over the rooftops of the city of Ravenna, gaining speed, sliding across tiles. If anyone saw my movement, they would attribute it to their imagination, or perhaps the wine in their skins. Or, if they were smart, they would attribute it a member of the nine Families, and they would turn away. It was said that to lay eyes upon a clipper while they were about their bloody business invited death. We didn't go out of our way to disprove the story. Fear made our jobs easier.

I reached a single-story building, dark behind its locked door. An art dealer, and the shop did indeed sell portraits, beautiful oil paintings with thin brushstrokes.

A hidden latch on the roof of the shop opened a secret

door. I dropped inside.

There were many such shops within the Ravenna city limits, all hidden storage points for the Saldana Family. There were safe houses for the Da Vias too, though I'd never seen one.

They were a closely guarded secret.

Most were simple places where one could change from leathers into something more appropriate, say, for meeting one's secret suitor for dinner. A few contained hidden entrances into a Family's home, the place where we lived, where we dined together and slept and were tutored as children. Our literal home. If a Family found another's Family home, there would be trouble.

Generations ago there had been twelve Families. Two of the three lost Families had been destroyed when another Family discovered their home. The current king, as a disciple of Safraella, had no authority over the Families and their relationships with one another. When he'd become king, he'd sworn an oath to remain unbiased in matters of the nine Families. If a Family wanted to war with another, the king could not intervene unless their feuding endangered people outside of the nine Families, the common.

All the Families were adversaries, of course, but some more than others. And sometimes it seemed the Da Vias and Saldanas were feuding the hardest, though maybe that was because we shared a territory.

I tossed my dirty leathers into a cupboard reserved for my things. My brothers Rafeo and Matteo also had cupboards in this shop, along with our cousin Jesep. We were the only active Saldana clippers, though my mother and father would take a job if needed.

Since the plague, Mother often reminded me of my duty as a Saldana woman, to swell our ranks with as many children as possible.

I slid into a red velvet gown with a low bodice fastened along the ribs instead of the back for the type of self-dressing I often had to accomplish. My dirty-blond hair fit snugly into a silk snood, netting it away from my face, and a pair of flat lambskin ankle boots finished my attire. Nothing too fancy, since it was only dinner with Val. And because the Saldanas couldn't afford better at this time.

I slipped a dagger into my boot and secured a knife to my thigh. A clipper never went unarmed, even for dinner. I hung my mask and weapons carefully in my cupboard, then patted my chest, feeling the comforting weight of the key to enter our home around my neck. I never took it off.

I lifted my skirts and raced through alleys and backstreets, taking the shortest way to Fabricio's. Shops lined the streets—a locked flower stand, a bakery, and an alchemist's stand, his beak-shaped plague mask hung outside to show he was closed for the night. Ravenna was a night city, more than any other city in Lovero, but only the entertainment and refreshment establishments stayed open. The other businesses waited for the sun to rise to save on the cost of oil.

A salty breeze from the sea carried with it the sweet scent of the lantern oil used to light the streets. I inhaled and smiled. Ravenna was the most beautiful of Lovero's cities, and its life soaked into my skin and muscles. I reveled in running through its streets. I wouldn't want to be anywhere else in the world.

Fabricio's appeared before me, lanterns flickering. My breath eased in my throat, and I strolled casually to the front door. The restaurant pressed against the crumbling city walls. The walls had once been used to keep the ghosts out, but with Safraella the patron goddess of Lovero, the ghosts couldn't enter Loveran borders, even though the walls were cracked and collapsed. Ghosts could not cross onto holy ground, and now all of the country was considered holy. Before that, the ghosts would haunt the streets at night, stealing bodies and forcing people to hide in their homes. Now the ghosts just haunted the dead plains.

A small crowd of people waited at the entrance. A pinch-faced woman on the arm of a man dressed in colored silks too gaudy for the season glanced at my dress and sniffed.

Val dropped from Fabricio's roof to land beside me. The woman shrieked.

He wore black velvet with gold brocade visible through slashes on his sleeves. An elegantly stitched gray leather vest matched his knee-high boots. Diamonds winked in his ears, and a ruby ring flashed on his left pinkie. Val didn't purposely flaunt the Da Via wealth, but it was hard to ignore.

He scanned the crowd, including me.

I blinked slowly and nodded to him. A silent boast that said, *I beat you here.*

He nodded back, politely. *As expected.*

And though his eyes sparkled like his diamonds and a smile twitched at the corner of my mouth, no one would guess we were together. Which was how it needed to be. No one could know about us.

My breath caught in my throat as Val strode past the crowd to the doorman. The secrecy sent a thrill straight through the tips of my fingers.

"Ah, Master Da Via." The doorman bowed deeply. "How wonderful of you to think of us on this lovely night."

"My usual table, please," he said.

The doorman bowed once more. "Come, come, I will seat you immediately."

Val and the doorman disappeared inside. When the doorman returned, I stepped up next, earning a glower from the pinch-faced woman.

"Mistress Saldana, you grace us with your presence."

I glanced over my shoulder, and the woman's glower turned into surprise as she recognized my name. When our eyes met, she dropped her gaze. I smirked. Where was her haughty attitude now?

The restaurant was packed, tables filled with couples enjoying a romantic meal, or more lively guests whose libations caused them to laugh too loudly.

I scanned the room for anyone who might recognize me. Val and I had entered separately, but it never hurt to assess one's surroundings.

The doorman led me into a small, curtained-off room.

Inside sat a table for two. The curtain closed behind me. I waited three breaths before I tapped on the left-hand wall.

The wall slid aside, and I ducked through to an identical room so no one in the restaurant would see us seated together. This room housed Val, waiting for me, curtain closed against prying eyes. I slid the wall closed.

He took my hand and kissed it, his lips soft and warm against my skin. I pulled away but could feel the blush spreading across my cheeks. "Don't be ridiculous," I said.

He pulled out my chair and I sat down. He adjusted my snood, and his knuckles brushed against the back of my neck, lingering before he stepped away. I shivered.

We sipped the house wine and ate crusty bread and nutty cheese while we waited for our main course of duck in fig sauce.

"Did your father truly speak to the king about marking kills?" he asked. "Because my aunt won't be happy about that."

"Does Estella truly believe not offering the coin will not offend Safraella?" Yes, Family came before family for clippers, but allegiance shouldn't ever come blindly.

"I don't know what Estella thinks. And I'm not going to ask her."

A waiter appeared and served the duck. The greasy skin of the bird crackled, still hot from the fire. The scent of fresh rosemary and olive oil floated past me, and my stomach rumbled.

I was tired, and not just from the poison. "Why are we even talking about this? I don't have any sway over my father. And we both know your aunt is crazy."

He reached across the table and squeezed my hand. Heat trailed down my body, and I squeezed back.

"That she is," he said. "A man-hating old bat. But I suppose we have your uncle to thank for that."

I pulled my hand away and drank my wine. "We don't talk about Marcello Saldana."

"Which is funny, because my aunt rarely shuts up about her hated ex-husband. But don't let anyone else hear you speak against Estella so. She's the head of our Family for a reason, and the others would not stand the insult, even from a Saldana."

"You mean *especially* from a Saldana."

He grinned.

We attacked the bird, talk subsiding. When full, I set my napkin on the table and watched Val as he finished off the wine in his glass. He smiled. I used to think Val was vain and spoiled and self-indulgent. Now . . . now I felt the same way, but there was something to be said for capturing a vain man's gaze. And once I'd gotten close, it became apparent that much of that vanity was a shield he used to keep people away. The Da Vias were cutthroat, even in their own Family, and he had few people he could fully trust.

From outside our room a waiter's voice crept past our curtain as he spoke to another server. "Mistress Da Via would like her duck more rare."

We glanced at each other, and Val rubbed his eyes. "Damn it."

I peeked past the curtain to the main room. Off to the right, at a table by herself, sat a woman heavy with child. I closed the curtain. "It's your sister."

Val groaned and got to his feet. He glanced out the curtain. "What is she even doing here? She's going to have that baby any day."

"Well, pregnant women *do* have to eat," I suggested. Not that I had any love for Claudia Da Via. From everything Val had told me, she could be humorless and cruel. Which made it even more shocking, he'd said, when she'd wound up pregnant while unmarried. The pregnancy was fine, any Family would welcome an addition to the fold. But she'd refused to tell anyone who the father was, even when Estella had commanded her, except to say he was another clipper. It had become a bit of a scandal, everyone wondering who the father could be. Val thought it was probably someone from one of the lower families, a Gallo maybe, and that she was too ashamed to admit it.

"Do we wait her out, or sneak away?" I asked.

"If we wait, we'll be here forever." Val straightened his vest. "No, I'll distract her while you leave quietly."

I slipped back to my original room. Once there I watched through a gap in the curtain for the best time to leave unnoticed.

Val strode over to his sister and stood at her table. She looked up and scowled.

Claudia couldn't find out I had come here with Val.

Families could never work together, because it would give the allied Families too much power over the others. But clippers almost always married other clippers. The marriage usually bought a generation or two of peace between their Families, a temporary halt to any feuding.

Val leaned closer to Claudia, both hands flat against the table. They spoke, but were too far away for me to hear what was said.

Clipper marriages were always carefully arranged. It would take months to decide which clipper would join which Family and who would pay a dowry. Sometimes a Family would lose money *and* a member, but these were usually the lower-ranked Families, and giving up so much often meant they gained status, and maybe an increase in rank. Everything was decided between the Family heads.

Of course, sometimes clippers married non-clippers. Rafeo's wife hadn't been a clipper, but she *had* been a cleaner, so she'd known what she was getting into. Cleaners were their own guild. They dealt with the aftermath of our duties, removing and cleaning bodies and notifying families of their loved ones' demise.

Our mother hadn't been pleased, since Rafeo's chosen bride didn't bring any money or status, but Mother had relented when their marriage produced a son almost immediately.

Through the gap in the curtains, I watched as Val and Claudia argued. She placed a hand on his elbow, and he jerked it away.

"Because Mother and Father aren't here!" Val snapped, his voice rising above the sound of the other diners. Claudia jerked him closer, whispering harshly.

Time to take my leave.

I stepped past the curtain and strode calmly and confidently to the front door. The only people who gave me a second glance were those of the common who recognized me as a Saldana.

Outside, I walked into an alley across the street. I waited only a few moments before Val found me. Anger flowed through him, visible from the tension in his shoulders and neck.

"What was that about?" I asked.

"Nothing." He waved his hand, dismissing the fight with Claudia. "It was only stupid Family stuff. I don't want to talk about it."

I took his hand and stroked his knuckles. He didn't have to tell me, but I wanted him to know I was there for him, regardless. "I'm sorry. I didn't mean to pry."

He sighed and rubbed his face with his palm. "It really was nothing, Lea."

"Okay. But even if it was something, you know you can tell me, right? I'll keep your secrets."

He snorted. "You're my only secret."

Behind Val, a man walked across the street. He wore

a brown robe and a strange cylindrical hat. He carried a wooden staff with some sort of green gem at the top.

"What is that?" I stared at the man as he slipped into a back door of the restaurant.

Val looked over his shoulder. "What?"

"A strange man just walked into the restaurant."

He shrugged. "Don't know. And perhaps we should take all this drama elsewhere?"

All thoughts of the strange man escaped me as my skin flushed.

Val offered me his hand and I placed my palm in his, the tough calluses on his fingers pressing against my own. His hand was warm, and his pulse beat rapidly in his thumb. His lips parted.

My own pulse raced, and we left the alley. We needed to find somewhere more private. I desperately wanted to get him alone.

We stumbled a few streets away and ducked out of sight into an empty garden.

In the shadows, he pushed me against a brick wall, lips crushed against my neck, one hand releasing my hair as his other slid down my bodice to my hip. I held my breath until I was dizzy and had to break away for air before I pulled him back to my lips.

This was what I loved about him. How quickly he could make my heart pound, my breath catch. Being with Val was like the best kind of job, an exciting chase followed by a satisfying capture.

I slid my hands beneath his shirt, running my fingertips across the smooth skin of his stomach. He flinched.

"Your hands are cold," he murmured against my throat.

"I need you to warm them up."

He reached for my fingers. I made a token gesture of trying to avoid him, but when he clasped my hand with his own, I let him pull me against his chest. His well-worked muscles made his body lean and hard.

He pressed his lips to mine. I returned the kiss, hands gripped on his arms. He made me feel wanted, beautiful. Heat rushed across the skin of my throat and up to my cheeks until they burned. Val's lips scorched my blood like the most exquisite poison in the world. But only one tasted sweet.

four

VAL TORE HIS LIPS FROM MINE. "STAY OUT WITH ME tonight."

I kissed his jaw. He still smelled like his leathers. "I have a curfew. My parents would suspect something."

He ran his fingers through the back of my hair. "Break it. For me."

I snorted. "Like you break your rules for me? Marking your kills, for example?"

He pulled away. The humor had disappeared from his eyes. "That's different. That's *Family* rules, not family."

"Sometimes Family and family are the same thing."

He scowled. "Don't be naive. You damn well know Family comes before family."

I released his hand. I wasn't a child, and I wouldn't be patronized. "Not to me. Not when you're asking me to disobey my father's rules."

Val set his jaw stubbornly.

But I could be stubborn, too. "He's right about marking kills. The cleaners will find my coin and spread word that the Saldanas killed a man tonight. That coin will give my kill a faster rebirth, will buy us respect and fear from the common."

We stared at each other. Marking a kill wasn't worth so much anger. Neither of us could resolve the politics between our Families.

Val tried to ease things with a grin. "Let the Family heads worry about this. Things will be finished soon enough."

He held out a hand, and I took it automatically. He pulled me close against him. "Now, where were we?"

I smiled, but dropped my gaze. It was so easy for him to brush things off. To simply forget the argument.

"I think"—I swept a speck of dirt from his chest—"I was on my way home."

He frowned. "It's not that late. We can spend time together. Take a walk along the pier maybe. We could watch the sun rise." He flashed his dimples because he knew I loved them.

"My mother would have my head. And my father would probably support her."

He snatched my hand again, tugging on it, but I held my ground. I wouldn't be bullied or persuaded in this.

"Please don't go home. Come on, I'm begging you."

He had to be kidding. "Yes, that's clear." I jerked my hand free. "It's not very attractive. I'm going home, Val. I'll see you tomorrow. Maybe."

"Lea, I'm trying to do the right thing."

Whatever that meant. Pushing me wouldn't get him the results he wanted. "I'm worn out."

Val pinched his lips together, but I was too tired to care about his hurt feelings. It wasn't always about him—where we should eat, what we should do, when to end the night.

"You'll need this, then." He held up an iron key. I clasped my hands to my chest, but my key was gone.

I stomped over and ripped the key from his fingers, the chain glinting in the moonlight. "You damn well know lifting keys is off-limits," I hissed. When had he even taken it? The restaurant, when he'd brushed my neck with his fingers. I glared even more.

He shrugged. "I saw an opportunity and I acted."

"Well, now I'm seeing an opportunity and leaving."

"Fine." He held up his hands, eyes cold. "Do what you want. Sleep well." He stormed away.

The urge to call after him crawled its way up my neck, but my key felt heavy in my hands. He knew the rules we'd established. Keys were off-limits because they were connected to our Family homes. Not that Val or any of the other clippers knew where we lived, but still.

The safety of my Family wasn't a joking matter.

I retraced my earlier path to the art shop's hidden entrance. When I stripped out of my dress, something fluttered to the ground, a flash of white in the dark. I scooped it up. A white poppy, pressed between the pages of a book until it had become as delicate as lace paper.

The white poppy was the symbol of the Da Via Family. Val must have slipped it to me sometime during dinner, a gesture of affection for me to find later.

I twisted it in my fingers and sighed. He tugged me so many different ways. But it had been a tiring night, and I didn't want to fight with Val. I wanted to rest.

I tucked the poppy into my spare saddlebag. It could wait there as a surprise for another day.

I finished changing and traveled to a secret Saldana hatch hidden behind a bush at the corner of a church dedicated to Safraella. It was apropos, my brother Rafeo would say. Then I would laugh at him and tell him he sounded much older than his twenty-four years.

I dropped inside and closed it above me. The black tunnel smelled damp, but I could find my way even blind.

A slight brush of air against my cloak told me I'd reached the first break in the path. There were many such splits, set to confuse and disorient any intruders who managed to discover the tunnel. The wrong path led to dead ends, tunnels that dropped into pits, or labyrinths to confuse even the cleverest.

The stone tunnels went on for what seemed like miles, but in truth the correct tunnel was just over a mile long, leading me to another hatch and the Saldana home. I climbed a short ladder and used my key. The hatch popped open. I ascended to the tunnel room, where all the myriad underground entrances to our house eventually ended.

I hung my cloak on a hook beside my brothers' and pushed

my mask to the top of my head. Masks were personal identifiers, both of ourselves and our Family. Safraella's face was formed of the bones of Her mother, the goddess who had breathed life into the sky. All disciples of Safraella wore bone masks when doing Her work. Even the king wore a bone mask during trials or funerals.

The smooth masks covered our entire faces, a blank facade except for the slashes used for eyeholes. The right side was always the color of the bone. The left side was decorated accordingly. Each of the nine Families had a color. The Saldanas were black. Any of the common looking upon our masks could identify which Family we belonged to by color alone.

The pattern, however, was purely personal—used to identify the individual clipper behind the mask. Even if I couldn't recognize Val from the way he stood—cocky and self-assured, arms loose and ready—I would recognize him by the red checkered pattern on the left side of his mask. Just as he would recognize me by my black azalea flowers.

Outside the tunnel room, my boot heels sank into the plush rug of a well-lit hallway. Our home was a house within a house. From the outside, one would see an empty building. It was only behind those walls that the Saldanas' real home hid. None of our rooms had windows or doors to the outside, though there were concealed skylights. The only way in or out was through the tunnels.

A servant waiting in the foyer handed me a glass of mulled wine. I sipped, its warmth spreading down my chest and limbs. The fight with Val had worked its way beneath my skin just as much as the poisoning, pulling on my muscles until they ached. My bed, with its soft covers, would be a soothing balm. I intended to sleep well past morning.

From around a corner a child raced toward me, nightgown and long, curly hair flapping behind him.

"Aunt Lea!" He crashed into my legs.

"Emile." I set my wineglass on a hall table. I peeled him from my legs and picked him up, feeling the lovely weight of him in my arms. "What are you doing up so late?"

He laughed, squirming in my arms. From around the same corner his nursemaid, Silva, appeared with my brother Rafeo.

"There you are, you naughty child." Silva took Emile from me and hurried down the hall.

Rafeo put an arm around my shoulder and pulled me close for a kiss on the cheek. I squeezed into his comfortable warmth.

"Thanks, Donna," he said. "We've been trying to catch him for five minutes."

I rolled my eyes. Donna was Rafeo's nickname for me. It wasn't enough that I'd been named Oleander after a poison. No, I had to have a poisonous nickname too.

When I'd been younger, Rafeo had been my mentor. My first kill had been using poison, a belladonna concoction. I'd been so excited. I'd wanted to show how well I'd studied. But the poison didn't take, at least not all the way. The man was dying, but slowly and in pain.

Excitement had turned to fear. I'd wanted Rafeo to fix it for me, but he'd pressed a dagger into my hand. *What you do for him now is a mercy,* he'd said. *It is the most beautiful gift you can grant someone, a quick end to pain. He will be with Safraella, and She will grant him a better life.*

It had been hard, to use that dagger, but Rafeo had been right. Serving Safraella was difficult work. But there was beauty and mercy in the shadows, too.

I leaned my head against his shoulder. "A little late for a four-year-old's bedtime, isn't it?"

"Tell that to him."

A door opened and my mother stepped out, searching the hall with a frown, her blond hair plaited down her spine. How someone as regal as Bianca Saldana could ignore all the exquisite fashions of Lovero, I'd never understand. Even the most common housegirls were wrapping or netting their hair, and yet she still preferred the ease of braids and ties.

Rafeo sighed, and we stepped apart. Separated, one of us would be more likely to escape. The other would have to serve as a sacrifice and take the lecture stoically.

"What is going on out here?" Mother's harsh whisper filled the space. She was still dressed in an evening gown, which swished against the carpeted floor. "It's much too late for games in the halls."

"It's my fault, Mother." Rafeo held his hands before him, heroically accepting Mother's ire. "Emile got away from Silva, and Lea helped us get him to bed, that's all."

She sniffed and glanced at me before turning fully on

Rafeo. "You must get that child under control. He's far too old for these sorts of games. He must conduct himself in a manner befitting a Saldana."

"He's only four."

"Exactly. The children are never too young to begin learning about Family responsibilities."

An image of Emile dressed in tiny little leathers and wearing a small bone mask, decorated with puppies, came to mind. I bit my tongue to prevent a laugh from escaping.

Mother turned her gaze on me. Damn. I'd missed my opportunity to leave.

"And what are you doing home so late? Jesep and Rafeo were back hours ago."

Rafeo stepped behind Mother, crossed his eyes at me, and then left me alone with her. Ass. I would make him pay.

"I took some food after my job, is all," I said. Sometimes the best way to deal with Mother when she was in one of her moods was to go on the offensive. "I needed it to offset the loving poison you dosed me with."

She ignored my comment. "Food? Where?"

"Fabricio's."

Her lips tightened, carving lines in her skin. "I don't want you lining the Da Vias' pockets. Our Family will not help them in their grab for status."

It always came down to what was best for the *Family*.

"Now. The Caffarellis have put in a claim for you for their son Brando."

My breath left me in a rush of air. A claim had come in for

me. For marriage. With Brando Caffarelli.

Mother had been born a Caffarelli and had only become a Saldana after she'd married my father and their union had produced a child—Rafeo.

Brando, Brand as everyone called him, was tall and handsome and well established as a clipper. He had blond hair, like my mother, like all the Caffarellis, and I knew Mother had imagined the towheaded babies we'd produce.

Brand, though, was the son of Mother's oldest brother. "He's my first cousin!"

"Oh, be calm. His mother's not of the Families. He has enough outside blood that it's not a concern."

"What about Valentino Da Via? He's closer to my age." As soon as the words had left my mouth, I knew they were a mistake.

Mother pursed her lips and her eyes widened. "Never. Never will the Saldanas make another union with the Da Vias."

My uncle Marcello had been married to Estella Da Via before I was born. Then something went wrong and no one would speak about it, but the Saldanas and Da Vias had been at each other ever since.

Mother regained her composure. "The Caffarellis are willing to let him become a Saldana *and* offer us a small dowry."

I paused. A clipper usually joined another Family officially when a marriage produced a child. Then negotiations would decide which clipper changed Families and who paid a dowry. But the Caffarellis were willing to give us Brand and money if we agreed to this union. How was I worth so much?

Rank, of course. The Saldanas were the first Family, the Caffarellis the fifth. If we agreed to the marriage, their rank would rise drastically, perhaps enough to surpass the Bartolomeos and the Accursos.

The Saldanas as the first Family, and my father as our head, held the most power over the nine Families, but the main reason why we were the first Family was my father's close friendship with the king.

"All of that aside"—my mother flicked her fingers in the air—"it is a serious claim and we should consider it. Safraella knows we could use the money almost as much as we could use the addition to the Family. That plague may as well have killed us all unless we increase our numbers and funds. It's a miracle the other Families haven't made a move against us."

My stomach sank whenever she spoke like this. Like our rank compared to the other Families was more important than the people we lost. "They wouldn't dare, Mother. Not with Father's friendship with the king."

Mother raised an eyebrow. "It doesn't matter that your father was the king's foster brother and his personal guard until Marcello almost ruined this Family. If the other Families were to take a stand against us, Costanzo Sapienza would not stop them. He would not save your father over the lives of the common, over the safety of the country."

I dropped my gaze. When the king had bowed to Safraella

on behalf of the entire country, She had become Lovero's patron. Before that, people had worshipped whichever god they wanted, and the stone walls had tried to keep the ghosts out. Now almost everyone in Lovero worshipped Safraella, and the king had become our wall. His faith, his belief on behalf of all of us, kept the ghosts away. If he were to falter in his faith, the ghosts would find their way back inside.

"Why is it just me?" I changed the subject. "Matteo is older."

"Don't for a second think you're so special. Just because you're not privy to our conversations doesn't mean I'm not discussing marriage prospects with Matteo. Or even Rafeo. Two years has been long enough to grieve."

Another door down the hall opened and my father stepped out, his dark, curly hair pulled back respectably in a tie. He wore a pair of glasses to help him with reading in the lamplight.

"Ah, Lea. I'll take your report, if your mother can spare you?"

Saved by my father once again.

Mother dismissed me with a wave of her hand. "Go speak with your father. But we are not done with this talk. You're plenty old enough to contribute to the growth of this Family."

I tried not to shudder. Marriage prospects with *anyone*, even Brand Caffarelli, were something I was not remotely ready to discuss.

My father held open his office door while I walked in. I

took a seat and pulled off my mask.

Papers and parchments lay scattered across his desk. A small stack caught my eye: letters from priests putting in their bid to be the new Saldana Family priest. I picked up the one on top, sent from a priest named Faraday from a monastery on the dead plains. We'd been without a priest for two years, but it wasn't as easy as just choosing anyone. The Family priest was as good as family. He would live with us, counsel us in all matters, keep Family records. He had to be a good fit.

Father sat across from me. "Actually, I don't really need your report right at this moment."

I smiled. He always knew the most tactful way to interrupt Mother's tirades. "We might as well finish it so we don't have to work in the morning."

He dipped his pen in the inkwell. "You mean so *you* don't have to work in the morning. The work for me, my dear, never ends."

Father scratched the nib across the paper as I told him about my successful night.

He sighed and set his quill aside. "He didn't pay a lot, of course," my father said. Suicide requests usually didn't.

"I thought you were going to have Matteo take over some of the paperwork," I said. "He'd excel at it."

Almost as if he'd heard us, Matteo stepped into the office. I nodded and he sniffed, once.

"Lea," he said. "Got home late enough, I see."

"Matteo. Didn't go out at all, I presume."

"Children, please." Father removed his glasses and pinched the bridge of his nose.

I'd never gotten along with my brother Matteo. He was strict and humorless, so different from Rafeo and me. As a child, I used to dream about him leaving the Family, joining another. Of course, now I understood things were complicated.

I exhaled. Losing Matteo, losing any of us when our Family had already lost so many, would put us further in a bind. Maybe Mother was right. Maybe it was time for me to grow up and do something for the Family for a change.

I thought about Val, the smell of his skin, the taste of his lips, and the feel of his embrace. We couldn't always have what we wanted. I knew this. Sometimes, we had to give up what we wanted to get what our Family needed.

Even if that meant marrying Brand Caffarelli.

five

LATER, I WOULDN'T BE SURE WHAT HAD WAKENED ME: the smell of smoke, or the sounds of violence outside my room.

In the end, it didn't matter.

I rolled out of bed, alert. The acrid scent of burning wood and cloth reached me even through my closed bedroom door.

I jerked open a drawer in my bureau and dragged on a pair of leather pants beneath my nightgown, not only for ease of movement but also for the pockets they afforded me. I grabbed any knives in my end table, far too few for comfort, and cursed my sword, still resting in the weapons room.

A sudden bang exploded against the door. I dropped into a defensive stance, knives in hand. My key thumped against my chest from its chain.

No one burst through. Gray smoke flowed under the door.

I snatched my mask from my bedside table and jammed it over my face. Its familiar smell enveloped me. I breathed deep. Whatever was happening outside my room, I could handle it. I was a clipper. A Saldana. I had no fear. Right?

The door handle burned my palm. I yelled and pulled away. Sloppy, Lea. I needed to get my wits about me. I slipped my sleeve over my skin and jerked the door open to face the fire.

Flames crawled across the walls. The Saldana Family tapestries burned merrily as the hall and rooms filled with smoke. With no windows in the house, the smoke had nowhere to go. The fire would burn until it consumed all the air in the house. My Family's remaining wealth, all our beautiful things, surrendered themselves to the flames.

A hall door creaked and fell inward, covered in flames. Go! Move! Do *something*!

I dashed from my room. My mask protected me from the smoke. It wouldn't last. It couldn't last.

"Mother!" I shouted. "Father!" Had they fled and left me alone?

The flames licked the ceiling. Before long they would rain onto me. I had to get out of here. I had to reach the tunnels.

I raced through the halls, stopping only to check the bedrooms. In Emile's room his nursemaid Silva leaned over his bed, a knife plunged into her back. She'd been dead long enough for her blood to soak his bedcover, turning it scarlet.

I clenched my hands into fists. She had been kind, and caring, and now she was dead. There was nothing I could do for her, but maybe she could help me. I removed the knife. No markings, no sigils or crests. No sign of who owned this knife. Of who was attacking us.

Did Rafeo have Emile?

Jesep's and Matteo's bedrooms were engulfed in flames, and I couldn't see inside.

I stumbled down the stairs, coughing as the smoke snaked its way beneath my mask. There wasn't much time, but I needed to find my Family. I wouldn't leave without them.

In the stairwell another body lay slumped against the wall. Rafeo. A wordless shout escaped my lips. I dropped beside him. He wore his leathers, and a crack ran along the white side of his mask where his mouth would've been. My fingers pressed against his neck. Nothing, then a pulse, slow and weak. My hand came away coated in the deep red of heart's blood.

He groaned, and relief washed over me like a gale before a storm.

Stay calm. More than anything I had to stay calm. Rafeo needed me.

"I'm here, Rafeo." I threw his arm over my shoulder. Rafeo was not a large man, no Saldana was, but even with all my strength I couldn't bring him to his feet, not without his help.

"Rafeo." I struggled to lift him. "You need to help me. I can't do this without you."

He coughed behind his mask. His knees bent, and together we got his feet under him.

Reaching the bottom of the stairs was not easy. Rafeo kept tripping, threatening to drag us both down, but somehow we made it. Only one more hallway to the tunnels. If we could reach them, I could stash Rafeo safely and return to search for everyone else.

The fire wasn't as bad downstairs, though it was spreading quickly. It must've been set on the upper level to allow the attackers time to escape. Someone had found their way through to our home. It was the only explanation.

Rafeo stumbled beside me. He tugged me with him as he leaned against a wall.

"No, Rafeo. We're almost to the tunnels. You need to help me."

Behind us, a door crashed. I turned, dropping Rafeo as I pulled out my knives.

Three men had kicked it down. They wore leathers and bone masks. Another Family, then. The worst possibility. I peered through the haze, but the smoke obscured the colors and patterns of their masks.

They approached, swords held before them. I had no sword, only knives. They were bigger than me, with longer reaches. I was outnumbered and wearing my tattered nightgown.

I swallowed, my mouth and throat dry. Maybe this was it. Maybe this was how I would die.

Rafeo groaned again. I glanced at him. The leathers on his chest were slick and wet.

I closed my eyes. Nothing to do for him. Not unless I

could somehow drop the three clippers.

A shriek filled the air. From the stairwell a figure landed on the back of one of the men. Daggers plunged into his neck. The man collapsed, dead, and my mother turned her attention to the man on her left. He blocked her dagger thrust at his gut.

"Mother!" I screamed. The third clipper swung at her from behind. She bent backward. The sword barely missed scraping across her bone mask. She moved like a water serpent, all fluid attack.

I raced toward her. Where was Father?

"No, Lea!" She blocked the sword swings with her daggers. "Take Rafeo and flee."

I stopped, torn. I could disobey her, run to her aid, and fight beside her. End those who were destroying our home, killing our Family.

I faced Rafeo. He didn't move. His heavy breaths struggled against the smoke and his wounds. My mother needed my help, but Rafeo needed me more. He couldn't help himself. I would return for my mother.

Rafeo was even less responsive. His feet tangled together as I dragged him closer to the tunnel room and the safety found there. My heart was heavy with dread.

A loud crash exploded from upstairs. The house shook. Behind us, the ceiling collapsed. Broken beams spilled across the hall, covered in flames and fire from above.

"Mother!" The smoke and flames were too thick to see

past. She would be unharmed. She would be safe. I had to believe it.

I shouldered open the tunnel room door, dragging Rafeo beside me. A hatch lay open—the one the other Family had used to breach our home. The same one I'd used earlier tonight.

Had I forgotten to lock it behind me?

All this was my fault.

I kicked the hatch shut, cutting off a startled yell from the dark tunnel.

Someone pounded on the hatch, trying to break through. I tipped over a cloak cabinet. The wood clattered and cracked as it blocked the hatch. Any surviving attackers in the house would have to take their chances with a different tunnel.

All the other hatches were locked. No one had been through them yet. I chose one and climbed down the ladder. The tunnel was cool and dark and, most importantly, empty of attackers and flames. I reached for Rafeo. The weight of his body crashed into me. We spilled to the tunnel ground in a heap. I crawled out from under him and closed the hatch.

Rafeo groaned at my feet. My body burned and ached. I couldn't lift him anymore. I'd used almost all my strength getting us this far. I grasped his wrist and dragged him down the tunnel. His body painted streaks against the dusty floor until we reached the first split. I pulled him into a dead end.

"You'll be safe here," I said. He showed no sign of hearing me.

I stood. I had to help Mother. To find Emile and Father and Jesep and Matteo and anyone else still inside the burning house.

Rafeo grabbed my wrist, jerking me off my feet.

"Rafeo." I crouched beside him, squeezing his hand with mine.

He kept a firm grip on my fingers, struggling to remove his mask with his free hand. He finally lifted his mask off his face and dropped it to the ground. It clattered loudly in the silence of the tunnel.

A slight glow from the fire trickled down to us from the edges of the hatch.

"Oh, Rafeo . . ." A deep gash stretched across the left side of his throat. A slow, steady pump of blood escaped him. His dark leathers were drenched with it.

I slipped my hand from his grip and pressed tightly against his wound to stop the bleeding. The blood seeped through my fingers.

He stared at me, then gave a small smile before he pushed me away, his hands fluttering against mine like moths against a lamp glass.

"It's all right," he whispered. His voice had no strength, and his eyes wouldn't focus on me. I slipped off my own mask and clutched his hands, his blood slick between us.

"Rafeo, please hold on." My voice broke, and tears dripped off my chin to land on his chest. How could this be my joyful, beautiful brother? How had we come to this? Had Safraella forsaken us?

No. Safraella was the goddess of death, murder, and res-urrection. This dark work belonged to Her as well, even though we were Her disciples.

He took a deep breath. Then another.

"Da Vias," he said.

Rafeo exhaled and died.

I clutched his hands to my heart. I bent over him, my forehead resting against his blood-soaked leathers. I tried to sing him my nursery rhyme, tried to tell him he'd be safe and warm once more, but my throat closed and I wept for my brother. Wept for all of us. We were lesser without him. The world was lesser without him.

It took me far too long to gain control of myself, but when I'd finally stopped my tears, I closed Rafeo's eyes and dug around in his leathers until I found a coin. I placed it in his mouth.

It was fine. I would miss him—gods I would miss him—but he would be reborn. He was favored of Safraella. She would provide him with a good, new life. Maybe one without so much blood.

I grabbed my mask and left Rafeo in that tunnel. I'd come back for him later, but for now it would have to serve as his tomb.

I returned to the hatch, pausing at the bottom of the ladder to ready my knives.

They would pay for Rafeo. They would pay for it all, even if it cost me my own life.

I climbed the ladder and reached the hatch.

It wouldn't budge.

I used the butt of my knife to pound against the wood. The sound thumped dully. Something must've been resting on it.

No. No, that wasn't possible. I could not be trapped in the tunnel. Not when my Family needed me!

I pulled myself up the ladder, crouching below the hatch and using my shoulder and back to push against it. The hatch creaked. A small shaft of light stabbed into the darkness.

The air exploded in fire.

I screamed and fell to the ground, covering my head with my hands. An image flashed in my mind, of my hair catching fire and it consuming me. I batted at my face and head, but there were no flames.

I caught my breath. The hatch was closed again, sealing me off from the fire raging above. I was cut off from the house. From my mother. From everyone else trapped inside.

There was no way back, and I was alone in the tunnel with my brother's body.

six

THE TUNNEL OPENED INTO THE BOTTOM OF A FALSE well, and I climbed my way to the top. By the time I stumbled into the city, the sun had risen. Yellow light reflected off the tiled roofs.

Dried blood and black smears from the tunnel covered my white nightgown. I stank like filth. I couldn't be seen in public.

I blinked, and tears pricked my eyes again. *Please, please let the others have escaped.* Just because they hadn't used my tunnel didn't mean they couldn't have reached another. There were six in total. Surely someone had gotten away. Surely I wasn't alone. . . .

Shut up, Lea! I lifted my mask and rubbed my eyes. A clipper shouldn't act this way. I needed to get control of myself. When I controlled myself, I controlled my situation.

I replaced my mask and took a few deep breaths.

First, I needed a change of clothing.

I headed to the closest safe house, a tapestry dealer a few streets from the well. Moving quickly, I managed to avoid being seen. Ravenna may have been an all-hours city, but the early morning was typically reserved for bakers and shop owners.

I slipped through the hidden entrance of the shop, its interior dim in the morning light.

I stripped, throwing the stained nightgown and pants as far away as I could. My mask rested on a table while I pulled everything of use from my cabinet.

The buckles, straps, and pockets on my leathers hid every knife in the cupboard. I tucked the small purse of money in my waistband, then ransacked Rafeo's cabinet for his weapons and money as well, strapping a spare sword on my hip.

I paused before Jesep's and Matteo's cupboards. They'd been at home. I'd leave their cabinets be, in case they'd escaped the fire or the attackers.

The attackers . . . Rafeo had mentioned the Da Vias before he died.

I closed my eyes, sifting through memories of the fire, and the clippers in the smoke. Masks definitely, blank of any features. One side white and the other mottled with dull color. It was no use. The smoke had been too dense to identify the Family.

Of course, Rafeo might have been addled from blood loss. But he might have seen clearly. Maybe Val had been part of it. Maybe Val had snuck into my home while I slept to murder me and my Family.

No. No, it wasn't possible. A vain, selfish show-off he might be, but he loved me. He wouldn't betray me. . . .

I shook my head.

I'd find answers about the attackers later. First, I needed to discover if my Family had made it out. My mind flashed to little Emile, his long, curly hair and his bright smile. He must've been so scared. Surely, even the members of another Family would pause before slaughtering a child of only four years. . . .

I needed answers. I grabbed my mask, my thumb rubbing over a split on its surface.

I flipped it over and traced the crack near where the mouth would've been.

Rafeo's mask. I'd taken Rafeo's mask instead of mine in the dark of the tunnel.

Gone were my black flowers and vines, replaced by tiger stripes.

I bit my lip against the building tears. Maybe it was meant to be. Maybe this way Rafeo could live through me.

From the front of the safe house a door opened, followed by the sound of shutters banging aside as the shop owner prepared for business.

I thrust the mask over my face. Time to go.

I stepped away from my cabinet as the shopkeeper pushed his way into the room.

His mouth dropped open before he lowered his gaze. His face blanched white. "Oh! I'd heard you were all killed! That the home had been discovered and the Saldanas slaughtered.

Oh, it does my heart good to find you here!"

Word traveled quickly in Ravenna, especially when it involved a fire that could easily spread to other buildings.

I freed a knife and pressed it against his throat. "No one must know I was here, do you understand?"

"Oh! Yes, I do. I will protect your appearance here as surely as I protect this location."

Someone had sold our Family out to the others. I stared him in the eyes, searching for a hint of betrayal.

No. None of the shopkeepers knew the location of our home. They only kept our belongings safe, to gain favor from Safraella.

I sheathed my knife. It was a testament to the man's loyalty that he didn't check his neck for blood.

From the hidden entrance, I slipped into the alley.

I spent the entire day traveling shadow to shadow, searching the hatches for signs of my Family. The first I checked was the entrance the attackers had used, the one hidden by the church.

I didn't get too close. Someone would be watching, waiting to see if anyone would appear. I wasn't stupid.

I clutched the key hanging from my neck and examined the entrance from a hiding spot. The bush that hid the hatch had been hacked apart, and the door had been chopped into slivers of wood.

Last night Val had dangled my key before me. And then hours later my Family was dead. Or, if Rafeo was wrong, and it wasn't the Da Vias, then I must have left the hatch into our house unlocked. Either way, everything had happened because of me.

I wrapped my arms around my stomach, trying to calm my twisting gut. Answers could come later. I lived. It was up to me to try and save what was left of my Family. Failing that . . . I'd cross those fields when I reached them.

The other tunnels remained undiscovered. I traveled through each, following them until I reached the hatches at the other end that led into the house. None would open, even with my key. No one had escaped through them.

I was the only remaining Saldana.

I sat at the bottom of a hatch and removed my mask, breathing freely in the damp air, which stank of smoke and burned things.

I pictured the house. A burned-out wreck, down to the beams. Or maybe the fire had somehow been contained, only burning everything inside. The plush carpets. The furniture and our belongings.

The people . . .

No. Don't think about it, Lea. Don't think about them. This couldn't be happening. Not to me.

I rubbed my eyes and pulled my mask down. Crying wouldn't lead me anywhere. I needed a plan. I needed to *fix* this!

My joints creaked as I stood. I also needed sleep. And food and a bath. Those were the first things. Then I'd choose my next steps. Decide who to kill first, and how.

Because someone would die for what they'd done to the

Saldanas. And this time I wouldn't kill just in service of Safraella. No. This time it would also be for me.

⬥

I slipped through the streets, passing through shadows cast by lamplight until it grew dark enough to travel by rooftop. It was quicker to travel above, especially early in the night when the streets were crowded with people. I stopped at every safe house, collecting all my spare money and anything else I might need, and then I headed southeast, toward the border of the city of Ravenna. The closer I drew, the sparser the buildings. Finally I had to climb down to the street level and make my way between shadows and trash-filled alleys. The streets weren't safe.

Around the corner a group of revelers blocked my way. Their raucous laughter echoed off the snug walls of the garden I slipped inside to hide. A wrought-iron bench further blocked me from their view. I pulled my cloak tight as they traveled past the gate. The women wore luxurious dresses, made from the finest velvet and lace, their collars reaching to the tops of their heads and their hair wrapped intricately with ribbons, beads, and gems.

I'd never wear anything like that now. Not that I'd ever had an opportunity to own something so fine, even for the balls at the palace where we were often invited. There would be no more balls for me. No more beautiful things.

I glanced out from my hiding spot. At the rear of their group I caught a quick flash of a man in a cylindrical hat, staff at his side. I looked again.

58

Nothing. Only my tired eyes playing tricks.

When the group turned a corner, I escaped my hiding place, staring in the direction they'd gone. Echoes of their revelry reached me in staccato bursts. It must've been easy, to be a commoner. To know if they were murdered at the hands of a clipper, they would be reborn as an infant into a better life. To know there was someone who would seek vengeance on their behalf or take their life if their sadness was too great. To not worry about gods and their demands and Family ranks.

This far south I could smell the brininess of the sea on the air. I inhaled deeply and pictured throwing myself into its depths, letting myself sink to the bottom and the peace and quiet found there.

I shook my head. A common life wasn't for me. It never had been. I just needed some sleep. Things always looked different when I was well rested.

Before me stood an inn tucked away in a corner of the city. I hid my mask in my cloak, but it would be clear to the inn owner I was a clipper. I didn't have any common clothing. I'd have to be gone as soon as possible in the morning before the owner had a chance to wag his tongue.

I used part of my money to rent a room for a night and asked that a hot bath be drawn. I smelled of smoke and fire; this was obvious even before the innkeeper wrinkled his nose. It was on my hair, my skin, inside of me. Maybe I'd never be clean of it.

My room was small, but the mattress was free of bugs and

lice. The innkeeper offered me a key to the bathing room, and after I stashed my belongings, I went straight there.

The tub was dented and rusted in spots, but hot steam rolled over its edges. I climbed in and sank up to my chin, letting the water soak away my aches and pains. I scrubbed my skin with rough soap, concentrating on my hair, which stank the most.

Once out of the bath I stood in front of the mirror, staring at my reflection.

I still looked the same. Everything had changed. Everything. And yet my face stared back at me the way it always had. My eyes were still brown, my hair was still long and blond.

I ran my fingers through the strands, pulling apart any tangles. It wasn't fair. I was different on the inside. I should look different on the outside.

I dug through my leathers until I found what I was searching for.

The knife sliced my hair easily and the chunks fell across my bare feet, piling to my ankles before I was finally done.

I left it long enough to pull back to keep out of my face when I wore my mask, but barely.

There. Now the girl who looked back was someone different. Just like the girl on the inside.

In my room I crawled under the blankets, pulling my knees up against my chest. My muscles still ached, weary from everything, but my mind wouldn't be still.

All I could picture was Val in the alley, dangling my key

from his fingers before I'd snatched it back. He had taken it from me at the beginning of dinner, at a restaurant his Family owned. Anyone could have made an imprint of it while we dined, while he stroked my fingers. And then we'd fled to the alley and he'd kissed me, all while his Family plotted to destroy mine.

My fault. All my fault.

Tears soaked into the pillow beneath my head. I wept steadily. My grief stretched on and on, endless. When I'd manage to regain control of myself, my body, I'd remember someone I had lost: my father, my mother, Matteo, or Jesep. Emile. Rafeo. Then the tears would start again.

I'd left Rafeo in the tunnel, and I'd left my mother in our burning home. I was alone now. The only Saldana remaining, and I'd gotten my Family killed because I'd loved a boy in secret who used that love to destroy me.

I cried until my cheeks burned from the salt, until my skin chapped and my head pounded. Then, finally, my body empty, I slept.

seven

†

STALL OWNERS CLOSED UP SHOP BELOW MY OPEN
window. I'd slept through the rest of the night and the day.
My eyes were sticky and sore with dried tears. My muscles
begged me not to move.

I'd never slept so heavily before—like I'd slept for years.
I scrunched under the blankets. Maybe I could simply not
wake up. Ever.

Footsteps pounded outside my room as other guests went
about their business. It was no use. I couldn't stay like this. I
couldn't give up.

I climbed out of bed, the wooden planked floor rough
beneath my bare feet. I stood in front of the mirror over the
bureau and smoothed my newly shorn hair.

What would I do? The only thing I *could* do.

Kill everyone responsible.

I jerked on my hair, pinching my scalp. I pictured Val in
his leathers, leaning against an alley wall as he kissed me. I

saw him laughing, his smile lightening the mood. Then my chest constricted as I pictured Emile as he tried to outrun bedtime. And my father, removing his glasses and massaging the bridge of his nose where they always rubbed him sore.

I pictured Rafeo dead in the tunnel, his leathers soaked in blood, his skin cold.

My throat burned. I coughed, then swallowed. If Val had been a part of the fire, I'd have to kill him. If he'd helped kill my Family, then he deserved to die. It was that simple.

Even if I loved him.

Even if more killing wasn't the answer.

I paused, my fingers entangled in my hair. "I'm a clipper, a disciple of Safraella," I said to my reflection. "Murder is always the answer."

I pulled out my leathers and set about dressing myself. I needed to verify that it *was* the Da Vias who'd attacked us. Then I'd make a plan. The Da Vias numbered over fifty active clippers. I couldn't take them out one by one. They'd catch on.

No, I needed to kill them the way they'd killed us.

If I found their home, I could burn them out.

If only I had help . . .

The Caffarellis. Maybe I could reach out to them. There had been the marriage prospect, and my mother had belonged to them, once.

But why would they offer aid? The Da Vias were now the most powerful Family. The Caffarellis ranked fifth. They couldn't defeat the Da Vias even if they agreed to help me.

Probably they would just hand me over to the Da Vias to curry favor.

I tightened the buckles on my boots until my calves ached. No other Family would assist me. Not now, even if they hated the Da Vias.

No. I couldn't trust them. I couldn't trust anyone ever again.

I could give it all up. Bury my clothes, the mask. Become a different person. I could be a glassblower. A seamstress. No one need ever know who I was, what I could do.

Safraella would know. I couldn't abandon my duties to Her and Her subjects.

I paused. My mind turned. I did need help, though. Someone who couldn't abandon me. Someone who could help me fix things.

Time to visit the king.

The three Loveran cities that bordered the fields in front of the dead plains, Ravenna, Lilyan, and Genoni, pressed against one another like drunks in a barroom, their boundaries blurred by buildings that spilled across the city lines. Lilyan was smaller than Ravenna, but because the Caffarellis didn't have to share territory, like the Saldanas and Da Vias in Ravenna, they had more space. The southern cities and territories spread out more freely, with farmland and room between them.

The king's palace, located in Genoni, sat in the center of Addamo territory. Even if I could avoid the Addamos, and they were lacking in the skills of stealth and fighting technique, it would take too long to travel on foot. I'd need my horse if I wanted to speak to the king, Costanzo Sapienza.

As we did with our myriad safe houses, the Saldana Family hid stables throughout the city, moving our horses between them as needed. I headed to one as the shadows and dark night kept me hidden from the common. And the Da Vias.

I reached the stable and slipped inside.

Surrounded by the sweet smell of hay and the sounds of sleeping horses, I made my way into the secret stalls where three horses were kept well groomed, exercised, and fed.

My gray gelding, Dorian, nickered softly as I tacked him up. In the next stall Rafeo's stallion, Butters, stomped his hoof, anxious for a night ride himself. Rafeo never believed in giving animals serious names. The final horse was Matteo's gelding Safire, who ignored us all in an attempt to sleep.

I led Dorian out of his stall. Butters whinnied loudly.

"Butters!" I whispered. "Quiet yourself!"

He kicked at the stall door, the loud banging waking the other horses. If he kept it up, he'd wake the whole neighborhood. Better to bring him along, even as just a packhorse.

I tied Dorian to his stall door and tacked Butters up as well. He barely calmed, even when he realized he was coming. Rafeo thought . . . *had* thought . . . spirited horses were funny. I just thought they were a pain.

I threw the extra bags and weapons onto Butters but kept my spare money on Dorian.

Something slipped from a saddlebag and drifted to the

ground. The white poppy Val had left me.

I stared at it between my boots. My throat tightened. It would be so easy to crush it beneath my heel, to grind it into the ground until it was dust.

But maybe Val hadn't done anything. Maybe Rafeo had been wrong.

I picked it up, then replaced it in Butters's saddlebag. I could deal with it later, once I had some answers and some help.

We left the barn, Butters tied behind Dorian. I smacked Butters when he tried to bully his way to the front, and he finally got the message.

The horses' hooves clopped loudly on the flagstones as we took darkened backstreets. Butters grazed from any gardens we passed.

We crossed the city line into Genoni. I exhaled. The Addamo Family was smaller than the Da Vias, so chances were slight that I'd meet one of them, even though Genoni was half the size of Ravenna.

The palace sat on a hill in the center of the city, lit with giant lanterns, glowing brightly even against the lights of the city. It looked warm and welcoming, like a single coal burning in a brazier, but I'd be turned away if I approached the front gate at this hour.

They were not clippers, the Sapienzas, not part of the nine Families. The king was a disciple of Safraella solely to keep the angry ghosts outside the crumbled city walls.

My father had explained that before the Sapienzas had

seized the throne in a coup, the cities had been overrun by angry ghosts. The only things that could stop the ghosts were moving water, sturdy walls, and extreme faith in Safraella. People were afraid to leave their homes once the sun set.

The common people worshipped dozens of gods, though there were six predominant Loveran gods, including Safraella. Countless gods promised afterlives, some more desirable than others, but not many offered such a fair trade as Safraella: a new life in return for a death.

Finally, the Sapienzas managed to gain the support of the most powerful of the nine Families, and together they took the throne for the Sapienzas. Costanzo's agreement with the Families was that he would follow Safraella, building altars for Her throughout the country and donning his own bone mask—the royal family's color was gold, of course. And the common followed suit, abandoning their gods and turning to Safraella, the god their new, just king worshipped.

So pleased was Safraella by the king and the country's devotion to Her that She drove the ghosts out onto the dead plains, granting Lovero Her patronage, and Ravenna had become a city that thrived on nightlife and entertainment for those who had spent so long locked behind doors.

I stashed the horses in an abandoned garden, tied to a pergola, and gave each a bag of grain to keep them occupied. They were trained to wait patiently for their riders.

The palace was massive, as any good palace should be. Its walls soared into the sky, flecks in the stone sparkling against the lamplight like stars. The palace was the crown jewel of

Lovero, set against the rubies and emeralds of the cities and cradled by the sea.

I waited for the patrolling guards to turn their backs before I scaled the wall and dropped into the courtyard. I was allowed to be here; I just couldn't let *anyone* see me. Guards' tongues wagged as much as courtesans'.

I scurried across the courtyard to a special door reserved for clippers. I'd never had to use it. But my father had made sure we'd all known about the door and the correct protocol. One never knew where a threat to the king could appear, he'd said, and we had to be prepared.

I entered, walking up a set of stairs to a small room decorated sparsely with only a desk and two chairs. I lit the small lamp on the desk and found an alcove in the wall. Beside it were nine candles, each adorned with a strip of ribbon. Nine candles for nine Families. Three empty candleholders reminded us of the lost Families. I supposed soon it would be four.

I chose the candle tied with a black ribbon and lit it before I set it on a tray in the alcove. With a push, the alcove twisted on a hidden axis and the candle disappeared as the wall rotated. A special messenger would see the candle and tell the king someone from the Saldana Family awaited him.

I took the chair in front of the desk and sat, expecting a long wait.

The king was the religious leader of the common, but not over the nine Families. We were Her disciples and served Her before all. If Costanzo Sapienza were to lose favor with

Safraella, the ghosts would no longer be kept out of the country. The walls would need to be rebuilt, and people would need to return to staying indoors at night until the king could regain Her favor.

A creak sounded behind me. I turned. A tall, dark-haired man entered the room through a secret door. Costanzo Sapienza, the king.

I'd met him before, of course, at balls when my parents introduced me. He was a man with an easy smile and sadness in his eyes. None of the children his wife had given him had survived past their infancy, though she was pregnant again now and confined to bed.

He closed the door and faced me, smiling. When he saw my mask, the smile vanished. He put a hand to his brow and closed his eyes.

"You must forgive me," he said, his voice gruff. "When I was told the black candle had been lit, I was sure it was my friend Dante coming to reassure me of his continued good health. But you must be his first son, Rafeo."

He shook his head and walked to the other side of the desk, taking a seat.

I pushed my mask to the top of my head, then slipped it off, my newly shorn hair coming to rest against my cheeks and chin. "Actually, it's Lea."

He blinked and leaned back in his chair. "I apologize again, then. I must have confused your masks."

"No, you weren't confused." I turned the mask in my hands and examined its design and the crack across its surface. "This was my brother's mask. I couldn't save him, so I wear it now, to honor him."

He ran his fingers through his dark hair. "Then Dante and Bianca?"

"I searched . . ." I paused, my breath suddenly heavy in my throat. "I searched but could find no sign that anyone else escaped." My fault. It was my fault they were dead.

He nodded as if he expected this news.

"It doesn't mean anything, though," I added. "They could have gotten out before me. They could be safe. . . ."

He folded his hands in front of him on the desk. "Truthfully, I'm surprised to see any Saldana remaining. I was told the whole Family had been destroyed in their home."

I leaned forward. "Told by whom?"

He waved his fingers at me. "I cannot divulge that information."

"I need to know who killed my Family!"

His eyebrows arched in surprise. "How is it you do not?"

I settled against my chair. "It was dark, there was so much smoke. I couldn't make out their masks. Rafeo, before he died, said it was the Da Vias. Is this true? Please tell me if this is true." *Please let it not be true.*

He didn't respond, but the dark look on his face was all the confirmation I needed.

My stomach dropped. To know, to actually *know* it was the Da Vias who had killed us . . .

Yes, there were the Family politics and the struggle for rank and power. Objectively, it made sense that the second

Family would destroy the first when the first was low in numbers and wealth. But Val . . . didn't he love me? Had it all counted for nothing?

I closed my eyes. What hurt more? The death of my Family, or the cold betrayal?

I needed to breathe. In and out. Just like that.

We were the first Family, and yes, the Saldanas and Da Vias shared Ravenna as a territory, but that had been the way of things for generations. There was bad blood because of the failed marriage between Estella Da Via and my uncle Marcello, of course. But that had happened decades ago, and they hadn't moved against us in all that time. What had changed to make the Da Vias decide to end us now?

The plague, of course.

The plague had weakened the Saldanas, almost crippled us. And the plague had put Estella Da Via in charge. She wanted change, while the Saldanas followed the old ways, and as long as we were the first Family, we made the decisions. With us gone their territory would be larger and they would become richer and none of the other Families would be strong enough to face them alone. No one would punish them for what they'd done to us. They could take what they wanted—and Estella wanted to be in charge and wanted the Saldanas gone. It had taken her only two years to work out a means to do so—using Val to get to me.

I looked back at the king, who was watching me thoughtfully.

"Will you help me destroy them?" I asked.

Surprise flashed across his face. "No. No, I can't do that."

"But you were friends with my father. And they murdered him! Murdered him while he slept!"

"Lea, I cannot interfere in Family politics. I cannot show bias. The other Families would come for my head, and then where would the country be?"

"It wasn't his fault! It was my fault. I trusted . . ." My words caught in my throat, and I clutched the key at my chest. "Didn't you love my father?"

"Of course." He sighed. "Dante Saldana was a brother to me. I would've done anything he asked."

"Then help me with this!"

"No. This is something Dante would *never* have asked. He helped put me on the throne for the good of everyone, not for himself or his Family. And I'm not sure how he would feel about his only daughter planning to take on the most powerful of the Families."

"I have no choice. Safraella demands it of me." Did She? Because maybe I was actually doing this for myself. It didn't matter. I'd murdered in Her name before, and I would do so again. The only difference this time would be that I'd take personal satisfaction in sending the Da Vias to face Her.

"Be that as it may, there are other ways you could appease Safraella. You could pledge yourself to the church. Or you could continue on as a clipper."

"Live my life cloistered away? Never. And the Families— the Da Vias—would never allow me to continue to serve Her as a clipper. They would not rest until I was dead."

"You could marry into another Family. Surely one of them would be glad to have you."

"I have no rank now, no status. And any Family that took me on would have to face the wrath of the Da Vias." I shook my head. "None of them will take that risk for me." And they couldn't be trusted.

"No, this is what I must do. Alone, if need be. I'm the only Saldana left, anyway."

He shifted in his seat, tapping his fingers together. "Fine. I see you cannot be dissuaded from your path. And that is your right. But you don't have to do it alone. You are not, in fact, the only Saldana left."

My heart skipped a beat. I leaned forward.

"If you're interested, I can tell you where your uncle, Marcello, hid himself after leaving Lovero."

My uncle Marcello. My stomach knotted. No one else had survived then. The king was referring to my traitorous uncle, who was better left forgotten. We did not speak of him.

I was truly alone.

The king leaned back in his chair. "The Da Vias and possibly even the Maiettas would pay dearly to learn where he is—"

"I will not sell out my uncle, estranged though he may be, to the Da Vias to save my own life. I will not give them the opportunity to shed any more Saldana blood."

The king held up a hand. "You misunderstand. I offer you his location only if you wish to seek him out for help or

Family obligation. Nothing more."

"No," I said. "I could not trust him."

The king sighed. "Lea, I know the disaster surrounding Marcello was before your time, but I knew him quite well, and Marcello Saldana *was* trustworthy."

I'd thought Val was trustworthy. I stood and picked up my mask. I was done. There was nothing the king could do for me. *Would* do for me.

He took a quill and a scrap of parchment from a drawer, as well as an inkpot. "If you change your mind, last I'd heard, this is where you can find him."

He passed me the slip of parchment. I read the words. The city of Yvain in Rennes, Lovero's neighboring country. I dropped the scrap into the lamp, and the flame burned it to ash.

The king stood and walked to the hidden door. He pressed on a latch and slid the door open before he stepped through. He paused, looking back at me.

"Besides," he added, "Marcello Saldana would know how to find the Da Vias' Family home."

He closed the door, and I was left alone.

eight

†

I WALKED THROUGH THE STREETS OF GENONI, AVOID-
ing the large crowds this time of night. Maybe the king
couldn't help me, but calling on him had been the right
thing to do. Even if I'd thought of Marcello, I hadn't known
where to find him, or that *he* knew how to find the Da Vias.

Marcello had to help me. We were blood, after all, family, even if I'd never met him, even if he was disgraced. And
he'd once been Family, too.

Yvain, a tiny city, sat on the border of the country of
Rennes, Lovero's nearest neighbor. It would take a day to
reach it, but if I traded off between Butters and Dorian, I
would make better time. The more I thought about it, the
more it seemed like a good idea. I'd reach the city of Yvain,
find Marcello Saldana, enlist his help in destroying the Da
Vias, then return to Lovero together and burn them out like
the rat's nest they were.

I closed my eyes and pictured them dying, their leathers

soaked with blood, their eyes sightless, their breaths stilled. My vision drifted toward Val, and I snapped my eyes open.

I'd have to be quick about this. Sooner or later the Da Vias would learn I'd survived, and then they'd be after me. And if they chased me to Yvain, it could lead them right to Marcello. If the Da Vias could find him, they would kill him, too.

I'd collect the horses, find somewhere to hide for the rest of the night, and head out at first light when it was safest. If I had to stop, there were monasteries scattered on the dead plains.

I returned to the garden and found the horses waiting patiently. I freed Butters from the pergola and tied him to Dorian again.

I paused, the back of my neck shivering beneath my hood. Someone was watching me.

I scratched Dorian's chin, my actions casual and unconcerned. Three of them, at least. Two on the roof of a nearby house and the other on the ground, hiding, poorly, behind a bush near the entrance. Terrible skills. Even Val could get closer to me, and he barely tried.

I bent over, lifting Dorian's hoof, to give the appearance of freeing a wedged stone. I slipped my hand under my cloak and secured a pair of daggers. I didn't have room in the cramped garden to unsheathe my sword.

I waited, certain one would make a move while I was "distracted." It was what I'd do. Nothing happened.

Time to take the lead, then.

I stood and faced the entrance and the clipper hiding there. "Well come on, then!" I yelled. "You're here for me, aren't you?"

The two on the roof looked at each other. The third revealed himself at the entrance to the garden. They watched me silently. I'd taken them by surprise, and they seemed unsure how to proceed. Rank amateurs.

The clipper before me stepped closer. The light from the moon showed brown splotches, reminiscent of ink blots, decorating his mask. Family Addamo, then. Alexi, to be specific. The other two I didn't recognize. Mother always tried to get me to memorize every mask, to be able to recall every clipper in every Family by their masks alone, but I could only remember a select few from each. Unlike Rafeo, who knew every single one.

I loosened my spine. I could take Alexi, even with two others backing him.

Alexi lifted a knife and tapped it against his mask.

"You've taken us a bit by surprise," he said. "We expected Rafeo." He pointed his dagger at my mask.

I shrugged. "Sorry to disappoint."

"Oh, I wouldn't say we're disappointed. The Da Vias will want to hear that a Saldana survived, and whether that's Rafeo or you, doesn't really matter to us. Either way, the Da Vias will be the first Family, and we'll have earned their favor. And you'll be dead."

Above me, one of the Addamo clippers slid closer—a move he probably thought I wouldn't notice. No wonder they were only the seventh Family. I tightened my grip on my knife. "You can give it your best attempt."

I whipped the knife at the two on the roof. The first clipper dodged, but the one behind was midstep. My knife struck the tile roof at his feet. I grimaced behind my mask. Knife throwing had always been my weakest skill. But the Addamo clipper lost his balance on the steep roof. He stumbled, tripped, and fell off the edge, landing with a loud thump on the flagstones below. He rolled onto his side and lay still, the ground spreading with blood beneath his head.

One down, even with my feeble knife toss.

Alexi rushed me, switching his grip on the knife in his left hand. He jabbed. I blocked and kicked at his knee. He twisted, but not fast enough. My foot hooked behind his ankle, and I pulled him off balance. He stumbled behind Butters, who swung his rump, excited by the commotion. Alexi fell to his knees.

I sliced through the rope securing Dorian. I was holding my own, but I didn't want to be denied a quick escape.

The remaining clipper jumped to the pergola and dropped behind me. He aimed a kick at the back of my knees. The kick connected, but I rolled with my knees bent, freeing myself from the close confines of the garden.

Finally, in the street, I found space to unsheathe my sword. I let it ring against its scabbard. The sound bounced off the brick walls of the houses around me.

Alexi, on his feet again, and the other Addamo approached

me cautiously from the garden. I waited, steadying my staccato breathing.

I twirled my short sword in my hand, a move of bravado my parents would have been disgusted to see.

Behind them, Butters and Dorian wandered into the street.

"Come on." I gestured the Addamos closer with the dagger in my left hand. "Or do the Addamos lack the edge to take a lone clipper outside her territory?"

My taunt did its job. Alexi charged, freeing his sword, the other clipper a step behind. Alexi lunged sloppily at me. I leaned away, dodging the swing, and jerked my knee into his gut. His breath left him in a whoosh. He stumbled, barely managing to keep hold of his sword. The other clipper rushed at me. This time I twisted inside his reach. A quick jab at his throat with my left hand and his life was over. He stumbled backward. His sword fell to the street with a clatter as he struggled to keep his life's blood from pouring out of his neck.

Movement behind me. Dumb, to be distracted by my kill. But dumb of Alexi to come at me with such an obvious move. The Addamos had no grace.

I twisted. Alexi raised his sword over his head. Again, I stepped closer, and thrust my sword up under his ribs. He coughed, sword tumbling from his fingers.

I jerked my sword from his body as he collapsed to the street.

I wiped my sword and dagger clean as I caught my breath. It had been easy to kill them. Much, much too easy. I sheathed my weapons.

If this was an accurate representation of the other, lower-ranked Families, then the king was right. The only Family who could've ever expected to take out the Saldanas was the Da Vias. And they'd only been able to do so because of me.

Above me, a boot scraped on tile.

On the roofs, more clippers stared at me behind their quiet bone masks. Addamos, each one. I couldn't take on the full dozen threatening me now.

The clipper in front, the leader and probably Alexi's father, Nicolai, stepped closer, his hand raised in a signal to the rest of his clippers.

I took a step backward, toward my horses waiting for me in the street. I slipped my fingers in one of my pockets, closing my fist around two small spheres.

The Addamos watched me. My muscles flinched. They were hesitating, and the tension burned through my limbs. I couldn't stand the waiting. . . .

I pointed at Alexi and the other clipper, dead at my feet. I shrugged. My flippant attitude would force their move.

Nicolai's hand dropped and the Addamos charged, jumping off the roof.

I cast the spheres at the ground. Smoke bombs. The thin ceramic casing shattered, combining the two liquids inside and creating a thick, gray smoke.

I turned and leaped onto the nearest horse—Butters. He

was still tied to Dorian's saddle. I swore as I sliced through the rope.

The first of the Addamos dashed through the smoke, but quick pressure to Butters's right side signaled him to kick out with his hooves, scattering the clippers.

Then we were free. Butters's shod hooves clattered against the flagstones, Dorian behind us, as we raced away from the Addamos.

Butters was fast, almost too fast, racing down an unfamiliar street in the middle of the night. Ahead, a group of revelers appeared. We ran through, dispersing them and their screams of alarm.

I aimed Butters straight, trying to get as much of a lead as possible. This was Addamo territory; they'd catch me, given enough time. I had to get free of Genoni. If I couldn't escape them, no one would make the Da Vias pay.

I shook my head. I'd killed three members of their Family, all while in their territory. They'd chase me even after I left Genoni. Simply leaving the city wouldn't be enough.

I glanced behind me. Dorian paced Butters, dutifully following. Maybe I could buy myself some time. . . .

"Dorian!" I called his name over the sound of their loud hooves, and his ears twitched in response. I shouted the command for him to turn right. He tossed his head, warring with his desire to stay behind Butters, but I had trained him well. He swung down a side street, away from us.

I lost sight of him. *This is their fault—the Da Vias. One more beautiful thing gone from my life.* Tears pricked my eyes. *Don't think about it.* He was a good horse. Someone would give him a good home.

At the next fork, I swung Butters north, away from Ravenna and my home territory. Some of the Addamos would've gone ahead to the city limits to catch me there. Hopefully this change in direction would shave off a few pursuers.

There! Before me stood the old, crumbled city wall. Behind it lay the end of the tightly packed buildings of the cities and the start of fields, spread through the valley until the river cut across them. That was my destination—the river and the bridge that spanned it.

We hit the fields and I leaned forward in the saddle. Butters took the cue gladly and raced faster.

A shout from behind. I spared a glance. From two different streets Addamos poured from the city, seven of them, each mounted on a horse of their own. They whipped their mounts in a desperate attempt to catch me.

They could do it, too. Butters was fast and willing, but their mounts were fresher, and they knew the quickest path to reach the bridge.

A whistle shrieked above me. I hauled left on Butters's reins, and only my quick reflexes saved us from the arrow. Butters slid to the side, almost losing his feet. I kicked him to regain his lost speed.

I stared over my shoulder for the archer.

There were two of them, their horses moving slower as their riders used both hands to pull on their bows.

I kneed Butters farther left, placing myself directly in front of the closing front runners, blocking me from the view of the archers.

Only a few yards ahead stood the bridge over the river. They wouldn't follow me across it. They couldn't. Only someone with nothing to lose would cross the bridge at night.

Someone like me.

All bridges over the river were crooked, with sharp turns in the middle before they continued on.

Spirits, like people, need bridges to pass over rivers, but they could only cross moving water in a straight line. The bridges zigzagged, to prevent the ghosts from reaching the cities.

An arrow slammed into my shoulder. I slipped left and lost my grip. Only my thighs squeezing Butters's barrel kept me in my seat. He stumbled again, compensating for my sudden shift in balance. Then we were on the bridge. Butters cut the last corner with an awkward leap. He landed, and I slapped painfully against the saddle. We'd done it. We'd crossed the river.

I'd reached the dead plains, home to angry ghosts.

nine

†

I DIDN'T SLOW BUTTERS UNTIL WE WERE SAFE FROM the Addamo archers. I stopped him with a tap of my legs and my voice. He halted, his head hanging as his sides heaved.

Bonelessly, I slid to the ground, my knees almost giving way beneath me. I leaned against Butters and examined my left shoulder.

The arrowhead had pierced me through the top of my shoulder, the metal tip protruding from the front of me. The injury wasn't life-threatening if I could treat it and it didn't become infected. I wouldn't treat it here, though. Not until I was safe.

The Addamos sat on their horses on the other side of the river. My gamble had worked—they wouldn't come after me into the dead plains, not at night.

I hadn't entered their city with the intent of killing three of their members. That had come about in self-defense. If they had any honor, they'd take this as a lesson to train their numbers better.

They watched me for a few more moments, and then, as one, they turned from the river and headed back into the city.

With a knife, I sliced off a strip of fabric from the bottom of my cloak. I tied it around my back and left arm with help from my teeth, immobilizing my arm across my chest to prevent further injury. Blood seeped into the makeshift bandage. I paused to catch my breath. I didn't have much time. I'd left the Addamos behind, but what waited for me on the dead plains was much worse.

"Plains" was a misnomer. The long grasses before me rolled over gentle hills. Their peaceful appearance belied their true nature. But returning to Lovero now would be a death sentence. The Addamos would be watching for me. And soon they'd inform the Da Vias. Luckily, the three Addamos who knew I wasn't Rafeo were dead.

The pain in my shoulder settled into a fierce ache. Regardless of my injury, I had to keep moving if I wanted to have a chance.

The dead plains were dotted with shrines and monasteries dedicated to Safraella. If I could reach one, I'd find sanctuary.

I remembered the stack of paper on my father's desk, the bids for our new Family priest. I scanned my memory of the one I'd examined, searching for the location of the monastery. Northwest of Genoni.

Mounting Butters with a single arm was difficult, but after

much swearing and kicking, I managed to climb into the saddle. I rested, then nudged Butters forward. We headed northwest. I kept my eyes peeled, watching the dark landscape for movement.

Everything was wrong. Nothing was the way it was supposed to be. Why had this happened to me? How had my life come to this? Fleeing in the night, injured and alone.

My fault. All my fault.

But, also, the Da Vias'. I tightened my fist on the reins. Butters flicked his ears. It was their fault, too. *Don't forget that. Don't forget this feeling, the rage flowing in your blood.*

Val. His actions had condemned me to this fate. If I could just speak to him, hear his side of things—no. *Don't be dumb, Lea.* Nothing he could say would fix what had happened. Even if, more than anything, I wanted to feel his arms around me, telling me everything would be all right. That no one would find out about us. That we'd be safe together. But now I was alone and I'd never be safe again.

Ahead, something lay in the tall grass. Butters snorted, and we approached cautiously. Nothing moved other than the grass in the wind.

I knew it would be a body. I looked down as we passed. A man, dressed in cheap silks that fluttered around him in the night breeze. He lay facedown, his head turned to the side, dirt pressed against his mouth and open eyes. Nothing marked him, as if he'd dropped dead from a failed heart. It wasn't his heart, though, that had brought his death.

Anyone could become a ghost. People who died out of

favor with their gods, people who didn't worship a god, even people of good faith who died with too much rage or despair in their hearts. It was why we left the coins on people we clipped. It acted as a balm to ease their rage, to signal to Safraella that they'd been murdered for holy reasons and deserved a chance at a new life.

Movement to my left. I turned slowly, trying not to draw attention.

A wisp of white, a figure floating in the night across the field. An angry ghost. The dead plains were full of them.

Many gods had their own personal hells they could damn their followers to, but Safraella did not. If someone was devoted to Safraella but died out of favor, they entered a sort of purgatory. Ghosts congregated on the dead plains, waiting for a person to stumble upon them so they could steal the body and turn that person into a ghost.

But a ghost could never again be a person, and after a day or so it would abandon its stolen body—often on the dead plains, like the body in the tall grass—and begin its search anew, endlessly looking for the life that had been taken from it.

I shivered. The angry ghosts were dangerous. They could use their rage to move objects, or they could rip your soul from your body. No one would ever willingly face a ghost. The ghosts were why the Addamos had let me go.

I ducked my head and asked Butters to speed up. So far the ghost hadn't noticed me. Sunrise was only an hour or two away. If I could pass through unmolested until then, I could travel to Yvain and find my uncle. Luckily, the Addamos didn't know where I was headed, but there were only so many places one could go to from the plains.

Butters huffed, his breath steaming in a puff of white in the cool spring night.

To the right, more movement. Another ghost, heading south toward the river.

I hunched in my cloak. My shoulder burned and my vision faded. I bit my lip until my sight cleared. I needed to stay in control or I wouldn't make it out of the dead plains.

But maybe . . . maybe it would be okay to not make it out. Maybe it was what I deserved for the deaths of my Family, an afterlife spent wandering the dead plains as a ghost. . . .

No. If the ghosts took me, then no one would make the Da Vias pay for what they'd done.

Butters shook his head, the metal buckles on his bridle tinkling quietly. I held my breath as the closer ghost paused, then turned toward me.

Oh gods . . .

The ghost shrieked—a guttural screech that echoed across the field. It rushed my way, its white, glowing form spread out behind it like morning mist.

I kicked Butters. He jumped into a canter.

Ghosts were dead. They never tired; they would keep coming until the sun rose or I could find safety.

The angry ghost caught up to me. My voice evaporated in my throat and my fingers clutched the reins until pain rushed through my fingers. I stared at the ghost as it kept pace with us, the rage on its face, the darkness in its mouth as it howled at me. It had been human, once. A woman. A faint outline glowed where her throat had been slashed. Someone had taken her life, but not someone in my Family. We marked our kills to avoid creating angry ghosts. But ghosts didn't follow logic, or mercy. They followed their rage until it led them to a person.

The ghost reached for me. I jerked Butters away, my shoulder stretching with fresh, hot pain. Her fingers passed through the saddle. She shrieked louder, her screams reverberating in my skull.

More ghosts appeared; she'd called them in her rage. They raced to us and Butters flattened his ears, snorting, his eyes wide and white. Every hoofbeat pounded through my shoulder until my body was awash with agony.

Their screeches deafened me. They seeped into my body until I clenched my eyes shut and screamed at them, trying anything to get them to stop their terrible cries.

I leaned over Butters and forced him faster. He broke into a wild gallop. My thighs strained, and it was all I could do to stay on, one armed.

The ghosts fell behind, and for a moment it seemed we would outrun them all, but they rallied and raced after us.

Butters's breaths beat beneath me, matching the rhythm of my own heart. A rock flew out of the night and struck Butters on the hind end. A ghost had thrown it.

Butters bucked, squealing, and I slipped across the saddle, losing the reins completely. Only my feet in the stirrups kept me from spilling off. I lunged for the pommel and grasped it tightly, gasping as spots flashed before my eyes.

With no pressure on the reins to slow his headlong gallop, Butters flew across the plains. His blond mane whipped painfully against my face as I crouched over his neck and struggled to keep my grip on the pommel. At this speed, falling off could be a death sentence, even without the arrow in my body. If I didn't crack my skull or snap my neck, I was loaded with sharp objects, any of which could lodge fatally in my flesh.

I used my left hand, still bound across my torso, to dig through a pouch on my waist for a Saldana Family coin. I clutched it tightly in my palm and prayed to Safraella.

A ghost appeared beside us. Its spectral hands reached for me. I twisted, but its fingers slipped into the flesh of my thigh.

Icy pain cracked through my body, radiating from where the ghost touched me. I shouted as the cold spread through my leg. The ghost pulled its hands away, but with it came a transparent image of my limb, the ghost's fingers wrapped tightly around it as it tried to tug me from my own body.

"No!" I yelled. I couldn't fail my Family. "No!"

The coin in my hand grew warm. Then hot. It burned, erasing all other pains. I struggled to open my hand, to be rid of the coin, but my fingers were paralyzed.

I screamed, leaning over Butters, clutching my burning hand to my chest. I turned my face away as the ghost slowly pulled my soul from my body.

The pain in my hand stopped, like a quick breath. An

explosion of light erupted from my skin, catapulting the ghost away.

Salvation appeared before me: the monastery, nearly hidden amid a grove of old oak trees.

I put my burned hand out of mind and focused on the reins bouncing on Butters's neck. I counted to three, then lunged for them, the leather slapping into my palm. I hauled back, trying to slow Butters, to show him I was in charge again. He tossed his head, his mouth and eyes wide, but his ears flicked backward and he slowed.

I turned him toward the monastery as a small group of ghosts passed us by on the right and flowed around the trees.

A thunderous crack split the night and a tree jerked, showering the field with new leaves as the ghosts fought to knock it down. The tree creaked and toppled over, right in our path.

We couldn't stop—we were going too fast.

I leaned forward over Butters's neck again, loosening the reins until he reached the downed tree. He bunched his legs and we flew over the tree trunk, the ghosts behind shrieking in renewed anger and rage.

We raced through the gates of the monastery, free of the mob of angry ghosts.

ten

✝

AT THE SOUND OF BUTTERS'S HOOVES CLATTERING ON the stone entryway, the priests of Safraella rushed outside carrying lanterns.

The angry ghosts milled around the fence surrounding the monastery, held back by the priests' faith and the holy ground, blessed by Safraella.

The priests reached my side, and I slid off Butters into their capable hands.

"Sister, how do you come to be here so late at night?" The speaker was a man with dark skin, and hair clipped close to his scalp. He had brown, kind eyes with laugh lines around the edges.

"You mean so early, Brother," another one said. To the east, the sun crested the horizon and the wailing ghosts faded away in the soft light of morning.

My legs wobbled, but the priest helped me to stand. "I fled across the dead plains."

He called for another priest to tend to Butters, whose chest heaved as he tried to regain his breath.

"You have been arrow shot!" he exclaimed.

I laughed. Surely he knew I was aware.

"Come, Sister." He lent me his shoulder. "We will tend you inside. I am Brother Faraday. When you are treated, you should tell me your tale, for it must be full of adventure and daring."

I glanced at him and his eyes sparkled. He was younger than I'd first guessed. Maybe only a few years older than me. "I know you."

His left eyebrow arched upward.

"I saw your request to become the Saldana Family priest."

"Ah!"

Inside the stone walls, candlelight filled the halls with a soft yellow light. Faraday led me past a great room with a stone altar at the far end and into a small chamber with only a table and chair.

A few priests hovered in the doorway, peering past one another at me.

Someone outside huffed, and the men parted to allow a priest with a bucket of hot water and towels draped over his arm to enter. Two others followed.

One of the priests, who introduced himself as Brother Sebastien, cut my cloak away from my body, carefully removing it so it wouldn't catch on the arrow shaft protruding from my shoulder.

He examined the wound. "There's no easy way to do

this. We'll have to force the arrowhead the rest of the way through your flesh. Then we'll be better able to remove the shaft."

I slipped off my mask. Another priest took it reverently.

"We'll have it cleaned and repaired," Brother Faraday said.

"No!" My shout startled them. I lowered my voice. "Cleaning is fine. But the crack . . . leave it. It's a reminder for me."

The priest carried my mask away.

"What have you done to your hand?" Brother Sebastien seized my wrist.

I'd almost forgotten my hand. I turned it over and with some effort managed to peel my fingers open.

"What is this?" Sebastien plucked the coin carefully from my scorched palm and passed it to Brother Faraday. My burned skin cooled painfully in the air. It was red and raw. Brother Sebastien dabbed at my hand with a damp cloth.

Faraday cleaned the coin under the light of a lantern.

"It's a holy coin," I answered. "I was clutching it in my fear."

"But why are you burned?" Faraday asked.

I shrugged, then hissed in pain from the movement.

"I don't know how it burned me," I replied to Faraday. Sebastien cut away my leathers and started to clean my shoulder of blood. "I didn't think I'd be able to reach the monastery before the ghosts stopped me. I clutched the coin and pleaded for Safraella to save me."

Faraday paused in his examination of the coin and stared

at me, his gaze so intense I fidgeted in my seat.

Sebastien pressed his hands against my shoulders, holding me in place. "Miss Oleander, I must implore you to remain still."

"You recognize me?" I asked, surprised.

"The coin and the mask are Family Saldana, though the mask belongs to Rafeo Saldana. The late Rafeo Saldana, if I've judged things correctly." He glanced at me, then returned to my shoulder. "There are only two women in the Saldana Family, and you don't look nearly old enough to be Bianca. Therefore, Oleander."

"I go by Lea," I mumbled.

"Yes, well, perhaps you should return to your discussion with Brother Faraday, as this next part will be . . . unpleasant."

Sebastien shoved the arrow the rest of the way through my shoulder.

I grunted and the room rolled. Sweat broke out on my forehead and my stomach contorted.

Sebastien broke the shaft and removed the arrow from my shoulder.

"Some stitching on both sides and you'll be back to normal in no time," he said. "As long as you refrain from heavy use of this arm. I take it you are right-handed? Good, then it shouldn't be so difficult."

Brother Faraday diverted my attention while Sebastien set a needle to my skin. "The coin itself burned you? After you prayed to Safraella?"

"Yes. I couldn't release it."

"But the ghosts still chased you? I don't understand what this means. . . ." The last bit he addressed to himself, his gaze retreating inward. Sebastien finished the stitches in my back and moved to the front of my shoulder.

"While it was burning me," I continued, "a ghost tried to pull me out of my body, and something pushed it away."

That drew Faraday's attention. "What do you mean?"

"I'm not sure I can explain. There was a flash, like embers maybe? And the ghost was thrown away from me. I didn't pay the flash much attention. I was trying to stay seated on my horse."

"A miracle?" he asked. "You held off a ghost by the strength of your faith alone?"

There had been stories and tales of priests or clippers so devoted to Safraella or their own gods, so favored that the gods protected them from the ghosts. They could walk the dead plains at night, unmolested. Those of incredible, fervent faith—saints or those who saw the goddess herself in a vision—were sometimes granted true resurrections and brought back to life in their existing body. It hadn't happened in hundreds of years. I scowled. "I'm no saint."

Faraday blinked rapidly. He flipped the coin in his palm. "Do you mind if I keep this?"

I waved his question aside. "Have it. I have a pouch full of them. They're really only worth the value of the coin."

"To you, maybe, but to me it is apparent you had an experience with the goddess Herself, that She somehow deigned to answer your prayers. You must be very special, Lea Saldana."

Sebastien, finished with the stitches in my shoulder, dressed the wound with a foul-smelling salve, and wrapped it tightly with white cloth. He moved on to my hand, cleaning it with another damp towel before slathering the burns with the same salve, wrapping my hand and pronouncing me mended.

"I don't see that I'm favored by Safraella," I responded to Faraday. "Two nights ago my whole Family was slaughtered by the Da Vias. If She loved us so, then why did She let us be destroyed?"

Faraday closed his fingers around the coin. "Yes, I can see how that would be . . . upsetting. But do you not also see how you were the sole survivor? How you escaped the slaughter of your Family?"

I shook my head.

Luck. It had been only dumb luck that had saved me.

And since everything had been my fault, the luck tasted like dry ashes in my mouth.

Brother Faraday showed me to a room. It was small, and sparsely furnished, but the bed was clean and my body sank into it. My mind, however, could find no rest.

I was surrounded by men of faith, servants of Safraella, and yet I'd never felt so alone. The pain in my shoulder and hand paled against the pain of my heart. Before, whenever I'd felt sad or lonely, I'd talk to Rafeo, who would be quick to cheer me with a joke. Or I'd find Val, who could make my body tremble with well-placed hands and lips.

But Rafeo's voice had been silenced. And the love between Val and me had been a lie.

My shoulder ached as my thoughts plagued me, and finally, after close to an hour, I sat back up.

Someone pounded on my door, but before I had a chance to answer, Brother Faraday slipped inside, latching the door behind him. He held a robe and a wide-brimmed hat in his arms.

"Brother Faraday?"

"There's no time," he whispered, handing me the clothes. "The Addamos have come looking for you. Well, looking for your brother Rafeo."

I jumped to my feet. "What?"

"Put on the robe and hat. We're going to sneak you out. You'll have to leave your horse—Butters, was it?—but we'll take good care of him. The rest of your belongings have already been packed."

"I don't understand." I slipped the rough wool over my head. "How did they find me so quickly?"

"They must have left at dawn to get here so soon, though I suspect they're checking as many monasteries as they can. And they haven't found you yet. But they might if you linger." Faraday opened the door a crack and peeked out. He glanced over his shoulder, and after I tugged the hat in place, hiding my hair, he gestured for me to follow him.

Voices trickled around the corner of the empty

hallway—Brother Sebastian arguing with someone.

Faraday held up a hand and we ducked into an alcove. I clutched my key around my neck and listened carefully.

It wasn't an argument, it was an interrogation from an Addamo clipper.

"He had to have stopped here," the clipper's voice echoed.

"I'm sorry, Brother, but no man called on us last night."

The front door to the monastery opened, and another Addamo walked in. Faraday and I pressed our backs against the wall of the alcove.

"There's a palomino stallion in the stables, well-bred," the new clipper announced. "Could be the same one he was riding."

"Well?" the first Addamo asked Sebastien.

I chanced a look. Sebastien bowed his head. "The horse wandered onto our land this morning. He had no tack to identify his owner. We are planning to keep him until his owner claims him. It is only right, considering how finely bred he is."

"It's awfully convenient."

"I'd actually say it's inconvenient," Sebastien said. "Both for you and for the owner of the horse. Are you truly confident this clipper braved the dead plains at night?"

"Of course we are. He was arrow shot by one of my men. We watched him ride into the dead plains north from Genoni."

"Perhaps he succumbed to his wounds? Or the fury of the ghosts? An injured man is more at risk for possession.

Or maybe he returned to Lovero, through a different gate."

The Addamos paused as they thought this over. "The Caffarellis could be hiding him," one mumbled to the other. "Maybe he circled back on foot to the Lilyan gate."

"Why don't you come this way and I will get you some refreshments," Brother Sebastien said.

One of the Addamos made a frustrated sound, followed by footsteps as they trailed after Sebastien. "The Addamos would pay handsomely for any information, of course."

Whatever Sebastien said in reply was lost as they left the room.

Faraday and I waited a few more moments to make sure it was safe for us to move.

"You could've told them about me," I whispered.

He shrugged. "Like the king, we do not support one Family over another. They should know this."

"But by helping me, aren't you supporting the Saldanas?"

"Haven't you heard? The Saldanas are all dead, wiped out by the Da Vias. Anyway, it's a disgrace they offered us money like we're some sort of commoners. We, too, are disciples of Safraella, even if we don't murder in Her name. Sometimes clippers forget this."

I smiled. "When you're a clipper, you're schooled to think highly of your own importance."

He peeked around the corner, then waved me forward. We scurried out to the yard. There a wagon waited, hitched to a chestnut mare. In the back rested my two bags, though the saddle and saddlebags had been left behind.

"Come." Faraday gestured as we rushed to the wagon.

"Won't we look suspicious?"

"We're just two priests, going about our duties."

Priests inside the city walls generally tended to the common, accepting offerings of blood or bone from people who hoped to gain favor from Safraella, seeing to their spiritual needs.

The monasteries on the dead plains, though, served many purposes, including offering sanctuary for travelers. But their two main duties as priests of Safraella were to play the role of cleaners on the dead plains—finding any bodies and returning them to their families if possible—and to pray for the angry ghosts.

At night, the priests would gather at the gates and pray for the angry dead, pray for their torment to end, for Safraella to offer them a rebirth so they could stop their endless searching for a body. No one knew if it worked, but the priests had faith.

"I have to say, I never expected a clipper to ride here in the middle of the night seeking safety." Faraday took the driver's seat and adjusted his own hat. I sat on the bench beside him. "You certainly brought much excitement with you."

"I apologize."

He smiled. "It has been liberating. A nice change of pace. Sometimes, things can get boring."

I yawned and regretted my lost rest. "What? At a monastery in the middle of the dead plains, surrounded by angry ghosts?"

"Yes, well. As you may have noticed, the ghosts aren't very good conversationalists."

He flicked the reins and we moved forward, leaving the monastery behind. "Where is it you're headed?"

I paused. Faraday had only helped me. And he was a priest. Of course, I'd trusted Val, and look where that had ended.

But there was no point in lying, not if I wanted to reach my destination and find my uncle. He was the key to the Da Vias and my revenge. "Yvain," I finally admitted.

"Then we'd better move a little faster." He clucked his tongue and the horse sped up.

eleven

†

YVAIN WAS A CITY AS DIFFERENT FROM RAVENNA AS
the dead plains monastery was from the palace in Genoni.
Where Ravenna was a city of nightlife, masquerades, and
carnivals, Yvain was tiny and quiet, more provincial, with
fresh flowers in the window boxes of every house, and fragrant red mosses growing between the cobblestone streets.

I hated it immediately. There was no life to the people.
No sea air and the sweet smell of the lantern oil. No fashion
and pride in what they wore. In Yvain, the women didn't
even cover their hair, and beneath the cloying smell of the
flowers, the warm stench of sewage from the canals drifted
everywhere.

Walls divided the city from the dead plains, since Rennes
was not a country that bowed to Safraella. Ghosts could not
pass through walls, and the city walls kept the dead plains
ghosts out, but anyone who died within the city, behind the
walls, and became an angry ghost would be trapped inside

the city with everyone else. So like the old days of Lovero, people stayed inside their homes once the sun set.

"Why doesn't their regent simply bow to Safraella?" I complained as the wagon slowly made its way into town behind a line of people entering the city before the sun set.

Faraday shrugged. "It's a question of geography. Lovero is pushed against the sea on the south and west, and bordered by the dead plains on the north and east. When the Sapienzas took the throne, the people supported a royal line that would bow to Safraella and free the country from the menace of the ghosts. But Yvain is the only city in Rennes pressed against the border of the dead plains. It's more easily managed with the walls, and any ghosts inside Yvain can't get farther into the country because of the canals. To the ghosts it's a labyrinth of waterways."

"It still seems it would be a good idea to follow Safraella."

"The people of Yvain, and Rennes as a whole, find our devotion to a goddess who deals in death and murder to be macabre at best." Faraday chuckled.

"She offers resurrection."

"Yvain's patron is Acacius, a minor god of crops and debts. It's why they have flowers everywhere. And you will find honorable people here. If they accrue a debt, they will do anything to repay it. If they are devout, Acacius gives them their own version of eternal life, by making them one with the land and plants and animals."

"I'm sorry," I scoffed. "But I'd rather deal with blood and death and return as a person than water some pretty flowers and pay my debts and come back as a wheat field."

"Well, you are biased. But for them, becoming part of the land is a form of immortality. They would rather try to live full lives here and now than be faced with death and murder only to be reborn and have to face it all over again. Acacius offers gardens and farms, trees and flowers. You will find little hunger in Rennes."

We struggled to break free of the crowd, Faraday steering the wagon past the heavy gates of the city walls. He shifted in his seat. "You don't have to go after the Da Vias, you know."

I stiffened. I hadn't told him my plan.

"Don't be alarmed. It just seems your most likely course of action." Faraday grinned. "But no one seems to realize you, Lea Saldana, survived the attack on your Family. Very few people get such a clean chance at starting over."

I pushed my growing anger aside. "You're suggesting I give up serving Safraella? You? Her disciple?" My whole life I'd been a clipper. If I gave it up now, no one would avenge my Family. Memories of the Saldanas would fade, until we'd simply become another of the lost Families. "Being a clipper is a calling."

"Oh, I understand a calling. But can it truly be counted one if you're born into it? Did your mother or father ever ask if you wanted to be something else?"

I snorted. "Who would give up a life of money and power and respect?"

"Those things are gone with the lives of your Family.

Those things are fleeting, as you can see. Intangible."

I looked away, scanning the faces of the crowd around us. They blended together until I didn't truly see anyone. "I do not care for the turn of this conversation, Brother."

Faraday held up a hand in surrender. "I apologize. I forget you are not of the church and unused to discussions of philosophy and faith. I spoke out of concern for a sister and that is all."

"Whatever my plans are, they are well considered." Find Marcello. Enlist his help. Kill the Da Vias before they realized I'd survived their attack. Simple.

Faraday nodded, then drove the wagon down a street almost as busy as the entrance. He pulled the wagon off to the side and stopped.

"Here we are." He gestured to a small building to his left. The setting sun highlighted a carving on the door, a blank bone mask. This was a church of Safraella.

"They allow our churches here?" I asked.

"Clippers are not allowed in Yvain, of course, but they do permit a few small churches. Mostly for the use of the monasteries. We return as many bodies from the dead plains to Rennes as we do to Lovero, but many of us can't make the trip back to our monasteries in one day. I'll stay here for the night and head back in the morning. There is plenty of room for you, too. The Brothers will be happy to welcome you."

It would be easy to walk into the church, get a good night's sleep, then find my uncle in the morning.

But the Addamos were already after me. If they had sent

members to the monasteries, then next they'd be heading for the nearest cities, including Yvain. And the first place they'd check would be the churches. Anyone could be made to talk. Anyone.

"This will be where we part ways," I said.

Faraday's smile dropped, but he nodded.

I jumped off the wagon and grabbed my two bags. "Thank you, Brother Faraday. I wish I could offer you something. In the past I would've granted you good grace with the Saldana Family. I still could, but it's not worth much these days."

"I'll take it." He leaned over me. "You may be the only Saldana now, but I do not think your Family's story is complete."

"Well, it's kind of you to say so, anyway. If ever you need assistance, Brother Faraday, you need only ask it of a Saldana. There. Now it's official."

"Thank you. Look for a letter from me. I will write with any information about your situation. Good luck, Lea Saldana."

He clucked the horse forward into a small alley beside the church. I fought off a yawn. My shoulder, hand, and entire body ached from the Addamos and ghosts. I'd need to find somewhere to rest.

Around me, the streets grew empty as the sky grew darker. Unlike Ravenna, there were no crowds of people waiting for the moon to rise. The few who remained headed for inns, lit brightly against the encroaching darkness of the streets. Building after building held businesses where they'd offer to lend money if paid back with interest. In Lovero, if people didn't pay their debts, someone typically hired a clipper to pay them a visit.

I walked along a canal, bags heavy in my hands, wrinkling my nose against the smell. The small boats people used as transportation were tied against docks and buildings. Lanterns adorned many of the boats, but for what purpose in a city that hid from the night, I didn't know. Perhaps Yvain had carnivals like Ravenna, and they decorated their boats with flowers and fires. *Remember why you're here.*

I couldn't care about masquerades or good food or flirting with boys. None of that meant anything anymore. Maybe it never had. Maybe if I'd been more like Matteo, focused on my studies, I would've been able to save my Family. To save Rafeo, who was lying alone in the tunnel.

I could still do it. If I worked hard, became the best clipper, maybe She would undo what had happened. Maybe She would return my Family to me. *Even just Rafeo. If I could have Rafeo, I could serve You better.*

No. It was impossible. True resurrections never happened. Or at least hadn't happened in hundreds of years. It was a stupid thing to wish for, but I couldn't help it. I missed them so much. So much.

This was my punishment. My terrible secret. Val had brought about my Family's death. They were gone forever and I was alone and this was my burden to bear.

I shook my head, freeing it from heavy thoughts, and found a dark alley to hide in. Safe from prying eyes, I changed out of the garments the monastery had provided and slipped into my familiar leathers. My boots buckled tightly against my calves and the belts fit snug around my waist, though they were too light without their customary weapons. I opened my second pack and slipped on every knife I could fit around my waist, in my boots, and on my arms. I sheathed my short sword and filled a pouch with a fair selection of my favorite poisons. After a moment of thought, I included a few smoke bombs as well. This was a new city, a new country. Better to carry a bit of everything and not need it than to regret something left in a pack.

There were no clippers in Rennes, or anywhere else other than Lovero. There were only nine Families, and we all called Lovero home. Maybe one day, if worship of Safraella spread past Loveran borders, there would be clippers in other cities, but for now I was alone.

I pulled on my cloak, fingering the small stitches a priest had used to close the arrow hole. My shoulder ached fiercely. Finally, I slipped on Rafeo's mask, inhaling deeply the smell of fresh oil used to clean it. I was safe now, behind the mask. And it was time to get to work.

I tied a rope around my bags so they would hang below me, then approached a nicely pitted wall, easy for climbing. I'd get to the roof, stash my belongings for now, and then explore the city and try to learn its ways. Maybe, if I was truly lucky, I'd actually find my uncle tonight and I could be back on my way to Ravenna with him tomorrow morning. Of course, chances were it would take a few days of searching and questioning the right people. After all, he'd been a Saldana once and could hide effectively.

I yawned. Or maybe I could just find somewhere to get some rest first. Yes, I wanted to find Marcello as soon as possible, especially since the Addamos were after me—and it was only a matter of time before the Da Vias learned about me, too—but I would be of no use exhausted.

I tightened my grip on the wall and pulled myself up.

My shoulder exploded in pain. I gasped, dropping to the street. I clutched my shoulder and closed my eyes until the pain faded to a steadier ache.

Damn it. I was too tired, and not thinking straight. My shoulder couldn't support me so soon after being stitched up.

I looked up at the roofs. I would find no sanctuary among them tonight. I'd have to find somewhere else, somewhere other than the churches or inns where the Addamos would be sure to look.

As much as a bed called to me, I couldn't take the risk.

I leaned against the alley wall, my muscles sagging, my body begging me to rest, to sleep.

The city remained empty except for a few people heading quickly to their destinations. It was so unlike Ravenna, where there was nothing to fear in the night. Well, except for the clippers. But now, with the hush and the quiet floating across the streets, gooseflesh broke out on my skin. I'd never seen people live this way.

A scream stabbed the night.

That was more like it. I turned, trying to pinpoint the

sound. Muffled shouts were followed by scuffs on cobble-stones. I grabbed my bags and rushed down the streets, my fatigue forgotten in the moment.

The noise stopped.

Ahead of me, a man stepped out of an alley, rubbing a hand through his white hair. I paused and he turned, catching sight of me. His face blanched and he shouted, then fled.

In Ravenna, people feared my mask, but they also respected me. Here, the man had just reacted in terror.

I let him race away. I had no reason to chase him.

I stepped into the alley, and there lay a body.

I approached it, waiting for any movement, but none came. I knew now why the man had fled so quickly.

The body was that of a young man, not much older than me. He had smooth brown skin and a dusting of hair over his lip. He had been stabbed in the chest three times, and his blank eyes stared at the dark skies. His coin bag lay beside him, torn during the struggle and empty.

He had been murdered for money.

A sudden surge of anger filled my chest. I should have chased after that man. I should have made him pay for what he'd done to this boy. I was a murderer, yes, but I murdered in the name of a god, and the deaths I brought came with the promise of a new life. What did this boy's death grant him?

He had been killed for no higher reason. He had been murdered in cold blood for a few coins.

The boy's blood seeped into his linen shirt, and I remembered how Rafeo's blood soaked his leathers, his hands weak and cold in the tunnel.

My leathers felt suddenly tight around my chest, and I fumbled around in my pocket until I pulled free one of my remaining Saldana Family coins.

My burned hand ached when I looked at it, but I leaned over and placed the coin in the boy's mouth, humming my song. Maybe it wouldn't work. Maybe he followed Acacius and his soul had already been reborn as a shrub or something. But if he hadn't, then maybe Safraella would see my coin and give him a new life.

Behind me, I heard a noise, like a puff of air, or a loud exhale. I turned.

A ghost floated at the entrance to the alley, staring at me.

My blood froze and my hand instinctively dropped to the sword strapped to my hip. Not that the sword would do anything.

The ghost charged, its high-pitched shrieks bouncing off the walls and filling the alley.

I grabbed my bags and ran. After the dead plains I knew the ghost was faster than me, but the alley ended at a canal, and maybe a crooked bridge stood nearby.

I reached the canal. My boots slid to a stop at the edge. I looked left. Right. No bridges. Nothing. I was trapped. The ghosts couldn't cross the water, but neither could I.

The ghost's screams reverberated loudly. My head pounded with the beat of my heart.

In the middle of the canal a boat floated listlessly, loosely moored to my right. It was far. Too far to reach, but I had no other choice.

I whipped my bags across the water. My shoulder burned with fresh pain, but both bags landed in the bottom of the boat with a loud *whump*.

I jumped.

My body crashed into the boat. My arms barely managed to grasp the side. My legs and hips splashed into the water, almost capsizing the boat. My shoulder screamed in agony, but somehow I managed to pull myself over the edge, crashing into the bottom.

I cradled my shoulder, biting my lip beneath my mask. I rocked back and forth, trying to prevent the tears that threatened to escape.

This was just physical pain. It was nothing. I would not waste my tears on it.

I took a few deep breaths, then pushed my cloak off my mask. I peeked over the edge of the boat.

The ghost floated at the end of the alley, stopped by the flowing water of the canal. It moaned steadily, staring at the boat. Like the ghosts at the monastery gates, it would wait for me all night.

I leaned back, slumping against the boat. Finally, I rolled over and covered myself with my wet cloak. It seemed I'd found my place for the night.

twelve

†

I AWOKE TO THE SOUND OF CANAL BIRDS SQUAWKING in the air and voices drifting over the water. I was lost, but then I remembered the murdered boy and the ghost and my restless night in the boat.

I groaned and rolled over. Above me, the gray of early morning blanketed the sky. I'd wasted the whole night, but at least the ghost would be gone.

The voices came again. I blinked, trying to focus, and then peeked over the edge of the boat.

Three men in the alley stood over the body of the boy. They wore gray-and-blue uniforms with round hats. Yvain lawmen.

I couldn't make out their muffled words, but it suddenly seemed important to find out what they were saying.

I reached my arms over the boat and grasped the moor line. I dragged the boat closer to the alley.

"It's different from the others," one lawman said. "I think

this was just a regular robbery gone wrong. Nothing else is missing but the coins."

"Not all the coins, though," another lawman said. They turned to look at the third lawman, who held a gold coin in his fingers, examining it. My gold coin. The one stamped with the Saldana Family crest that I'd slipped into the boy's mouth last night in a fit of exhaustion and stupidity. They didn't worship Safraella in Yvain, so chances were they didn't appreciate a murder.

"What do you make of it, Captain Lefevre?" one asked.

"It's Loveran." He flipped the coin over. "See this stamp? It's a crest from one of their clipper Families."

"Clipper?"

"Their assassin Families, who serve Safraella by murdering people." One of the lawman spat to the side, but lawman Lefevre continued, "They clip people's lives short."

Lawman Lefevre was either well educated in Loveran customs and culture, or he'd spent some time in my country.

"Then what is it doing here?"

Lefevre whistled a short tune, turning the coin in his fingers again. "They only leave these coins on someone they've killed, so it means this boy wasn't killed by our mysterious serial murderer, but instead by a Loveran clipper."

I hadn't killed the boy, though. I'd only tried to make his passage to his next life easier. It was a kindness, what I'd done for him.

The third lawman grunted. "So, not only do we have our own serial murderer on the loose, but now we have a

Loveran one as well?"

"Seems so," Captain Lefevre said. "And the clipper will be a professional killer, proficient in all manners of murder."

Beside me, a canal bird landed on the edge of the boat. I looked at it, and my movement sent it skyward in an explosion of feathers and shrieks.

All three lawman looked up at the sound. Their eyes followed the bird before settling on the boat. Where I lay hidden, arms grasping the moor line to keep me in place, masked face peeked over the edge to eavesdrop.

One gave a wordless shout. All three rushed to the end of the alley and the canal I floated in.

I swore and dropped the moor line. The boat began to drift away.

"Stop right there!" one shouted.

I declined and instead grabbed my closest weapon, my favorite stiletto hidden in my boot. I sliced and sawed at the moor line, but the rope was thick and crusted from the canal water.

The two junior lawmen found a boat pole in the alley and used it to snag the moor line. They hauled on the rope, and my boat jerked toward them.

Captain Lefevre stood at the edge of the canal and stared at me, twisting the coin in his fingers.

I eyed the rope, and then the water. There was no guarantee if I jumped into the canal that they wouldn't follow me. And I had two bags of weapons and belongings that would weigh me down.

I used all my strength and pressed the edge of my stiletto

into the fraying rope. My shoulder stretched painfully.

The rope snapped. I almost fell into the canal at the sudden freedom. Shouts erupted from the alley, and I scrambled to my knees. The sudden slack had caused the junior lawmen to tumble to the ground.

My boat drifted downstream. The fallen lawmen scrabbled to their feet and ran out of the alley. Captain Lefevre continued to stare at me, a slight smirk on his face.

"I'll be seeing you later, clipper," he shouted. He turned and walked away, whistling a tune that echoed around him.

I somehow managed to steer the boat down a side canal away from the lawmen. As soon as I could, I pulled myself to the streets and escaped the boat, shoving it on its way.

The lawmen would still be looking for me. They didn't know my identity because of my mask, so I'd be safe without it, but they'd surely recognize my mask again if they saw it. I'd need to be careful, stay in the shadows. Which meant I needed to find somewhere to hide, somewhere I could stash my belongings to keep them secure.

My shoulder ached. Everything about me ached after the night spent in the boat, but getting to the rooftops was the safest option. The lawmen likely wouldn't look there.

I scurried down the dark alleys, avoiding the main streets and the people starting to fill them. I wore my leathers and cloak and mask, and even if I hid my mask and cloak in my bags, my clothing would still look odd. And people remembered oddness and would talk. Better to wear the mask and have people remember that than take it off and have people remember me.

Down another alley, bordered by a canal, leaned a pile of pallets and refuse against a single-story building. I rotated my arm and grimaced at the pain, but this would be the most help I'd find.

I once again tied my bags to me, and then tested the resiliency of the pile. It wobbled with my shoves but seemed fairly stable. I'd have to take care and take my time.

The pile turned out to be easy to climb. The nooks and crannies of the refuse made for plenty of hand- and footholds. And though my shoulder protested the entire time, my night of sleep must have done some good, because I was able to keep going until I found myself at the top of the pile.

From there I could reach the rooftop with my fingertips. I threw my bags up and then pulled myself after them. I sat down to catch my breath and let my pounding shoulder rest.

Where Ravenna's roofs had been angled and tiled, Yvain's roofs were flat and uneven, the difference in height between each building varying greatly.

I grabbed my bags and headed for another roof, jumping the gap easily. I landed hard. The roof creaked below me. I stumbled away just as a rotten part of the roof collapsed. A puff of dust erupted from the new hole.

I set my bags down and approached cautiously.

The rest of the roof seemed stable. I peered past the dust and darkness to find an empty and abandoned room. Maybe this was just what I needed.

I dug through my bag until I found my grappling hook, and then used my rope to slide down into the dark room. If this didn't work out, I'd face a hard climb back up. . . .

The room was empty and abandoned. The windows and door had been boarded up, the floor and walls covered in dust and cobwebs.

It was perfect.

No one had been in here for a long time, which meant no one would start poking around now. The boards covering the windows were rotted and they easily popped off the nails holding them in place. It would be simple to slide them on or off the nails, to replace them while I was inside or gone to make it look like nothing had changed. I arranged my two bags in the corner. Then I stared at them.

Now what?

I'd found somewhere safe to stay. Well, safer anyway. A ghost wouldn't find me in here. But there were lawmen after me now, for a crime I didn't commit. And I couldn't walk around Yvain dressed as I was.

My stomach growled. I sat on the dusty floor and went through my things. I had two purses of coins, but one contained my holy coins, which weren't for spending. I poured the money from my other purse into my hand and counted. I had maybe enough to buy some food and local clothing but not much else.

I'd thought I was poor before. But the hard times my Family had fallen on were nothing to what I was feeling now. I'd never gone hungry at home. I'd just always compared myself to Val and the wealth of the Da Vias.

I swallowed and returned the coins back to their bag. The Da Via wealth would only grow, now that they didn't have to compete with the Saldanas for jobs.

They had so much money already, though. Of course, I didn't know the other Da Vias. I only knew Val, and he wouldn't have been part of murdering my Family just for the chance at more wealth. Or, at least, I'd *thought* I knew Val.

But the Da Vias had gotten in somehow, and I kept picturing Val returning my key to me after he'd lifted it at dinner.

I clutched the key against my chest. The house was gone, of course. The key was useless, with nothing left to lock, nothing left to protect. But I couldn't give it up. It was all I had left of my home. And its weight served to remind me what I needed to do.

I needed to find my uncle, enlist his help and his knowledge of the Da Vias. And then kill them all.

thirteen

IT TURNED OUT FARADAY AND THE OTHER PRIESTS HAD
done more than just pack my belongings. I found some bread
and hard cheese, a skin of wine, and Butters's saddle blanket all tucked inside. I wished I'd known about the saddle
blanket before my cold night in the boat, but now it would
serve as a bed.

I made a quick meal of the food and mapped out my next
steps.

I would go out when the sun set—sticking to the roofs as
much as possible to avoid any more ghosts—and begin my
search for my uncle. The lawmen had mentioned the mystery of a serial murderer. If I were a gambler, I'd put money
on it being my uncle. He must have created some way to
find jobs. One didn't give up being a clipper just because
he'd been ousted from his Family and home.

The second plan, though, the most important one, was

harder. I had to find the Da Vias' Family home. Then I had to find a way to get inside. Both of these were things my uncle could help me with.

There were over fifty Da Via clippers, which didn't even include those who were too old, or women who were pregnant or had recently had a baby, or even younger children who weren't clipping on their own yet. Somehow my uncle and I would have to kill all of them before they dropped us.

I closed my eyes and pictured slipping my knives into their hearts, cutting them down with my sword, forcing them to drink my most painful poisons. They deserved it and worse for what they'd done to the Saldanas.

I took a nap, using the robe I'd worn to escape the monastery as a pillow. I slipped off my mask, tucking it safely beneath the robe, my fingers tracing the crack along its surface. My injured shoulder pulsed with the beat of my heart, lulling me to sleep.

I dreamed of Val. His lips on my skin, his calloused hands on my flesh, and when I woke, my body burned, missing him. But my heart burned more with missing my Family.

My muscles creaked, still stiff and sore, but the nap had helped to clear the last bit of cobwebs from my head.

I tightened my cloak around my shoulders and loaded up my weapons. The empty room had grown even darker with the setting sun. It couldn't be that hard to find one old clipper in a city that abhorred death.

I slipped out the window. It was time to hunt.

Nothing.

I found nothing in my night of hunting.

I'd traveled along the rooftops, searching the dark alleys and streets for signs of my uncle, for bodies or sounds of death or any clue, really, that somewhere in the city a clipper conducted business. But all I found were ghosts, lazily traveling the streets, doubling back when they came to a canal or crooked bridge.

I clutched my hands into fists. My burned palm ached.

As sunrise approached, I headed back to my safe space, dejected that my plan of *find my uncle* wasn't as simple as I'd initially hoped. He could have easily been out and our paths could never have crossed. I needed to know where to search.

Secure inside my empty room, I changed from my leathers into the only other clothing I had: the robe given to me by Brother Faraday. I would draw attention, but I had no other choice.

When the sun rose, I slipped outside again. The brown robe tangled in my feet, and I stumbled in my secluded alley. I brushed my hair out of my face and strode down the street like I was of noble birth, instead of a dirty girl in an ill-fitting robe.

People were about their business early in Yvain. I garnered a few strange looks, but I just concentrated on blending in with the crowd, searching the shops and wares. Many of the clothing shops looked too expensive. I clutched my purse in my hand. Val had so easily lifted things off me, I couldn't risk an actual pickpocket stealing my remaining funds.

I discovered a store with simple dresses and stepped inside. It didn't take long to find something I could afford—a plain purple dress, with no real shape—and though the shop owner offered to tailor it so it fit better, I couldn't justify the cost.

It didn't matter anyway. So Lea Saldana was walking around the streets of Yvain in an ill-fitting dress barely adequate for the common—who was left to care? All my beautiful things were gone with my home, with my Family. I didn't deserve anything more.

While I paid, the shopkeeper and her assistant gossiped steadily about the city and people they knew. At a break in their conversation, I made my move.

"I heard some lawmen say they found a body the night before last."

The shopkeeper clucked her tongue. "It's been terrible lately, I swear."

Her assistant shook her head. "It must be that serial murderer everyone's talking about."

"Serial murderer?" I prodded.

The shopkeeper rolled her eyes. "Nothing but rumors, my dear. No need to worry your pretty head."

"I wouldn't be so sure," her assistant said. "There have been a lot of bodies found in the north corner, and not all of them are ghosts or robberies. My brother said people have been sliced open. I don't know of any street thug who carries a sword."

She was right—that didn't sound like a robbery gone wrong. It certainly didn't match the robbery and murder I'd seen.

"It's a shame. Even if we didn't have the ghosts, good people still wouldn't be safe at night."

The shopkeeper shrugged. "The solution is the same as always: stay inside after dark."

Her assistant hummed an agreement.

I collected my change and bag and thanked the women.

Outside, I bumped into a plump woman in a yellow robe. She faced me and smiled brightly, her cheeks rosy, her brown eyes practically sparkling in the sunlight. "Hello, child! Have you come to hear the word of Acacius?"

To the right stood two other women in the same robe, holding baskets filled with fruit.

"No, thank you. I follow a different god." I clutched my bag and tried to step around.

She turned with me. "At least take some food." She forced three pieces of fruit into my hands, their thin lilac skins bruising and splitting with her verve.

The fruits were heavy in my hand, probably filled with sweet flesh and juices. My stomach groaned. "You're just giving away this food? To anyone?"

"Acacius loves his children, and his love provides us with food to fill our stomachs and our souls." Her smile could have scared away the night.

A pair of large hands clasped over my fingers and the fruit.

I turned, yanking my hands free from the boy who now stood beside me, abandoning the fruit to him in my anger.

Long, dark, wavy hair—fighting to escape from a tie— brushed against his tan skin. A strong jaw was hidden behind a short beard on his chin, and a neck that was too long offset a nose that was too large. Maybe not so much a boy, actually.

"What they don't tell you"—he leaned closer to me—"is that Acacius is also a god of debts, and taking the fruit is an act of worship. You will owe them a debt."

The woman smiled tightly. "Lending to someone and having them give back what was given to them are all ways to show Acacius our devotion. He rewards us with this bounty." She held the basket out to me, but I kept my hands away from the fruit.

"The devout of Acacius always collect on their debts," the boy said quietly, "because collecting the debt is also an act of worship."

"I follow a darker god," I said to the woman.

She frowned, and the boy replaced the fruit into her basket. She turned her back on us, and just like that, I was forgotten.

My hands were sticky from the fruit, and it took almost all my willpower not to lick my fingers.

The boy placed a hand on my shoulder in an attempt to lead me from the Acacius women. I jerked away from him. "Don't touch me."

His eyebrows rose in surprise. "I meant no disrespect."

Whatever else he might have said remained unspoken as he looked over my head. He narrowed his eyes. I turned.

There, in the center of the street market, walked the lawman from the other night—Lefevre. He scanned the crowd, examining each person as he passed. He was searching for someone. Me, maybe. Or perhaps the serial murderer.

The crowd gave Lefevre a wide berth. It was a warning to me that the people he was supposed to protect did their utmost to stay away from him.

Lefevre's eyes swept over the women of Acacius and then me. He couldn't have recognized me without a mask, but his gaze lingered. I dropped my eyes. Let him think me demure, weak. If he thought I was just a poor girl on the streets, he wouldn't pay me any mind.

Lefevre continued on his way.

I exhaled and turned to the boy, but he had vanished.

I frowned. He'd moved surprisingly quietly for someone so tall. He'd both appeared and disappeared without my notice.

Hunger must have driven me to slip. I would need to get myself under control.

It wasn't until I'd left the street market that I discovered the three pieces of fruit hidden in my bag with my dress. The juices had stained the fabric.

I headed to the north corner of the city where most of the bodies had been found. Not that I expected to discover anything during the day, but if I familiarized myself with this part of the city now, it would be easier to search for my uncle once the sun set.

I ate the fruit as I went. It was as sweet as I'd imagined.

To my left a woman sold flowers. "Roses for love," she called. "Pennyblooms to keep the ghosts away!"

She had a bundle of Tullie blossoms, and their sharp fragrance caused me to gasp, fruit forgotten in my hand. My mother had worn a Tullie blossom perfume. I stood in the middle of the street and inhaled deeply until I became inured to the scent of them. My eyes burned with tears. I didn't know if I wanted to purchase the flowers and bring them back to my dusty, hidden space, or if I wanted to hack and slash at them until they were nothing but scattered petals on the cobblestones.

I walked away, finishing the last piece of fruit.

A shadow flitted across the wall of the building to my left. Then again, a moment later. Someone was following me. He wasn't being sly about it either. I glanced over my shoulder. A tall man casually strolled behind me, hands in his pockets, face hidden in the shadows.

I chose a side street. He turned as well.

I scanned my surroundings. I could lose him on the rooftops, but it would draw attention. The wrong kind of attention.

I traveled deeper into the maze of buildings stacked on top of one another. The cramped streets were filled with cascading flowers in window boxes, as if the Yvanese couldn't have enough flowers in their lives.

I could kill the man. It was within my skills as a clipper. But the lawmen were already searching for me for a murder I didn't commit.

Another turn. A canal stretched before me, the road ending at its murky waters.

I needed to get out of this dead end before I was trapped.

The man turned the corner, blocking me in.

Too late.

I faced him, my back straight, chin held high. He didn't frighten me. If he saw this, he would think twice about whatever he had planned.

I let a dagger pocketed in my sleeve slide into my palm. I tucked it behind me, waiting for the man to step from the shadows.

He paused, then continued his casual walk in my direction, whistling an unfamiliar tune.

He stepped into a shaft of light. I released my breath. It was the lawman, Lefevre.

"Lawman." I nodded in greeting. "I seem to have lost my way."

"It's Captain, actually. And I suppose our ways can be rather confusing for a foreigner."

I blinked.

He smiled, a glimpse of white against his olive skin. "Your accent and clothing give you away. Lovero, yes? Though I didn't know they had adopted the robes of their priests as fashion."

I flushed. I hadn't known I had an accent.

"I lost my belongings, and the priests were kind enough to clothe me temporarily." I raised my dress bag in front of me. "But I'm afraid I find your streets and canals most confusing."

"Ah, I see." He stepped closer. I clenched my hidden

dagger. "You must be new to town, if you're just now replacing your clothes."

He hadn't worded it as a question, so I didn't respond. I held my eyes wide and innocent.

"I was born in Lovero, you know," he said. "My mother was a devout follower of your death god."

I held my tongue. Let him continue to fill the silence if he must.

"Perhaps you can help me with something, Miss . . ."

"Lea." As soon as I said it, I cursed myself. I should've lied about my name, called myself Jenna or Marya or anything. He had an unsettling manner about him I didn't understand. It tripped me up.

"Miss Lea, then. It's been a long time since I've called Lovero home, and I have a few questions."

There was nothing I wanted to help him with. "I must really be on my way. I promised I would return these robes to the priests, and the church is so far from here. I would hate to be caught on the streets when there are ghosts about."

"I'm not afraid of the ghosts. It will only take another moment of your time, and then I will send you on your way." He stepped closer still. My body tensed.

I didn't know what game he was playing, only that there *was* some sort of game. He couldn't know I was the clipper who'd fled from the body. I'd worn my mask.

I needed to get out of here. I could slide past him and run, but that would only indicate me as suspicious. Better to keep up with the act of a little lost girl, asking a lawman for assistance. "How can I help?"

He reached into his pocket, and I held my breath.

His hand emerged. In his palm rested a gold coin, stamped with the Saldana Family crest. My coin. I flinched. A slow smile spread once more across Lefevre's face.

"Ah, I thought you might recognize this."

"Any Loveran would. You should be rid of it. It does not belong to you."

"Oh?" He flicked the coin between two of his fingers. "And who does it belong to?"

"Safraella."

He tilted his head. "I don't understand."

I examined his face before I dropped my gaze to the coin. If he was faking his confusion, then he would make any stage player envious of his skills.

"That coin belongs to Safraella. It is a bribe, to request that She resurrect someone quickly. The coins are placed on dead bodies by clippers. If you are not a child of Safraella, you should not have taken the coin. You could draw Her ire, or the ire of one of Her disciples. It would be best for you to make that coin a gift at Her church."

He examined the coin between his fingers. "And this stamp, this Family crest, if you could just tell me which Family this coin belongs to and how to reach them, then maybe I can converse with them. Lovero may be a country of murder and death, but here in Rennes, our laws and gods are different."

"I can't, I'm sorry."

"You do realize it is illegal to impede a lawful investigation, yes? I could bring you to jail for refusing to answer my question."

"I'm sorry, Captain Lefevre, you misunderstand. It's not that I won't help you, it's that I can't. That coin is stamped with the Saldana Family crest, but there are no Saldanas left."

He stared at my eyes. I let him see the truth in them, showed him that in this, at least, I was not a liar. He scowled. "Well, isn't that awfully convenient."

"Hmm." I thought of Brother Sebastien and how he'd dispatched the Addamos. "I would say it's awfully inconvenient for you and your investigation."

He closed the coin in his fist. "The Saldanas made their home in the city of Ravenna, right? They share territory with the Da Vias, if I recall."

It was clear he knew more about the Families than he'd let on. He'd been testing me. Or trying to catch me in a lie.

Lefevre snapped his finger. "I know. I'll send a letter to the Da Vias, perhaps. Ask them about this coin. I'm sure they'll help."

I bit the inside of my cheek, desperately trying not to give anything away. If he really did send a letter to the Da Vias, they would know I was hiding in Yvain.

I smiled. "The Da Vias are not known for their love of the common. I do not think they would help you, even if they could. Now, if you would be so kind as to point me to the main street?"

He stepped in front of me, so close his warm breath

brushed across my face. It would have been easy to slip my knife between his ribs.

"I think you're hiding something from me, little girl. And until I find out, you won't be able to shake me. As a lawman I see terrible accidents all the time."

I clenched my jaw.

"People slip and fall into canals, never to come up. It happens every day." He flicked a lock of my hair and stepped away, his smile like a knife slash in his face. The smile I realized, too late, was his own mask.

I'd underestimated him. He was not a man to toy with.

"You can find your own way home," he said. "I hope you're fast enough to outrun the ghosts." He walked out of the alley, whistling once again until he was gone from sight.

I took a deep breath and released it. No one had ever threatened me before. The lawmen in Lovero would never dream of wielding their power like that over people, because they could never be sure someone they had wronged wouldn't hire a clipper to seek vengeance. Lefevre was the first person to show me what a man could do if his power wasn't held in check.

I could only hope his threat to send a letter to the Da Vias was a bluff.

I pocketed my dagger. I needed to locate my uncle and leave this city before I found any more trouble.

fourteen

THE WIND LIFTED, THE CORNER OF MY CLOAK AND I
jerked it under control, shifting my weight. I'd been sitting
on the rooftop of this damn inn since late afternoon and
nothing even remotely interesting had happened in this dull
city. I could have taken a longer nap and missed nothing.

Below me in a square, women washed their laundry in a
fountain. The women in Yvain wore long skirts and short-
sleeved blouses with shawls around their shoulders. I'd had
to leave my hair uncovered, and more than once my long
bangs had flopped into my face.

Stupid Yvain with its outdated fashions. I tugged the cloak
around my shoulders, and my injured arm flared in pain. I
should've been home in Ravenna, listening to music and
revelers instead of watching the common go about their
chores. I missed the smell of the sea and lantern oil. Yvain
smelled of rotting fish and canals, and the common seemed

to think putting flowers everywhere could somehow disguise the stink.

Thinking about Ravenna made my chest ache. I needed to find my uncle and go home where I belonged. Ravenna was all I'd ever known and I missed it, like another piece of my life had been stolen from me.

Children played in the water of the fountain or ran through the streets, hitting one another with rags and sticks.

Don't think about Emile and how he'll never get a chance to play games like this. How he'd never get a chance to dance with a girl at a masquerade or steal a kiss under the colored lights, their masquerade masks lifted, their lips pressed together.

I blinked, my throat tight. There was no use crying about it, wishing for things to be different. What was done was done. I could only worry about the future now, and how I could best make the Da Vias pay.

As the sun sank, the women gathered their laundry and children.

"Hurry now, before the ghosts take you," one woman said to her dawdling daughter. Once darkness spilled across the streets, Yvain seemed as empty as the dead plains.

I sighed and picked at the hem on my cloak. My shoulder ached and itched. I stifled a yawn under my mask. If my uncle had been in Ravenna, I could've found him immediately. Rafeo would've known what to do. Rafeo would've found Marcello by now.

Below me a man stumbled out of the inn despite the late

Yvain hour. He tripped and laughed uproariously. I frowned. I'd never alter my state of mind so much. Someone could be watching from the shadows, knife in hand and poison in their pouches.

On a rooftop across the street a shadow moved. I stilled my body, sinking deeper into myself. My spine pressed against the chimney of the inn as my cloak obscured my outline. I waited.

The shadow moved again and revealed itself to be not a shadow but a person, hiding in a hooded cloak similar to mine.

My uncle, Marcello Saldana.

He crouched on the edge of his building. The moonlight reflected brightly off the silver buckles on his boots and the weapons on his belt.

I frowned. Sloppy. Amateur mistakes. The cloak was to prevent accidental reflections and no clipper would ever leave the shadows if they had a choice.

Marcello watched the drunken man below. For a moment I recalled a similar night when I'd watched my own "drunk" stumble in the streets while Val snuck up on me.

Val. My heart clenched at the memory of his hazel eyes, his bright smile, the feel of his breath on my skin. But there was no Val here. And this time I was the hunter.

My uncle jumped off the building in a brazen move. He was either crazy or idiotic, and I scrambled from my post to peer down into the street.

Marcello landed directly on his target, slipping his knife

into the man's neck. The mark barely had time to react before he was dead on the ground, my uncle standing over him.

I quietly slid off the roof. No need to give away my advantage. Marcello nudged the dead man with a boot and grunted in satisfaction. He flicked his cloak over his shoulder and returned his knife to his belt. He froze at the prick of my dagger against his windpipe.

"So sloppy," I whispered, loud enough to be heard through the mask.

Tension rippled across his body. He was taller than me by quite a bit, taller even than Val, but I'd spent enough time sparring with Val to handle someone with height on me.

His left hand twitched, and he moved it slowly toward his belt. A lefty then.

I tapped his wrist with a second dagger. "I wouldn't try it."

He opened his palm and raised his hand.

"Who are you?" His voice rasped as he tried to disguise his anger.

"I am death," I whispered. "I am Safraella, come to collect what I am owed."

He tried to turn his head.

"Ah, ah." I pressed my dagger into his skin. His hood slipped, and the corner of his face caught the moonlight.

He wore no bone mask.

He wasn't a true clipper then. He wasn't my uncle. Just someone playing at murder.

Heaviness spread through my limbs. This had been my

only lead. And now it was nothing.

I used my foot and shoved the false clipper in the back of his knees. He stumbled away from me. I wasn't threatened by this fool.

He got his feet under him and pulled out his own knives. His eyes widened as he took in my leathers and the bone mask hiding my face.

My own eyes widened behind my mask. It was the boy from the market, who had stolen the fruit for me.

"You're a clipper." His mouth tilted in a crooked smile. He looked down at the knives in my hand, then returned his own knives to his belt. He held his hands before him, weaponless. Dumb, to trust me. Still, I relaxed my stance.

"You could teach me," he said.

I wasn't a nursemaid. I was a clipper. I didn't have time to teach anyone anything. I needed to find my uncle, and though I'd missed my mark with this false clipper, I was willing to bet he knew where my uncle was. "I won't be teaching anyone anything."

"That's unfortunate." His eyes flicked to the left. Right. He was stalling.

I pointed my dagger at him. "Don't move."

Around me flashes of light burst in the night: *pop, pop, pop, pop.*

Smoke gushed from four different spots on the street until I could see nothing.

I spun around. He hadn't thrown any smoke bombs. He had to have people with him, helpers.

But there was no one. No sounds, no movement, no attacks from different quarters.

How . . . ?

I charged through the smoke, my mask mostly protecting me from the bitter taste and smell. I dashed left, down an alley, the route I would've chosen had I been him.

I'd picked correctly. The fake clipper stood at the end of the alley, canal at his back, trapped.

His teeth flashed. He was missing his first molar on his right side. "You found me."

His tone reminded me of Val, all cockiness and self-assurance. Tricking me once was not a cause for so much bravado. If he kept it up, he'd wind up dead.

"It wasn't hard."

"After meeting you in the market today, and then seeing you here, I think I prefer you without the mask. Much prettier."

My throat tightened. He knew who I was?

He pointed to his left hand. I glanced at mine and the burn on my palm. I flushed. I'd skipped my gloves because they'd been rubbing painfully against my still-healing palm.

Seventeen years in Lovero and never once had anyone seen my face unless I'd wanted them to. And now, after only a short time in Yvain, some faker had seen me. My parents would've been ashamed. Rafeo and Matteo, too. Not that Rafeo would have said so to my face.

I ground my teeth together. "I can tell you're not a real clipper," I said.

"How's that?"

"To a real clipper, the bone mask is the most beautiful face of all."

He blinked. "My name's Alessio, by the way. Les."

He waited for me to respond, and when I didn't, he continued. "It appears I just keep running into you, Clipper Girl. I think it's a sign from the gods. A sign you are meant to teach me your ways. Invite me into your Family."

I snorted. I couldn't help it. He seemed so serious, but any Loveran knew you couldn't simply be *invited* into a Family.

His smile collapsed, and I felt a twinge of sympathy. Why did I even care? He was no one to me. I needed to focus. The only thing that mattered was making the Da Vias pay.

"You're right," I said. "I think it *is* a sign from the gods."

He cocked his head.

"It's a sign you need to tell me where to find your teacher."

He tensed, his body taut with energy and danger. I tightened my own muscles, prepared to match him. Clearly I'd struck some sort of nerve.

"Are you even sure I have a teacher?"

"You're sloppy. You have no grace about you, and you've displayed, more than once, your ignorance regarding clippers. But you aren't untrained, only unfinished. Someone had to teach you the basics. Maybe someone who didn't want to talk about his former life as a clipper. Someone who felt betrayed and hurt by his Family. Someone named Marcello Saldana."

He held his breath, studying me. He exhaled. "He never told me he was a Saldana."

I lowered my knife. I'd done it! I'd found my uncle. "I need to speak with him urgently."

He shook his head. "No. He doesn't see anyone."

I pointed my dagger at him, staring him in his eyes. They were dark, and he had surprisingly long lashes. "I could make you tell me."

He shrugged and raised his arms. "Then what are you waiting for, Clipper Girl?"

I slid my right foot forward, weapons held before me. "Have it your way."

I dashed at him. His eyes narrowed before he dodged away. I swiped with my left knife. My shoulder erupted in pain, and a few stitches popped. The copper scent of blood seeped into the night air. I hissed, missing my strike.

He pushed himself off the wall and twisted closer to the canal, facing me. He held his own knife in his left hand now, a monstrous cutter almost eighteen inches long and slightly curved. Where in the hells had he hidden such a large weapon?

Blood soaked through my leathers, and he glanced at my shoulder. Concern flashed in his eyes. "You're hurt."

I used his distraction to strike at his ribs. "Worry about yourself!"

He glared and hooked my ankle with his foot, a move I knew only too well. A wolfish grin spread across his face.

"Wait!" I shouted.

He yanked and I fell, plunging into the dark waves of the canal.

fifteen

†

THE WATER WAS FREEZING FROM SPRING RUNOFF, AND it saturated my clothes. My cloak and boots weighed me down. I struggled, kicking against the fabric as I reached for the surface.

I broke through and took a deep breath. I grabbed the edge of the canal and searched the alley, but Alessio had fled. He seemed to enjoy starting things, but never stuck around to see them through.

"Typical." I pulled myself from the canal, grimacing at the muck now coating my leathers. I squeezed my hair to prevent it from dripping into my eyes any further.

Damn him. Damn everything in this whole damned city. This whole country!

I'd been on my own for days now and nothing had gone right.

My shoulder bled. I pinched my eyes shut and took a few deep breaths. My chest felt tight against my leathers. My eyes stung. *Don't think about it, Lea. Don't think about anything. Just get to your safe house, get clean and dry. Things will look better.*

On the way back home I scoured the street where I'd confronted Alessio. Casings from the smoke bombs he'd somehow managed to use against me littered the cobblestones. I picked one up and sniffed. It smelled strange, a chemical I didn't recognize. The casing was surprisingly brittle, and it crumbled between my fingers with barely any pressure. How did he stop them from breaking in his pouch? And how had he thrown them without me seeing him do so?

I remembered the flash, too, at the very beginning. I'd never seen smoke bombs put off any light before.

Mysteries. He had cloaked himself in mysteries. I would have to keep my eyes wide open when I dealt with him again.

At my safe house, I removed the boards blocking the window and climbed in tugging the boards back into place. I dripped filthy, smelly canal water across the dusty floor. At a stack of old crates I slipped off my wet leathers and cloak. I yanked my mask from my face. It stared at me with Rafeo's tiger stripes. I set it gently on the ground.

My shoulder burned with fresh pain. Where some of the stitches had popped, my flesh looked red and inflamed, though any bleeding had slowed to a trickle. Removing the bandages, I prodded the wound gently and was rewarded with a pinch of pain. Wonderful.

I hung my bandages up to dry and returned to my monastery

robe before collapsing onto my saddle-blanket bed.

I'd only had a single lead, and it turned out to be nothing. Well, not nothing. A false clipper with a crooked smile. But not my uncle, whom I still needed to find.

I rolled onto my side, the heavy key around my neck resting against my chin. This wasn't working—what had made me think it would be easy to find someone who'd remained hidden for decades? I couldn't do anything right, starting with keeping my Family safe or trusting someone I'd believed I loved to not murder my Family while we slept.

Thinking about Val made my chest tighten, my skin flush. I shouldn't have spared a single thought for him. His Family killed my Family. He should be dead to me.

But maybe *he* didn't have anything to do with it. Yes, he'd lifted my key, but maybe he wasn't even there.

He had to have known. He could've stopped it, or at least made an effort.

He could've warned me.

I probably wouldn't ever be sure.

I rubbed my face with the palm of my hand, my calluses dragging against my skin.

There was no point in wondering about things. Val was a Da Via. Even if he wasn't involved, he hadn't done anything to stop what had happened. We were done, he and I. I had to kill his Family. I *would* kill his Family. I would make them bleed and choke and beg for mercy. As for him, I'd cross that crooked bridge later. Right now I needed to come up with a new plan.

The fake clipper was the key. He wasn't the lead I'd expected, or wanted, but he was still a lead. He could bring me to Marcello, even if he didn't realize it.

All right. I'd been delayed only a few days. And yes, the Addamos were after me, and I'd be a fool to think the Da Vias wouldn't be after me soon, if they weren't already, but I needed to keep my head down and find my uncle. And when I did, he would help me find and kill the Da Vias. Everything else was just distraction.

I didn't know anything about my uncle. My father refused to speak of him, and all my mother ever said was he'd been exiled from the Family for killing his uncle, the head of the Saldanas at the time. Killing your own Family members was an anathema, so it was no surprise he was banished. And none of the other Families would take in a cast-out clipper.

Why he had killed his uncle, his own flesh and blood, was a mystery to me. The Da Vias and Maiettas were somehow involved.

He'd murdered his own blood, but I couldn't help but think about how much I wanted to see him. Not just for my plans, but because he was all that was left of the Saldanas besides me. He was a link to everyone and everything I'd lost. I closed my eyes and clenched my hands to my chest. My grief was all I had left of my Family.

I exhaled slowly and released my fists. My burned palm ached.

I hadn't gotten any real sleep in much too long. I'd need to catch up if I wanted to accomplish my plans for tomorrow.

I tucked my legs underneath my robe and thought of a boy with a long neck and a crooked smile.

Tomorrow, false clipper. *Tomorrow I'm coming for you.*

———⊰⊱———

The next night my newly bandaged shoulder felt bulky and awkward under my leathers. I ignored it and instead relished the feel of the tiled rooftops beneath my boots as I headed north once again.

My uncle lived somewhere in this city. Alessio knew where. All I had to do was find him and follow him until he led me to Marcello.

Alessio thought he was a clipper, and maybe he had some natural talent for it, but he had no idea what it was like to deal with a *real* Loveran clipper. Probably even fumbling Alexi Addamo could've given Alessio a fight.

I reached the street near where I'd found him yesterday. I crouched behind a chimney, arranging my body and legs so I'd be ready to spring at a moment's notice. No more taking things easy. This was a job. Alessio was my mark.

Patience was the first thing I'd learned as a child. Even before I began my training as a clipper at age six, my parents and nursemaids and tutors spent what seemed like hours each day, teaching me to wait quietly for the things I wanted. Looking back, I appreciated this early lesson. Especially since the streets of Yvain were so quiet and still once the sun set.

If I ever had children of my own, I'd definitely make them sit quietly before they got to have fun. All day long if I had to.

Of course, that life was over. When I found Marcello and killed the Da Vias, I would probably die in the fight. There was nothing left for me anyway.

It was a few hours past midnight when a man appeared below me. He hastened across a central square, pulling his felt hat low against the breeze.

It was strange to see someone out on the streets at night, but perhaps he had an emergency, something worth braving the ghosts for. The man walked quickly, trying to stay within the lights of any street lanterns that remained burning.

Run home, little man. There are worse things out tonight than angry ghosts.

The man vanished down a dark alley, his footfalls on the cobblestones quickly disappearing with him. A moment later a shadow appeared down the street, cast from above.

I shifted my position quietly and watched.

Alessio crept about on the roofs.

I exhaled behind my mask; my muscles trembled.

Alessio followed the man who'd crossed the square. And I followed Alessio, careful to keep him in my sight, but far enough away to keep his attention off the roofline.

He took his time as he stalked his prey, content to wait in the shadows as the minutes ticked by.

Damn. He wasn't actually that bad at this, the stalking part anyway. Maybe he was unfinished, but he was a better clipper than I'd given him credit for. Of course, my uncle had trained him, so he had to have some Saldana skill.

The man walked across the street, following the light of

the streetlamps until they ended and he was forced to walk in the shadows.

Something flashed on the street. The man shouted but was immediately engulfed in smoke.

Alessio once again performed his showy trick of leaping blind from the roof. He disappeared into the smoke, landing presumably onto his mark to kill him with a single stroke.

The smoke cleared.

Alessio knelt beside the corpse. As he rifled through his mark's pouches, robbing the man, a bitter taste crept across my tongue. Robbing the dead was deplorable. Not even the lowest of the nine Families would sink so far.

Of course, in Lovero the coin flowed more freely to clippers. Maybe Alessio didn't have many contracts to fulfill.

Alessio dragged the body deeper into the shadows. After a quick look around, he climbed to the roofs and headed north.

I smiled behind my mask. Finally! He had to be heading home, and his home had to be with my uncle.

I trusted that Marcello, banished or not, still kept to the clipper ways. And clippers didn't live by themselves. It simply wasn't done. There was no safety in it. If my uncle was Alessio's trainer, and I didn't think Alessio had been lying, then they had to share a home.

Alessio led me deeper into Yvain, where the buildings were not as well maintained and only every other lamp had oil enough to light the streets.

I wrinkled my nose. My uncle must have truly fallen low

if he couldn't find better accommodations.

I thought of my own abandoned building. That was different, though. I'd had no choice. Alessio dropped off a roof and entered an alley. I waited another moment before doing the same.

The alley was empty. Alessio had disappeared.

I searched the roofs above me, making sure he hadn't doubled back, but no, the roofs were as empty as the alley. He'd vanished like an angry ghost at dawn.

I walked farther into the alley, carefully examining the street. There. A sewer grate suspiciously clear of debris and filth. The Saldanas had always used tunnels to reach their home, and old habits died slowly, if they died at all.

I squatted beside the grate. There didn't seem to be any lock. I tugged on the bars and it swung up easily, its hinges well oiled.

I guessed if they were the only clippers in a city, they didn't need locks.

I dropped into the tunnel. It wasn't anything like our tunnels in Lovero. Those had been designed to confuse and kill intruders. This one seemed to travel in a straight line. I trailed my right hand across a smooth surface until the tunnel ended at a ladder and another grate.

I climbed the rungs and carefully peeked out.

The grate opened into a small room, similar to the tunnel room in my home. The room was dim, the floor, walls, and ceiling nothing more than the stonework of the tunnel, but past a doorway a fire roared in a large hearth.

Alessio stood just a few feet away from me. Only my many years of training prevented me from rapidly closing the grate. The movement would attract his attention faster than the slight gap I peered through.

He stood before a small altar, dedicated to Safraella. He used a knife to cut his finger. When his blood welled up, he rubbed it over a coin and placed it on the altar. It was an old way of worship, but perhaps it was all he knew.

He left, disappearing into the room with the hearth and fire. I watched quietly. Rushing things would only lead to mistakes.

Alessio passed in front of the tunnel room. He'd removed his cloak and was unlatching the buckles securing his leather vest across his chest. He stepped out of sight, and I took the moment to slip out of the tunnel, hiding in a dark corner.

"He didn't have much," Alessio said, but from my corner I couldn't see whom he addressed. I needed to make some decisions about how to proceed. I could simply walk in and announce myself. Or wait until the fire died down and ambush them. No, that would be dangerous, and I didn't want to hurt anyone. I just wanted what I came for, the location of the Da Vias' home and Marcello's help.

I slid to the edge of the doorway, pressed against the wall. In the other room, coins clinked as they dropped into a dish or bowl. A sigh followed, and I could imagine Alessio stretching his arms the way Rafeo used to, when he had finished a job for the night and was glad to be home.

"Any troubles?" It was a man's voice, low and gruff. Marcello?

Alessio hesitated. "No. It's been quiet these last few nights."

Liar.

"No trouble at all?" Footsteps clicked on the floor of the room.

"I'll be right back," Alessio said. I heard the sound of splashing water.

Strange. Alessio was keeping me a secret.

The tip of a knife pricked against my throat and I froze. I turned my head, but the pressure increased and I stopped.

"Come out slowly," a voice said from the other side of the doorway.

I'd lost my advantage.

sixteen

†

I COULDN'T SEE HIM, THE PERSON WITH THE KNIFE against my throat. He hid on the other side of the doorway.

I stepped from the tunnel room, my hands held before me as the knife pressed on my throat. The light from the great room burned brightly against my eyes. I shut them against the glare until the pain passed.

The hearth with a fire was in the center of the massive room. The areas surrounding it were broken into sections, each "room" separated by tapestries and silk screens decorated with dancing women, Loveran fountains, and masks.

In front of the fire rested two chairs and a sofa, as well as a small table where a book lay facedown, its spine protesting the treatment.

An unmade bed hid behind a tapestry displaying blond and brown wirehaired retrievers, and behind the fireplace sat weapons racks, clipper training tools, and stands. I hadn't been gone from Lovero for long, but seeing these little reminders of its rich culture made my stomach coil with longing for the home I'd left behind.

"Keep moving," the voice said behind me.

"What's going on?" Alessio stood in front of the hearth, wearing only a pair of trousers and a pendant around his neck, his damp hair dripping across his bare chest. I looked away from him and tried not to think about Val or Val's bare skin.

"Look what I found sneaking about."

"How did she get in?" Alessio stared at me with his mouth agape.

"I came through the tunnel."

The knife pressed tightly against my throat. "I don't remember saying you could speak."

"But how did you find it?" Alessio asked me.

"Alessio!" my captor snapped.

"I followed you," I answered.

My captor inhaled, then shoved a fist into my spine, marching me forward. Did he really think he could handle this situation with a single measly dagger? Time to regain my advantage.

I dropped, bending backward. The top of my head shoved against his chest.

He stumbled away, his dagger scraping across my mask.

I yanked out a dagger of my own. Alessio stared at me, in shock. My captor climbed back to his feet. He turned to confront me.

My breath caught in my throat. I lowered my weapon.

It was like seeing a ghost. Tears filled my eyes as I raised my weapon again. I'd given a lot of thought to little Emile, Jesep, and my parents. And Rafeo, who'd died in my arms. I'd grieved for them, but seeing this man before me, this man who could've been my father, showed me how much I wasn't done grieving for them. Showed me I'd never be done grieving for them.

He resembled my father, but the lines on his face were deeper, his hair longer and grayer, and he didn't wear my father's glasses.

"Is that any way to greet family, *Uncle*?" I asked.

"Family? Pah." He spat to the side and slapped aside Alessio's offered hand of assistance. "I have no family."

I closed my eyes. I'd expected him to be difficult. I just hadn't expected him to get the drop on me.

"Uncle?" Alessio looked between me and Marcello. He settled on me. "You didn't tell me you were related."

"It was none of your business," I snapped. "And you never asked."

"You've been fraternizing with her?" Marcello sneered at Alessio. "How quickly the apprentice turns on the master."

"I haven't done any such thing." Alessio scowled at Marcello, then walked to a chair in front of the fireplace and pulled a worn cotton shirt over his head.

"This is why I said no jobs. This right here." Marcello pointed at me. "And now you've brought trouble back to our home."

Alessio sighed and waved his hand in my direction. "Clipper Girl, you can lower your weapon."

"A clipper never lowers her weapon while a weapon is trained on her," I quoted my father, and nodded toward the dagger still gripped in Marcello's hand.

"Master, please."

"A clipper never lowers his weapon while a weapon is trained on him." He mocked me.

Alessio threw his hands into the air. "By the gods, it's like reasoning with stubborn tigers! Master, I'll vouch for her. And Clipper Girl, you are a guest in our home."

He was right. It was incredibly rude to draw weapons on the lord of a manor. And besides, I hadn't come here to fight. I'd come here for help.

I kept my eyes trained on Marcello as I slowly lowered my weapon. He sheathed his dagger and I followed.

"I won't deal with anyone hiding behind a mask," Marcello announced.

I hissed. My mask was a holy symbol of Safraella Herself! "You blaspheme."

He smiled slowly. "No masks allowed in our home."

Alessio sighed. "Clipper Girl, please humor him. I've seen your face before, and apparently he's your family."

I hated them. I hated that they had so much power over me, that because I needed them, I had to do what they said. I was powerless, like the night of the fire.

Just give them what they want. The faster I cooperated, the faster I could get back to the plan. And I didn't have time to waste. I pushed down my hood and slid my mask to the crown of my head.

I stared at them, daring Alessio to brave a cocky comment, daring my uncle to gloat. A single wrong word and I'd show them what someone behind a mask could *truly* do.

"You are Bianca's daughter, Oleander," Marcello said. "I can see much of her in your face. Not so much my brother Dante."

"Oleander." Alessio smiled slowly, and no matter how hard I searched I couldn't find malice or jest in his grin. "One of the prettiest of the poisons."

"Lea," I snapped. "Only my mother called me Oleander."

Alessio inclined his head. "*Kalla* Lea."

Marcello glowered, and I agreed. I didn't approve of Alessio calling me something in a language I didn't speak.

"And why have you come here?" Marcello strode to the kitchen. He lifted a carafe of amber liquor and poured a glass. "Has Dante come to his senses and sent you to fetch me home? Surely if you've come to end my life you would've done so by now. Unless the Saldana standards have fallen so low?"

I glared at him. Anger seeped through my limbs like hot honey. My cheeks burned and tears pricked my eyes. I blinked them away. "My father is dead."

Marcello exhaled through his nose. "I see." He took a drink. "Was it illness? An accident?"

"It was the Da Vias," I spat. "They killed us. Everyone. My father and mother. Rafeo, Matteo, Emile, and Jesep. Even the servants. I am the only Saldana left."

Marcello stared at me blankly. Tension coated the air as

Alessio glanced between the two of us.

Marcello looked at the glass in his hand, watching the amber liquid slide across its surface as he rotated it in the light. His breath sounded rapid and harsh.

He screamed, a loud, guttural noise from deep in his body. He threw the glass across the room to shatter in the fireplace, the liquid hissing and sputtering in the flames.

Alessio covered his head when the glass soared past his face. He spun toward Marcello. "Gods, Master!" he shouted, but the anger leaked out of him as he saw my uncle's state.

Marcello stood unmoving, but his body shook as tears poured down his cheeks, tracing the lines of his face like a river through sand.

He wept for them. He wept for our Family. Would he weep so easily if he knew it was my fault? If he knew I'd trusted Val, which brought about their deaths? I pressed my hand to my chest, feeling the key tucked beneath my leathers.

"Gods damn the Da Vias." His voice hitched in a sob. He sank his face into his hands. "Gods damn them all."

Alessio approached my uncle and, when he met no resistance, escorted him to a chair in front of the fire. I followed quietly behind and sat in the other chair while Alessio visited the kitchen and returned to my uncle with another glass of liquor.

"Drink this, Master," he said quietly, pressing the glass into my uncle's hand. There was real tenderness in how Alessio cared for him. They must have been together a long time, only the two of them, a sad little clipper Family in a country where the people feared the night. It must've been lonely.

"So this is why you came, niece?" Marcello's voice was gruff with tears and grief. "To torture me with memories?" He drank, the liquor splashing against the whiskers on his chin.

I shook my head. "No. Truthfully, I did not come for you at all. I came for me. I seek help."

He glanced at me out of the corner of his eye, then returned to staring at the fire. He took another drink. "And what could I possibly have that you would value? Tell us, *kalla* Lea," he mocked. "Tell us what it is *you* need."

As if he had the right to be angry. He wasn't there when our home burned. When Rafeo's blood spilled across my hands.

"The Da Vias," I said. "You're going to help me kill them."

He turned to me, surprise flashing in his eyes. And then he laughed in my face.

seventeen

†

A RAGE FLARED ACROSS ME, SO BRIGHT IT BLINDED ME.
I lunged to my feet, the heavy oak chair screeching like a cat
in an alley as it slid across the stone floor.

Alessio jumped to my side, hands at the ready to stop me
from grabbing my weapons. But I didn't need a weapon for
this.

I slapped my uncle across the face.

The crack echoed dully against the stone walls until the
only sounds remaining were the popping of the fire and
Alessio's sharp intake of breath.

Marcello's face was streaked red where I'd struck him.
He gingerly brushed it with the tips of his fingers before he
faced me.

"Get out of my home," he said quietly.

"How dare you." My voice scratched against my throat.
"You weep for my Family, *my* Family, and rage at the Da
Vias, but when I call on you for help, you laugh in my face?

You are not a Saldana. You were not there when we needed you the most. You gave away your name when you murdered your own uncle."

"I said get out!" Marcello screamed.

I raised my hand to strike him again, but Alessio grabbed my wrists, dragging me away. He was stronger and taller than me. And I was full of grief and rage, and Father always said strength comes only with a cool mind and heart.

"Come." Alessio pulled me toward the entrance, not roughly, but with a firm grip.

I yanked my hands away from him and jerked my mask down so he couldn't see the tears struggling to fall from my eyes. "I know the way," I snapped.

He followed as I entered the tunnel room and lifted the grate.

"You shouldn't come back, Lea," Alessio said. "And—"

I slammed the grate behind me, cutting off whatever he planned to say. I didn't care to hear it. Damn them both to the dead plains.

I ran through the tunnel, trying to burn the anger and pain out of me with every step. I flung myself into the darkened alley.

The sun would be up in an hour or so, and I needed to get home.

Home. If I ever had another one. Would I ever be able to return to beautiful Lovero and live the life I'd once had?

There was no turning back, now that I'd started down this dark path. I had to continue on. I had to kill the Da Vias.

I reached my safe house, feeling the stretch and pull in my shoulder as I climbed to the safety of the roof.

I sat on the edge of the roof, mask pushed to the top of my head, knees pressed against my chest, and tried not to think about how badly things had gone. If I hadn't been so quick to anger, so quick to let grief consume me, maybe I could've convinced my uncle to help. Instead, I'd been brash and bold and *entitled*, and there was no way he'd help me now. And I needed him. I couldn't face the Da Vias alone, not if I actually wanted to succeed.

I dropped my head onto my knees. *Rafeo . . . what do I do now?* I blinked rapidly at the tears welling in my eyes. *I wish you were here. You'd know how to fix this.*

Across the canal flashes of white between the buildings illuminated the ghosts prowling the streets. They were terrible, the ghosts. I knew this firsthand, but in the earliest hours of the morning, when everything was still and with enough distance between us, they had a sort of beauty about them as they floated quietly on their way.

Back home I used to sit on the roofs whenever I was upset and couldn't bring myself to go home. It was how Val and I had started our secret relationship. During the plague there were so many common asking us to release their loved ones. And I'd spent the night sneaking through open windows, finishing people who were delirious and coughing up blood, finishing children or babes still in their cribs, and though I knew it was a mercy I performed, the children always weighed the most heavily on me.

I couldn't go home, not and face my cousin whose parents were dead, my brother whose wife lay feverish in her bed as she slowly succumbed. And so I sat on the roof and watched the stars quietly until I heard a noise behind me. I turned and saw a figure standing on the other side, lost in his thoughts. After a moment I realized his shoulders shook not from the cold, but from tears.

I'd tried to leave quietly, to let him have his privacy, but he heard me and turned. I recognized his mask right away—Valentino Da Via—and though his mask hid his face, his eyes were lined with red.

We stared at each other for what seemed an eternity.

And then I realized my own throat was tight, and tears slipped quietly down my cheeks.

"I just couldn't go home yet," I said to him, my voice breaking.

After a moment he'd nodded, and we'd sat side by side, watching the stars, listening to the sounds of the sea, saying nothing. And everything.

I swallowed and took a deep breath. Yes, everything was my fault. Again. But this time I could fix it. I would win over Alessio and then return with him to Marcello and ask him to reconsider. I would make my case. I would not let Marcello anger me. With Alessio on my side, I would urge him to see reason and to help me kill the Da Vias.

The sun crested the horizon, turning the twists and bends of the canals golden with its light.

I used the rope dangling from the hole in my safe house

and slipped inside to change out of my leathers. I would take a short nap, then return to Marcello's home with the sun. Apologies were always easier in the dark, but I had no choice. I was running out of time.

I dreamed of the fire. Only this time the smoke was a living thing, its tendrils shaped into the hands of infants, their tiny fingers grabbing onto my nightgown, trying to pull me deeper into the chalky darkness of the ashes.

I woke and found my room dim, hidden from the dawn sun.

My muscles ached and my eyes were heavy. My encounter with Marcello had drained me more than my most difficult job as a clipper.

I ran my fingers through my hair and threw on my single dress before I made my way outside.

I took backstreets whenever I could. After Lefevre had followed me from the market, he could be watching for me. To do what? I wasn't sure. But I didn't trust that he wouldn't follow through on his threat and send the letter to the Da Vias. Better to stay hidden.

When I reached the alley with the secret grate, I leaned against a wall, determined to wait as long as it took.

The alley, the street leading to it, and the nearby canal were particularly quiet. No people about their business cast suspicious eyes on me, nor were people using the canals for travel or trade. Marcello had picked his home well.

The sun had climbed to midmorning before the grate in

the alley opened slightly. It stopped, but then a hand pushed it open the entire way.

Alessio pulled himself through and got to his feet, brushing off his clothes. He'd layered a brown vest over a hunter-green tunic in the outdated style of Yvain. His pants and boots were serviceable and clean, and the threads on his vest, while simple, were carefully stitched. Not a lot of money, then. But enough to keep him looking respectable.

I tried to tuck the stain on my skirt behind other folds.

At least Alessio hadn't shaved. The stubble across his jaw and cheeks gave him a rakish, instead of sloppy, appearance that matched his seemingly carefree smile.

A smile he kept to himself when he discovered me waiting. "You came back." His shoulders slumped. "Just go home, Clipper Girl."

I pushed myself off the wall. "I have no home to go back to."

His face flushed at his gaffe, but he didn't say anything. He left the alley and I followed after, rushing to catch up. His long legs made his stride much lengthier than mine.

"And I can't go anywhere until I get what I came for," I continued.

"What do you even need his help for anyway? He's an old man and you're a real clipper."

I couldn't ignore the stress he'd put on *real*. But there was no point in keeping anything secret anymore. Without Marcello, I had no plan. And with no plan, the Da Vias would win.

"He's not that old. And I need him to tell me how to reach the Da Vias in Ravenna. To help me kill them all. I can't do it alone." Whether I could do it even with help remained a mystery. But once I got Marcello, we could work on a plan together.

Alessio looked at me, a strange expression on his face. We left the backstreets and entered a main road, with people heading to the nearest square and day market. Alessio fell in line behind the crowd, and I followed.

"I could help you kill them."

I narrowed my eyes. "Why?"

"Because you need the help."

No one simply offered to help without an ulterior motive. "Acacius is the god of debts. Are you sure you're not trying to accrue some favor?"

He frowned. "I'm devoted to Safraella."

I pursed my lips. There was nothing he could gain from helping me.

"When I was young," he interrupted my thoughts, "someone once helped me for no other reason than just to help me. I try to do the same when I can."

"You don't know what you're offering. What you'd be getting yourself into."

"Well, my master won't help you. At least, not with killing the Da Vias. He doesn't leave the tunnels anymore. Not for the last few years."

"Why?" I asked.

"He's worried people are searching for him. He stays hidden."

"What people?"

Alessio didn't respond. We reached the square and broke free of the crowd. He led me around the market.

"And where are we going?" I asked.

"Breakfast." He waved his hand at a small café before us.

My stomach grumbled at the smell of warm baking bread. I tucked my hair behind my ear. "I don't—"

"Judging by how desperately you eyed that fruit the other morning," Alessio interrupted, "I'm betting you haven't taken time to enjoy the finer points of Yvain, one of which is our food. And it's my treat."

"Why did you steal that fruit for me?"

He shrugged. "You looked hungry. Like you do now."

He pulled out a chair for me, and I hesitated. My funds were so low, and I *had* been neglecting regular meals. But I didn't want to be beholden to him. I already needed his help with Marcello. . . .

"I don't bite, Clipper Girl," he said.

"That's not my name." I sat down. It would be stupid of me not to take advantage of the free food. The Da Vias would be well fed when I faced them.

"*Kalla* Lea, then."

I ignored his correction. I had to remain on his good side. "He could be right, you know."

Alessio sat across from me and signaled a waiter. "Who?"

"My uncle. People could be looking for him. *Are* looking

for him actually, just not very actively."

Alessio snorted.

"It's true," I said. "The Da Vias have never really stopped their search for him. Which is another reason why he should help me."

"If he stays put, he's hidden."

"The Da Vias are after me. It's only a matter of time before they realize I'm here. And once they do, they'll be crawling all over this city. It won't be safe for anyone."

He scratched the stubble on his jaw. "I don't think that will convince him. Once he's made up his mind, he rarely budges."

I could be stubborn too, though.

The waiter delivered some sort of pocket bread stuffed with meat and fruit. I wrinkled my nose.

"Trust me on this," he said. "It'll change your view of Yvain."

Good food, and it was good food, always put me in a better mood. The lamb had been perfectly seared and seasoned with lemons, olives, and unfamiliar spices that left a pleasant, sweet taste lingering in my mouth. The fruit had been soaked in wine and burst with flavor. Alessio was right. I'd been missing out on some of Yvain's finer points. There may not have been many, but the food might have been one. And maybe the flowers, too. They smelled nice, after our meal.

"Didn't I tell you?" Alessio smiled as I licked my fingers clean.

"Yes, you did. You were right. I haven't eaten this well

since before . . . well. Since before." It had been with Val, actually. At Fabricio's.

I would never again dine with Val. Our secret meals, filled with laughter and flirting and stolen kisses, were gone forever, like my Family. I pressed my hand against my stomach, the Yvanese food like a stone in my gut. It wasn't fair, that I could miss him so much.

"Sorry," he said.

"What do you have to apologize for? You didn't kill my Family."

"This is the second time this morning I've said the wrong thing to you, and there you are, lost in your memories."

I shook my head. "It's not your fault. Almost everything reminds me of them. And that night."

Like how Rafeo would've taken huge bites of this pocket bread, while Matteo would have picked it apart and eaten only the bits he liked. And how none of them would ever get to taste it, and how I couldn't even tell them about it, couldn't tell anyone about it because there wasn't anyone left to tell. It was just me, alone, desperately trying to get some fake clipper to like me so he would put in a good word with my uncle, who'd turned out to be nothing like the Family I'd lost.

"Still," Alessio said, pulling me from my thoughts. "I meant no harm."

I cleared my throat. "The other night. And last night, too, you used some sort of smoke bombs. But I never saw you throw them. And they were different, too. They flashed."

Alessio smiled widely. "That's my own invention. It's effective, isn't it?"

"But how did you throw them without me seeing?"

He took a sip of his water. "I didn't. They were in place beforehand. They're timed to go off. Actually, the ones you saw firsthand were a little late."

Timed smoke bombs. My mind raced, thinking through ways they could be of use. The possibilities were astounding. Especially if they could be rigged for something other than smoke—

Wait.

"They flashed when they first went off."

He nodded. "The time bombs use a different chemical reaction than the regular smoke bombs. It's actually a small fire that's extinguished by the smoke. They're mostly free of danger."

A small fire extinguished by the smoke. "Could it be a bigger fire?" I asked. "Something that isn't extinguished? A kind of firebomb?"

His eyebrows creased, and he stared at me. "I don't know. Maybe. Why?"

"You asked me if I would train you that first night. Isn't my uncle training you?"

"This seems an abrupt change of topic."

I stayed quiet, waiting for him to respond. He took another sip of water, organizing his thoughts. "My master hasn't been a clipper in close to thirty years, and I had to beg him to teach me, *beg* him. Finally he relented, because he thought it would keep me safe. When he discovered I'd started taking jobs last year, he stopped all my training. He doesn't approve, thinks I'll get hurt or worse. When I saw you that first night . . . you're the only true clipper I've ever met."

He watched people as they walked past our table. "All I've ever wanted to be was a clipper. And I thought, here's someone who can teach me. *Truly* teach me, if she's willing."

"Why would you want to be a clipper?" I asked. I'd been born into this life. And, yes, in Lovero most people would claw at the chance to join a Family, for the power and wealth and status. But there was no prestige for clippers here.

His eyebrows twitched. "When I was a boy," he started slowly, weighing his words, "my mother was robbed and murdered. And I was orphaned and living on the streets, hiding in dark corners once the sun set, raging over the man who had taken my family from me, terrified of the angry ghosts and despairing of loneliness. And then my master found me.

"He brought me to his home, a hidden palace beneath the streets of Yvain, and he fed me and clothed me and kept me safe. And as we grew closer he told me about his life before, and of Safraella, and I knew that was where I belonged. Serving a goddess who would promise me another life after this one, if I followed Her dark design. If my mother had been Her follower, I would've slept easier after her death, knowing she had been granted a new life.

"This is why I want to be a clipper. My master, he gives me glimpses of what that life can truly be, but he keeps me from fully embracing it. You could give it to me. You could teach me. We could rebuild your Family."

Rebuild my Family. All I'd been thinking about was destroying the Da Vias. I'd assumed I'd die in the process. But if I didn't and I killed them all and still lived, if Alessio was right, maybe the Saldanas could still be one of the nine Families.

It wouldn't be the same, without my mother and father, my brothers, my cousin and nephew. And the Saldanas would never be the first Family again, not in my lifetime. Not even with the king's good graces. But maybe we could reclaim our territory, return to our duties of serving Safraella. Move past the horror of that night.

No. It wasn't possible. My Family was gone forever. Destroying the Da Vias was my only goal. Recapturing all I'd had before was a daydream, nothing more. There was no point holding on to that dream.

But without Marcello's help, it would be impossible to take down the Da Vias alone.

I glanced at Alessio. He was unfinished, but he'd shown some skill. And he knew the secret to making those timed smoke bombs, which could maybe be modified to better fit my needs. He had offered to help me kill the Da Vias. He said it was for no ulterior motive, but I couldn't trust him. He wasn't Family or family. If he was going to help me, it needed to be some sort of equal exchange. No one was owing anyone in this city of flowers and debts.

"I came here for two reasons," I said. "The first was to

locate the Da Vias' Family home, and a means to get inside. The second was to convince my uncle to help me kill them all."

"I already told you, he won't help."

I held up my hand, forestalling him. "Maybe I don't need him."

Alessio blinked. "Well, what's the alternative? Sit here until they find and kill you?"

"What you said earlier—"

"About me helping you?"

"I'm not a charity case. It would be an equal exchange. I could train you. . . ."

Alessio leaned forward. "If you train me, I will help you kill the Da Vias."

I ignored my churning stomach, the part of me that said he wasn't good enough, that it would take time to prepare him to fight so many Da Vias, time I didn't have. That I would be training him to greet his death. He desperately wanted to be a clipper, he'd said so himself. And what was I, if not a bringer of death?

Most importantly, I needed him. I would make the Da Vias pay, no matter who fell along the way.

Time to reel him in. "Will my uncle let you just leave? And I still don't know how to find the Da Vias. Maybe this is a bad idea."

Alessio waved his hands. "Don't worry about that. If you train me, I will get the information you need from him."

"And you'll need to teach me how to make those smoke bombs."

"Absolutely."

"But they need to be firebombs instead of smoke bombs."

His smile faded as he scratched his jaw, thinking. "I don't know . . ."

"I need them. It's no deal without it."

He shook his head. "It's not that I'm unwilling, I've just never attempted it before. It's going to take some trial and error on our part."

"How long will it take?" I asked.

His eyes connected with mine, dark brown even in the morning light. "How long will it take you to train me?"

"A lifetime."

Alessio paused, thinking this over. "You train me, and when the time comes, you take me with you to help kill the Da Vias. I get the information from my master somehow, and we work together on making those firebombs."

"As soon as you can. The longer we stay here, the more likely we won't ever leave."

He nodded, lost in his own planning. I stood, and he scrambled to his feet.

"Clipper Girl . . ."

"I'll see you on the rooftops near your home at sundown for training."

eighteen

I SAT ON THE FLOOR OF MY HIDING PLACE, THE EVENING sun prodding its way past the boards in the windows. I'd slept through the afternoon, but I didn't feel well rested. I never felt well rested anymore.

Three things I needed. Three things before I could return home: the location of the Da Vias from my uncle, at least one working firebomb from Alessio, and help from either. Or both. But preferably help from my uncle, who had at least been a real clipper in his youth.

Three things reminded me of the children's stories my father used to tell me. It seemed those characters always needed three things too: three kisses, three magic cakes, three breaths from a corpse. But the heroes of those stories always succeeded, and I'd already failed my Family. And I didn't think there'd be a happily ever after at the end of my tale.

When dusk arrived, I changed and climbed to my roof.

Alessio waited for me, dressed in his full leathers. I scowled behind my mask. "How did you know where to find me?"

He shrugged. "I followed you that first night to your . . . home. After you climbed out of the canal."

"I watched my back. You couldn't have followed me."

"I can tell you're not from around here," he said. "You forgot to watch the canals."

My eyes flicked to the canal behind me. Damn. He was right. I *had* ignored them.

"That one there"—he nodded—"actually leads to the one near my alley. It's much quicker to travel by canal if you know your way around them. Safer too."

"People could see you if you go out too early," I said. "You should wait until the sun sets."

He shook his head. "The only people left out at dusk are drunks and prostitutes. And they stay away from the canals. Now, what are we going to do tonight? Pull a job? Race across the roofs? Spar?" He rotated his shoulders, loosening his joints.

His excitement grated on me. "I want to see your weapons."

"What? Let's work one of my jobs or something!"

"You asked me to train you, so we're doing it my way. Let me see your weapons."

He sighed and took a seat on the roof, folding his long legs beneath him. I did the same, sitting across from him.

He emptied his pockets of small throwing knives and needles made for quick punctures. He pulled out wire for garroting and a stick used to assist in a fight. The last weapon was his huge knife, the one he'd brandished in the alley. It was close to eighteen inches long, and judging by how carefully he set it beside his other weapons, it was his favorite.

"Is that all?" I asked.

"Isn't that enough?"

I poked through his collection. Everything was serviceable and well maintained, but his collection was limited.

He chuckled in disbelief. "What else could I need?"

I dug through the pouches and pockets in my leathers and cloak and through my sheaths and weapons bags, which held much of what he'd laid before me, but also included brass knuckles, multiple knives, daggers and stilettos of varying weight and length, a collapsible blow dart tube and darts, a set of bolos on the off chance my mark fled, my sword, and of course, my large pouch of poisons.

"Why would I ever need all of this to drop a mark?"

"Not all of this is for marks. Some of this is for other clippers."

His eyes flicked to mine. "Is that a common problem in Lovero? Clippers killing clippers?"

I wiped a speck of dust off the blade of my sword. "I'm here in Yvain, aren't I?"

He nodded and returned to examining my weapons. "And this?" He pointed at the pouch.

"My poisons. Where are yours?"

He shook his head. "Master refused to teach me. He said I was more likely to poison myself or him than a mark."

"Hmm." A lot of clippers disdained poison, thinking it weak, or requiring no skill. But the truth was the opposite. Poison took more skill and knowledge than any of my other weapons. And often it took much more skill to get close enough to a mark to poison them, unseen, and escape, than it did to, say, leap off a roof, land on a mark, and sink a needle into their heart. "Where's your sword?"

"I don't have one. Just my cutter." He tapped his knife affectionately.

"Well, if we're going to make a true clipper out of you, you're going to need a sword at the least. Every other clipper will have one, and I don't care how long your arms are, that cutter's not going to pull it off against them."

He probed at the gap in his teeth with his tongue. "Master has a few in our weapons storage."

"Then I'll expect you to bring one tomorrow."

He smirked, then turned away.

"What?" I asked.

He shook his head, hiding his smile. "It's nothing."

I felt my cheeks redden beneath my mask. "Tell me!"

"It's only . . . look, it's nothing. You just sounded like my master right then."

"Oh. Well, our Family's training has been handed down through the generations, so I'm sure what I'm telling you is very similar to what he was told. He's been stopping himself from teaching you too much. Which is stupid. Why would he teach you enough to get in trouble but not necessarily enough to get out of trouble?"

His eyes narrowed. "I can get myself out of trouble."

I waved my hand. "That's not what I meant and you know it. I simply mean, it seems sloppy to train someone without finishing them. It's dangerous. And cruel, too."

"He's an immovable rock when he wants to be. There was no changing his mind no matter how hard I pushed."

If Marcello was really so stubborn, then how would Alessio get the Da Vias' location from him? How would I change his mind and convince him to join me?

Les continued, "And then I'd start to worry he'd grow so angry that he'd leave me like he'd left his family in Lovero, and I . . . I couldn't have that."

I had a hard time believing my uncle would abandon Alessio over an argument. "He didn't leave his Family. He was banished. Didn't he ever tell you?"

Alessio shook his head. "No. He just said there was a falling-out with his Family and that he couldn't ever go home again. Will you tell me?"

"I don't know."

His eyebrows creased. "How can you not know?"

"It was before my time. All I know is he was forced out for killing the head of our Family, his uncle. I don't know why he did it, what could have driven him to take his own Family's blood, but we weren't allowed to speak about him."

"Ever?"

I shrugged. "Ever."

"That seems cruel."

"He killed his uncle, his own flesh and blood. There is cruelty in that, too."

We stared at each other. We had reached an impasse. This training session wasn't starting as I'd imagined. One more thing I couldn't do right.

Rafeo would make a joke, but I didn't know any jokes. Father and Matteo would've known better and wouldn't have found themselves in this place of pregnant silence.

"Can I see your mask?" Alessio's question jostled me out of my rumination.

"I suppose." I lifted it off my face and handed it to him.

He examined it closely in the fading light. "It's cracked."

I nodded. "I think it happened in the fight. Or the fire. I'm not sure which."

He rubbed his thumb against the crack and across the eye-holes. I was glad of the darkening sky so he couldn't see me blush.

"Why did you pick these stripes?" He traced the black marks on the left side of the mask.

"I didn't."

"Don't you choose the pattern? Or am I mixing it up with the color?"

"No, you're right. The color is signified by Family. Black for Saldana; red for Da Via; orange for the Accurso in the region of Brescio; gray for Bartolomeo, who cover Triesta to Parmo; purple for Caffarelli in the city of Lilyan; yellow for Maietta in Reggia, Calabario, and Modeni; brown for Addamo in Genoni; blue for Zarella in the farmlands; and green for Gallo in the far south. Sapienza, the royal line, has gold, though they don't actually clip people. Their masks are for ceremony only.

"The patterns are up to each individual, but the slashes aren't mine. The mask isn't mine."

"Do you often trade masks?"

"No, we don't trade masks. It's my brother's mask. Rafeo. I got them . . . confused."

My chest tightened at the memory of the dark tunnel, and my brother alone down there, my mask resting beside him. Maybe my mask comforted him the way his mask comforted me. I hoped Safraella had given him a fast rebirth. He had probably been reborn already and was being cradled warmly by his new mother. I hoped his new life offered more peace than his last one.

Alessio looked at me. "He died in the fight?"

"Yes," I whispered, not trusting my voice any louder.

He nodded. "I'm sorry. I understand what it's like to lose your family. Someday it won't be so hard, and you'll be able to think of them without the pain." He handed the mask to me.

I held it in my lap. "When we were children, once, travelers passed through Ravenna with their menagerie. They had caged tigers. I'd never seen anything like them before, and never since. No books or tapestries could convey the colors, and the way their muscles rippled beneath their fur and stripes, and how their gold eyes stared at me. They were so beautiful.

"Rafeo . . . Rafeo could not stop talking about the tigers. I think they changed him, changed the way he saw the world, saw his place in it. He earned his mask two months later, and it was no surprise when he requested a tiger's black slashes." I rubbed my thumb over the black marks on the mask.

"My family were travelers," Alessio said.

I raised my eyebrows. "Really?"

He smiled and gestured to his face. "Can't you tell from my handsome nose? My coloring?"

I looked at him closer. Of course I had noticed his skin color, his nose, but I hadn't known they were markers of some kind. I shrugged. "I haven't met a lot of travelers."

Travelers were so called because they would travel across the dead plains without fear. One of their gods protected them from the ghosts. They were menagerie people, keeping dangerous animals and bringing them to cities for shows and viewings. Most of them hailed from Mornia, a country to the east, where they lived until they needed funds. Then they would gather and put on a tour until they made enough money to return home.

He glanced at the mask again. "What did your mask look like?"

"It had azalea flowers."

"Because they're poisonous?"

I nodded. "Truthfully, they never meant as much to me as Rafeo's tiger stripes did to him." I put it on and then slid it to the top of my head.

"When will I get a mask?"

I sighed. "I don't know. You should've had one by now.

As clippers, we're given one before we go on our first solo job. In Lovero, there are tradesmen who craft the masks for the Families. They're made from the bones of oxen that are raised on feed blessed and sprinkled with holy blood. It's a secret craft only they practice. I don't even know where to begin here in Rennes. Did you ever ask my uncle about it?"

"He refused. You heard him. He doesn't allow any masks around him. He wouldn't even show me his. Sometimes, when he's really drunk, I hear him cursing Safraella. Sometimes I hear him begging. I think the mask reminds him of Her and brings about dark thoughts."

I shook my head. "He does himself no favors in Her eyes."

"I don't think he wants to. He punishes himself."

I understood that. But for my atonement I'd rather do something, work toward killing the Da Vias instead of getting drunk and raging at the night.

"Training me was a sort of penance," Alessio said, "but he refused to train me all the way. Perhaps he looks at me and sees a path to redemption. Or maybe he was just a lonely man who found a lonely boy and figured they could find safety from the ghosts together."

I smiled. "You could be a poet, with words like that."

He returned my smile, and I felt it deep in my stomach. "*Kalla* Lea, I could be a lot of things, if I so chose. But I choose to be a clipper."

I climbed to my feet. "We'll start with poisons."

He smiled even more brightly and leaned forward. "Anything you can teach me, Clipper Girl."

"As much as I can until we leave."

His eyes darkened, but he climbed to his feet and nodded. "Until we leave."

Behind him, a flash of white light appeared in the alley beside my safe house. The light moved, then vanished behind a building before reappearing.

I walked to the edge of the roof for a better look. I tightened my arms around myself, my fists clenching. The ghost was so close this time.

"Sometimes the streets are full of them," Alessio said quietly as we watched the specter drift away, looking for a live body it could take as its own. "Even I don't venture out on nights like that."

I remembered the horrible screams on the dead plain, the black emptiness of the ghost's open mouth as she reached for me, the iciness of her fingers as they slipped through my flesh, trying to claim my body as her own. I remembered hiding in the boat on my first night here, the ghost waiting for me.

I released a breath I hadn't known I'd been holding.

We watched the ghost together. Alessio began to hum a song under his breath. I glanced at him, but he didn't seem to notice. I forced myself away from the edge.

I thought I had conquered my fear of the ghosts, but when I opened my fists, my nails had dug grooves into my palms and I hadn't even felt it. Not even on my burned hand, which ached from the pressure.

nineteen

THE NEXT MORNING I OPENED THE DOOR TO THE MAIL
office, and the sound and smell of pigeons assaulted my
senses. The front of the shop was small, no more than ten
feet wide and fifteen feet deep. At the back was a wooden
desk, kept clean but scratched by long years of use. Behind
the desk were cages and cages of pigeons. White pigeons,
blue, green, all of them cooing and bobbing and making a
racket. Small feathers drifted out of their cages and floated to
the floor. I covered my nose.

I shook the handbell on the desk. A portly man with
glasses and a balding crown stepped out from a side door. He
pushed his glasses farther up his nose and broke into a grin.

"Hello, milady. What can I do for you today?"

"I'm expecting a letter." Or at least Faraday had said he
would send me a letter. I didn't have an address here in
Yvain, so I had been checking the post office every few days.

"Of course, of course." He pulled out a ledger book and

dipped his quill into an inkwell before he flipped to a blank page in the middle of the book. He scratched something into the ledger. "Name?"

I blinked rapidly. I couldn't imagine Faraday using my full name to send a letter, on the off chance it was intercepted.

"Miss?" the clerk asked, glancing over his glasses.

"Oleander," I said. Maybe it would be enough, since it wasn't common.

He lifted his eyebrow but said nothing. Postmen took an oath. Any letters remanded to them were kept secret, as were destinations and origins. "I do indeed have a letter for an Oleander. Delivered yesterday."

My stomach fluttered.

"Do you need it read to you?" he asked.

"No."

He turned and paged through envelopes and letters in a bin behind him. He grunted and pulled one free, setting it on the desk. "Will you be sending a reply?"

I shook my head.

"Two gold," the postman said. I widened my eyes, and he lifted his eyebrow again. "Is something the matter?"

"Two gold is a lot. Why is it so expensive?"

He shrugged. "Postmaster owes a debt. I don't set the prices, miss."

Two gold would make a significant dent in my remaining funds. Most of the gold I'd brought with me from our stashes I'd left in Dorian's saddle packs. I had the Saldana stamped coins, but I couldn't use them. For one thing, they were holy coins, not meant for spending. And I couldn't take the chance of anyone seeing them. Since Lefevre had found the coin I'd left on that murdered boy, I'd hidden the coins in my hideaway for safekeeping.

But Faraday might have information regarding the hunt for me. I couldn't risk not hearing from him. No. I had to bite my lip and accept the cost.

"If you can't pay now, you can open a tab," the clerk said. "Pay your debt later."

Debts again. It had to be exhausting being Yvanese and having to juggle debts left and right. How anyone remained in good graces with their god was beyond me.

I sighed and poured two gold coins into my palm before passing them to the postman.

"Thank you so much for your business, and stay safe from the ghosts."

I took the letter and slipped out to the streets. The flecks of quartz and mica in the mail office's walls sparkled in the light of the afternoon sun. I took back ways and alleys to my safe house and slipped inside. It was almost too dark to read inside, but I felt safer.

The letter was from Faraday, of course, and I exhaled slowly as I opened the seal. His precise handwriting spilled across the page. I read his greeting:

They know.

My stomach sank. I scanned the rest of the letter, then realized I hadn't absorbed any of it, so fully had my fear overwhelmed me. I took a deep breath and read the letter carefully again.

They know.

I don't think they know who they're chasing, but they know someone survived their fire. Word is they're scurrying around the city like terriers tracking a rat and that they're considering a bounty on you. It's only a matter of time before they catch your trail. I would recommend you finish whatever business it is you're conducting as soon as possible and flee before they find you. Or someone finds you for them.

Expect another letter from me soon, with more information.

I will remind you it is not too late to return home, live a new life. I fear, though, that window will soon close and you will be committed whether you are ready or not.

I will pray for you, though I do not think She deals in the kind of mercy I'll ask for.

Yours in faith,

F

I crumpled the paper in my hands.

So the Da Vias knew I'd survived their attack. They must have spoken to the Addamos. But maybe the Da Vias didn't suspect it was me. Maybe the Addamos confused the situation and told them I was Rafeo. If they had counted and identified bodies, they wouldn't have found Rafeo's or mine.

But even if they thought I was Rafeo, that didn't give me much of an advantage. Perhaps they would be surprised when they discovered the truth, as Alexi Addamo had been, but it wouldn't change anything. They'd have to kill me no matter who I turned out to be, and I'd be easier to kill than Rafeo, who had been the best of us.

I was running out of time.

———

I leaned back against the wall of my space, trying to calm the fear and anxiety that had crept over me after Faraday's letter.

A thump came from above. I jerked my stiletto from my boot and scrambled to my feet.

Alessio peered down at me from the hole in the ceiling, an amused expression on his face. "I didn't mean to startle you."

I resheathed my stiletto, trying to decide if I was embarrassed. Clearly I was on edge from Faraday's letter, but I'd rather overact to nothing than underreact to an actual threat.

He dropped through the hole, dust puffing around his boots. He was dressed in green trousers and a matching vest covering a loose-fitting linen shirt, his pendant resting against his chest. He looked clean, freshly washed, with his hair pulled back tightly in a tail and the short beard on his chin neatly trimmed.

Alessio looked me up and down, taking in the same stained dress I'd been wearing, and tried to hide a grin. He turned and examined my space, the empty floors, my saddle-blanket bed, my bags of weapons and supplies. Everything I owned, except for Butters stabled at the monastery.

"Is this where you've been staying?" he asked.

"And?" I snapped.

"Nothing. Four walls are always better than none once the ghosts come out."

"What are you doing here, Alessio?"

"Les," he corrected. "I want to show you something. And we can get some food on the way. My treat."

This was the second time he was giving me food. Third if I counted the stolen fruit. "Are you courting me?"

He smiled, that ridiculous crooked smile of his. "Do you want me to court you?"

I stiffened. "Les . . ."

He held up his hands. "Lea, I simply want to make your stay here in Yvain easier. That's it. If you're not at your best, then your training won't be your best either. I'm sure you're starving, and honestly, I could use the company."

"Are you going to show me how to make the timed bomb?"

He at least had the decency to feel embarrassed, judging by the way his throat turned red. "No, we can't during the day."

I glared at him. He had to be delaying things. I didn't know why, but I couldn't trust him.

"We had a deal," I said. This was taking too long. I hadn't accomplished anything yet, and Faraday's letter urged me to hurry. I couldn't spend any more time here.

"I know. We can work on it tomorrow night."

"Tonight."

He shook his head. "It'll take me time to get all the supplies we'll need. But tomorrow night. I promise. Now, let's get something to eat before we starve."

He was intentionally delaying things. I didn't want to wait another night here. I wanted to head home to Lovero. I wanted to kill the Da Vias.

For now, I would stay on his good side. If I couldn't get the bomb tonight, then maybe I could work on one of my other necessities. And Les was right. I was famished.

I smoothed the skirt of my stained dress. I desperately missed my closet of clothes. Each dress I'd owned I'd picked out myself, and they had been tailored to accentuate my good bits and hide the not-as-good bits. And wearing the same clothes over and over again just made it easier for Lefevre to spot me in a crowd. I needed a change, but for that, I would need more money. But there was nothing I could do about that problem.

I gestured to the back window. "Less chance someone will see us."

We slipped outside, replaced the boards, and headed toward a city square. Alessio kept up a steady stream of chatter, pointing out landmarks and interesting facts of the city, and I nodded when it was appropriate and asked the occasional questions to make it seem like I was interested, but mostly I was lost in my own thoughts.

It seemed so natural to spend time with someone, a boy, Les, in broad daylight. Val and I had hidden in the shadows, kept everything secret. Which had been exciting, but looking back, it had also been stressful, sometimes, and tiring. It would've been nice to have Val court me for real, to go out in public with him and not worry about who might see us.

It didn't matter. I couldn't be with Val anymore. His Family had destroyed mine. Regardless of how I felt about Val, salvaging our relationship was not possible.

That didn't mean, though, that I wanted someone else. I glanced at Les, his long neck, his large nose. He winked at me and pointed to a building where a priest had held off a dozen angry ghosts, armed with nothing but his faith, until the sun had risen hours later. Les was funny and kind, and he actually seemed to understand some of what I was feeling. But he also held the keys to the Da Vias, and I wasn't here for friends.

Les paused and handed a beggar woman a coin.

"Why did you do that?" I asked when we were far enough away.

"Because she needed the help."

"But she'll probably just spend it on chetham leaves or something else."

"Or maybe she'll spend it on food, or a warmer shawl, or to pay back a debt she owes so she can greet Acacius gladly at the end of her life."

I turned away from his eyes and how they seemed to see right through me. There was no point to helping that woman. She wouldn't give Les anything in return.

"Here we are." Les flourished his hand in front of a small street vendor, serving skewers of lamb. He bought us each one, and then led us away.

"Alessio!" a man shouted, and Les waved at him.

"A friend of yours?"

He shook his head. "No friends. Only me and the old man. People don't stick around." He cleared his throat and suddenly seemed older.

"How old are you?" I asked.

"Nineteen. You?"

"Seventeen."

He nodded. "I'm sure you had a lot of friends left behind. You're just short of royalty there."

I shrugged. "I learned very young they were more interested in what I was than who I was. Maybe they're hoping for favors from Safraella, or from a Family. Maybe they're more interested in the wealth and power. And even if they aren't, it can be difficult to keep any friendships because, try as they might, the common can't fully understand. My brother Rafeo was my greatest friend. Then my cousin, Jesep. And my suitor, Val. I spent a lot of time with him."

He paused so slightly it was barely noticeable. "Suitor? You must really miss him."

"No." I brushed the sides of my dress. "He was a Da Via. I'd rather avoid seeing him again for the rest of my life."

Les paused and watched me. His study made my nerves twitch, and when I was nervous I blushed.

"Was he there?" he asked. "The night of the attack?"

I stepped over a cracked cobblestone. "I'm not sure. I didn't recognize anyone. I didn't even realize they were Da Vias until Rafeo told me. I confirmed it with the king."

Les tripped. "Did you say *the king*?"

I nodded.

"I was mostly joking when I compared you to royalty earlier. . . ."

"Well, any clipper can speak to the king. He's a disciple of Safraella too. And my father and Costanzo Sapienza were good friends since childhood. My father helped put him on the throne."

Les nodded, his eyes wide as he took this in. "How would a relationship with another clipper work? I thought the Families were all at war with one another."

"Some of the Families have good relationships. Gallo and Zarella, for example."

"But weren't you always worried your suitor Val was planning something?"

I blinked. "In hindsight maybe I should've been more worried. But I'd known Val my whole life and we shared a territory, Ravenna, so there was overlap." I picked a speck of lint off the sleeve of my dress. "No one knew about us. We kept it secret. There was no love between the Saldanas and Da Vias."

Alessio tugged on the pendant resting on his chest and led

me down another side street. "But what about that saying I've heard . . . 'Family over family.' Doesn't that mean you really *should* fraternize with each other?"

"Mm." I pushed my hair behind my ears. "What that means is you put your clipper Family before your blood family. So if your father tells you one thing, and the head of the Family tells you another, you do what the head tells you."

"That seems backward."

"Everything we have is due to Family. My status doesn't come from being the daughter of Dante and Bianca. It comes because I'm a member of the Saldana Family. Anyone who joins us, through birth or marriage or adoption, is named Saldana. That's Family. That is more important than blood ties. It has to be if we're to survive the way we have for generations."

Les scratched his jaw, lost in thought.

Speaking too much about the Nine Families turned my stomach. I stopped. We were wasting time I didn't have. "What are we doing?" I asked. "What did you want to show me?"

"This." He stopped and waved his hand before him.

Resting on canal waters that twirled lazily before us, moored to the alley so it wouldn't float away, bobbed a boat.

twenty

"A BOAT."

"My boat, yes. It's clear you don't know anything about our canals or boats, so I thought I'd show you how to work one and map out some of the waterways."

"I know how to use a boat. Ravenna has a seaport."

"Canal boats are different. You steer them with a pole while standing, but they're flat bottomed and they rock easily. It takes skill to stop from falling in." He untied the boat and held the rope in his hand.

"I don't have my own a boat, though."

"Then borrow one. They're tagged and someone will return it to its owner." He tapped the boat and a symbol carved into the prow, declaring who it belonged to. "Returning it will accrue a debt and the common enjoy a debt."

What could teaching me how to work a boat gain him? "Why would I even need to know this? It's not like I plan on staying."

"Because the canals are the best way to escape the ghosts," he answered.

I thought of my first night here and knew he was right. Still, I hesitated.

He sighed. "Remember how I said my mother was murdered?"

"Yes."

"I'm only half traveler, on my mother's side, and the two of us were visiting Yvain with my grandfather. I think they were looking for my father, so she could leave me with him. When she was murdered, we had to identify her body. My grandfather wanted her to be carted home. He told me to stay at the law office and wait for him while he made arrangements with her body. And he never came back."

"He *left* you there? Alone? How old were you?"

"Seven."

I tried not to picture little boy Les, sitting on a chair, knowing his mother was dead and waiting for someone to come for him. My chest ached for that child.

"So the lawmen kicked me out onto the street. The sun had set and they were tired of watching me and there's no love for travelers here. I hid beneath a bush, trying not to cry. But the ghosts found me. They always find you. I had to outrun them until finally I just spent the night in a canal, hanging on to the edge and swimming into the center if one came too close to me. That went on for a week or two. Then I met your uncle and he took me in."

The boat had drifted, and he yanked the rope to bring it

closer. "So now you know. When I say the canals will keep you safe from the ghosts, you can believe me."

He gestured for me to get on the boat. My burned palm throbbed, and I tightened my hand into a fist. Any escape from the ghosts was a skill worth having.

I stepped onto the boat and it rocked immediately, threatening to spill me into the water.

Les jumped in beside me, a long canal pole in his hands. "I'm going to push us around a bit. You should stay standing so you get a feel of the boat and how easily it shifts. This canal leads to our home, and I'll show you how it connects to your place, too."

"Why? I already know how to find your home."

He grinned. "In case you need another way to reach me."

I scowled. He was too familiar with me sometimes. "So, your grandfather," I said. "You were family. How could he abandon you like you were worse than livestock?"

Les pushed the boat roughly, and I swung my arms out to keep my balance.

"My family wasn't very accepting of me, being a half-blood. Every day I'd clean the tiger cages and dream of getting closer to them, of taking care of them. But my family made me stay away. All the men and women who worked with the tigers scarred their forearms with tiger claws, to mark their important status." Les gestured to the top of his forearm, dragging his fingers like claws across the skin. "As you can see, no scars for me, because taking care of the tigers meant you belonged. And I didn't. I was less than them, not worthy.

"And here, in Rennes, they weren't accepting of me either. Only your uncle didn't seem to care about my heritage." He leaned forward, using the pole to drag the boat around a corner.

"Safraella doesn't care," I said. "A death is a death. Marcello would have been raised to believe so, too."

"While my grandfather spoke to the lawmen about my mother, before he left, I snuck in to see her. She always wore a pendant. Said it was a gift from her grandmother and contained old magic. I wasn't allowed to touch it because I was only half traveler."

He lifted the pendant I'd seen before from under his shirt. It was a disc-shaped agate, with shades of blue radiating out from the center, polished to a high sheen.

"I took it, to remember her by. I didn't know I'd never see any of my family again, but my grandfather didn't notice what I'd done. I'm sure he was angry when he got home and saw her pendant missing. It's all I have left of them. All I have from my previous life."

I raised my eyebrow, trying to lighten the somber mood we'd fallen into. "Was that your first time being a thief?"

He chuckled. "No. Travelers worship three gods. One of them, Boamos, is a god of thievery and wealth. I'd definitely dabbled before. I daresay He—and my mother, actually— would have been quite pleased at my little act." He flicked the pendant.

"What does *kalla* mean?" I asked.

He jerked the pole and the boat tilted sharply. Only my

quick reaction kept me on my feet. He smiled slowly. "That's for me to know. Unless you speak Mornian."

His mood seemed to have lightened. This was probably the best chance I'd get to broach the subject. "Les, do you think I could speak with Marcello again?"

He blinked, and his smile vanished. "I told you, he's forbidden you to return."

"I know, but what would it hurt to try again?"

"He could leave. Just slip out when I'm not home, disappear on both of us."

"Would he really do that?"

"It's his favorite threat."

I frowned. A threat wasn't anything, though. It could have been false, an easy way to keep Les in line. Les said Marcello hadn't left the tunnels in years, and I doubted seeing me again would be the final pressure to crack the egg.

"What if I promise this would be the last time? I could speak with him quickly, then leave. Let him think it over on his own terms. I can control my temper." I could convince him to help me. I knew I could.

"Why are you in such a rush anyway?" Les asked.

I didn't want to think about the letter, about the Da Vias searching Ravenna for me, discovering I'd come to Yvain. I just had to hope it would take them longer to find me than me to find them. "Sooner or later the Da Vias will find me here. I don't have any time to waste."

He watched the swirls on the canal water.

"Okay," he finally said. "One more try. But you will have

to be polite and respectful, even if he's drunk. Even if he's an ass. If you're not, he won't even listen to what you have to say."

I nodded eagerly. "I can do that."

We continued down the canal, lost in our thoughts. After a few moments the silence slipped into awkwardness. Les poled the boat and began to hum. I watched him.

"Do you always sing to yourself when thinking?" I asked.

He blinked. "I guess so. I've never really thought about it before. I used to sing in the tiger cages. And when I was hiding from the ghosts in the canals. I suppose it's just a habit."

I thought about humming my tune when marking a kill. It seemed we had something else in common.

"And here we are." He poled his boat to a mooring and I saw that we'd reached the street next to their alley. Time to speak to Marcello.

Les tied the boat off and jumped out. I followed behind, but the boat rocked suddenly and I stumbled. Les grabbed my hand, steadying me. He laughed, his hand clasping mine, and I laughed too. I couldn't remember the last time I'd laughed. I'd forgotten how good it felt.

Les's smile faded and he stared at me. His fingers stroked mine.

My breath caught in my throat and my cheeks burned. I pulled my hand free. "I think that's enough for now."

The wind blew a strand of his hair across his throat. Les rubbed his neck and nodded. "You're absolutely right. I'm sorry."

Was he? Because I didn't have time for this. I needed to concentrate on the Da Vias and nothing else.

Even if, for an instant, I remembered how it felt to have a body pressed against mine, how it felt to feel so alive when Val kissed me and showed me how beautiful he thought I was.

But that wasn't for me. It wouldn't be fair, to feel so alive again, when my Family was dead because of me.

twenty-one

†

I SAT DOWN ON A CHAIR ACROSS FROM MARCELLO. HE glared at me while Les poured tea. Then Les disappeared into one of the back areas, leaving us alone.

I couldn't decide if he was being polite, or a coward.

"I thought I told you to get out." Marcello sipped at his steaming tea.

"You did. And I did. And now I've returned."

Marcello set his cup down. "What do you want this time, *niece*?" he sneered. "Get it out so we can all get on with our pathetic lives."

"I don't have a life anymore," I said. "The Da Vias took it from me."

"That's why I included you in the *pathetic* part."

I dug my fingers into the arms of my chair, trying to rein in my temper. Marcello's eyes flashed to my hands, and he grinned slowly.

He was trying to get a rise out of me, trying to make me

angry so he would have an excuse to throw me out again. I wouldn't let him beat me.

"They lit the house on fire," I said. "While we slept. They came inside and set the fire and waited for us to flee our beds before cutting us down."

Marcello tapped the arms of his chair. "That is what the Da Vias do. They are sharks in the sea, always circling, always waiting for an opportunity to taste blood."

"I left my brother's body in the tunnel," I continued. "I left my mother in the house, fighting Da Vias, while the roof collapsed and surrounded her with flames."

"Maybe you shouldn't have abandoned her, then."

I bit my cheek until the taste of blood bloomed across my tongue. "Emile was four years old. Jesep was sixteen. Matteo was nineteen. Rafeo was twenty-four and already a widower."

"So? What's your point? Death comes for all of us. You of all people should know that Safraella sees not age, nor wealth nor creed."

I needed his help. Why was it so hard to appeal to his sense of justice? "Help me, please. They were your family, even if you were no longer Family," I said. "They were your blood."

"Pah." He shook his head.

I leaned back. "Maybe you are too much of a Da Via."

He slammed his fist of the arm of his chair. "Don't you dare call me a Da Via!"

"You were married to Estella Da Via. I know that much.

And there you sit, choosing them over us."

"I'm not choosing anyone. There's no point to your little plan of vengeance. It doesn't matter."

"They were my Family!" My voice cracked shamefully, and I flushed.

Marcello eyed me. "And you were lucky to have them when you did. Not everyone in this world is so blessed. You should count yourself further blessed that you survived while they didn't. Forget about them. They will surely be reborn—if they haven't been already—and won't have a single memory of you. Flee from here, from Lovero. Find some man to straddle and make yourself a new family. It's the only way you'll achieve any peace in this life."

I glared at him. "I don't need peace in this life. I need vengeance."

He got to his feet. "Well, you won't find any help here. I need you to leave now. And you're not welcome back, niece."

I stood. More than anything I wanted to hurt him, to claw his eyes, bury my stiletto in his unfeeling heart. But I had promised Les I would behave, and he was my only hope now of getting the information I needed from Marcello.

"My father would be ashamed of you," I said.

Marcello smirked. "He already was. Now leave."

He turned his back on me and headed to the kitchen.

I waited for my anger to abate so I wouldn't lose my temper again before I strode from the fire. On a small table sat a dish filled with coins, the coins Les had been stealing from his marks. Marcello and Les weren't even using them.

I needed clothing. And food. And money to claim any further letters Faraday might send me. I couldn't just sit around, begging for Marcello's help, waiting for the Da Vias to find and end me. I had to do something.

I scooped coins into my hand and shoved them into my purse. I didn't take them all, but enough to get by. One way or another, Marcello was going to help me.

In the tunnel room I jerked the grate up. Suddenly Les's hand was on mine, closing over it and the grate. His palms and fingers were warm, and calloused, but his grip was gentle. I glared at him, the coins heavy in my purse.

He gave me a sympathetic smile and mouthed a silent apology for how Marcello had treated me.

I wanted to be angry at Les, too, but he seemed sincere in his apology, just like he seemed sincere in everything he did. My rage began to fade, and I nodded. It wasn't his fault, anyway. He had warned me.

"Later tonight?" he whispered.

For a moment I wanted to tell him no. I wanted to walk into the middle of the street and wait there until the Da Vias found me and sent me to meet Safraella like the rest of my Family. It would be so much easier.

But my Family would be ashamed of me, and regardless of how Marcello felt, I knew if I added more shame on top of my guilt, I wouldn't meet Safraella when my life ended. My heart would be so full of despair that I would wander the dead plains as a ghost in my own personal hell.

"Only if we work on the firebomb," I said.

Les tightened his jaw but then finally nodded. I knew he'd just been trying to delay things. I pulled my hand out from under his. He closed the grate quietly behind me.

———◆———

My sour mood—tinged with the despair I was trying not to acknowledge—followed me out of the tunnel. It was late afternoon, but the Yvanese continued with their shopping at the markets, using every moment of daylight available to them. I slid into the crowd, heading back to my safe house, lost in my thoughts. People packed the market. More than once I had to bite back a vicious barb, or an equally vicious elbow aimed at a person who'd gotten too close. People spoke quickly, conversation limited by daylight. Cart vendors called out their wares, telling people if they couldn't pay now, they could pay later with interest. Debts were accepted everywhere.

I'd failed with Marcello. Again. And I knew I wasn't going to get a third try. All I had now was Les. He would have to get the information from Marcello, which meant I had to keep training him, keep in his good graces, remind him that Marcello was holding him back and it was in his best interests to help me.

Even if it wasn't. Even if helping me could get him killed.

My stomach rumbled, the tea I'd drunk with Marcello doing nothing to ease my hunger pains. Before me stood a vendor with more of those meat pies Les had introduced me to. I had money now. But I couldn't just spend it on anything. If I used a small bit to buy one pie, I could eat half now, and half later.

The stall owner held up his fingers for a price, and I reached for my coin pouch.

It was gone.

I felt around my belt, but it was nowhere to be found. I twisted to search the crowd behind me.

To my left, someone whistled a familiar tune. I turned. Captain Lefevre. He smiled when I made eye contact.

"Ah, Miss Lea. Have you lost something?"

I swallowed. He could have been following me the whole time. But I hadn't done anything to give myself away. Unless he'd seen me crawl out of Marcello and Les's tunnel. But I would have noticed that. . . .

"I seem to have lost my money purse." I patted my hip. "You don't think it was stolen, do you?" He had to realize I was faking my naïveté, but if other people in the crowd were listening or watching, I wanted to be clear on how I presented myself in case he publicly accused me of anything.

"Perhaps this is it?" From his fingers swung my money pouch.

"Yes!" I smiled sweetly and reached for it, but he turned to face the stall owner.

"How much does she owe you?" he asked. The stall keeper held up one finger.

"That's quite all right, Captain Lefevre," I said. "I can pay the fine gentleman."

Lefevre smiled at me again, his sickly sweet grin. He dumped my coins into the palm of his hand. He poked through them, examining each one closely, before he finally removed a coin and handed it to the stall keeper, who pocketed the money and passed me the meat pie.

Lefevre dumped the money into my pouch and cinched it. He held it out to me. I reached for it, but he clasped my hand with his own.

"You must be more careful with your coins, Miss Lea. You never know when they'll draw someone's attention. Someone who's looking for you, maybe."

He stroked my palm with his thumb, tracing the healing burn. I jerked my hand away, yanking the pouch with me. Lefevre smiled even more brightly.

"I'll try to keep that in mind, Captain Lefevre."

I slipped away from him, determined that he wouldn't catch me unaware again.

Les's hands shook as he tried to pour a concoction from a bottle into a vial. The harder he tried to still his fingers, the more they shook.

The moon shone down on us as it made its way toward the horizon. The canal waters sparkled with its light, creating starbursts in the streets. Something I'd never see in Ravenna.

Finally I grabbed his hands and took the bottle away from him.

"If you're not careful, you'll spill it," I snapped. "Some poisons only require skin contact, and if you spill those, you'll be dead."

Les sighed and jerked his hair tie off before running his hands through his hair. "I'm no good at this. I don't have the patience for mixing poisons."

I poured the poison carefully into the vial, then stoppered it with a cork. I passed it to Les. "Mark the top with a symbol. It should be unique to you, so no one else can use it."

He pocketed the vial before tying his hair back once more. "How do you have so many recipes and antidotes memorized?"

"Because I've been doing this for over ten years. But you don't need to be a master poisoner to use poisons. These ones are easy to craft and simple to use. You could coat your cutter with one, and a shallow cut would become a mortal wound. Poisons are versatile and have more uses than just dosing someone's food for a quiet kill."

Les shook his head slowly. "I'll never be the kind of clipper you are."

I didn't like the turn of this conversation. If he thought he wasn't getting a good value, he might decide not to help me. Yes, he'd originally offered to help me for no other reason than just to help, but I still didn't trust that intent.

Then again, I knew how Les felt. Rafeo had been an amazing clipper. Everything came easily to him. Matteo and I struggled to even come close to his skills. Matteo especially took Rafeo's skill as a personal insult, as if Mother and Father had somehow contrived to make him look bad. But not even Matteo could stay angry at Rafeo for long.

"Let's work on the firebomb," I said. "That's more

important than poisons."

Les grabbed a satchel he'd brought with him and set it between us. I sat down across from him. He laid out a blanket and set down different spheres, some ceramic, others metal. Beside the spheres he placed small jars filled with different-colored powders, and a few more with liquids.

The materials looked similar to the ones used to make smoke bombs, but when I picked up one of the ceramic spheres, it wasn't divided in the middle.

Les pointed at my chest. I looked down and found my key loose from my leathers. I tucked it back in.

"What is it for?" he asked.

"My house."

"I thought your house burned down."

I nodded. "It did. I just . . . couldn't bring myself to get rid of it. It's all I have left."

And it served as a reminder, so I'd never forget that my secret had destroyed everything. I glanced at Les. He was so eager to assist me, a stranger he barely knew. A girl who had invaded his home and stolen from him, and yet here he was, back to helping me again.

Would he be so eager if he knew the truth about me? That the murder of my Family was on my hands?

Les smoothed the blanket. "Okay. Well, timed smoke bombs are similar to the throwing kind. The ceramic shatters and the chemicals combine and smoke appears."

His flashed his hands before me, mimicking an explosion.

"For the timed ones, though, we have to use some different chemicals and different layers."

He picked up a jar with a clear liquid and placed it in front of me. "This will eat through metal. Not immediately—and how fast depends on the type of metal, the amount of solvent, and so on. It takes a lot of trial and error, and even then sometimes it doesn't turn out right."

He glanced up at me, and I nodded to show I was following.

"Besides metal, it will also eat through flesh and fibers. Wood. Fabric. But it can't go through glass." He flicked the jar with his finger, and it pinged quietly.

Ate through flesh. I immediately thought of different ways to use it. Perhaps a thrown vial at an enemy as a deterrent. "Where did you get this?"

"It's a traveler recipe. It's something we've—they've—kept secret for hundreds of years." He pushed the jar aside. "So, how the timed smoke bomb works is, I fill one of these small metal spheres with the powdered smoke agents. Then I place it inside one of the ceramic spheres."

He showed me how the ceramic sphere was actually two pieces, tightly fitted together like a puzzle. The metal sphere fit inside the ceramic halves, and he closed it up. "I fill the ceramic with the liquid smoke agent and the acid. They don't like each other, so they stay unmixed, and the acid picks and pocks at the metal until it's breached. The acid and the powder also don't like each other. That's where the flash comes from. When they mix, the acid is burned up, exploding the ceramic casing, and then the remaining powder and liquid combine to make the smoke."

"Okay." I nodded. I'd made smoke bombs before, and with all my poison and antidote experience I understood how chemicals mixed in different ways reacted to different things. "What's all this for, then?" I pointed at the remaining powders and liquids he'd placed on the blanket.

"These are the combinations we're going to try, to see which ones will make the biggest fire that will burn the longest."

Les grinned and I did too, though my grin came from picturing the Da Vias, trapped behind the flames of their burning home.

twenty-two

†

WE SPENT HOURS TRYING DIFFERENT COMBINATIONS, our hopes high. But after a few hours of frustration and frayed tempers, we decided to try again later and went home for some much-needed sleep.

In the morning I headed to a different market to look for clothes. The old one had good prices, but I didn't want to face the women of Acacius again.

It didn't take me long to find a shop. I bought two dresses and changed immediately. I was almost tempted to throw out the stained one, but even if I didn't wash it or ever wear it again, I could use it as a blanket or a pillow on my saddle-blanket bed. There was no point in being wasteful.

I used some of my coins to buy a filling lunch, one that would hopefully last me the rest of the day. Then I headed to the mail office. Faraday had said he was going to send me another letter, so I wanted to keep checking.

It was the same postman as before, and he bobbed his head

as I entered. "Oleander, right?"

I nodded and he flipped through the envelopes in the bin. He pulled one out, then glanced at me over his shoulder before returning to the letter.

"Is it for me?" I asked.

He faced me, letter held at his thigh. "Do you go by any other names?"

Another name. Of course I did, but why would Faraday use it when he'd used Oleander before? "Lea," I said. I would've forsaken the letter before I risked giving him my last name, too.

The postman set the letter on the counter. He pulled out his ledger and made a mark on a line. "Two gold again."

I passed him the coins and he slid the letter over to me.

"Thank you." I walked out of the shop into the bright afternoon sun.

The letter was addressed to me, but I understood why he'd hesitated before handing it over. It had my name, Oleander, written on the front, but someone had crossed that out, a single black line through the letters, and replaced it with Lea.

I sat on a bench outside and cracked the seal of the letter, the pages unfolding in the gentle breeze.

A pressed white poppy fell into my lap.

I couldn't breathe, couldn't feel my heart beating, couldn't do anything but pinch the poppy between my two fingers.

I opened the letter and read.

Maybe this will find you. If you're even in Yvain. If you're even still alive. I don't know. I must be an idiot to think this letter will go anywhere. But I found this flower in a saddlebag kept at a monastery, and I couldn't believe it was simply a coincidence.

Maybe it is, though. Maybe I'm just crazy.

But if you are alive and do get this letter, I want to say ... I want to say a lot of things, actually. And I wish I could say them to you, but I guess if this is the only chance I have, then I'd better take it.

I'm sorry. I know it doesn't mean anything, and maybe it doesn't even matter because you're dead anyway and this letter will go nowhere.

But if you are alive, and you do get this letter, please be careful. I've spoken to the Addamos, and they've scoured the dead plains. Yvain is the only place they haven't searched yet. It won't be long before the rest of my family catches on. We're close. We won't give up. Better for you to disappear, to vanish and never come back.

That was it. No signature. Nothing to tell who had written it, but I knew the letter came from Val. If he'd found the flower in Butters's saddlebag, it meant the Da Vias were closer than I'd thought. If the Addamos had steered Val to Yvain, enough to send a blind letter anyway, then the others would be close behind.

Dumb. I was so, so dumb. I should've destroyed the poppy when I'd found it after the fire, should have crushed it. But I'd kept it, put it aside somewhere I wouldn't have to look at it anymore, so I wouldn't have to feel the things it brought to the surface. And now here it rested in my fingers, a reminder of all the mistakes I'd made, that I continued to make, and the consequences that seemed to never end.

A shadow fell over the letter. I looked up. Les stood before me, blocking out the sun.

I squinted. "What are you doing here?"

He glared at me until I shifted. "You stole from us."

I narrowed my eyes. So that was the way this conversation was headed. I took a breath. "I needed the money. It was just sitting there. You weren't using it."

"Oh, of course," he scoffed. "You *needed* it, so you just took it because *we* weren't using it. It all makes sense. I thought you were a thief, but now that you've explained it, I see I was mistaken."

"That's not—"

"I don't even know what's worse," he interrupted, arm cutting through my words. "The fact that you're still going to want me and my master to trust you, to help you, after all this, or that you didn't trust *me* enough to just ask for the money in the first place."

I blinked. If I had asked him for it, I would have been beholden to him. I couldn't let him hold that over my head. We had agreed to an even exchange.

216

"My master will never help you now." He paused and rubbed the back of his neck. "I would've given it to you," he said. "I wouldn't have even asked why you needed it."

"Clothing," I said. "And food."

He shook his head. "It doesn't matter."

Of course it mattered. It wasn't as though I'd stolen the money to spend on frivolous things like necklaces or lace. I had spent it on things I truly needed.

"I trusted you."

My body froze at his words. He had trusted me. What had I done to engender such blind faith?

But maybe the better question was, why had I broken it? I'd become a thief, something I would have never done before.

If I looked in a mirror at this moment, I didn't think I'd recognize the girl who looked back.

"We're done, Lea." Les turned his back on me.

"But—"

He didn't even wait to hear what I had to say. He just walked away, slipping into the crowd.

A gust of wind swept through the square. It tore the pressed poppy from my fingers and sent it after Les until it, too, had vanished.

That night I waited for Les on the top of my safe house.

He never showed.

⸻

Sometimes I found it hard to sleep at night. I was so used to later hours working as a clipper that when I didn't have to work—or like tonight, when I'd made a mistake and driven Les away—the still quiet of the night wasn't the lullaby I sought.

Especially in my little safe house, where my bed was a saddle blanket on the hard floor, and the old, rotting walls creaked and groaned with every breeze.

I rolled over, trying to cover my ears, to give me some peace from the noise. But the groaning grew louder.

A white glow seeped in, past the gaps in the boards, followed by a slow, soft moan.

It hadn't been the wind or the wood making the noise.

A ghost hovered outside my window, and though it couldn't see me, didn't know I was inside, I still tucked my knees against my chest.

The ghost moaned again, and my stomach tightened. Ghosts were terrifying. And malevolent. And this one would rip me from my body if it could catch me.

But they were also heartbreakingly sad. Who knew what this one mourned? The loss of its body, of course, but maybe it, too, mourned the loss of something more. A mother or father. A husband or wife. A child. Maybe just the sun, or the light, or something I couldn't even understand, being alive.

"Ohhhhh," it moaned again, like the women who wept and wailed at the cribs of the infants I had released during the plague. Like Rafeo when his wife had taken her last breath.

I shut my eyes and covered my ears, but no matter how hard I tried to hide myself from the ghost, that sound crept into me, filling me up, until I knew I would never be free of it.

I had to make things right.

As the morning sun slipped past the slats of the walls of my safe house, I pulled on one of the new dresses, then thought better of it and slipped back into my stained one.

I would return to Marcello's home, and though I couldn't repay the money I'd spent, I could at least return what I had left. And then I would beg for their forgiveness. No matter how I tried to rationalize my actions, Les was right—it was thievery, plain and simple. I'd already lost so much, and I refused to lose any more of myself. I wouldn't be a thief.

I climbed out the window. The day had dawned cool, and a soft mist floated above the canals, drifting into the alleys and streets.

I'd have to wait for Les to come out. I couldn't just barge into their home or let myself in.

I walked through a square, and even though it was early enough that the market hadn't fully opened, the common of Yvain were already about their errands and plans for the day.

I cut through the crowd, ignoring the bakers with their iced buns and sweet rolls for breakfast. Ignoring the looks my stained dress garnered from the better dressed women. None of that mattered. Only one thing mattered, and that was killing the Da Vias.

The crowd thinned around me and I slipped into a side street, following it along the canal that led to Les and Marcello's alley. I turned down the dead end and stopped, prepared to wait all morning if I had to.

The grate above the ground squeaked. Maybe I wouldn't have to wait long after all.

"Miss Lea," a voice called to me.

I spun. Lefevre waited at the entrance to the alley.

"Captain Lefevre." I glanced at the grate, but if it had been about to open, it was now still. Lefevre seemed to be everywhere I went, always present, always spying on me. It made the back of my neck crawl.

"I thought it was you." He stepped into the alley, walking closer. "I could tell by your dress. It has a stain on it, by the way."

I blushed, wanting to cover the stain with my hand. "An unfortunate accident."

He nodded. "It's early in the morning to find yourself lost in an alley."

I smiled. "I just get turned around easily," I said. "I can hear the market but I can't seem to find it."

"Ah. Then let me escort you." He held his arm out for me.

I would have done almost anything to avoid taking his arm, but I had to keep playing this role of innocence, even if he didn't believe me. And I had to lead him away from the entrance to Les and Marcello's tunnel. If he found them, it would put an end to all my plans.

I clutched his arm and he led me from the alley.

"You were really quite near." He leaned close to me. His warm breath brushed against my neck. "Just a few streets off."

I was sure he could hear my teeth grinding. "I would have stumbled my way there eventually."

"And I don't know that you should be walking about on your own. There's a serial murderer on the loose."

"Is there?" I played dumb. It was clear Lefevre suspected I was the clipper he'd seen my first night here. But I wasn't sure if he suspected me of also being their serial murderer.

"I only arrived a few days ago," I said, "so I hadn't heard anything about it." That should clear me of any suspicion.

"Yes. When the priests lent you a robe. I spoke with them, though, and they don't seem to remember anyone arriving in the last few days."

He'd been checking into me, asking around. He was dangerous, in more than one way.

I bit my lip in fake concern. "It was a visiting priest from a monastery. His name was Faraday. He can provide you more information, if you'd like."

"I'll seek him out, then." He led me around a corner and the market spread before us, the crowd growing.

I released his arm and fought the desire to wipe my fingers on my dress.

"Thank you, Captain Lefevre."

"It was my pleasure, Miss Lea. I'll be seeing you around. Stay safe from the ghosts."

It was a common Yvain good-bye, but Lefevre made it seem like a threat. I bowed my head and pushed my way into the crowd. I couldn't return to Les and Marcello now, not with Lefevre so clearly watching for me during the day. I could feel his eyes on my back, and it took all my willpower to calmly stroll through the market.

I was frightened of very few things, but Lefevre was slowly making his way up the list.

twenty-three

†

THE SUN SET, AND I CLIMBED TO THE ROOF OF MY SAFE house. Lefevre wouldn't be watching for me at night, so I was hoping to return to Les and Marcello's and ask for their forgiveness. Time was running out.

A thump behind me. My hand dropped to my stiletto, but then I realized it was Les. I grunted and got to my feet.

He stared at me, his hood casting his eyes in shadow. My mask covered my face, but it didn't hide my eyes.

"You came," I said.

He didn't say anything. Finally he sighed. "I saw you this morning. With that lawman. Lefevre."

"I didn't mean to draw him to your entrance," I said. "I was coming to apologize. To give back the money. But he's been trailing me since I arrived. I led him away as best I could."

"I followed you two. You could have told him the truth. About his serial murderer. About me."

Lefevre was after me for the murders Les had committed. Lefevre had the right motive in mind, but the wrong clipper.

I paused. This could be some sort of test for me. If I said the wrong thing, maybe he would leave again. "Why would I do that?"

"Who am I to you? And telling the truth would make things easier for you."

He was right. Telling Lefevre that Les was his serial murderer, and even where he could find Les, would get Lefevre off me. But I needed Les and Marcello, more than I needed to be free from Lefevre.

"I need you," I said.

He dropped his head, but not fast enough for me to miss the twitch of his lips. "All right. You give me the coins back, and I'll still help you."

I shoved my hand into my purse and scooped out the remaining coins. I poured them into his palm.

"Is this all of them?" he asked.

"Everything I didn't spend."

He nodded and slipped them into his own pouch. "Then we're back on equal footing. At least between you and me."

It was so easy for him to forgive what I'd done to him and Marcello. I wish I could forgive as easily. But all I could do was remember the horrible things done to me and my Family and focus on my revenge. It had been my fault, though, what had happened. And maybe Les wouldn't be so forgiving if he knew the truth about me.

I sighed. "Les, I—"

224

Les held up a hand, cutting me off. "I said we're good. I don't need another explanation. Let's just get back to work on the firebomb."

He watched me and I watched him until finally I dropped my head and nodded. It didn't matter if he knew the truth about me, or what he thought about me. All that mattered was killing the Da Vias.

False dawn crept over us, and I stifled a yawn.

"Maybe this is hopeless." Les ran his hands through his hair before he retied it out of the way. "Maybe I was wrong to think this would work."

"No. It's not hopeless. We just need to keep trying." I sprinkled a little bit of a gray dust into a mound. "Don't give up on me yet."

Les shot me a sideways glance and I flushed. Why I had said that, I had no clue.

"What is the purpose for this firebomb anyway?" Les asked. "I mean, I'm guessing you want to set fire to somewhere without having to be there?"

I measured out some of the acid, careful not to spill any on my hands or leathers. I had long since put my mask aside. "I'm going to burn the Da Vias out like they did to us. I'm going to sneak into the center of their home, leave this as a present, and then just wait at the exit for them."

Saying it out loud felt good. And if I was lucky and it worked like that, there was a chance I might emerge from this plan alive. At the least, I probably wouldn't burn to death.

"You mean *we*, right?"

"What?"

"*We're* going to burn them out. And *we're* going to wait for them at the exit."

I nodded. "Yes, of course."

Les wrinkled his brow but didn't comment. I changed the subject.

"How do you get your jobs? I've seen you on two now. How did you know someone wanted those men clipped?" My pile of grains and acid flamed for less than a second, then fizzled out.

"There's a building near the town square with a single brick that's loose and hollowed out behind. Anyone who has a job can leave me a message and the money behind that brick, and I collect the jobs and there you go."

"Aren't you worried someone will see you collecting the letters?"

"No, the letters drop down a hole. I'm sure people think the letters sit behind another brick, but they fall beneath the street. There's a tunnel that leads to them. I check it every few days."

"But if it's illegal, how do people know about you?" I poured more gray dust and added some of the black powder. "Do you have a lot of jobs? Well, maybe that's a dumb question, since you're the *serial murderer* and all that."

He grunted. "Sometimes I go months with nothing. Sometimes, like this week, I have two or three. Just because murder is illegal doesn't mean people aren't willing to pay to put an end to someone for one reason or another. Most of my jobs are people who have caused a grave offense. How does it work in Lovero?"

"There's a guild with offices throughout the country. Anyone can walk in and request a job. They can open it to any Family or request a specific one. The guild contacts the Family when there's a personalized request. Otherwise, we can check with the offices when we're looking for work. The guild withholds payment until the job is completed. That way they can return payment to the client if a clipper refuses a job or it fails."

He shook his head. "It's so strange to me, how candid your country is about murder."

"Murder is worship. You either become a clipper and do it yourself, or you allow clippers to do it for you. And maybe one day it's your life they take. But if they do, you know Safraella rewards those who follow Her."

"Rewards them with death, you mean."

"Everyone dies. You could turn into an angry ghost and rage across the dead plains for all eternity. Or you could die at the hands of a clipper and Safraella will grant you the gift of a new, better life. Loverans understand this. And besides, you have a lot of murder here."

Les guffawed, and I shot him a look.

"Oh, you're serious?" he said. "How can you even compare?"

"Loverans are generally safe from clippers if they don't anger someone enough to pay to have them killed. Here, I could walk home in the evening and some stranger could murder me for my purse or any other reason."

"I don't see how hiring a clipper in Lovero would curtail violence," Les said.

"Because people talk. And if I wronged you, you would pay to have me killed and you would be right to do so."

"Doesn't it just start a cycle of murder and vengeance? What if my family hired someone to kill you after you had me killed?"

I shrugged. "Sometimes that happens. More so before. Now people understand that the murder of a loved one is an act of worship, that they'll be granted a new, better life."

Les shook his head. "You make it sound like Lovero is so morally superior, because everyone follows Safraella, but here you are, plotting to kill the Da Vias because they murdered your Family."

I grimaced. He'd hit on an uncomfortable truth. "It's not the same."

"Isn't it?"

"The Da Vias killed my Family, yes, but only a fool would think they did it as an act of worship. Maybe that's what they want the common to think, but the other Families know that the Da Vias attacked us because they were the second Family and we were the first and by killing us they got power. Anything else was just a bonus."

"Won't the other Families punish them, then? Why wouldn't they just rise up together and put a stop to the Da Vias if they're so power hungry and less than faithful?"

"The others are cowards. Most of them, anyway. They feel safe at the bottom. And they'd need proof. Right now they may know the Da Vias killed more for themselves than Safraella, but without proof, they would never rise up against them."

"Then it sounds like Rennes and Lovero have more in common than you thought."

I ignored this barb and instead dripped a bit of the acid onto my dust pile. It flared up immediately into a bright flame.

I shouted and Les scrambled over. "What did you use?"

"Just the acid and those two powders!" I grabbed the jars and sprinkled a bit more of the dust onto the flames. They burned gleefully. With this mixture we could make a timed firebomb, not just a smoke bomb.

Les grabbed my hands and we jumped and danced around the fire, laughing and cheering. "Thank you," I said to him.

He grinned. "For what?"

"For making me laugh."

Together we watched the flames flicker in the early morning, and for a moment all the pain and guilt and loneliness from missing Lovero and my Family and Val just disappeared into the night sky with the embers of the fire—until it seemed the fire might burn another hole in my roof and we were forced to put it out with the bucket of water.

I clutched the jars of powder in my hands. This plan could work. This plan *would* work.

I would have my vengeance.

twenty-four

†

I DREAMED OF THE FIRE AGAIN. BUT THIS TIME WHEN IT tried to pull me into its flames, Les was there, and he threw a bucket of water on it and the fire vanished.

I awoke to the setting sun and stared at the ceiling above me.

Eleven days. Eleven days since the Da Vias had murdered my Family. I was so close. And I couldn't deny that I had Les to thank for it. He'd helped me create a plan to kill the Da Vias. And he'd gone home last night determined to get the Da Vias' home location from Marcello.

Something stirred in my stomach, and it took me a moment to realize it was eagerness to see Les again. Yes, he would hopefully bring me good news, but also because it seemed when I was with him, I didn't think about my Family as much.

Or I did, actually, but sometimes it didn't hurt quite so badly.

I got dressed and climbed to the roof, determined to refocus on my goal.

A few hours later I stopped my pacing and stared at the canal beside my building.

Les was late.

I sat down, soaking in my anger as it got later and later and he didn't appear.

Maybe he'd quit on me. Maybe he'd seen the seriousness of my firebomb plan and decided it was too much for him. Or maybe he was still mad about the stolen coins and he couldn't forgive me as easily as he thought.

My stomach sank. He'd seemed just as excited as me at our accomplishments. I couldn't imagine him suddenly changing his mind.

It didn't matter. Either way it was a lack of respect. And I didn't have time for it. The Da Vias weren't going to slow their search for me just because I was stuck waiting for Les.

I climbed to my feet, determined to hunt him down and drag him out of Marcello's if needed, when he appeared on my roof.

"You're late." I crossed my arms.

I thought he'd be apologetic. Instead, almost visible waves of anger rolled off him. It took me aback. I'd yet to see him really angry. Annoyed, yes, like when I'd first approached him, and disappointed when I'd stolen the coins, but never angry.

"Can we just get to work?" He rolled his shoulders and avoided my glare.

"Why were you late?" I wasn't going to let this go. Not until he apologized at least.

He sighed. "It's nothing. I'm sorry. It won't happen again."

That was easier than I'd expected. And then I understood. It wasn't his fault. "Did Marcello find out I'm training you?"

He pinched the bridge of his nose, a gesture so reminiscent of my father that I had to take a slow, deep breath to loosen my throat.

"You're late because you were arguing with him," I said. "About me."

I could see the truth written in his face. "I was trying to get the Da Via location from him. He doesn't know about the training, but he *now* knows I've seen you since that last time you spoke. He was . . . not happy."

"I'm sorry," I said.

He waved my apology away. "You have nothing to apologize for. It's my fault, and really, it's his fault for being so angry about it. He still sees me as a child, as that boy he found. When he's reminded I'm not, it shakes him."

My skin itched with the desire to leave, to take the firebomb and Les and head home to Ravenna. "Did you get any information out of him, at least?"

"No. I even told him if he just gave you what you wanted, you'd leave. But he doesn't want to give in to you. Feels like you're pushing him too hard."

Of course I was pushing him! What didn't he understand about the Da Vias coming for me and how that would be bad for him, too? His stubbornness overrode his sense of safety.

Les would have to try again. He would have to keep trying until he got what I needed. It was the only option.

"Can we do some training?" Les asked. "Otherwise I'll
never be able to compare to you."

Training wasn't really wasting time. If I was going to bring
Les with me, the more he trained, the better he would fare
in the fight to come. But after his failure to convince Marcello to give me what I wanted, everything felt like a delay.

If I was going to send Les to try again, though, I needed
to keep him on my side. Which meant keeping him happy.
And if training was the way to do that, then it was an easy
enough task. And sometimes it was even enjoyable.

"You can't liken yourself to me," I said. "I was born into
this life. And you are more skilled than you give yourself
credit for. I'm sure there's something you excel at."

He smiled at the praise. "Why didn't you ask sooner?"

At our spread of weapons, he picked up three knives well
balanced for throwing. I groaned quietly behind my mask.

He set up a target across the roof, then stood beside me.
He whipped the knives one after the other in rapid succession. Each struck the target near the center. Les strode across
the roof and retrieved the knives before he returned to me.

"What do you think?" he asked.

I waved my hand. "Yes, yes, you're good at knife throwing."

He held out a knife to me. "There must to be something
you can teach me."

I didn't take the knife. "No. You looked fine."

"Lea, you're supposed to be training me."

"I am, I just . . ." I rubbed the crack on my mask. "I'm not the best knife thrower."

Les leaned closer. "I'm sorry, what was that? Did you just admit to being *bad* at something?"

"I never said I was perfect."

Les laughed louder than was necessary. I turned my back on him. "We're done for the night."

"Lea, no, wait." He grabbed my elbow. "I'm sorry, I didn't mean to insult you. I just honestly never guessed I'd be able to best you in anything. Come on, don't leave me. I'll give you some tips. No teasing. I promise."

He passed me a knife. I sighed and showed him what I could do. It was worse than I remembered. I didn't even hit the target. The knife skidded across the roof until it crashed into the rest of the weapons.

I frowned, but Les only nodded thoughtfully. "Take off your belt and weapons. They're throwing off your balance."

I did as he said and pushed my mask to the top of my head. He handed me another knife and this time he stood behind me. He lined his arm next to mine and grasped my hand and the knife.

His body felt warm and hard, pressed against mine.

"It's a smoother motion." He moved my arm with his. "Clean and quick. It doesn't have to be powerful. That can come later."

I let him instill the rhythm in my arm. He began to hum quietly, and when I was ready, I released the knife. The hilt crashed into the target and the knife dropped to the ground, but at least I'd actually struck what I was aiming for.

I smiled and Les whooped, spinning me around, my hand still in his grasp.

"See!" He grinned and squeezed my fingers.

This. It was so easy to feel carefree around him. But that wasn't for me. I pulled my hand free, and the smile faded from his face.

"Something's bothering you," he said.

"It's nothing."

"Oh, it's clearly something."

I returned to the knives, packing them up. "It's nothing and it's everything. We're running out of time here and Lefevre's poking around, following me. I made a mistake when I first arrived, and now he's trying to trap me or trick me into making another so he can pin a murder on me. Yours, actually. Well, not only yours."

He straightened and frowned. "That sounds like more than nothing, Lea."

"No, it's fine. Really. I can handle him. And I don't plan on staying long enough for him to charge me."

He rotated a shoulder. "What if the firebomb fails? Do you have a backup plan for the Da Vias?"

"None of that matters unless Marcello tells you where to find them," I snapped.

Les waved his hand at me. "I know, I know."

I shrugged. "I might just walk in there and face them head on."

"What?" he barked. He opened his mouth to say something else, but then he closed it and looked away.

"What were you going to say?"

"Nothing." He shook his head and smiled at me. But the smile was forced. He was trying to be nice, but he was keeping something hidden.

"It's not nothing," I said. "Don't lie to me."

His smile vanished. "I'm not a liar."

"Yes, you are. I can tell you're hiding what you really think."

His eyes flashed and his jaw tightened. I was so used to him being friendly and nice that this new Les made me step back. "Fine. Lea, you're crazy. You'll get yourself killed."

I narrowed my eyes. "Well, until you get the location of the Da Vias, none of this even matters! And so what if I die? I don't see why that's any concern of yours."

"You don't see . . . Lea . . . Argh!" He threw his hands into the air, then snatched his cloak from the roof and walked away from me.

"Where are you going?"

He looked over his shoulder. "For someone so smart, you can be ridiculously idiotic sometimes."

He jumped to the nearest roof.

Blood rushed to my face. How dare he? I was his teacher— he couldn't speak to me like that!

"Les," I shouted. "Alessio! Don't you walk away from me!"

He stomped away faster.

I pulled my mask down and raced after him, trying to

close the gap. He sped up, determined to get away.

Oh no you don't!

He couldn't outrun me, not when I was this mad and this determined to catch him.

He dropped off the roof into an alley between the two buildings. I blindly jumped after him, trusting there would be ground beneath me.

I landed in a crouch. The alley was a dead end, empty except for a door boarded up with a single piece of lumber. Alessio stood before me. I grabbed his shoulder.

"Les, what the—"

He gripped my wrist and pulled me beside him. "Shut up!"

At the entrance to the alley floated the white specter of an angry ghost.

It was a man, or had been a man at one time. I could clearly see his trousers and vest. He hovered quietly and seemed asleep, or adrift.

My heart raced. Being so close to one again brought back memories of my flight across the dead plains. My burned hand pulsed in pain, and I clenched it into a fist.

"Where's the nearest canal?" I whispered.

"Just stay quiet. Maybe it won't see us."

We stood still, the sound of my heart and quiet breathing matched by the sound of his. We huddled like statues, willing the ghost to leave. Les clutched me to his side, the solid strength of his body pressed against mine. I pictured the celebration on the roof before, my hand in his, his arms around me like they were now.

I blushed behind my mask and pulled away.

"Lea, don't—"

The ghost blinked its phantom eyes and faced us.

Maybe it couldn't see us in our leathers against the dark alley.

It screamed, a sound that emanated from somewhere in the heart of it. It raced our way.

"Oh gods!" Les shouted. He squeezed his eyes shut against the ghost. He was so frightened of it, so scared. And I was too. But it was my fault, and if I could distract it, he could flee.

I pushed Les aside and confronted the charging ghost. Les grabbed my right hand, shouting something in my ear, but I focused on the ghost.

I remembered the ghost who tried to pull me from Butters's saddle, remembered how tightly I'd gripped Safraella's coin and prayed for Her to grant me a fast rebirth. I prayed again, now, and stepped forward. I met the shrieking ghost with my hand across its chest, willing it to stop its attack.

The ghost shot away from us, repelled out of the alley and out of sight, leaving nothing behind but a quickly fading echo of its screams.

My chest heaved with rapid breaths and my mouth ached from dryness.

"Lea . . ." Les loosened his grasp on my hand. "What did you do?"

My arm flopped to my side and I swallowed deeply. I shook my head. It was a good question.

He stepped beside me. "How did you do that?" His voice was tinged with awe and something else. Fear maybe.

"I don't know. I'm not sure it *was* me."

"I don't understand. . . ."

I lifted my mask to the top of my head and brushed a lock of hair from my eyes. "It happened once before. I was on the dead plains, racing from the ghosts."

"Wait. You crossed the dead plains at night? Are you crazy?"

"I didn't have much choice. It was face the angry ghosts or face the Addamo Family."

"I don't—I don't even know what to make of that, so I'm going to set it aside for now." He made a motion of pushing something invisible away. "Let's get back to how you saved us from that ghost."

"It wasn't me. I think it was Safraella."

He gestured for me to continue. I sighed.

"When I was on the dead plains, I was injured and the ghosts were trying to pull me from the saddle. I thought I was going to die. And I was upset I wouldn't have a coin for Safraella, for a fast rebirth. Which was stupid. I'm Her disciple. I don't think She would begrudge me a coin in the midst of fleeing for my life." I shook my head. "Anyway, I managed to clutch a coin in my hand. And it burned me."

I slipped my glove off and stuffed it in my belt. He took

my left hand gently and traced my healing palm and fingers with his own. Val used to trace my knuckles with his thumb. I was glad for the darkness in the alley so Les couldn't see the color that had risen to my cheeks. I took a breath.

"How did it burn you?" He followed the shallow shape of the coin around my skin. I pulled my hand away.

"I'm not sure. I spoke to a priest at a monastery on the dead plains. He wasn't sure either. Maybe some sort of holy fire? He'd never heard of anything like it happening before. But when my hand was burning, a ghost reached for me and suddenly it was gone, flung away across the plains. Before I had time to think about it, I was in the monastery." I shrugged.

Les stared at me. "That's it?" He shrugged, mocking me. "You can just shrug it off?"

"What do you want me to say?" I snapped. "That I understand everything about Safraella and how She works? Or that I have some sort of magical clipper magic and you will too, as soon as we somehow get you a mask?"

He tightened his lips. I'd hit a tender spot. He *had* thought one of those things.

"I don't understand how you can do something so amazing," he said, "like stopping an angry ghost, and just shrug as if it's no big deal. As if you're not worried about it, or fanatically curious. You did something amazing, miraculous, and you treat it as an irritant at best."

"Because I don't have time to figure it out! I don't have all the answers, Les. In case you haven't noticed, I'm barely getting by. I just need to focus on doing what I came here to do."

"Killing yourself, you mean."

"What?"

"That's what you came here to do, right? Find the means to kill yourself at the hands of the Da Vias?"

He was ridiculous. He didn't understand anything. "I don't *want* to die."

"Don't you?"

He stepped into my personal space. He was so much taller than me, but I stood my ground. I wasn't that easy to intimidate.

"There are other solutions, if you'd only stop and think."

"I don't have the time!" I yelled. "The Da Vias already know a Saldana survived the fire. If they haven't spoken to the Addamos yet, they will soon, and it will be obvious I came to Rennes. The Da Vias aren't the Addamos. They have more clippers, more money, more resources and power. If they want to find me, they will as soon as they connect all the loose threads I've left trailing behind. I have to get to them before they reach me, otherwise it's all pointless. Otherwise it's all been for nothing and the Da Vias will have won."

"I'll be with you, though. It won't just be you, alone. That could change the outcome."

I shook my head. "I came here looking for Marcello not just because he knew how the find the Da Vias but because he was a Saldana clipper with skills that should at least match my own. And I needed him to help me. Even with my training, Les, you're a half clipper at best."

Behind us, the sun crept above the roof of the buildings, casting beams of light in the shadows. We'd stayed out too late. We needed to get to our homes.

"No one's going to be ready for this, Lea. Not even you. And damn you for writing me off like that!"

I stepped back at the anger in his voice.

He followed me, leaning over to look in my eyes. "You don't get to roll over people. Just because you have permission to end lives doesn't give you the right to destroy them first."

He was breathing heavily, staring at me. Was he right? I thought over the path I'd traveled to get here.

The Addamos . . . I'd definitely done some damage there. But they'd brought it on themselves. They were the ones who'd attacked me.

Brother Faraday had said priests weren't allowed to take sides, but he'd bent the truth for me.

Les was wrong. "You don't make any sense. I'm making you a better clipper. How is that a bad thing?"

He closed his eyes. "Do you really not see it, *kalla* Lea? Are you truly that blind?"

I'd been blind to things before, and I'd made terrible mistakes. "Maybe I am blind," I whispered, "but you don't understand."

"*I* don't understand? Lea, I think I probably understand better than most."

"No, you can't. It's my fault."

"What's your fault?"

"My Family. Their deaths." I coughed and took a breath. "Val took my key from me. He must have made a copy or something. And because he was a secret, *my* secret, I didn't tell anyone. The Da Vias got inside because of me."

There. My darkest, heaviest secret bared for his judgment. Now he'd see me for the failure I was.

Les rubbed his neck. "It's not your fault."

His words hit me like a gust of cold air.

"You didn't kill your family, Lea, the Da Vias did," he continued. "Lay the blame where it belongs, not at your feet, but at theirs."

I exhaled slowly. He made it sound so easy. But it *was* my fault. I'd had a hand in the deaths of my Family. When I closed my eyes, all I could see were their faces, and then I couldn't help but imagine their last moments. Had they burned to death, their skin crackling, their lungs filling with black smoke? Or had the Da Vias killed them first, their knives and swords carving into their flesh? Had Emile been scared? Had he cried, fat tears rolling down his face as he called for his papa?

And how could Les just push my failings aside like that? Like it didn't even matter to him.

To our left someone applauded slowly. I yanked my mask down as we turned.

"Bravo. This has been better than a stage play." It was Captain Lefevre and six other men. "And look, you even have costumes." He gestured to our leathers and my bone mask. I cursed my damn foolishness. We should've been long gone before the sun had ever risen so high.

I'd played right into his hands, standing in a secluded alley, with no witnesses to whatever he planned.

twenty-five

†

'LEA, LEA, LEA.' LEFEVRE STEPPED INTO THE ALLEY
with his men behind him. None of them wore uniforms.
This was about something else, then, and not the murder
investigation.

One of the men was a giant, nearly filling the small alley
space. Beside me, Les moved closer.

"I knew there was something off about you," Lefevre said.
"But I didn't expect all this." He waved a limp hand in our
direction.

I dropped my hand to my sword.

Gone.

I closed my eyes. I'd left it on the roof when we were
knife throwing.

Les tensed beside me. He realized the same thing. All I
had was a single stiletto in my boot.

Sloppy. So sloppy.

Rafeo would be so disappointed in me. I'd let Yvain make

me soft. I'd let Alessio make me soft. Never in my life had I been caught without my weapons, and here I was, in my *leathers,* no less, about to reap the consequences. I deserved it.

"That first night," Lefevre continued, "when you fled from my officers, I thought I'd never see you again, at least, not like this. I recognized you as a clipper, of course, even without the coin you left on that body. But I was always raised to think highly of clippers. You were supposed to be these terrifying agents of a dark god, so when you escaped us, I thought you were gone for good. And yet here you are, standing in the open for anyone to find. And it turns out you *are* that raggedly dressed girl in the market. I wasn't sure, you know. I thought you were just covering for the clipper, but you have the mask and everything."

"What do you want, Lefevre?"

"What do I want?" He tapped his chin with a finger. His men chuckled and grinned. They didn't realize what they were getting themselves involved in. They probably saw a girl and a boy having a fight in an alley. They were in for a surprise.

"So, my hunches were correct. There's a bounty on your head, Miss Lea. It turns out the Da Vias in Ravenna lost someone. A Saldana clipper. And they're willing to pay quite a bit for her return. Lea Saldana has a nice ring to it, by the way."

I raised my hands. "I don't know what you're talking about. I don't know the Da Vias and they won't pay anything for me."

Lefevre smirked. "You aren't a very good liar, Miss Lea.

Even hidden behind that mask of yours. And anyway, being a lawman doesn't pay very well. If the Da Vias are paying, I could use the boost to my finances. And an end to the serial murderer."

"I told you that isn't me."

Lefevre snorted. "Oh please. You can give up the charade now."

"She's not lying," Les said beside me. "I'm the murderer you've been looking for. You don't need her."

What was he doing? Telling the truth wouldn't gain him anything. Unless . . . unless he *wasn't* trying to get anything out of it.

Lefevre rolled his eyes. "You? Really? You don't even have a mask."

"North quarter, ten days ago. Northeast by the lazy canal, four weeks ago. A woman, six weeks ago by Upsand Downs."

Lefevre's smirk vanished. "It seems I was mistaken. I can admit when I'm wrong. But I still need the money. You'll just be an extra bonus for my reputation as a lawman."

His men moved forward.

"I'm giving you a final chance to walk away," I said. "This won't go the way you want. If you walk away now, everything can be forgotten. Otherwise I'll have to kill you." I showed him my conviction in my eyes, so he'd understand I could murder him with no more than a flick of my wrist. That his blood across my face would be like the spray of the sea to me, wet and warm and nothing more.

His men paused and glanced to Lefevre. He barked a

laugh, his eyebrow raised in disbelief. "Oh, Lea, you ignorant girl. *I'm* not going to fight you. I'll be leaving you in the capable hands of my men. After all, the sun's up and I have work to do and lawbreakers to catch." He waved his hand, and his men flowed toward us. "Keep her alive," he commanded as he turned to walk away. "Kill the other one."

The men charged as Lefevre whistled and left the alley behind. I barely had a moment to yank my stiletto from my boot before they were on us.

Six against two. If it had been me and Val, we could've handled it. But it was me and Les—unfinished and unarmed—trapped in a cramped space with no quick escape. I had to keep him safe.

Before the first attacker reached me, I twisted my body and shoved Les farther into the alley. He grunted in surprise and I imagined his anger once he realized my plan, but I didn't care. When this was over, I'd rather have him alive and angry than injured or dead. The thought of him dead was like a kick to the stomach.

I blinked. When had that changed?

The first man swung at me with a cudgel. I barely managed to block his swing. The blow vibrated up my arm. Pops in my shoulder told me more of my stitches had snapped. I brought my knee into the man's gut and his breath exploded over me in a whoosh, stinking of liquor and rotting teeth. I shoved him into the man directly behind him. They tumbled to the ground in a tangle of limbs, tripping up a third man.

Another attacker swiped at me with a knife, aiming for my

face. Dumb. Even if I hadn't managed to dodge his clumsy attempt, my mask would deflect any strokes. I grabbed his arm and pulled it sharply backward. Braced against my left elbow, his joint cracked and snapped. The alley filled with his screams and the sound of his knife clattering to the ground.

Movement over my shoulder. I shifted to the left, blocking Les in the alley, keeping him behind me. His rage-filled eyes shot murder at me from beneath his hood, but I didn't have time for him.

I smashed the heel of my boot into the throat of another attacker. His neck crunched. He collapsed against a wall, hands clawing at his throat as he struggled for breath he would never find.

The first three attackers got to their feet and changed tactics, coming at me together instead of individually. It actually made things easier. They got in one another's way and I ducked and weaved and stabbed, all while blocking Les, keeping him away from the center of the fight. The alley was so cramped, the fewer clippers in the mix, the better. This way I didn't have to dodge Les, too.

Blood dripped off my mask and leathers. Its rich scent filled my mouth and nose as I caught my breath. Four of Lefevre's men lay dead or injured on the ground when the giant finally waded into the fray. He was close to seven feet tall and wide as a cart. Not fat, simply thick with flesh and muscle. The attacker with the fractured arm pressed against the wall as the giant charged, bellowing like an enraged bull.

I stepped back, trying to give myself space, but I bumped against someone.

"Les!" I screamed, pushing against him.

The giant leaned over and rammed his shoulder into me, connecting sharply against my breastbone. If I hadn't been wearing my leathers, padded to protect me, the bone would have cracked.

He launched me into the air. I flew into Les and we crashed into the wall, Les's body shielding mine from the stone building. I heard, rather than saw, his head strike the wall. The loud crack bounced around the alley.

We collapsed to the ground.

"Les!" I grabbed his leathers. He didn't respond, either unconscious or . . .

No! Don't think it, Lea!

The giant grabbed my shoulders. He yanked me from Les, tossing me like a log onto a fire.

I landed on the body of one of the men I'd killed. Before me lay his cudgel, resting in a pool of thick blood. I snatched it up as the giant bellowed over me.

I rolled and threw the cudgel overhanded. The weapon struck him dead in the forehead.

The snarl across his face vanished as his jaw slackened. He stared at me in utter shock. Then his eyes rolled up in his head and he fell, crashing onto the alley floor.

I struggled to my feet, my body aching and my breath sharp in my chest.

Lefevre's last man cradled his injured arm against his ribs, whimpering. I faced him, stiletto in hand.

He fled. When he reached the alley entrance, he began screaming for lawmen, shouting about murderers and ghosts and other unintelligible things.

If the lawmen showed, it'd be over. We needed to flee.

I stumbled over the bodies toward Les. I crouched and pushed the hood off his face.

His eyes were closed, but he was breathing. I released my own breath, not even aware I'd been holding it. He wasn't dead. I hadn't gotten him killed.

"Les." I tugged on his leathers. "Alessio!"

He moved his head but didn't wake. I lifted one of his eyelids. He moaned and feebly struggled away from my fingers.

We needed to leave. Now. Any longer and we risked being caught by the lawmen.

I grabbed one of his long arms and draped it over my shoulder. I braced my back against the wall of the alley and stood, pulling Les with me.

He was too heavy. I needed to find the strength to move him. I couldn't be weak now. I tugged on him and called his name, and he seemed to wake enough to get his feet under him.

We stumbled deeper into the alley to the boarded-up door I'd seen when we'd first dropped into this alley. It didn't matter where it led. It had to be better than walking the streets in the open.

The board was rotten and old and it took barely any effort to yank it down. Les leaned on me more and more the longer I supported him.

The lock had failed years ago and I pushed the door open, heaving Les with me into the dark and gloom.

Dust coated the air. I coughed heavily behind my mask, and for a moment, I was back in my home in Ravenna and it wasn't dust in the air but ash, and it wasn't Alessio I carried but my brother Rafeo, bleeding his life away. A sob escaped me, but I kept us moving through the building as tears blurred my vision and my breath burned my throat.

Les fell and dragged me with him.

"Alessio!" I yelled, but he didn't respond. He lay on the ground like a dead man. I couldn't continue to carry him like this. I needed a solution.

I examined the dark, decrepit building. It had been a house once, for a family maybe, with children and laughter and warmth.

Rotted carpets were spread across the floors, large sections torn away to reveal the wood beneath, and black wallpaper peeled off the walls like the rind from an orange. A rickety staircase led to a second floor, but most of the steps were missing, stolen for firewood perhaps.

In a corner, concealed behind a collapsing wall, stood an old cupboard and a pile of blankets. We had to hide and pray the lawmen wouldn't find us.

I grabbed Les under his arms and dragged him to the cupboard. I pushed him inside and ran to the main hall.

Anyone looking for us would be able to follow the drag marks and footsteps in the dust to the cupboard. I'd have to lay a false trail.

I pushed my weight against the half-collapsed wall in front of the cupboard room. It creaked, then crashed onto the cracked tile of the floor, covering my drag marks. A storm of dust exploded into the air and I coughed. I climbed over the debris and snatched a moldy blanket.

In the hall I used the blanket to fake more drag marks as I headed away from the room and to the other side of the building. I found another boarded-up door and rammed it down. It spilled me into an alley. This one, though, had a canal running along the end of it.

I dragged the blanket after me, creating an extended trail of dust. Then I lobbed the blanket into the canal's waters.

The abandoned building was easy to scale, even with my shoulder and its fresh pain, and I dashed as fast as possible to the roof to keep my false trail intact.

In the square, a troop of lawmen made their way toward the scene of the fight. I'd run out of time.

I raced across the roof and scurried down into the alley, recklessly jumping the last story. The hard cobblestones jarred my ankles and back. I leaped into the house as the light in the alley dimmed from the lawmen's entrance.

When I reached Les, still hidden in the cupboard, I climbed in with him, pulling his long legs against me so the cupboard door could close on our tangled bodies.

The air and dust were thick inside. The gods themselves

had to hear the beating of my heart as I tried to keep us quiet and still.

Les groaned beside me. I covered his mouth with my hands, the hair on his face sharp against my burned palm.

Shocked shouts drifted in from the alley. The lawmen had found the bodies.

They rushed into the building. I drew Les tight against me and kept my hand over his mouth.

My breath against my mask sounded like bellows pumping in my ears. They'd hear me. They couldn't not hear me. I squeezed my eyes shut and concentrated on Les's warm breath against my hand.

"Look!" a voice came. "Over here!"

Footsteps pounded through the building, and then silence again. I swallowed, my throat like a desert.

More footsteps, casual this time, as if the person strolled along a park instead of an abandoned building.

All my life I'd fought and killed people but had never experienced fear as I did then, hiding in the cupboard, praying we wouldn't be discovered.

The man whistled. My blood turned to ash. Lefevre.

He knew he was looking for me. Knew I was responsible for the dead men. *His* dead men.

He paused and hummed to himself, as if he'd found something interesting. He had to be examining the collapsed wall, and if he looked too closely, he would see the cupboard hidden in the dark corner.

I clutched the key around my neck.

The floorboards creaked. Then more footsteps arrived, less frantic this time.

"Couchier found a blanket in the canal," the new speaker announced. "Looks as if they fled that way."

"Show me," Lefevre said. They left the building.

I nearly collapsed with relief. We weren't safe yet, but they'd bought my ruse.

Alessio groaned again. "Don't leave me, Lea." His words were quiet and slow.

I whispered in his ear, pulling him tighter against me, trying to keep him still. If we could hide here until the lawmen left, we could escape to somewhere safer.

I closed my eyes.

At this point, anywhere would be safer.

twenty-six

†

WE HID IN THE CUPBOARD LONG PAST THE TIME WHEN the alley emptied. I didn't trust that the building wasn't being watched. I didn't trust that Lefevre would let this go.

Finally, we had to take our chances. We couldn't stay hidden in this cramped cupboard. Les kept falling in and out of consciousness. He needed help.

I pushed the door open and tumbled into the dusty room.

My limbs and joints screamed at the sudden freedom. I struggled to my feet, groaning and stretching before I pulled Les out.

He grunted and stirred. "Where are we?" He barely opened his eyes.

"We were hiding." I crouched and helped him to stand. He hunched over, hands on his knees.

"We have to go now. It's not safe, Alessio." I ducked my head beneath his so he had to focus on me. "I need you to help me now. I need you to stay awake."

He moaned and we trudged through the home, his feet tangling in debris.

We were close to my safe house, only a few blocks away. But I couldn't convince Les to climb to the roofs, and there was no way I could get him there alone. That left only one place.

We reached the other side of the building. I released Les and left him to lean against a wall while I scouted our path.

A cart vendor selling fish blocked the front of the empty alley. Finally, a bit of luck.

I scurried to the canal and leaned over its waters. A canal boat bobbed calmly, secured to a building on the other side. I gripped the wall and climbed across its crumbling surface to the boat. The boat rocked. I took a moment to capture my balance before untying it from its mooring. I used the long pole to push it to the alley entrance and Les.

He leaned against the wall and sighed, his eyes closed tight. He'd vomited while I'd been away.

"Come." I guided him out of the house and to the boat.

"I'm sorry," he mumbled, and my heart sank. He shouldn't have to apologize. This was all my fault. Like everything else.

"It's all right," I murmured. I helped him step across the gap. He almost toppled, but I kept my grip on him until he settled in the middle.

"Lie down," I encouraged him. I covered him with both our cloaks so he looked like a pile of goods or laundry instead of an injured person.

I removed my mask and tucked it carefully beside him.

There was nothing I could do to disguise my leathers, but I'd simply have to hope I wouldn't encounter any lawmen patrolling the canals.

I pushed the boat away from the alley and used the pole to steer it north, the slight current of the canal helping to ease us along as I silently thanked Les for showing me how to use the boat and which canal led to their home.

How had I gotten myself into this mess?

The same way I'd gotten myself into all these messes since the attack. I didn't stop and think things through. No matter how many times I remembered I wasn't in Lovero, I kept making mistakes over and over. I trusted people, and it led to more trouble.

I'd trusted that Lefevre was the kind of lawman I'd find in Lovero, but instead he'd proven to be crooked. I'd trusted Les, but he'd gotten me so angry that I'd left my sword behind when I chased after him. And why had I even bothered to chase him in the first place? Because I needed him.

My stomach jumped, and I swallowed.

But it was true. I *did* need him. He was my only link, now, to Marcello, and Marcello was my only link to the Da Vias. It was nothing more than that.

Everything in my body froze as my thoughts twisted and turned. Les had been understanding, though. He'd seen his mother murdered, had been orphaned like me. He knew how it felt. And he hadn't cared, when I'd told him about my shame. He hadn't turned away in disgust and in fact had offered help.

Being around him eased the loneliness that had been threatening to drown me since the night of the fire. I missed Rafeo. I missed everyone. I missed Val and I *hated* Val and everything just hurt all the time. But Les somehow made that pain fade, at least for a little while.

I gave the boat another push. Maybe I'd lost sight of things. My goal had to be killing the Da Vias. I looked down at Les, hidden in the boat.

He stirred. "Where are we going?"

"I'm bringing you home."

"Marcello will be angry."

"He's always angry." I paused. "Why did you do it? Why did you tell Lefevre you were the murderer?"

Les rolled over. "It was the right thing to do," he mumbled.

I poled us under a bridge. He'd put me before himself. I'd never known anyone who helped people just because he wanted to help them, and yet Les did so again and again. And it wasn't just me he helped.

He made me want to . . . I wasn't sure. Do something or be someone different.

To trust him fully, anyway. It was the least I could offer him in return.

Somehow I managed to reach Marcello's. I helped Les off the boat, my arms aching from steering it down the canals.

Getting Les into the tunnel was easy. Getting him up the ladder at the other end was not. His feet slipped off the rungs and he kept apologizing. He sounded so genuinely ashamed that guilty tears came to my eyes until finally I called for help.

The tunnel room above us flared with light, and a shadow stepped into the room.

"I thought I said you weren't welcome here," Marcello said from out of sight, his voice stern.

"It's Alessio," I said. "He's hurt."

The grate opened and Marcello leaned over us, lantern in hand, looking so much like my father. He glared at me, but then Les apologized again and I almost went berserk, prepared to scream and threaten my uncle, anything really, to make him *help* us.

Marcello set his lantern on the ground. He crouched, and together we lifted Les up the short ladder into the room.

He vomited again, and Marcello looked worried. I pulled myself out of the tunnel and into the room.

"What happened?" he asked me.

"We were attacked. He cracked his skull on a stone wall."

Marcello swore. He used his shoulder to escort Les out of the tunnel room and into their great room. He gestured at the lantern. "Bring the light."

We walked past the fireplace to the curtained-off bedroom area. Marcello helped Alessio to a bed, and Les sat on the edge.

"Hold steady," Marcello said. He bent Les's head forward and prodded the back of his skull.

Les flinched, but Marcello forced him still and continued

to feel beneath his dark hair.

Finally, he stood, satisfied. "The bone isn't fractured. He'll heal with some rest. Help me get him to bed."

I unbuckled his leathers and pulled them off his arms and chest, being careful not to bump his head or snag his pendant.

When I'd seen him shirtless before, I'd stared. Now he looked so tired and hurt that there was no excitement in seeing him, only more guilt.

Marcello tugged off Les's boots and pants while I removed the tie in his hair. I always hated sleeping with my hair pulled back. It gave me a headache.

His hair was soft and smooth as it slipped through my fingers. Les lay down, and my uncle covered him with a blanket.

"Sleep for now, Alessio," Marcello murmured, pushing the hair off Les's face. It was a surprisingly gentle and loving gesture from a man I'd seen mostly rage and anger from. "I'll have to wake you occasionally, to make sure you're healing right."

Les mumbled something in a language I didn't speak, and my uncle leaned closer. When Marcello looked at me with a calculating expression, I turned away, giving them their privacy.

"Yes, I understand." Marcello kissed Alessio's forehead, and we left him to rest.

I walked to the fireplace and collapsed into a chair. Fatigue covered me like a shroud. Since the fire it seemed I always found myself on the edge of exhaustion.

I set my mask on the table and rubbed my face. My hands were filthy, but I didn't care. It was time to stop caring about a lot of things.

Marcello handed me a glass with amber liquor. I drank it and it burned down my throat until it settled into a deep warmth in my stomach. He took a seat, eyeing his own glass before drinking.

I placed the empty glass on the table, and my left shoulder burned with pain. I gasped and sat back, bringing my hand to it.

"You're injured." Marcello stood.

"No, it's nothing. I just . . ." I closed my eyes and sighed. "Can you help me remove some stitches? They've mostly snapped at this point."

He set his glass down and walked away.

I undid the buckles of my leathers, letting them slide around my waist. I sat half-dressed, wearing only my leather trousers and my under-leather camisole, but I was so tired it didn't matter. The fire kept the room warm, and more than anything I wished to bathe, to curl up in a bed somewhere and maybe never wake.

My shoulder was red and inflamed, but the wound in front appeared closed, a pink scar stretching smoothly across the flesh. I looked down and gasped.

Beneath my loose camisole and across my chest, from below my breastbone and up to my clavicles, stretched a violent purple bruise from when the giant had rammed into me.

I pressed against the bone, and pain flowed across my tissue. I bit back a whimper.

Marcello returned with a medical kit. He glanced at me. "What's the key to?"

I looked at my key hanging around my neck. "My home."

He didn't comment. Instead he pulled out a small scissors and examined my shoulder.

"What happened?" he asked gruffly. He began to snip and pull out the threads on the back of my shoulder.

"I was arrow shot, crossing the dead plains. The damn Addamos were chasing me and were too cowardly to follow me past the river."

"That's not what I meant."

Oh. I sighed. "I don't . . . I'm not even certain where to start."

"How about you start with how you let my boy crack his thick skull almost wide open."

I held back a laugh. I didn't think my uncle would appreciate it. Not that I thought Les would appreciate Marcello calling him a boy. Or thickheaded.

"We were training. But then he was angry at me and tried to leave, and I followed him."

"Les does not have a temper. What did you do to anger him so?" He clipped out another stitch.

"I don't know. And before I got a chance to question him further, we were confronted by a ghost."

Marcello's scissors hovered over my shoulder. "In the streets?"

I nodded.

"How did you get away?"

I paused. If I told him the truth, it would lead to more questions. Questions I couldn't answer. But I knew he'd be able to tell if I lied. And remaining truthful with him was probably my last chance to get into his good graces. I couldn't afford another misstep.

"It vanished before it could hurt us. I can't really explain it."

"It vanished in the sunlight, perhaps?"

I shrugged, and my uncle grabbed my shoulder, holding me in place. "In the sunlight, they simply fade away. This was something else. This was violent. I sent it away, somehow. Or Safraella did."

He grunted disapprovingly and glared at me until I turned away. He moved to the stitches on the front of my shoulder.

"We were foolish," I continued. "We'd left our weapons behind and were arguing in an alley and a lawman, a crooked lawman named Lefevre, found us. He'd brought men, and they attacked."

"You were unarmed?" He stopped in his ministrations. He took a few steadying breaths. "How could you be so incompetent? How did you even earn your mask?"

My turn for a deep breath. I had stay on his good side. I needed him more than ever now. "I already said it was foolish. This place, this city, it pushes against me. It makes me sloppy."

He snorted. "And this lawman attacked you because . . ."

"Captain Lefevre wanted to give me to the Da Vias for

coin, and he wanted Les for his murders. I warned him away, but he didn't listen. There is no respect for clippers in this city. No respect for Safraella."

He set his scissors down and I examined my shoulder. It looked much better. Marcello sat in his chair and returned to the liquor in his glass. "Well, what did you expect? That you'd come here and the people would fall to their knees at the sight of you? That they would turn their eyes to Safraella and forsake their own gods? You are a foolish child."

My cheeks burned. "Foolish I may be, but I am no more a child than Alessio is a boy. I am the head of the Saldana Family, and though I receive no respect from the people of Yvain, I command it from you, Her disciple. And someone who should know better."

He rolled his eyes and sipped his drink before he motioned for me to continue with the story.

I took a moment to calm myself. I didn't know this man who shared my blood. I didn't know if he purposely aimed to anger me or if he truly meant the things he said.

"I tried to keep Les safe. I kept him out of the fight, though I knew he would not thank me for it. But when the giant attacked me, I crashed into Les and he took the brunt of our fall. After that we had to hide from lawmen until I could get him here."

"What happened to the men you fought?"

"I stopped them."

"How many were there?"

"Six. Though one fled, injured. And I can't be sure the

ones I dropped were all dead. I didn't have time to check."

"Six men. And you were unarmed and trapped in an alley."

"I had a stiletto."

He stared at me, then downed his drink in a single gulp. "Who was your teacher?"

"My brother Rafeo. And my father and mother, of course."

"Your brother."

I nodded. "Matteo, my other brother, wouldn't bother. Sometimes I would spar with Jesep, too. Or Val."

"Val. I do not recognize this name."

"Valentino Da Via. He's my suitor." What I said hit me like a punch to the gut. "Was my suitor."

His eyes widened and showed a touch of that rage I had witnessed before. "You were fraternizing with the Da Vias? Did your parents know?"

I exhaled, trying to tread carefully. He could explode again. Throw his glass into the fire and scream his rage once more.

"No. I hid it from them. There was no love between us and the Da Vias. I think my father had tried to buy peace between us when I was younger, but it didn't work."

He took a breath. "Dante was always something of a fool, though maybe he'll have more wisdom in his new life."

I bristled. "Don't speak of my father that way."

Marcello smirked. He opened his mouth to counter but then seemed to deflate. "I suppose you are right. It does me no good to speak ill of the dead, even if they brought about their own demise."

"My father didn't bring about his death. The Da Vias did." And me. My fault.

He rubbed his forehead, smoothing out the lines, before he ran his fingers through his hair. "What do you know about me, Lea? How did your father speak of me?"

This was an odd turn of conversation. "He didn't speak of you. Only my mother did, and that was to tell us to never bring you up."

He nodded slowly. "Your father was a great many things. He was my brother and I loved him, but sometimes he believed in peace too much, saw the good in people even when it was nothing more than a mirage. It was your father's misplaced belief that the Da Vias could be reasoned with that led to the death of your Family."

"No." I shook my head. "I don't believe you. What could you know of it anyway?"

"What could I know of it? Everything." He settled in his chair, his hair resting against his shoulders. "The Da Vias killed the Saldanas because of me."

twenty-seven

HIS WORDS WERE A SLAP TO THE FACE. HE WAS RESPON-
sible for the Da Vias' attack on us? That couldn't be true. "I
don't . . . I don't understand."

"When I was younger, much younger, I was married to
Estella Da Via, as you know. It was not a marriage of love. It
could not be, from me, but the heads of our Families wanted
a child from our union, of Saldana and Da Via lineage, and
peace between us, if only for a time, and I was nothing if not
obedient."

He shifted in his seat. "No child came, even though the
years passed as they do. And any ease between us rotted away
until the core was nothing but resentment and blackness.
And so I found someone else.

"He was a Maietta, and he was beautiful and full of grace
and wit, and never before had I loved someone so well."

My uncle's eyes sparkled as he remembered his long-ago lover.

The memory smoothed his face, made him appear younger.

"We kept it secret, of course. I was married, and the head of the Saldanas, my uncle Gio, was not tolerant of men who desired other men. But they found out, of course. My wife. My Family. Such anger from them all. My wife blamed me for the lack of child she'd been promised. Of course, how could she know who was to blame? Sometimes children are not born to a married union, and it is the way of Safraella. And I don't think our scarcity of love for each other helped.

"I blamed her for wasting some of my best years, for sinking her talons in and dragging me into the dark pit she had created. It was she who had driven me elsewhere. I refused to reconcile. No threats from her Family or mine would make me turn away from Savio."

He rubbed his jaw with the palm of his hand, lost in the tale. I thought about how it must feel, to love someone so well but to be told to turn away from them. I'd kept Val a secret purely because of that reason. But maybe it hadn't been love between us, or at least on his part. Not if he could betray me so easily. Maybe I didn't really understand true love, like Marcello described. Maybe love was less about feeling wanted and beautiful and more about feeling safe.

I glanced at Les, asleep on his bed.

"I don't know who planned it," my uncle continued. "Probably my wife. I do know, though, that it was her brother, Terzo, and my uncle Gio who murdered Savio. They didn't even try to disguise it. There were witnesses, and they were in Maietta territory.

"I'd never felt such pain. And anger and grief. And never since. My uncle Gio thought that would be the end of it. That by removing Savio, he had effectively ended the problem. So confident was he that when I approached him in our home it never occurred to him I'd come to kill him.

"It was much easier than I thought it would be, spilling the blood of my family. Truly, I felt nothing. And I certainly felt nothing when I killed Terzo, my wife's brother.

"After that, things were a little . . . complicated." He waved his hand in the air. "Dante took over as head of the Family. The Da Vias felt their honor had been damaged, and the Maiettas were calling for a blood price for the death of Savio. I probably would have left on my own if Dante hadn't disowned me. There was nothing left for me anyway.

"As far as I know," he said, "Dante paid the Maiettas their blood price."

A blood price to the Maiettas would have been a large sum of money. Maybe that was where much of the Saldana fortune had disappeared to.

"I'm sorry," I said.

He paused and appeared taken aback. "For what?"

"For Savio. For the way you were treated by people who should have loved you and stood by you no matter what."

He grunted. "Yes, well. Family before family, of course. There was no real way to ease the Da Vias' anger. They are quick to cast blame and slow to forget. Even if Dante tried to smooth things over, I don't see how that would have worked. Estella felt I had personally shamed her, and nothing less than my head would've appeased her. She blamed Dante for letting me leave instead of turning me over to them. And then she started to blame Safraella."

"Estella Da Via is a lunatic," I said. "And now she's the head of the Da Vias."

"That's unsurprising. She was not all that stable when I left. I heard she never did produce any children, to her eternal shame."

"How did you hear that? And how did you know my name and know of my brothers? We weren't even born."

"Your mother sent me letters, sometimes. Though none in recent years."

"*My* mother? Bianca Saldana?"

He rolled his eyes. "Unless you have another mother I don't know of, then yes."

This . . . this flipped my world upside down. My mother had sent letters to Marcello Saldana, who we were told never to speak of. Who had brought shame to the Family. "Why would she do that?"

"We were friends. I was glad when she married Dante and joined our Family. I had great love for Bianca and my brother. It opened a wound I thought long healed to hear of their deaths at the hands of the Da Vias."

"Then why do you refuse to help?" I leaned forward. "Come with me! You know what it's like to need vengeance. You took yours but now stop mine. Give me the location of the Da Via Family home and we can make them pay for what they've done to our Family. I will make sure they never forget the Saldanas!"

"At the cost of your own life, you mean?"

I leaned back. "If need be. I'm not afraid to die."

He laughed. "No, of course you're not! You're, what, seventeen? And a *disciple* of Safraella. I'm sure you can't wait to meet Her cold embrace."

He mocked the gods too easily. "You step awfully close to blasphemy. I *am* Her disciple, and I'm confident She would offer me a fast rebirth."

"And then what? You die and are reborn? And what of the people you leave behind?"

"There are no people. Everyone's dead."

Marcello widened his eyes in a way that said he didn't believe me. He looked over to where Les slept.

My stomach coiled at the thought of Les. Of Les injured in the alley, of the brief moment when I'd thought he was dead.

"Dying is the easy part." Marcello got to his feet. "But what you leave behind is another matter." He glanced at Les again. "I fear you will destroy him."

"Me?"

"He is too kind to you. He thinks if he is kind, then people will like him. And if they like him, they won't leave. But that is not the way of things. You are a flame and he is a moth, drawn to you, unaware if he gets too close you will burn him up."

He'd struck dangerously close to my own thoughts

regarding Les. But I wasn't the only one to blame. "And you? You've given him a sword and taught him only enough to be dangerous with it, but not when to back away."

"Things were fine before you arrived," he countered.

"Were they? You never fought about it? You never threatened to leave, never held that over his head?"

Marcello was silent. He couldn't deny it.

I sighed. "Truly, Uncle, we're both at fault."

He nodded slowly. "We're Saldanas. Sooner or later we destroy the ones we love. Come, let's pour you a bath."

He walked behind the fireplace to another section of the room. Maybe he was right. It would be cruel, abandoning Les when he'd already lost so much. But I couldn't stand the thought of someone else dead because of me. And I couldn't let the Da Vias get away with what they'd done.

No. I had to continue with my plan. It was kill or be killed. If I did die, hopefully any grief Les felt would be lessened by the knowledge that I'd died on my own terms, confronting the Da Vias instead of waiting for them to take me in the night.

Still, I thought about Rafeo and my Family. My uncle wasn't wrong. Living, being the person who stayed behind while those you loved left, was not an easy path to take. Not at all.

Marcello and Les had a large copper tub hidden behind the fireplace. It didn't take long for Marcello to fill it, and while the water was lukewarm at best, the closeness of the hearth heated the tub and the water the longer I sat inside.

Before I climbed in, Marcello disappeared and returned with a stack of folded papers.

"Here." He handed them to me. "These are some of the letters your mother sent me."

I took them gently. Marcello left me to my privacy and I climbed into the tub, careful to keep the letters dry.

I could feel my mother in each piece of paper, sense her spirit as she chose what words to tell my uncle.

I read of her happiness when my brothers and I were each born, how eager she was to expand the Family. And her pride at Rafeo's marriage and the birth of Emile.

And then a final letter of grief, describing the plague that had swept the city, telling of the deaths in the Family, the loss of Jesep's parents, who I realized Marcello would have known, would have loved. Jesep's mother was my father and Marcello's younger sister. And Rafeo's wife, taken by the sickness just when it seemed it had finally abated.

The Family had been so weakened, she wrote, she didn't know how we would ever recover. And we hadn't, of course. The Da Vias took advantage of our weakness and destroyed us when we were too few to stop them.

Throughout the letters, though, my mother spoke of her love and pride in her children. How, even when Rafeo joked too much, he could always make her laugh. How Matteo's almost blind devotion to tradition and rules made him a precise and proficient clipper. And how my willful nature and stubbornness expressed itself in loyalty to the ones I loved.

The last line was brief. Just a mention of me, earning my mask, and how proud she was, and how she knew someday I would be the best clipper of them all if I could focus on what was important.

I turned the letter over, but that was all.

I set the letters on the floor and sank below the water. My mother had never spoken such words to me. She'd never told me how proud she was, and yet the letters had been filled with the eloquence of her love for me and my brothers. For our Family.

My heart and stomach twisted around each other, squeezing me with pain until I popped out of the water, choking for breath. It was an ugly trick of fate, to learn of my mother's love for me only after she'd left me behind.

I scrubbed at my hair and my skin, cleaning every inch until my flesh was pink and sore before I climbed out of the water.

Marcello had given me Les's clothing, a cotton shirt and pair of pants, to wear. Though they were freshly cleaned and folded, they still smelled like him. I held the shirt to my face, breathing in his cinnamon scent.

I had to roll up the pant legs and the sleeves and they were still too large, but the garments were clean and comfortable and I was happy to have them.

On the other side of the fire, my uncle slept in his chair. I let him rest, walking quietly past the tapestries blocking off the bedroom.

Les slept on his side, the blanket pushed below his arms, his dark, wavy hair resting on his shoulders.

I sat on the floor against the bed, my back to Les. I closed my eyes.

How had things gotten so confusing? It shouldn't have been this way. I should've gotten the information I needed, killed the Da Vias, and been done with it all, one way or another. But instead my uncle had told me the truth about our Family, and with Les, I had found something to ease my pain.

I closed my eyes against the tears falling down my cheeks. I was so tired of crying, and yet I couldn't seem to stop. I couldn't seem to do anything right. I wished Safraella would tell me which path to take.

"Don't cry, Clipper Girl," Les said quietly. He shifted in his bed and brushed my hair behind my ears.

I rubbed the tears off my cheeks and faced him. "I didn't mean to wake you."

He smiled tiredly. "Master said I needed to be wakened anyway."

"I'm sorry," I whispered. "I'm sorry I got you hurt."

"It's not your fault. I was in the way. I should've trusted you knew what was best in the fight."

"I should've trusted you to help," I said. "I should've trusted you."

"It doesn't matter." He closed his eyes and yawned, then shifted deeper into his pillow. His breath came slower as he sank toward sleep.

"Les," I whispered.

"Hmm?" he answered, barely awake.

"What does *kalla* mean?"

He gave a little smile. "Beautiful."

twenty-eight

†

MARCELLO THRUST A STEAMING CUP OF TEA INTO MY hands. "Drink this."

I'd fallen asleep on the couch in front of the fireplace. I sat up, brushing my hair off my face. My bones and joints ached, both from the uncomfortable couch and from the fight. It would be a couple of days at least before I could move without pain.

I sniffed the tea, then sipped tentatively. It was bitter and strong, but the warmth spread through my chest and limbs and soothed some of my aches.

"I've cleaned your leathers," he said, watching me drink. "When you're done with your tea, you should leave."

I finished the tea in a single, scalding gulp. "What time is it?" I asked, trying to cool my tongue.

"Past midnight. You'll be safe to return unseen to wherever you're staying."

"You let me sleep so long?"

"You needed the sleep."

I nodded. He handed me my leathers, and I walked behind the hearth to change. When I came out, he passed me my mask. It had been cleaned of dirt and blood, and I slipped it to the top of my head.

I glanced toward the bedroom and the tapestries. It was dark and quiet.

I'd made a decision before I'd fallen asleep. My stomach fluttered, seemingly warring with itself. It was easier this way, leaving without saying good-bye to Les. But a part of me, a very large part, had hoped he'd be awake. For what purpose, though, I couldn't say. Maybe he'd try to stop me, or force me to stay, or just make things different, somehow.

But Les was asleep. And things couldn't be different.

"You shouldn't see him anymore," Marcello said.

I closed my eyes. I couldn't argue against Marcello's opinion. Matters were only going to get worse. And in her letters my mother said I'd needed to focus on what was important. I had to focus on killing the Da Vias.

"Under two conditions," I said.

Marcello narrowed his eyes.

"The first is you have to finish his training. If you don't, he'll get himself killed and it will have nothing to do with me. He thinks you'll leave him if he argues too much about it, and that's not fair to him."

Marcello glowered, but then nodded.

"The second is the location of the Da Vias' Family home. I need it."

"No." Marcello sliced the air between us with his hand, a gesture I'd seen from Les. "I will not be responsible for your suicide."

"You could come with me. The last of the Saldanas together."

"Alessio would come after us."

"Then I can't leave Yvain. Not without the location of the Da Vias' home. And they're already coming for me. It's only a matter of time before they find me here. If you give me the location, I can get ahead of them, I can plan an attack instead of simply waiting to defend myself. If you give me the location, I will leave, and you and Alessio will be safe."

"You could flee. Give up on this ludicrous plan of yours. Revenge will not bring you peace. Revenge will not bring your Family back. I know this firsthand."

Marcello had succeeded at his revenge, had killed those who had killed Savio, his lover. So he had no right to try and convince me of another path.

"This is what I must do," I said. "There is no other way out for me. I do not seek peace. My peace died with my Family. I seek vengeance and I will have it, or die trying."

Marcello's shoulders slumped, and I could see his mind working. He knew the Da Vias coming to Yvain would be just as dangerous to him, and by association, Les. And the only way to be rid of them was to lure them away with me.

He walked into a back room. A moment later he returned with a key similar to my own. He handed it to me. "This is the key they used years ago. I don't know if it will still work, but it's all I have to give you."

"How do I find them? Where is their home?"

"There's an entrance in the north part of the city, at a restaurant. It's been too long and I don't recall the name."

A restaurant. The Da Vias owned two restaurants in the north part of Ravenna: Fabricio's and Luca. I had a hard time believing Val would bring me to dine at a restaurant that housed the entrance to his Family's home, but he was also cocky and self-assured. Either way, I would check them both and see what I could find.

I clenched the key in my fist. "Thank you, Uncle."

"Do not thank me. I take no joy in sending the last of my family to her death. But what's a little more shame heaped onto an old man who's spent his life drowning in it?"

"I go to end my own shame, Uncle." I pulled my mask over my face and left him in his home beneath the streets.

I climbed to the roofs of the city, my body complaining with every inch.

The night was quiet as I jumped and scaled my way toward my safe house. The moon had crossed most of the sky. It wouldn't be long before morning. I could leave Yvain with the sunrise.

Three things I'd needed before I could leave: the location of the Da Vias' home, the working firebomb, and help from Marcello. I had all but the last.

It had to be enough. I couldn't wait anymore, and Les was right, I hadn't persuaded Marcello. And I could no longer fool my conscience by saying I didn't care if I brought Les with me and he died. Because I did care. Somehow he had worked his way under my skin. Seeing him injured made me realize how much it would matter to me if I got him killed for my vengeance. He had helped me for no other reason than that it was the right thing to do. And now it was my turn to do the right thing and keep him out of my plan, keep him safe and alive here in Yvain with my uncle.

The only deaths I wanted on my hands now were the Da Vias'.

On my roof I collected and stored the weapons we'd abandoned. I placed Les's cutter and other tools in a corner under some burlap to keep them safe and easy for him to find later. I stared at the hole leading down to my little home in Yvain.

It was better this way. It would be easier to forget about Les, to go home and finish what I'd started. What the Da Vias had started. Even if he'd secretly been calling me beautiful.

I couldn't go inside yet. I needed more air.

I raced across the roofs of the city, the Yvain skyline lovely and still in the darkness of the early morning hours. I needed to move, feel my muscles stretch and burn in pain. I needed to focus on that so I wouldn't think about anything else. So I wouldn't think about *anyone* else. So I wouldn't think.

But I couldn't outrun my thoughts forever. When I was forced to slow, clutching my hand to my ribs to ease the stitch that had grown there, my thoughts appeared right where I'd left them.

I balanced on the edge of a roof, gazing at a canal that lazily swirled below me, a boat moored to the building, and a stone bridge connecting one side of the canal to the other.

Below, a man approached the canal. It was early for a commoner to be out. Maybe he didn't fear the ghosts.

He stopped at the edge of the water. He clutched something in his hand. A wooden staff. I blinked and peered closer. A tall, cylindrical hat rested on his head.

It couldn't be possible, and yet this was the same man I'd seen at Fabricio's with Val the night of the fire. He stood here, in Yvain, in the night.

Behind me, something crunched on the dirt of the roof. I turned.

Two men, both in leathers, their masks hidden in the shadow of the chimney they stood beside.

They glanced at each other, then stepped closer. Their masks came into view. One had swirls and the other grape leaves. Both patterns were the color of blood.

The Da Vias had found me.

twenty-nine

†

I DIDN'T RECOGNIZE THEIR INDIVIDUAL MASKS. RAFEO would have. He would have known instantly who stood before me, but there were over fifty Da Via clippers and I'd never been able to memorize every mask. These were probably some of Val's cousins, sent here to look for me. Maybe they were the only ones. Or maybe there were more.

It didn't really matter unless I came out the victor in this confrontation.

Three choices: I could run, I could hide, I could fight.

None of those options gave me a high chance of success.

Grape Leaves shifted his weight. The time for planning was over. I'd have to react now and hope it was enough.

"We didn't expect it would be so easy to find you," Grape Leaves said. He was tall and thin and had a rope wrapped around his shoulders and waist, one end tapered with a heavy stone weight, the other tied in a noose. "Of course, you made it easy, running around the rooftops like some sort of cat in heat."

I shrugged, using the movement to rest my hands closer to my sword and a dagger on my left. I'd learned my lesson about going anywhere unarmed.

The Da Via clippers saw the true intention behind my shrug and tensed.

"Honestly," I said, "the night air felt good. Attracting your attention was not a concern of mine. You didn't even cross my mind."

Swirls shifted his stance and glanced at Grape Leaves before returning to me.

"You're not Rafeo," he said, his voice higher than his partner's.

My cloak had hidden my shape from them. I inclined my head. "Very astute. Would you like a medal?"

They stared at me, making quiet decisions behind their masks. I shuffled through the possibilities. They could be planning an attack. They could be thinking of calling for reinforcements. Maybe they'd let me go, now that they knew I wasn't Rafeo.

I grimaced behind my mask. There was no way in hells they would let me go, no matter who wore Rafeo's mask.

"Though the Addamos pointed us to Yvain, it seems they've lied to us," Grape Leaves said.

"I doubt they did it on purpose," I answered. "They didn't seem to be the quickest larks."

Swirls brought his hand to his sword hilt and I reacted by unsheathing mine, loosening my wrist with a quick twist of the blade. I wouldn't let them take me unprepared. "Did they tell you how easily I dealt with them?" I asked. "Did they tell you how many of their dead and injured I left behind?"

"They didn't tell us a great many things, it appears," Grape Leaves said. "And because of that, I'll be on my way with a new message for the Family. But don't worry, *Lea* Saldana. Nik here can handle you all by himself."

Swirls unsheathed his own sword while Grape Leaves bowed and turned his back on me, trusting his partner's ability to handle things.

I didn't know anything about Nik Da Via. I didn't know where he stood based on skill. He could be showy or swift. Arrogant or quietly self-assured.

I did know, however, that I was unrested and sore from my fight the night before and I hadn't eaten anything in almost a full day. I didn't have much to give. I had to end this fight quickly. The longer I took, the better the chances I'd wind up dead. And I didn't want to die. Not yet.

Nik rushed me, and all thoughts disappeared as I adjusted my stance to defend myself.

He feinted to the left, but I didn't fall for it. I turned left too and swiped for his neck with my sword. He bent backward, flipping over completely. He kicked his leg at me. I jerked aside.

On his feet once more, Nik rushed me again, wasting no time. He attacked with exaggerated sword strokes, forcing me to block them or risk losing my head. I gave ground on the roof, sliding closer to the edge and the canal waiting below. He couldn't keep up these frantic attacks. They would drain him. But he might keep them up longer than I could defend against them. Every move I made sent a rush of pain pulsing through my muscles. Before long, Nik would notice I was injured and press me even harder. I needed to do something.

He lunged. I stepped away. Below me, the canal boat creaked against its moorings.

I released my left hand from my sword and found one of my long needles stashed in the lining of my cloak. I jabbed a pouch on my belt. The tinkling of broken glass told me I'd struck true.

I hid the now poison-coated needle beneath my cloak and waited for Nik to make another move. It came almost immediately. Instead of sliding left or right as he expected, I ducked. With a quick thrust I stabbed the needle into his thigh. He hissed beneath his mask and retreated, yanking the needle from his flesh.

"Is that the best you have?" He threw the needle to the ground. "This is what Lea Saldana has to offer?"

"No," I said. "This is."

I jumped off the roof, trusting that the canal boat was still in place.

I landed. The boat rocked and my ankle twisted sharply beneath me, a lance of pain shooting through my bones and calf.

A shadow from above told me Nik had taken the bait and followed.

When he landed, the boat rocked again, but Nik was unable to keep his balance. The leg I'd stabbed collapsed beneath him, and he shouted in surprise as I let the boat tip like Les had taught me and spilled Nik into the dark waters of the canal.

I sliced through the rope and shoved off, saying a silent prayer of thanks for the canals of Yvain. And to think I'd once hated them.

I flipped open my pouch of poisons and checked which vial had shattered. Pieces of glass lay against the other vials and the etched cork sat on top of the shards. Good. The needle had been doused in a nerve poison. Nik's leg and probably most of his right side would be paralyzed for the better part of a day. He'd be lucky if he didn't drown.

My boat floated away as I watched the ripples on the water to see if Nik would emerge.

His mask broke the surface, his hands splashing as he fought against his numb limbs to reach the edge of the canal.

"I'll kill you!" he shouted as I drifted farther away. He struggled to pull himself out of the canal. Finally he managed to flop onto the street. "You're dead for this!"

I pushed the boat around a corner. His threat held no new fear for me. The Da Vias already wanted to kill me.

My ankle pounded with pain, but when I tenderly put weight on it, it supported me. Not broken then, only twisted. Of course, it didn't really matter. The Da Vias were in Yvain, and they knew I was here.

I'd run out of time.

I steered the boat as close to my safe house as I could, then let it go, to drift freely on the canals. I stumbled onto the street, my ankle giving beneath me painfully. It would be a problem. I'd have to wrap it tightly and hope to avoid another fight until it had healed.

The sun had crested the horizon. Taking the roofs would have gotten me back sooner, but the Da Vias could be looking for me. They wouldn't be watching the canals, though. Like me, they'd assume clippers wouldn't use the waterways.

One more day. If I'd had one more day before the Da Vias had showed up, I would have been gone from here. They could have searched Yvain to their heart's content and never found me.

I limped down the alley toward the street that connected to my safe house.

I would need a disguise, now, to get out of Yvain. They would be watching the gates into the city.

Brother Faraday's robe could work again. Maybe. I'd have to be careful, though.

I turned the corner.

In front of me stood Lefevre in uniform and four other lawmen.

"Well, well, Lea. It seems we've caught you in a bit of a predicament." He smiled and tapped the basket of his rapier with a ring on his pinkie.

My first instinct was to run. To flee the way I'd come. But the alley ended at the canal, and I'd set the boat free.

I could fight them. I could kill them or disable them.

But I was exhausted and injured. Lefevre and the others wore rapiers, and though I had my sword and usual stiletto, I'd just fought with, and nearly lost to, Nik Da Via.

"What do you even want?" I asked Lefevre. "The Da Vias already know where I am. There's no money anymore."

Lefevre's face darkened at my news.

Another lawman shifted. "Did you honestly think you could come to our city, commit murder, and leave the bodies lying around and we wouldn't notice or care?"

They didn't understand. They thought me a common murderer. "I didn't kill that boy in the alley. The gold was a kindness I did for him," I said. "To grant him favor with Safraella, to earn him a fast resurrection. The only crime I saw was a lawman stealing a holy coin from a corpse because he wanted it more than a god."

"There were other murders," the lawman said.

He was right, of course, there were other murders. Lefevre's men. "They attacked me."

Lefevre's smile faded, and he dropped his hand from the basket of his rapier. "So, how do you want to handle this?"

I had nothing left. "I'll go quietly."

Lefevre scowled. He'd actually been looking forward to a fight. He grabbed my wrists and bound them behind me, then pulled off my mask. He was not gentle.

He leaned closer to whisper in my ear. "Maybe you could run from my men, but you couldn't run from me. Looks as if the little girl didn't know the rules of Yvain. My rules."

His hands brushed the nape of my neck and I shivered. He chuckled.

"Touch me like that again," I hissed, "and there will be nothing quiet about what I'll do to you, and you'll find no peace at the end of your life."

"What do you mean by that?" he growled.

"I am a disciple of Safraella, and I don't think She will look upon you with mercy."

"Is that true?" one of the lawmen asked, stepping away from me.

"Don't listen to her tales." Lefevre grabbed my arms and pushed me forward. "She's just a stupid girl."

"But all those men she killed in that alley . . ."

Lefevre laughed. "You really believe what those survivors told you? That she did it by herself? No. She had help. A man, I'm sure. Even the survivors said there was someone with her. I doubt she did anything more than cower in a corner."

A few of the lawmen nodded, but the worried one kept his distance. Smart of him. The more Lefevre talked, the more I regretted not sinking my stiletto into his heart when I'd had the chance.

He pushed me across the street, and the morning sun poured over us.

thirty

LEFEVRE AND THE LAWMEN TOOK EVERY OPPORTUNITY to parade me through crowds of people as we headed west into the city. There was no real point to the charade. The people didn't know me or what I'd done. All they saw was a limping, dirty girl wearing strange leather clothing. But Lefevre enjoyed the spectacle of it, enjoyed how people looked at him with respect and a touch of fear.

A man like him would never have amounted to anything in Lovero. Someone would've paid to have him clipped years ago. Maybe that was why he'd left.

Every time we approached another crowd of people I scanned their faces, looking for ones I recognized. But each face was a stranger to me, every eye soft, not hardened by Safraella's tenets.

Lefevre marched me to a squat brick building, its window boxes empty of the fragrant flowers that adorned the other buildings in the city. Inside, we paused so he could search me. He found my stiletto and dropped it into a box beside my mask, sword, and cloak. Another lawman carried the box into a small locked room. I marked its location in my memory.

Lefevre pushed me through a gate and around a corner to an empty row of cells with iron bars. He shoved me into the last one on the right, then slammed the door, locking me in. He motioned for me to turn around, so I did, and he released the bindings on my wrists. I rubbed the sore skin.

"I'd get comfortable while you can, Lea," he said. "You won't be here for long." He smirked and tapped the bars with his knuckles before he turned on his heel and walked out of the cell room.

In the evening the guards delivered what they considered "dinner": a piece of stale bread, cheese that appeared ready to grow mold, and a watered-down cup of wine.

I ate every crumb. Forget crispy duck skin, or flaky fish and cream sauce. Stale bread and moldy cheese were my new favorite foods.

I set down the plate and thought about my situation.

I thought of the way Lefevre had grinned at me, the feel of his hands on me. I couldn't let him win. But I was getting ahead of myself. First, I needed out of this cell and out of the building.

On the wall, directly to the right of my cell, was a small window about eight feet high. Most people would have a hard time getting through it, if they could at all, but I was a clipper and I wasn't very big. I just needed to unlock my cell without any weapons or tools.

The window creaked. I stilled.

The window, hinged at the top, pushed in and someone slipped through headfirst. He grabbed the sill and flipped over to land on his feet.

Les.

I scurried to the front of the cell, my hands wrapping around the cold bars. "What are you doing here?"

He glanced around the room, then fired me his crooked smile and approached the bars. "What do you think I'm doing here, Clipper Girl? Can't have you rotting away in prison."

He wrapped his fingers around mine, holding me in place as he stepped closer, until only the bars separated us.

My pulse quickened and my skin flushed. I dropped my gaze. It was too easy for him, too easy to make me feel this way. I would always be the better clipper, but he wielded a different power over me.

"How did you know I was here?" I asked.

He tapped my fingers with his own, and then released me and took a step away, examining the cell block.

"I went to find you. Thanks for packing my weapons, by the way." He patted his hip, where he'd strapped his cutter against his thigh. "But you weren't there. And then, of course, everyone in the market was talking about the murderer the lawmen had arrested."

"You shouldn't be here," I said. "You should be resting. I

294

can't believe Marcello let you leave."

Les rolled his eyes and rapped his skull with his knuckles. "It takes more than a brick wall to crack my thick head open. What's one more lump on this head of mine, right? And I snuck out."

He took everything so lightly. "You could've died."

His smile faded at my tone of voice, and he stepped closer to the bars again. "It's not your fault, *kalla* Lea."

"Don't call me that." I shook my head, my hair brushing against my cheeks.

"What? *Kalla?*"

"Beautiful."

He exhaled, a smile brushing his lips. "You figured it out?"

"You told me when you were injured. You shouldn't be so kind to me. I don't deserve it."

"Lea . . ." He sighed and pushed the hood off his head. "Since that first moment we met, when you held that dagger to my throat and threatened me and reminded me of how little I actually knew about being a clipper, I've been mesmerized by you. Even before I knew your name, I couldn't stop thinking about you. And then, when I did get to know you, the feeling just got worse. I cannot get you out of my mind. You fill me up."

"Les, I can't love anyone again. The last time I did, I lost everything—"

"No." He waved a hand at me. "You're not allowed to lessen what I've said by telling me how I've made a mistake, by coming up with some ridiculous reason why you don't deserve it. You don't get to decide that for me. Gods, Lea!" He threw his hands into the air. "You drive me crazy!"

My blood surged. He had no right to be angry at me. "I drive *you* crazy? What about me? What about how I feel? I come here with a mission, and then you show up and complicate everything! Look at us, we can't even go five minutes without fighting! This is really the last thing I need right now."

"Then what do you need?" He stared at me. "Because I'll give whatever you want. I would give my life if you asked it of me."

I stepped away. "No. Don't say that, Les. I have so much blood on my hands, and I don't want yours added to it."

He reached through the bars and captured my fingers, though I tried to pull free. "They look clean to me. You take too much on yourself. Your Family's death is not your fault. My injury is not your fault. The way I live my life is not your responsibility. Killing the Da Vias, you don't have to be responsible for that either. You can let it all go, Lea."

"Let it go? After all I've been through?"

"*Because* of all you've been through! Don't you think you've suffered enough? Whatever debt you feel you owe, it's been repaid. Leave the rest for the gods to sort out."

"But that's just it," I said quietly. "I am Safraella's mortal hands in this world. If I don't do this, no one else will."

He closed his eyes and leaned his head against the bars, pulling my hands to his lips. He kissed them, and everything in my body coiled and curled until I felt dizzy, until I felt like I'd never find my breath again.

"Then I will come with you," he said. "And you can't stop me. I will follow you no matter where you go."

Maybe it really was that easy. Maybe it simply came down to accepting his help, *truly* accepting it and not just deciding to use him for my own ends. Accepting him. If he could allow me to make my own decisions regarding my life, to take on the Da Vias even if it led to my death, then I had to let him do with his as he wished. I had no right to stop him, just as he had no right to stop me.

I nodded and leaned my head on the bars below his, clutching his hands tightly. "All right."

All my worry and stress melted out of me. Whatever happened, happened. I didn't have to keep Les safe. I simply had to deal with the Da Vias. Everything else was out of my hands. And it would be nice to have someone firmly on my side again. With Les, the loneliness that had plagued me since my Family's murder drifted away, set free on the night air.

From down the hall the gate unlocked, a familiar whistle echoing through the stone cells.

"It's Lefevre," I whispered. "You have to go!"

"I won't leave you here."

"Then don't. Just hide outside until he's gone. I don't plan on staying, but there's no sense in you fighting him."

He looked about to argue.

"Les," I hissed, jerking my hands away. "If you're going

to help me with the Da Vias, then you have to defer to my expertise. Starting with this."

He frowned, but nodded. He jumped and grabbed onto the windowsill and pulled himself through the window, closing it behind him as the gate opened.

I ran to my bed and lay down.

Lefevre stopped outside my cell and knocked on the bars. "Lea. It seems you have yourself a visitor."

A visitor. Who would visit me? I sat up and peered out of my cell.

A shiver ran up my spine, and I couldn't help the gasp that escaped my lips.

Val.

thirty-one

†

HE WORE HIS FAVORITE GRAY LEATHER VEST AND matching boots. His shirt and pants were navy blue with gold trim. His smile, when he saw me, rivaled the diamonds that sparkled in his ears.

"Lea," he breathed. His voice made me tremble. "I knew it."

I'd forgotten how beautiful Val was. I'd forgotten the richness of his cologne and the thrill that ran through me when his eyes reached mine.

But I hadn't forgotten my Family. And I hadn't forgotten Rafeo, dead in the tunnel.

I turned my back on him and sat on my bed. My hands shook. I clasped them together. Why was he here? And why did my traitorous heart skip when I remembered his low, throaty chuckle and the feel of his lips on mine? There couldn't be room left in my heart for Val. There just couldn't. Not after everything.

Val gestured for Lefevre to open my cell and let him in.

Lefevre complied, locking it again before he left us alone.

"You cut your hair." Val examined my face. "It looks nice."

"It wasn't meant to look nice," I snapped to hide the quaver in my voice. "It was meant to remind me I would never be the same." Tears welled in my eyes. I rubbed my face, trying to hide them from Val. I didn't want him to see me like this. I didn't want him to think he had any effect on me, even though I could almost taste him on the air, feel his hands on my skin again. "Why are you here?"

"I came looking for you. Well, Rafeo, actually. Me and some others. But then I found that flower in the monastery, the one I'd left for you to find later, and I . . . I hoped it meant it was you who had survived. That the Addamos had gotten it wrong. Did you get my letter? I sent you a letter. You probably didn't get it."

I'd never heard him babble like this before. He took a breath and composed himself. "And then I heard about the Loveran girl who'd been arrested for murder, and I knew I was right. That it was you we were tracking."

"So, what, you thought you'd come here and we'd talk or kiss or make up or something?" I looked at my legs, my feet, my hands. Anywhere except him. *Please, please just go away. . . .*

He leaned against the bars. His shoulders sagged. "What do you want from me, Lea?"

Want from him? I already had the key to the Da Vias' home. I knew the two places the entrance could be. I had a firebomb.

I had Les.

Val had nothing I needed. "I never want to see you again."

"After everything we've been through?"

I cast my eyes to his. This time I was able to hold his gaze without looking away. "Your Family killed my Family. Tried to kill me!"

He held his hands before him, palms up. "Lea—"

"You took my key," I interrupted. "Is that what you used to get into our house? The key you stole from me in the guise of our game?"

He didn't answer, but I could read the truth in his eyes, in the lines of his frown. I groaned. He had used me. I had loved him and he had destroyed me.

"How long had your Family known about us? From the beginning? Was it ever even a secret?"

"Of course it was! But they found out. A week or so before . . . before. It was do what they said, Lea, or die. Prove myself a Da Via once and for all. So I did what they told me."

I stopped shaking. I would be a statue. I would not let him affect me anymore. "Were you there that night? Did you fight my father or brothers in the dark smoke?"

"No! I wasn't there!"

I would never trust him again.

"I only learned about the full plan a few hours before," he said. "And when that happened . . ." He scratched the top of his scalp, mussing his carefully groomed hair.

"I asked you not to go home, Lea." He rested his head against the bars as he studied the ceiling. "I asked you to come with me, but you refused. I wanted to save you. To keep you safe."

My blood turned to cold silver in my veins. "You could have told me," I whispered. "I could have warned them, saved us all. . . ."

He shook his head. "I couldn't betray my Family. It was a test for me. If I had told you the truth, they would've had my heart. Estella does not suffer traitors in the Da Via Family."

"There were other options, Val," I scoffed. "There could have been other plans. But you chose to save yourself instead of saving me and my Family. And now you come here and expect me to be happy to see you? I don't ever want to see you again."

"Don't say that." His voice emerged quiet and small.

"I wish you were dead and gone from my life."

"It doesn't have to be this way. I've come here to bail you out. To take you home with me."

Back to Lovero, where lanterns lit the night and the sea air tasted of salt and brine.

But home was for family, and Ravenna was the place where my Family had died. It wasn't only angry ghosts that haunted the night.

"Your Family doesn't want to accept me," I said.

"They thought you were Rafeo."

Ah. They'd let me in not because I was somehow worth more than Rafeo, because my life had more value. No. They thought I'd be easier to control than Rafeo. They thought they could manipulate me with Val, like they had before with the key. They were wrong.

"Rafeo's dead. He bled out in my arms, and I have you and your Family to blame for that. I'm not going with you, Val. Ever. I'm going to kill your Family, and if you value your own life, you'll flee now while you can."

He glared at me. "You watch! Yvain will hang you from a noose as if you're nothing more than a common cutthroat! Is that what you want?"

I shrugged. "I couldn't stand to look at you for the rest of my life and remember how warm Rafeo's blood felt as it washed over my hands."

And I realized it was true. Yes, Val was beautiful, and once upon a time I'd thought I loved him, but now anything I felt was just an echo of that old Lea, the one who had died with her Family in the fire. Val didn't make me feel safe. Val didn't make me feel warm. And he only ever helped himself.

He banged on the bars with his fists. The frustration rolled off him like a cloud of black flies. "Why did you even come here, Lea? You wouldn't be in this mess if you'd stayed in Lovero!"

"And what was there for me?" I shouted. "Your Family, hunting me like a rat? The Addamos, trying for a piece of the prize? In Lovero, I felt like an orphan!"

He stared at me, his anger turning his hazel eyes black. Then his anger vanished.

"What?" I asked. "What are you looking at?"

He turned and banged on the cell door. "Lawman!"

"What is it?" I stood and grabbed his shoulder. Something

had changed. Two seconds ago he was practically begging me to forgive him, to go with him to Lovero, and now he was in a rush to leave. "Val!"

Lefevre walked down the hall, keys in hand. Val faced me again, taking my hands in his own. A war of emotions played over his face.

"I can't help you Lea, not unless you want me to. I wish you'd believe me when I say I love you and miss you and wish more than anything things hadn't happened the way they did and you'd come home with me. But I can't change the past, and I can't ask for your forgiveness, because I'm not sure I forgive myself."

Lefevre unlocked the cell, and Val slipped out. "Goodbye, Lea. I'll come if you need me."

He strode down the hall, his boots clicking sharply on the stone floor.

Lefevre faced me and grinned. "Lovers' quarrel?"

"No." I sat on the bed. There was no love left between us.

Once Val left, I mulled over everything he'd said. My Family was dead. His Family killed them. There was no reconciliation possible. There never could be.

Lefevre chuckled from outside my cell. I ignored him. But Val had been right. Two more lawmen soon arrived to help Lefevre escort me to wherever we were going.

"Ever seen a gallows before, girl?" Lefevre sneered as he locked my wrists behind me in a pair of shackles. He shoved me away from my cell.

"No," I replied. "In Lovero we trust steel or poison to do our death work. Rope is for sailors and the sea."

One of the lawmen laughed. We continued to march.

Outside, the sun brushed the horizon. It would set soon and then the ghosts would rise to search for bodies they could steal.

"We wanted to deal with you as soon as possible," Lefevre said. "You are more of a threat to the good people of Yvain than the ghosts."

My lip curled. "I only kill people who deserve it."

They marched me around a corner, and there, in the center of an empty square, stood a large wooden platform raised on stilts. Above it towered a beam with a dangling noose.

My heart beat faster. Val was right about one thing: this wasn't the death for me. I was a disciple of Safraella! About to dangle from my neck.

Lefevre shoved me forward. He and his men laughed when I stumbled, but I kept my feet.

We reached the stairs, and I stopped. My legs wouldn't move, my body wouldn't respond. I couldn't walk up those stairs.

The two lawmen grabbed me under the arms and carried me to the platform. I must have seemed a child to them, easy to manage. If I died here, then no one would avenge my Family.

I needed to do something. I needed to save myself!

I jerked my arms forward, trying to break free of the lawmen, but they squeezed their fingers deeper into my flesh. They dragged me to the noose as I struggled and kicked and tried to bite myself free of them. I would not go quietly!

We reached the noose, and Lefevre jerked it over my head. I swung my foot at him, trying to snare his ankle. He danced away.

Another lawman slipped a hood over my head. The musty burlap pressed against my face.

"It'll go quick," the lawman mumbled, tightening my noose. "A quick snap and it will be over."

Every breath pulled the burlap across my lips, but I couldn't slow my breathing, couldn't calm the racing of my heart. This was it. The end of it all.

A rushing reached my ears, the sound of my blood roaring through me. Then a man's shout from behind. A grunt and a loud thump. Yells and the smell of smoke erupted around me, heavy, even through the burlap covering my head.

Someone slammed into me. I staggered. The noose pulled taut against my neck, choking me. Below, something creaked, then banged.

I dropped through the floor.

I didn't fall straight down. Instead, my ribs slammed into the edge of the trapdoor, interrupting my fall and saving me from a broken neck. Pain erupted across my already bruised chest and vanished again as the noose around my neck tightened.

My throat closed up, the rope clenching my neck like a snake crushing a rat. My eyes bulged as I swung back and forth.

I kicked my feet viciously, trying to find anything to rest upon, to stop the choking, to free me.

Something above snapped. I dropped, crashing to the ground in a painful heap. My bad ankle twisted beneath me, and the burlap sack flew off my head to land in the dust at my feet.

I took a deep breath, coughing at the air that rushed into my wounded throat. Tears poured down my face, the salt reaching my lips. Dank smoke filled the air, an acrid smell that could come from only one source: a smoke bomb. I climbed to my feet. My ribs and ankle screamed at the movement. Above me, the lawman who'd showed me a touch of kindness lay dead, his body draped over the trapdoor, his throat dripping blood. Shouted commands from Lefevre bounced around me, but I couldn't see him through the thick smoke.

The noose rested against my chest, its end frayed from a cut. Someone had saved me.

Les.

I stumbled from the gallows, coughing with every step, my vision hazy. I needed to get out of here before more lawmen arrived. They'd already tried to hang me once.

"Lea Saldana!" Lefevre called from the smoke. He must have been searching for me. "I'll find you!"

I slipped down a narrow side street, the smoke abating the farther I got from the square. The little street was almost as dark as full night against the setting sun. The ghosts would be out soon, and injured and bound as I was would make me easy prey. I tripped, crashed against a wall with my shoulder.

I cried out at the pain from my ribs. At least one had to be broken.

Before me stretched a canal, its waters dark and still. I stifled a sob. I couldn't go back. The canal could keep me safe from ghosts, but I couldn't swim with my arms bound behind me. I leaned over the water, looking for a way across. To the left a bridge spanned the canal. The building beside me had a small ledge that traveled above the canal along the building's length, leading beneath the bridge.

I slipped onto the stone ledge, pressed close to the wall of the building. My tied hands unbalanced me, and I wavered on each step. If I fell into the canal, I'd drown.

Finally, I reached the bridge and slipped underneath to a shadowed, hidden area. I sat on the cobblestones and calmed my breath.

I'd never come so close to death before. I didn't care to repeat the experience. Ever.

I inched my arms beneath my legs until they were bound in front of me. Metal shackles encircled my wrists. I couldn't remove them without help, but at least now I could slip into the water and hang on to the ledge if I needed to.

I tugged the noose off my neck and tossed it into the canal. It sank slowly into the dark water. I leaned against the curved base of the bridge and closed my eyes. I needed to rest a moment, then figure out what to do.

Footsteps on the bridge. I stiffened. It was too late for a commoner. It could have been a prostitute, but more likely it was a lawman, searching for the prisoner who'd killed his brothers and escaped.

The footsteps reached the bottom of the bridge and paused. I could picture Lefevre searching the dark streets for me. The footsteps headed around the side of the bridge. I scrambled to my knees, watching, waiting.

A boot appeared. I jumped to my feet, hunched over in the tight space.

A face peeked under the bridge.

"Lea?" A whispered voice.

Les had found me.

thirty-two

†

'LES.' HIS NAME BROKE FREE OF ME IN A BREATH OF relief. I leaned against the bridge and slid to the ground.

He ducked under, his long legs bending as he hunched over.

"Sorry I'm late," he said. "I thought you might like these"— he passed me my weapons and cloak—"and this." He pulled my mask from under his cloak and handed it to me.

"How did you get this?"

He smiled. "Let's just say I'm overly familiar with the law office. And most of the lawmen went with you."

Les had known to bring my mask for me, had known it would make me stronger. A moment ago I'd been on the edge of panic. Then Les appeared and everything looked better.

He sat across from me. "I didn't realize the law moved so fast."

"I think they were worried I'd escape."

"You talked to your visitor for a while."

I pictured Les listening to Val and me. My stomach sank. It wasn't as if we'd said anything secretive, but Val had pulled a lot of emotion out of me, things I thought I was through feeling. "You could hear us?"

He shook his head. "I just waited for him to leave. He was in a hurry. Took off running as soon as he got outside. Afraid of the ghosts?"

I furrowed my brows. "That's unlikely."

"Anyway"—Les dug through his cloak pockets and pulled out a satchel—"look what I have!"

Lock picks. Relief spread through me, and I scooted closer to him. "Do you know how to use them?"

Les pulled my hands into his lap. He inserted the pick into the lock of the shackles. "It was the first skill I learned. Your uncle figured I couldn't accidentally kill myself with the picks."

He smiled, and some of my worry over Val vanished. Les had a way about him that made it easy to overlook the darker sides of life, even though his hands were as red as any clipper's. He began to hum as he worked on my shackles.

They were so different, Val and Les. Val was arrogant and believed everyone was below him. Les was kind to people, even those who tried to push him away. Val tried so hard to be the person he was, with his appearance and his manner. Les didn't try at all, and his nature came through in a way that made my heart stutter, my breath catch in my throat.

I'd thought I loved Val. But maybe that love had been

built on the prestige of his bloodline, his talents, and his wealth. Les had none of those things, and yet his very presence made me feel safe.

He glanced at me. "What are you smiling about?"

My eyes widened. "Nothing."

"Hmm." He twisted his wrist and the shackles popped open, tumbling to the ground. "And you're free."

He grabbed my wrists with his calloused hands and rubbed the feeling back into them. He leaned closer to whisper in my ear.

"This was my first jailbreak. I think you're a bad influence on me, Miss Oleander Saldana." We were so close I could almost hear his heart beating. His hands slipped down to mine, and he stroked my wrists with his thumb. I looked up at him.

He watched me, all traces of humor gone. Then his lips pressed against mine. He clasped my hands. I strengthened my grip around his, and for that moment everything else ceased to matter. All that mattered was Les—the way his beard scraped my skin and how his lips tightened in a smile against mine until he laughed and pulled away.

"This has been an excellent jailbreak."

He held out his hand. I took it, and he pulled us both to our feet. My ribs pulsed in pain, and I hissed.

"You're hurt." Worry flashed through his eyes.

"My ribs. And my ankle. Landed wrong on both. I'll be fine as long as we take it easy."

Of course, I couldn't take anything easy with my enemies

searching for me. "Come on," I said. "We've got a lot to do before we face the Da Vias."

I ducked out from beneath the bridge. Les followed and we fled the area, heading deeper into the city.

When we'd gotten far enough away from Lefevre and the gallows, we climbed to the roofs. Les had to help me up, and by the time we scaled the top I was winded and in even more pain. When we finally reached my roof, I slid my mask to the top of my head and pulled him toward me for another kiss. I didn't want to stop kissing him, didn't want to let him go.

We broke apart for breath. He tucked an errant strand of my hair behind my ear. "We should've been doing this all along."

"Probably. I just had some things to work out."

"And did you?" he asked.

I shook my head. "Not really."

He laughed, and we got to work organizing our weapons. Les handed me another stiletto for my boot. "Who was your visitor?"

I watched him dig through my packs. I sighed. "Val."

"Val. *That* Val?"

I nodded.

He snorted. "That must have been . . . interesting. What did he want?"

"Truly? I think he thought we could still be together."

Les glanced at me, then went back to sorting the weapons. "Did he actually believe you're so in love with him you could overlook the murder of your Family?"

"I think he meant what he said. That he was caught between his Family and me and had to make a quick decision. I was so angry at him, but is that fair? If our positions had been reversed, would I have picked him over my Family?"

"But what were his plans? That you'd go back with him and live among their nest of vipers and simply forget what they did?"

I shrugged. "I don't think he had much time to think it through. Until yesterday he thought I was dead."

"Yesterday?"

"I ran into a pair of Da Vias."

Les stopped what he was doing and stared at me. "So there are other Loveran clippers skulking around the city? That's it. You're coming home with me tonight until it's safer to leave tomorrow morning."

I shook my head. "No. Marcello won't allow it. We have an arrangement. . . ."

He narrowed his eyes. "Why don't I know about this?"

I could lie, but Les would probably drag the truth out of Marcello. "You didn't know because it was when you were injured."

"And?" He gestured for me to continue.

"And I promised him I'd stop training you, leave you alone."

"What?" He lurched to his feet.

"Les . . ." I rubbed my cheek. "He was worried about you. And I was worried about you, too. He just . . . we didn't want to see you getting hurt. More hurt."

After a moment Les's anger faded. "I know you were trying to look out for me, but I don't need you to."

"It seemed the only way at the time."

"The only way to what?" He sat down again.

I pulled out the key Marcello had given me before I'd stashed it with my weapons. "To get the Da Vias' Family home location. He only told me when I said I'd leave you alone."

Les watched me until I started to shift under his scrutiny. Finally he exhaled. "We can still follow your plan. Just because the Da Vias are here, it doesn't mean we can't destroy their home. It might make it easier, actually, with some of them here."

I paused. Val was here. And Nik and Grape Leaves. I knew how Nik and Val fought, and they were formidable. Presumably, Grape Leaves was, too. Three competent clippers not guarding their home. But both Grape Leaves and Val had left in a hurry. I figured Grape Leaves had gone to tell someone I wasn't Rafeo. But what had set Val off?

"Lea?" Les asked, but I waved him away. I'd missed something, something important. Val had left too quickly when he'd come to bail me out. Something had become more important to him than me.

His Family, obviously. He'd made it clear he'd choose his Family over me. But what exactly had changed? I sifted through our conversation.

He'd been angry about the murder charge, angry that I'd left Lovero . . .

I gasped and squeezed Les's arm.

"Lea, what is it?"

"They know." My limbs grew heavy, and I closed my eyes. "The Da Vias know about Marcello. They know he's here, hiding in the city. And they'll find him."

thirty-three

†

MARCELLO HAD STAYED HIDDEN FOR YEARS, AND I'D led the Da Vias to him.

At my words, only my grip on Les's wrist stopped him from running home.

"What are you doing?" He pulled his hood over his head. "We have to go! They could have him already!"

"No, we have to be smart." I tugged on his wrist, and he frowned. "I don't know how many Da Vias are here. At least three. Maybe as many as ten. They can cover more of the city than us. If we go tearing off without any thought, we could run into them. And if it's all of them, we won't win that fight. They'll kill us and take their time looking for Marcello. They know he's a Saldana and that we prefer tunnels."

Les rubbed his neck but nodded.

I released him. "We have to be careful so we don't meet

them. And we'll have to move Marcello, probably out of the city."

He shook his head. "He won't like that."

"He won't have a choice, not unless he plans to greet Safraella."

"They'll kill him?" Les asked.

"Yes. Maybe. Maybe they'll bring him home. Marcello told me the Da Vias killed my Family because of him, because of all this history between him and their Family. I'm sure there's some truth to it, but that can't be the whole story. No, something else was the final stab in the mark."

"So you don't actually know what they'll do?"

"Oh, they'll kill him. I'm just not sure if they'll drag him back to Lovero first."

"We can't let them take him." The worry leaked off Les like fog over the canals.

"We won't," I said. "We'll use our knowledge of the city. Let's take the canals. They won't expect that."

We armed ourselves with every weapon we could carry and traveled to Les's boat a few alleys away.

Les steered us north while I kept my eyes open for movement on the roofs. We were probably ahead of the Da Vias, but I refused to trust my luck. Better to assume they were scouring the city, looking for Marcello.

Yvain rested quietly. The moon was new and the bright pinpricks of stars filled the dark sky. I saw no ghosts and no Da Vias as Les quietly poled us to Marcello. Even if we reached him unmolested, we'd still have to somehow escape

Yvain. Now that the Da Vias knew Marcello was here, they would send for reinforcements, and they would watch the city day and night. But perhaps this could work to our advantage. If Les and I could escape to Lovero, we might have a better chance of destroying their Family home. And if we were successful, then Marcello needn't worry about the Da Vias anymore. At least most of them, anyway.

Les docked the boat and we got off, heading toward the tunnel entrance. We'd made it safely. I allowed myself a breath of relief. Safraella had been watching over us.

We turned the corner into the dark and empty alley. It stank, an acrid, smoky odor. I stopped. "Do you smell that?"

He sniffed the air. "Smells like smoke."

Something about the smoke . . . I had smelled it somewhere before.

I sniffed my leathers and found the same scent. The gallows. The smoke bombs when Les had rescued me.

"Where did you get the smoke bombs?" I asked.

"What?"

"When you rescued me, at the gallows. Where did you get the different smoke bombs? Yours didn't smell like that before."

Les stopped and stared at me. "Lea, *I* didn't rescue you."

From above, someone jumped into the alley. My sword was out instantly, my dagger in my left hand. Another figure climbed down the roof to stand beside the first. Nik and Grape Leaves, with his rope-bludgeon and noose tied around his shoulders and waist.

Beside me Les twirled his cutter in his hand, prepared to fight. It wouldn't only be the two of them. I spun. Four more Da Vias stood at the entrance of the alley, blocking us in. The Da Via on the left wore a mask with red checkers. Val.

Les and I stood back to back, our weapons at the ready. I could feel the tension in his body, pressed against mine, his muscles tight like viola strings.

Behind Val, a man approached. He stood to the side, but his cylindrical hat and wooden staff caught my attention. Val paid him no mind. He was with the Da Vias.

"Sloppy work, Lea." Val stepped forward. I could smell the smoke from the gallows still clinging to his leathers. His voice held no wryness or sarcasm, only a controlled fury. "You thought you'd beat us to him, but we're not some lowly Addamos. We're Da Vias."

"*You* saved me from the gallows." I glanced over my shoulder. Nik and Grape Leaves had taken out their swords but hadn't moved closer.

"I wasn't going to let you hang. And I figured you'd lead us right to Marcello."

I had to get the upper hand here. If I didn't, Les and I were dead. "I don't know what you're talking about."

"Gods, Lea, shut up!" Val screamed. I flinched against Les's back. He stirred but continued to watch Nik and Grape Leaves.

I'd tipped him over the edge. I had to keep him there. "Who's your lapdog?" I motioned to the man in the hat.

"A friend of the Family," Val said. "Don't worry about him."

"He was in Fabricio's the night of the fire." And just like that, I knew which restaurant housed the entrance to their home.

Val shrugged. "He gets around. He helps us get around. That's really all you need to know."

"He's the reason you're here?" I asked.

"No. We know Marcello Saldana is here," Val said. "It's the only reason you'd flee to Rennes. The only reason being in Yvain makes you no longer feel like an orphan. After all these years of searching for him and all we had to do was follow you."

"And you thought you'd bring Marcello to your lunatic of a Family head, hoping he'd prostrate himself before her, beg for her forgiveness?"

"I don't give a shit about any of that. I just do what I'm told."

I laughed. "Yes, that's been clear since the night of the fire."

Val jerked his sword out of its scabbard. The metal rang sloppily in the dark night. The Da Vias beside him followed his lead. "Fine then. If this is the way you want it, you have no one to blame but yourself."

I tightened my grip on my sword. Val charged. Les pushed off from me to defend against Nik and Grape Leaves. He was outclassed, but I couldn't think about him now. I could only help him if I survived.

Val lunged at me, the other clippers swinging left and right. I raised my sword to defend myself, but he feinted to the right and let another clipper rush in. It was a new move for Val. He'd always relished being in the center of the fight. He'd changed.

I barely had time to switch my stance. My sword blocked the attack of the Da Via with red diamonds on her mask. Our swords rang against each other. The echo bounced off the brick walls of the alley. My ribs roared in pain. My grip on my sword faltered. I twisted to protect my back from another Da Via with red splashes of color on his mask, like spattered blood.

He feinted, too. Someone's boot connected with the side of my right knee. Only my off-balance stance saved me from a broken joint. I stumbled away, barely managing to stay on my feet. My ankle ached at the rough treatment, and my ribs practically hobbled me. I couldn't fight this way. Not if I wanted to live.

Les parried Nik's blows. Grape Leaves circled behind him, taking advantage of Les's distraction.

I pulled out a knife. One smooth motion, clean and quick . . . I whipped the blade at Grape Leaves like Les had taught me.

The blade wobbled in the air. The dagger struck Grape Leaves between the shoulder blades, hilt first. Painful, but not damaging.

Nik Da Via shouted. Les had scored him on the arm.

Val looked over his shoulder at Les. He changed places with Nik, who turned to face me. I rushed after Val, but the three others closed the gap. I'd have to go through them if I wanted to place myself between Val and Les. We needed to get out of here.

I pulled out three smoke bombs. The Da Vias weren't the only ones who knew how to use them.

I hurled them between the legs of my opponents. They exploded, gray smoke flooding the alley.

"Les!" I stepped away from the smoke and the coughing Da Vias. "Les!"

A shadow dashed at me. I raised my sword.

Les erupted from the smoke. He grabbed my hand and yanked me after him. I gasped in pain.

We passed by the man in the cylindrical hat. He shouted to the Da Vias, but Les and I darted around a corner.

I couldn't keep up. This wouldn't work. The Da Vias would catch us.

"The canal!" I panted. We turned left and sprinted for the water and his boat where we'd left it. Les grabbed the pole and shoved us away from the street.

I struggled to catch my breath, my arm pressed against my side. Every movement sent pain coursing through my body.

"I'm sorry I hurt you," Les said as he pushed the pole. "I wasn't sure how long the smoke would last."

I took another deep breath, wincing at the pain. "It's all right. We had to get away."

He moved us quietly while my thoughts raced. They'd find the entrance to Marcello's tunnel. We'd led them right to it. We couldn't stop them, not without help.

"I scored one of them," Les said. I nodded. "I coated my

blade with poison, like you suggested."

I closed my eyes, calculating, trying to decide if the poison would work fast enough to grant us any advantage. They would still outnumber us.

Ahead, a bridge arced over the canal. Les pushed us beneath, into a deeper darkness. There was no way out of this, no plan I could think of.

We reached the other side of the bridge, and Les steered us out. A shadow flashed over him. I shouted a wordless warning, but the noose dropped over his head and pulled tight.

Les released the pole into the water and grabbed the rope around his neck, trying to free himself. I scuttled toward him, the boat rocking violently at Les's struggles.

The rope pulled him out of the boat and up to the bridge, his legs kicking as he hung in the air.

"Les!" I clutched my sword and lunged for the rope. But it was too high, and every second I wasted they pulled him closer to the top of the bridge.

Laughter and shouts echoed from above. The Da Vias, enjoying themselves while Les dangled, choking from the noose. I knew how it felt.

I sheathed my sword and jumped for the bottom edges of the bridge. My hands reached the stone and I clamped tight.

My side ripped with pain. My body fought against me, commanded me to let go. But if I dropped, Les would die. I managed to swing my leg and hook it onto the ledge. I took a breath, agony radiating everywhere, and pulled myself up. I flopped over the side of the bridge gracelessly.

Nik and Grape Leaves dragged Les onto the bridge. He lay sprawled on the ground, struggling with the rope. Grape Leaves drew the rope taut, the other end with the stone bludgeon resting at his feet.

"Looks like you caught a big one this time," Nik said as they watched Les fight against the rope. "Feisty, too." He glanced in my direction. "Nice of you to join us. You're just in time for the fun."

I struggled to my feet and hunched over as I pulled my sword free. Behind me footsteps pounded on the street. The rest of the Da Vias. I couldn't spare them any attention. I needed to save Les.

I lunged toward them. Nik laughed as I swung my sword. He jumped aside easily, but I wasn't aiming for him.

My sword bit into the rope, severing it. Les inhaled sharply and pulled the noose from his neck.

Grape Leaves shouted and jerked the severed rope toward him. He switched ends, grabbing the severed half and swinging the bludgeon in a circle beside him, slowly gathering speed. It whirred and buzzed the faster he spun it, until the rope was a blur of motion.

"You've made him angry now," Nik said to me. "That was his favorite one. He's had it for years."

"Too bad for him," I said, free arm clenched against my side, which burned with fresh pain. I couldn't straighten my body, could only face them hunched over like an invalid.

Les struggled to his knees beside me, coughing, tugging his hood back in place.

Behind us, I heard dirt shifting under feet. I turned. Two other Da Vias and Val stood armed and ready.

I charged them, a foolishly reckless move my parents would have been disgusted to see. But my parents were dead, and Les would be too unless I could stop this fight.

I swung at Blood Spatter in a wide and frantic arc, hoping my crazed attack would take him aback, force him to step away. But he was a Da Via, and they were the second Family for a reason. He stepped inside my arc. The pommel of his sword smashed against my solar plexus like a blow from a hammer. The air in my lungs rushed out of me with a cough.

Diamond Mask kicked the sword from my hand. It crashed against the cobblestone bridge.

A loud snap filled the air, followed by a booming twang. I turned. The stone bludgeon on the rope smashed into my right cheek. My head snapped back. Half of my mask shattered. Bone shards rained across me as I fell to the ground.

Everything faded to black. A smell like rotten fish wafted across me. Blurry shapes returned. Muted, dull sounds settled over me like raw wool. I blinked. Blood filled my mouth and I spat it out.

Someone leaned over me. Nik. I reached for him. He grabbed my hands and pulled me to my feet, twisting my arms behind me. In front of me a quick scuffle ended with Les in the same position, Grape Leaves securing Les's arms behind him.

Les and I were too winded and injured to speak. My face swelled. Was my jaw broken?

Val paced between us, his anger apparent with every pounded boot step against the bridge.

He stood in front of Les and jerked the hood off his head.

Behind me, Nik yanked the remains of my mask from my face. He dropped it to the ground and drove his heel through what was left of it. The tiger-striped bone shattered beneath his boot.

"You've been poisoned again," I said to Nik. My voice sounded slurred from the hit I'd taken. He paused, then looked to his arm.

"Huh. Well, knowing you, I'm sure you have an antidote somewhere in this pouch of yours." He tapped the pouch on my hip.

"Let us go, and I'll give you the antidote."

Nik laughed. "No deal. In a few minutes all your antidotes will belong to me. I haven't dropped dead yet, so I think I'll take my chances finding the right one in time."

Val slid his mask to the top of his head. His eyes flashed rage and hurt and betrayal, his brow dripped sweat. He pointed his sword at Les. "This is why you wouldn't come with me?"

Les thrashed against Grape Leaves, and Diamond Mask kneed him in the stomach. His breath escaped in a whoosh. He tried to double over but Grape Leaves held him too tightly. Diamond Mask wrapped his long hair around her fist. She jerked his head back and exposed his neck. The bruising he'd acquired from the rope stood stark and plain, even in the dark. His throat bobbed as he swallowed.

"You don't know what you're talking about, Val," I said.

"I saw you together on that roof, Lea. Kissing. I *saw* you! He doesn't even have a mask! He's a nothing! A fraud!"

"Let him go. He doesn't have anything to do with this. You're right. He's nothing. Only a fake clipper, living in Yvain."

Val scowled and shook his head. "You've always been a shit liar, Lea. Even now."

"What do you want, Val?" I asked. "I will give it to you. You want my pride? You can have it." Warm tears rolled down my cheeks to my lips. They tasted of blood. "Please let him go. Please. I'm begging you."

He blinked. "Yeah, that's clear," he said, his voice empty. "It's not very attractive."

His mockery pierced me like a needle to the heart, and I inhaled sharply. Nik leaned closer to me, his mask pressed against my ear.

"Watch this now, Lea Saldana," he whispered. "Because you'll be next, just as I promised before." He tapped my spine with the edge of a knife.

Val stepped before Les, sword in hand. His fingers tightened around the hilt until his leather gloves creaked.

Les twisted his head toward me. I stared at him, and grief and terror and loneliness and every dark emotion I was capable of feeling filled my chest until it seemed I would burst from it all.

Les winked at me.

Val drove his sword through Les's chest. He buried it to the cross guard, until the Da Vias restraining Les had to move aside or face the end of Val's sword.

Anguish erupted through me. I bit my tongue until it bled to stop the screams welling up from inside. I turned away, but Nik grabbed my skull and forced my head toward the scene, his fingers digging into my scalp.

Les coughed out a mouthful of blood. It spattered across Val's face. Val pulled out his sword. Les crumpled to the ground. His head moved once, and then he lay still.

My fault, my fault, my fault.

Only Nik's powerful grip on my arms kept me on my feet. "Very nice," Nik whispered to me. "Now it's your turn."

A sharp stab to the center of my back sank below my shoulder blades. I gasped as the cold metal slid into my body, shrouding me in agony, until my body arced against it.

Nik released my arms. I fell to my side on the ground, the cobblestones beneath my face damp from the canal.

"No!" Val screamed. Rapid footsteps closed the gap between us. I tried to reach the knife in my body, to pull it out, but my fingers scrabbled against my leathers, pain ripping through me with every twitch of muscle. I dropped my arms.

Val struck Nik, a loud crack bouncing over us. Val's fist crashed so hard into Nik's mask that it broke in half at the bridge of his nose. Nik's mouth gushed blood. He brought his gloved hand to his face and groaned. Blood Spatter took a step toward Val, but Diamond Mask pushed her mask to the top of her head, standing between Val and the others. It was Val's sister, Claudia, no longer pregnant.

"Nik had an agreement with Val," Claudia said. "Nik went against it, and Val was in the right to strike him."

Blood Spatter glanced between them, then shrugged and stepped away.

Nik yanked my pouch of poisons from my hip and walked off.

Val dropped beside me. I tried to push him away, but my arms bent like reeds in the wind. He wrenched the knife from me, ignoring my cry of pain, and threw it away. A dull ache spread across my body, replacing the sharp pain of the invading knife. Each breath became more difficult until I felt like I was drowning, as if the cold grasp of an angry ghost pulled me beneath the canals.

"Lea!" Val pulled me into his arms, tears running down his face. I turned to look at Les, lying on the bridge.

"I'm sorry!" He held me tight. "This wasn't supposed to happen, I swear it."

I wanted to tell him to leave me alone, to flee so I wouldn't have to look upon him any longer, but I couldn't find the words. The salty taste of blood coated my lips, and I closed my eyes. I was so tired.

"I found the entrance," a voice said from the end of the bridge. The man in the hat.

"Leave her, Val," Claudia said. "The sooner we can

be done with this, the sooner I can return to Matteo and Allegra."

My eyes snapped open at that. Claudia caught me looking at her and grinned. "What?" she asked me. "You thought you were the only Saldana with a secret lover?"

Matteo. My brother Matteo was alive. Marcello and I were not the last of our Family. And Claudia's baby . . . Matteo was the father, had been her secret all along. But he was a Da Via now. He'd turned his back on us.

It was too late, anyway. It didn't matter.

"Give me a coin," Val said to someone.

"You know Estella doesn't allow us—"

"I said give me a gods-damned coin!" he screamed.

A moment later his ungloved fingers pressed something against my lips. I let him slip the coin into my mouth. He sobbed and leaned over me, pressing his lips against my forehead. He gently lowered me to the ground. Then they were gone, vanishing into the streets that led to Marcello.

I rolled onto my stomach and agony shredded me, like my heart ripped free from my chest. I screamed against my closed lips. I needed to keep the coin safe. I had one last thing to do.

I crawled to Les, every movement agony, every second my vision growing darker. The sounds of the night faded until all I knew was the image of Les lying before me on the cold street. When I reached him, I brought my fingers to my mouth and pulled out the coin. It was stamped with the Da Via crest. I didn't need it.

I slipped it past Les's unmoving lips, his breath silenced. He was still beautiful, even in death. I would've wished something different for him. But Marcello had been right. I was a Saldana, and we brought destruction to those we loved.

The pain diminished. A final mercy in a life seemingly devoid of them.

I closed my eyes and waited for my breaths to stop.

thirty-four

PALE LIGHT SPILLED ACROSS MY FACE. I GROANED AND covered my eyes. It was too early. I wanted to sleep.

The light continued its push until I sighed and rolled over, peeling my eyes open.

I could see nothing except watery gray light. I blinked a few times, waiting for my eyes to adjust, to focus on something.

I pushed myself up. My nerves burned against my skin, in my muscles, my organs, my bones. I cried out and froze, trying to keep the pain at bay. After a moment the fire eased to a strong ache. Still painful, but manageable.

I turned my head slowly, searching for furniture, landmarks, a hint to discover where I was. But there was only the endless pale light and what seemed to be fog rolling in and out of the edge of the nothingness.

I struggled to stand, barely keeping my balance against the pain that blazed through my body. I glanced at my feet, trying to keep them stable. My legs were bare. I was naked. Scratches and bruises covered my body, the largest bruise flowing across my chest like a menacing ink blot and rolling down my left side to a violent mass of swollen and wounded flesh.

Something warm dripped down my spine. I reached behind me and my fingertips returned red with blood.

The knife. The knife that had pierced my body. That had killed me.

I was dead.

I looked around again. Nothing. No one. I was alone.

I swallowed. "Is anyone there?" My voice emerged hoarse and rough, like I hadn't spoken in years.

The fog shivered and spiraled and then blew away, as if a wind carried it, though I felt nothing. No one answered me.

Behind the fog stood a forest of trees, each one white and bare and stretching toward the sky. I looked closer. A forest, yes, but they weren't trees.

Giant bones were stuck in the ground and reached upward, swaying with the hidden wind. No mortal thing had ever possessed bones so large.

I took one tentative step toward the forest, bracing for the expected pain. Then another. I continued in this slow and agonizing manner, but I never drew closer.

I wrapped my arms around my stomach to lessen the pain.

"Am I dead?" I asked, not expecting an answer.

"Yes." The voice was soft and quiet and seemed to emanate from the trees before me.

"Who are you?"

"You know who I am, Daughter." The trees swayed.

And I found I indeed knew who the voice belonged to. "Can I see you?"

A pause, a hesitation. "I have driven mortals mad."

"I'm dead," I answered. "I'm not afraid."

Vibration in the trees, like a laugh. "I have watched you your whole life. So many think they do not fear death, but when their time comes, they beg it away. But not you. There was no fear with you."

"Will you show yourself?"

"So be it."

From the folds of the bone forest a figure stepped before me, tall as the oaks on the dead plains. My gaze brushed across Her limbs, Her body, unable to take anything in, unable to linger, to make sense of what I was seeing.

I met Her eyes and found a blank face with no features, made of nothing but smooth bone, empty, flat, barren. I'd never known something could be both terribly monstrous and terribly beautiful.

As I gazed upon the face of a god, of Safraella, my mind sank toward a dark vortex. The sound of a thousand storms, a thousand hounds baying in the night surrounded me, consumed me. I began to unravel, bits of me floating away until there, before me, was the memory of Les, his lips pressed against mine, whispering *kalla Lea*.

Everything snapped back into place. The bone trees swayed.

"Where are we?" I asked, watching the trees.

"A forest. A graveyard. A passage. This place is many things."

"A graveyard for what? Who do those bones belong to?"

Safraella shifted, Her arms stretching out at Her sides, as long as some of the bone trees. "My enemies."

Gods. This was their graveyard. The trees were the bones of gods.

I swallowed. "If I'm dead, why does everything hurt so much?"

"And whoever told you, little mortal, that death would not hurt?"

I nodded, trying to ignore the pain the gesture cost me. "Am I to be reborn then? Have You come to grant me a new life?"

She leaned closer. "Is that what you want, little clipper?"

It would be so easy, to be reborn as someone else, to forget everything that had happened in this life. To forget I was ever Lea. But it seemed like giving up. Like losing my Family again. "I only thought . . ."

"Yes?"

"It came so suddenly. The end. It seems unfinished."

"You are all unfinished," she said. "Like embers in the wind. You burn brightly in your own time, and then you are snuffed out. It is your way."

I looked down at my feet. The blood from my back dripped down my calves and painted my ankles red.

Safraella straightened to Her full height and displayed Her hand before Her. She held a gold coin between two fingers. I couldn't see the stamp on it, the Family crest. "You are due a resurrection, Daughter. But it does not have to be a new life."

My breath stilled in my chest, and I pushed aside the realization that I was actually breathing. "You could bring me back? As Lea? As myself?"

She inclined her head.

"Why? Why me? Why not my Family?"

"You have long been a favorite of mine, Oleander Saldana. Faithful to me even in the darkest corners of your life. There are others who have . . . drifted from my radiance. They forget their place. I would like you to be my reminder to them. A reminder of what it means to forget that I am a god and do not take kindly to those who no longer value my gifts." Her voice echoed among the trees like the final note of a bass drum.

"The Da Vias? Or are there others, too?" Like my uncle, who had refused to let me wear my mask in his home. She didn't respond. "Is that why, when the angry ghosts came for me, You protected me?"

"The ghosts are wayward children. Only those in my favor have the ability to send them on their path."

"And if I can't be the reminder the Da Vias need? If they refuse to hear Your word?"

"You will return them to me there, or you will return

them to me here." She gestured to the bone forest.

Kill them. The Da Vias. Because murder was always the answer.

Unless . . . unless I didn't return.

I could choose the peace that came with a new life, or all the death and blood that awaited me as Lea.

And Les. Needles pricked my chest when I thought of him lying dead on the bridge. If I went back, I would face the Da Vias, alone. How could I be Lea without him?

Safraella watched me. I could sense Her thoughts twisting like the earlier fog.

"What should I do?" I asked.

"Little mortal. Very few of you ever get a chance at a true choice. You would give it away so easily?"

I closed my eyes. "No." I shook my head. "I know what I have to do. I have to go back, be Lea still. Kill the Da Vias. But what about Marcello? They'll have taken him."

"What is that saying you're all so fond of? Family over family?" The bone trees rattled behind Her.

My thoughts raced. Matteo was a Da Via now. He was gone from my life just as if he had died in the fire. Marcello was no longer Family, but he was blood, was family. And I didn't want to be the last of my line. If the Da Vias killed him, they won all over again.

I would save Marcello. And I would kill the Da Vias. Only . . .

"How can I do it by myself?" I tasted salt against my lips. I'd been crying.

Safraella leaned toward me, Her tall body folding in on itself until Her giant bone face hovered before mine. She pressed the coin against my palm. For an instant I saw the Da Via crest on it. "And whoever said you had to be alone? I will grant you one member of your Family, if you ask it of me."

"A resurrection? Of my choosing?"

Everything had been my fault. Everyone was dead because of me. But if they were in my place, who would they choose?

I thought of Rafeo, my beautiful brother, cold in the tunnel, the best of us. I thought of little Emile, full of untapped life. Of my distant mother, who spoke of her pride in me in secret letters, and of my father, who tried to buy us peace, to keep us safe. How could I choose? How could I weigh and measure love so casually?

I thought of Les, dead on the bridge, offering to help me for no other reason than because I was someone who needed help. A boy who had been raised by my uncle, my family.

It was my fault too, what had happened to Les. Rafeo had died because he was a Saldana. Les had died because I'd kissed him on the roof.

"I choose Les."

"Did I not say a Family resurrection?"

I swallowed but stood my ground. "He is my Family now."

Safraella had no mouth. No eyes. But I could sense Her smile.

She leaned closer. She placed Her face against my forehead, and the brightest pain of all rushed through my body.

I closed my eyes and screamed and screamed until I could hear nothing but the anguish that burned through my flesh.

———⊰⊱———

Cold water dripped onto my eyelids. I blinked rapidly, trying to clear the liquid away. Rain, a slow, cold drizzle, coated the cobblestones, making them slick and shiny in the darkness. I lay on the bridge. The bridge where I'd died.

Safraella had resurrected me. A true resurrection, not just a rebirth like She granted everyone else.

I sat up, my hand rising to rub the water from my face, but my hand met a mask. I pulled it off and turned it around. It was a bone mask, perfectly flawless in its construction. Instead of a pattern, the whole left side was black. I ran my fingers over the color. It wasn't dyed like a normal mask. The color seemed to be part of the bone.

I slid the mask to the top of my head, and something burned in my mouth. I choked, spitting it into my hands. A gold coin. But I'd given Val's coin to Les.

I flipped it over. It was stamped with the Da Via crest. It grew warm in my hands.

I twisted until I spotted Les where I'd left him. His leathers were sopping wet, his hair plastered against his pale skin. At least the rain had washed the street clean of our blood.

The coin pulsed in my hands, still generating heat. I pushed Les onto his back and found a hole in his chest from Val's sword. I pushed the hot coin into his mouth.

I sat back, watching his chest for breath, wiping away the water that dripped down my face. It had to work. It had to.

Please. . . .

Les coughed, inhaling deeply. His spine arched against the cobblestones, his mouth wide with terror.

When he'd breathed all the air he could, he rolled over frantically, scampering toward the edge of the bridge. Rainwater coursed down his cheeks, and he scanned around him like a panicked animal.

"Les," I said quietly. "Alessio."

His eyes snapped to me, and the fear in them drained away.

"I saw . . ." He swallowed loudly. "I saw . . ."

"I know." I crawled to him, taking his hands in mine. The hole in his chest had vanished, and if I looked in a mirror, I expected my face would be free of bruises. Les breathed heavily, and then sobbed, fresh tears pouring down his cheeks.

"Gods, Lea . . . ," he choked out. He pressed his head to my chest and I pulled him close, holding him tightly until his shaking stilled.

The rain lessened, then stopped. All the while, Les and I sat on the bridge and stared at each other, lost in our own thoughts. We had to rise, to see what waited for us in Marcello's home, to once again plot against the Da Vias, but at this moment I felt no rush. Maybe looking upon Safraella's face *had* driven me mad.

"She told something," Les said, his voice low and quiet. "Told me to do something . . ."

He paused, struggling with whether he wanted to tell me or not.

"She told me to do something too," I said.

"I'm not sure if I can—"

"It's all right," I interrupted. "It's fine."

He nodded and took a deep breath. "She said She gave you a gift. A resurrection. Anyone you wanted."

I nodded.

"Why did you pick me?" Anguish filled his eyes.

I took his hand, squeezing it. "My Family . . . my Family is gone. They are my past. But you are my future. I couldn't turn my back on you."

"You gave up everything for me?"

I leaned my forehead against his. "It isn't worth anything without you. You make me feel alive when I've felt nothing for so long. When I thought I was done feeling."

He rubbed his face. "No one's ever come back for me before."

My heart twisted at his words. "I will never abandon you."

He pushed his fingers through my hair to my neck, pulling me closer. Kissing him then was better than any kiss in my life. Even though we were soaked and his lips tasted of blood, I would've spent the rest of my life kissing him there.

He shifted, tugging me closer. Something clattered to the ground beside us. We pulled apart. A mask.

Les turned it over. Black slashes covered the left side, like the claw marks of a tiger, but like mine the color was embedded in the bone, not dyed. He ran his thumb over the marks, then rubbed his unscarred forearm. "I don't understand."

"It seems you finally belong. Welcome to the Family, Alessio Saldana."

He laughed, a short bark of joy. He slipped the mask over his face. He nodded and we got to our feet. I pulled my own mask over my face.

"Time to get to it?" he asked.

"Yes." I nodded. "Time to face the Da Vias."

thirty-five

†

THE TUNNEL WAS DARK AND EMPTY AND STILL. WE made our way toward Marcello's home, neither of us speaking. It didn't seem there was anything to say. Either we'd find Marcello, or we wouldn't, and our next direction would depend on that.

Les climbed the ladder, carefully lifting the grate and peering through. It didn't seem like we'd been dead for long, but it could have been hours.

Les pushed the grate open, and it banged loudly against the stone floor. I flinched.

"Sorry." He pulled himself up.

Their home was dark and cool, the fire in the hearth extinguished. A fight had taken place: shattered glassware, shredded tapestries, furniture moved or destroyed. I stood in the center of the mayhem. My uncle had given the Da Vias more than they'd probably expected.

Les hurried to the bedrooms, then around the hearth,

searching all the different areas.

He stopped. "He isn't here."

"I don't see much blood. I think they took him."

"To Lovero?"

I nodded. "To Estella Da Via, the head of their Family."

"We have to catch them. If we can catch them, we can save him."

"The new plan is the same as the old. Get to Lovero, break into their house, kill them all."

Les rubbed his eyebrows. "All right. They'll head for the southern city gates then. They won't be able to cross the dead plains until morning. Not unless they want to face the ghosts."

"If we hurry, maybe we can catch them on the plains or at a monastery. Save my uncle before they reach Ravenna."

We left Marcello's home behind, pulling ourselves out of the tunnel and into the alley. A pink blush brushed the sky. The sun would be up soon. We'd been dead longer than I'd thought. Once it crested the horizon, the Da Vias would cross the dead plains, but the Da Vias thought we were dead. They had no reason to rush. It was our only advantage.

"We'll have to collect the rest of our things," I said. "And we'll need some horses to make it to a monastery before the sun sets."

"I'm not a great rider," Les mumbled behind his mask.

"Well, it's either that, or take your chances on foot." I looked over my shoulder at Les as I turned the corner.

I slammed into something and stumbled. Les placed a

hand against my lower back, keeping me on my feet.

"Well, well, well." Lefevre and more of his men blocked the street. "I've been looking for you, Lea."

—————

Lefevre approached and his men followed, grim expressions on their faces. None of them wore lawmen's uniforms, which meant this was personal.

"How convenient that I find you on the streets again," he said, "skulking in the dark."

I unsheathed my sword. "I don't have time to deal with your petty grievances. You missed your bounty. Now get out of our way."

I heard a noise behind us, but I couldn't risk taking my eyes off Lefevre and his men. Les looked over his shoulder, then tensed.

The men behind Lefevre shifted eagerly. Lefevre smiled, his teeth white and straight. "Oh, you're going to make time for me, little girl."

Les faced Lefevre again, cutter in hand, his expression hidden behind his new mask. "If you value your lives, you'll flee."

Lefevre laughed. His men joined in. "I've brought more men this time. And we're better armed. We won't fall for the same tricks as before."

"Last chance," Les said. I kept my eyes fixed on Lefevre, watching for the slightest movement that preceded an attack. Last time he'd let his men do the fighting. But this time he had a rapier strapped to his hip.

"I don't know where she found you"—Lefevre pointed a finger at Les—"but you'll die as easily as she. Kill them both."

Les grabbed my arm and spun us against a building. Our backs pressed against the rough stonework, my sword held before me.

Where we'd stood floated an angry ghost. It was small, the remnants of a child taken from this life too young. It could have been my nephew, Emile. Its ghostly form glowed with internal light as it stared at the men in front of it, a forlorn expression on its face.

It had been behind us the whole time, too small for Lefevre and his men to spot behind our bodies. Les had only seen it when he'd checked our backs. Now it blinked its dead eyes, shrieked loudly, and charged the group of men, its childlike innocence gone.

The men screamed in terror. Consumed by panic, they pushed and pulled, trampling one another in their haste.

Lefevre, originally in the front of the pack, now found himself at the crowded rear. No matter how much he bellowed for his men to make way, they didn't listen.

The ghost reached Lefevre, grabbing his wrist with its transparent hands. He froze. His men scrambled away, fleeing to safety.

The ghost pulled on Lefevre's wrist, and the crooked lawman's entire body trembled. Then Lefevre suddenly had two wrists, a flesh-and-bone one suspended before him, and a transparent one, trapped in the ghost's grip. As the ghost continued to pull, more and more of this transparent Lefevre appeared, emerging from his flesh.

Lefevre shrieked, his panic echoing off the buildings around us. He struggled but couldn't break free.

The ghost gave a final jerk, and Lefevre's spirit separated from his flesh.

Lefevre's body collapsed to the street.

The angry ghost dived at the empty body. Its form vanished inside his flesh. The body twitched, then shook. Finally it sat up, each eye blinking separately as it looked around.

Lefevre's spirit shivered in the air. He shrieked. I could feel his rage at the ghost child who'd stolen his body. I pressed myself closer to Les. He gripped my hand.

Lefevre's body rose to its feet and staggered around. It would never find coordination. It would never find speech or emotion or anything that had once made it human. It was nothing more than a shadow puppet. The ghost could not regain the life it once had, no matter how many bodies it stole from the living.

Lefevre flew at his body, trying to pull the ghost out, but he wasn't as strong as the child. It pushed him away, sending him floating toward us. His eyes widened in rage.

"You've done this to me!" he screamed, his voice an echo in the quiet night. Les twitched beside me. Soon Lefevre would lose all ability to speak.

I shook my head. "No. You've brought this on yourself."

He roared. I held my sword before me, sure he would

come for us, would try to steal our bodies as the ghost child had done to him.

To the east, a shaft of light crept over the roof of a building, illuminating the dark street. The sun had risen.

Ghost Lefevre vanished, leaving us safe once more.

Les breathed heavily beside me. My heart beat rapidly.

We pushed away from the wall, regaining our composure. The fake Lefevre stumbled around the street as it tried to gain balance, Lefevre's body shielding the ghost child from the sunlight. Undiscovered, it would stumble around like this for a few days until it would abandon Lefevre's body in search of a new one. But we were in the city. Authorities would find Lefevre's inhabited body and burn it outside the walls of the city, releasing the ghost to the dead plains.

"What should we do about that?" Les pointed at it.

I remembered the ghost child's face before it had attacked, how sad it had seemed. How unfair for one so young to spend eternity raging at the world. Surely it deserved a chance at peace, at a new life.

I walked over to Lefevre's body.

"What are you doing?" Les asked.

"Following a hunch." I pulled a Saldana coin from my pouch. I thought of Safraella in the fog of that dead place and Her kiss on my forehead—the pain and incredible heat. I remembered the coin burning in my mouth when Safraella had brought me back, remembered slipping it into Les's mouth and the breath that returned to him. The ghosts were wayward children, She'd said. Only those in Her favor could send them on their way.

The coin began to warm in my hand.

I reached false Lefevre and he faced me. His head sagged on his shoulders as he tried to control his neck. I touched his shoulder. He stilled, his eyes widening as he watched me.

"Be at peace," I said to false Lefevre. I pushed the coin into his mouth.

The ghost was ejected from the flesh. It reached out a hand, then dissipated in an explosion of mist.

Lefevre's body fell to the street.

"Did you clip it?" Les asked quietly.

"Yes." It would no longer be an angry ghost. I had sent it to meet Safraella in Her boneyard, to face Her judgment and be given a new life.

Les eyed me. I knew he was coming to terms with something. "Your conversation with Safraella must have gone much differently than mine."

I sheathed my sword and squatted beside Lefevre's body, searching through his pockets.

"Is this really a good time to rob the dead?" Les asked.

"I'm not robbing him." I pulled out the Saldana stamped coin he'd taken from the dead boy's body all those nights ago. "I'm taking back what's mine. Now let's get out of here before the decent lawmen stumble upon us with his body."

We climbed to the roofs and made our way to my safe house to prepare for the journey to Lovero.

thirty-six

ANARCHY GREETED US AT THE SOUTH GATE. CLOAKS hid our leathers, packs, and satchels stuffed with all the supplies we could carry, including the makings for the firebomb that we'd assemble later. Our masks were tucked away safely until we reached the dead plains. We'd expected to buy some horses and simply ride out of the city—now that the Da Vias had taken Marcello and fled home under the assumption they'd killed Les and me—but the gate was blocked with people milling around and lawmen interrogating the crowd. I stepped into a shadow, and Les followed.

"What's going on?" I searched the crowd for any clue to the uproar. People seemed to be gathered in groups, gossiping.

Les shook his head. "I've never seen anything like this."

An old man shuffled past, and I placed a hand on his shoulder. He turned his rheumy eyes to me.

"Excuse me, grandfather. What is the trouble? What is happening?"

He smiled a gap-toothed grin, pleased to be addressed. "Someone left the gates open, that's what!" he exclaimed. "Ghosts just walked into the city. Lots of people met their ends last night at their hands."

"Someone left the gates open at night?" Les asked, shocked. My neck prickled with dread.

"Isn't that what I said?" The old man squinted at him. "What are you, some sort of traveler? I can tell just by looking at you!"

I turned the old man away from Les, who rolled his eyes. "Do you know what happened?"

"I saw them myself! Heard a clatter from the streets and I looked out the window. A group of them, eight or nine at least, on well-bred horses. As soon as they got the gate open, they galloped out of here like ghosts were already after them."

No, no, no! "Did you see their faces, grandfather? Did they wear masks crafted from bone?" I clutched the man's hand between mine, his thin skin soft as expensive paper.

"Well, I can't say as they were made of bone, but they definitely covered their faces. They were dressed all in black, too. I told the lawmen, but they didn't think masks were important." He spat to the side, narrowly missing Les's boot.

I released my breath in a puff as any hope we'd be able to catch the Da Vias vanished. They'd left the city when it was still night. They'd reach Lovero a day ahead of us.

"I don't understand," Les said. He stepped farther away from the old man. "How could the Da Vias brave the dead plains at night?"

"They had a priest with them!" The old man pointed a bent finger at Les.

"A priest?" I asked.

"Yes! The priest had a hat and a staff of light. He lifted the staff high, and it surrounded them with light as bright as the sun. No angry ghost could reach them through that."

I felt as if I'd been punched in the gut. The strange man I'd seen at Fabricio's and in Yvain with the Da Vias—he was a priest. But not a priest of Safraella. When Safraella said the Da Vias had left the right path, She must've meant they'd taken up with another god.

I took a deep breath. Les squeezed my shoulder. This changed everything. Before, I was just going to kill them, make them pay for what they'd done to my Family. Now, now there were other gods, other priests involved. What had they granted the Da Vias in exchange for turning their back on Safraella? What if the Da Vias had some sort of blessing that would interfere with my plans? "Rot that Estella," I swore under my breath.

"Lea." Les leaned closer to me. "The plan's still the same. Get to Lovero. Find your uncle. Kill the Da Vias."

I took another breath and nodded. "Thank you, grand-father," I said to the old man. He patted my hand before he walked away.

From the center of the crowd, a whistle blew, sharp and

loud, followed by the voice of a lawman ordering the crowd to disperse. There was some grumbling and muffled protest, but for the most part the crowd went on its way.

We'd spent enough time in Yvain. I'd grown to like it—the canals, the flowers, the quiet cobblestone streets—despite my best intentions. But now it was time to return to Lovero and everything that awaited us there.

It took all my remaining coin and Les's to purchase the horses. The mare was sturdy and reliable, but the gelding was years past his prime and used every opportunity to slowly steer Les toward window boxes.

Les hadn't been lying about his horseback experience. Loverans were proud of their horses, but Yvain relied on its canals for transportation.

"Well, if we were taking boats, I might actually be of some use," Les snapped at me after I'd had enough and finally tied his horse to mine. The gelding tried to tug itself free until my mare flattened her ears and kicked at it in irritation.

The gate to the city had mostly cleared as people went about their morning errands, though a few gossipmongers hung around in small groups. We passed the city wall, the clops of our horses' hooves changing to thuds as they stepped off the cobblestones and onto the dirt road leading from the city.

We rode together quietly, lost in our own thoughts until I looked up and saw that the grasses of the dead plains had turned orange in the setting sun. Soon our path would be filled with the angry dead. And the Da Vias were still ahead of us. There was no way to catch them now. We'd have to hope that the Da Vias wouldn't kill Marcello immediately upon their arrival.

Safraella wanted me to remind the Da Vias of what it meant to serve Her. And I was happy to do it. All I'd wanted for so long was to kill them, to make them hurt like they'd hurt me. But if we couldn't get there in time to save Marcello, then what did it even matter? The Da Vias would have killed every last Saldana, even if I had been resurrected.

Brother Faraday's monastery appeared over a grassy hill as the sun touched the horizon. I kicked the horses to speed their steps, and we reached the gates before the sun fully set.

"Lea!" Brother Faraday shouted as he ran down the monastery steps. I pushed my mask to the top of my head. He clasped my hands tightly and smiled.

Behind us, other priests took our horses to the barn, Les's mount practically dragging his handler across the flagstones.

"I was worried," Faraday said to me, "when I didn't receive any letters."

"That was due to a lack of funds. I'm sorry to have caused you concern."

He turned to Les and inclined his head. "I'm Brother Faraday."

"Alessio. People call me Les."

"Alessio Saldana," I corrected, and Faraday's eyes widened.

I looked at Les. "You're going to have to get used to saying it sooner or later. And Brother Faraday, we've come for your help."

Faraday led us to a cozy room with a table and chairs. Another priest served a loaf of bread, cheese, and a carafe of cold well water. Les and I tackled the food together. Every bite of bread was so soft, like eating a cloud. The sharp, rich flavor of the cheese slid across my tongue, and the cold water from the carafe was so clean and refreshing I drank two glasses in rapid succession.

"Gods," Les said through a mouthful of bread.

"It's like tasting everything for the first time," I said.

Faraday looked at the two of us. He smiled tentatively. "I'm glad you find our meager fare so fulfilling."

I slowed my eating, savoring the flavors. "Something happened to us recently. It seems to have altered the way we experience food. I'm sure it will fade soon."

Les grumbled. "I hope we can taste some goose liver before then. Oh! Or some tender white fish baked in butter."

My mouth salivated, and I imagined seared lamb or juicy berries that popped between my teeth.

Faraday shook his head. "What happened to change your senses so?"

"We died," Les said.

"What?!" Faraday's chair scraped the floor as he scooted forward.

I sighed and set the cheese down. "It's true. We died. The Da Vias killed us."

Faraday's jaw dropped. "And She resurrected you both? *True* resurrections?"

Les shook his head. "No. She resurrected Lea. Then Lea resurrected me."

I flicked my wrist. "He makes it sound more impressive than it was. She granted me a single resurrection. I used it on him. It wasn't anything more."

"It wasn't anything more?" Faraday's voice squeaked in shock. "You were resurrected by the goddess Herself and She granted you a gift and you treat it so cavalierly?"

Faraday gulped in large breaths of air. I poured him a glass of water. He drank it quickly.

"Lea, this is a miracle you're speaking of. Nothing like this has happened in a hundred years. Not since Brother Pelleas saw Her face in a vision and walked the dead plains unmolested." He leaned forward. "Did you . . . did you see Her? Speak with Her?"

I nodded. "We spoke and I looked upon Her face. When I woke again, I found this." I slid my mask off my head and handed it to him.

Faraday ran his fingers gently across the flawless bone. He pursed his lips. "Lea, with your permission, I would like to record your experience. I've already written down what you'd told me about the coin, but I think I could write a whole tome on your life if you'd allow me."

"Brother, we have limited time here," I said. "The Da Vias have strayed to another god."

Faraday gasped. "How can that be? A Family of such

wealth and power, turning on She who has given them so much?"

"They have lost their way." I narrowed my eyes. "But I need to know what god they have turned to, to understand what we may face when we confront them. They had a priest with them who carried a staff of sunlight. It allowed them to cross the dead plains."

Faraday pushed his chair away from the table. "I'll be right back."

He ran from the room, his robe billowing behind him in his haste.

Les turned. "So. The food was amazing. Do you think other things could be amazing now that we're not dead?"

I studied his face. He grinned slowly. Heat rushed up my neck to my cheeks as we stood and reached for each other. I pushed his mask off his head to run my fingers through his hair. Les grabbed the back of my thighs and lifted me to the table. I wrapped my legs around his hips, pulling him closer to me. His fingers stroked the back of my neck. He kissed me on the jaw, trailing his lips across my skin. Nothing had ever felt quite like this before. Maybe it was the resurrection making everything more intense, like the flavors of the food. Or maybe it was simply the way my pulse raced when I looked at Les.

We both wore our leathers, their bindings tight against our bodies to protect us. I wanted to rip his leathers off, run my fingers across the smooth skin of his back, his chest.

Across the room, someone cleared his throat. Les paused, and I looked over his shoulder. Brother Faraday stood in the doorway, his eyes averted and his face red even through his dark skin. "I've found a book," he mumbled.

Les laughed and stepped away. I slid off the table and we returned to our seats. I righted my overturned glass as Faraday took a seat, pointedly not looking at me.

"Sorry," I said.

"No, it's fine. You simply . . . caught me off guard is all."

He opened the book, the leather cover banging on the table, and began to page through it. I stared at Les and he stared at me. Just the sight of him was enough to raise the heat of my blood.

"Here!" Faraday jabbed his finger to an entry on a page.

I leaned over. It was an illustration of a staff with golden beams of light radiating from a gem.

"Daedara," he said. "A god of the sun, mostly worshipped in the eastern part of the continent."

"Where the hells did they find him?" Les asked.

I shrugged.

"He was one of the six gods worshipped in Lovero before the Sapienzas took the throne," Faraday said, "but why the Da Vias have turned to him, I am unsure."

"I think I understand." I pointed at a line in the text. "Daedara is a god of fertility, also. Marcello told me Estella blamed him for not providing her with a child. But after he was banished, she remained barren. I don't think she was ever stable in her head, but I could easily see her transferring the blame to Safraella."

Faraday nodded. "It could be true, too. If Safraella could see how unfaithful Estella was, why would She bless her with a child?"

"But doesn't Daedara care that they're freely murdering people?" Les asked. "If they're not worshipping Safraella, then they're nothing more than common criminals."

Faraday examined the text closely, then shrugged. "He seems to be against the murder of children."

"Well," I said, "turning to Daedara seems to have done their Family some good. Their numbers have exploded. It seems their women barely have time to clip, so busy are they being pregnant."

Faraday leaned back. "But I don't think you need to fear anything from this priest of Daedara. Unless, like the ghosts, you fear the sunlight."

"Thank you, Brother." I inclined my head. "Should the Saldanas survive, I would welcome you into our home."

He smiled brightly and shut the book. "I may take you up on that, Sister. Truly your lives are full of adventure and intrigue!"

I grabbed my mask from the table. Les reclaimed his from the floor where I had knocked it. A tingle of regret traveled through me as I watched Les dust the cobwebs from it. He had waited so long for his mask, and I had pushed it aside as if it was a cheap trinket. Les didn't seem to mind, though.

He caught my eyes and winked before he pushed his mask to the top of his head.

"Now we must be off."

"But Sister, the sun has set and the angry ghosts wander the plains."

I clutched my key. There would be no more delays, not while Marcello still lived and I was so close to my vengeance.

I slipped my mask down my face. "If the lowly Brother Pelleas could cross the plains one hundred years ago, then surely a favored clipper can do it as well."

thirty-seven

†

WE GAVE THE MONASTERY LES'S HORSE. THEY LOOKED dubiously at the ill-tempered animal, but I reminded them they could sell him for the coin.

Butters had been kept well fed and maintained in my absence. He nickered when he saw me. We saddled both horses and led them to the gate, where the usual mob of ghosts had gathered.

"Are you sure about this?" Les asked. Butters tossed his head and stomped his hoof, either raring to go or trying to impress Les's mare. She stood quietly, her ears flicking at Butters.

"No." I stared at the ghosts. "But if it works, we can make up time."

The priests swung the gates open. The cacophony from the ghosts rose in volume. Even with the gates open, though, they could not cross onto holy ground. They pressed themselves against the invisible barrier, trying to reach us.

"Are you ready?" I asked him.

"What's the worst that can happen?"

"Your soul could be pulled from your body and you could wander the dead plains for a thousand years?"

"And that's why I keep you around, *kalla* Lea. For your sense of humor."

Butters huffed as we walked toward the dead plains. The moon was barely a sliver and already high in the sky. If this worked, we could push our horses and reach Lovero before the sun rose.

The ghosts stretched toward me, screaming. I urged Butters forward. The ghosts swarmed me, trying to be the first to claim my body, but when they touched me, they were driven back by a spark and flash of light, just as they'd been when I'd been attacked on the dead plains before.

"Les!" I glanced over my shoulder. He hesitated by the entrance. Then he shook his head and kicked his horse into the fray of ghosts. Miraculously, the ghosts swayed away. They could not touch him without being forced aside. We had looked upon the face of Safraella, and the ghosts could not rip our spirits from us.

Les directed his horse beside Butters. His chest heaved with heavy breaths. "I can't believe that worked."

"Let's go!" I kicked Butters, who leaped into a gallop, happy to be given the chance to run once more.

Les gasped as his mare followed. He had a tight grip on the her mane but didn't jerk her head. We trailed a stream of angry ghosts. The dead did not tire and did not forget their rage.

I slowed Butters a little so Les could catch up and ride beside me.

"Will we go straight into Ravenna?" he yelled over the sound of the horses' hooves.

"No." I shook my head. "They'll notice anyone who enters the city this late. We'll enter Lovero through Lilyan, then make our way to Ravenna."

We urged the horses faster, trying to outrace the ghosts. Any that managed to reach us were deflected by an invisible barrier that surrounded us like the monastery, hurling them far away into the plains with a flash of light. It was as if we were holy ground. They tried to throw rocks at us, branches, anything they could find, but everything was deflected away. Our protection seemed to make them even angrier, if that was possible. Maybe they could sense how Safraella had touched us, had given us a new life while they were trapped with their rage and grief. Maybe they hated us even more because of it.

Perhaps I'd possess this protection for the rest of my life. Though I supposed it could be stripped from me once I did Safraella's bidding. If it remained, I could travel anywhere by land, see the world and not have to worry about the ghosts. It was a heady realization, that I could be so free if I chose. If I survived.

We crested a hill, the horses' breaths blowing heavily. Before us spread the river and the many-colored lights of Lovero.

I slowed Butters, allowing him to catch his breath. The

ghosts circled, but none tried to touch us. Their screams, though, were the loudest I'd ever heard. "Is that Lovero?" Les asked.

"Yes." I pointed to the west. "Where the lights are the brightest, that's Ravenna, my city." I shifted my hand more to the east. "That's Lilyan."

"Will the Da Vias be watching the gate?"

"No. It's outside their territory. Unless things have changed since I've been gone. Lilyan belongs to the Caffarellis."

"Won't *they* see us?"

I shrugged. It was a possibility. But we had to cross into the country somehow, and the only three cities that bordered the dead plains were Ravenna, Lilyan, and Genoni. "I'd rather take my chances with the Caffarellis than the Addamos or Da Vias. We'll wait for daylight to slip into Ravenna. The Da Vias will be sleeping and won't notice."

I nudged Butters forward, and the ghosts chased us. The river wasn't far, and once we crossed the crooked bridge, they wouldn't be able to follow. Then it wouldn't matter how loud they wanted to be.

"It's beautiful." Les stared at the lights of my home. "I've never seen anything like it."

"Yes. It does have a kind of frantic, dark splendor. I've missed it. But it's funny—I thought I'd never get used to Yvain. The quiet way of the people and the nights, the stink of the canals, the flowers everywhere. But in Yvain, the stars are brighter."

"Also, Yvain has dangerously handsome clippers, which I think Ravenna was missing."

"Dangerously handsome?"

He held his head high and gestured to his face, his back straight.

"You're wearing your mask," I pointed out.

"Ah. Yes. But a clipper girl once told me the mask was the most beautiful face of all."

I laughed. The ghosts screeched and cried.

We reached the crooked bridge, and the horses' hooves clopped loudly against the stone. The ghosts tried to follow, but they couldn't turn when the bridge kinked to the left. They were stuck as we crossed the rest of the river.

They shrieked, more enraged now that we were escaping them. There were so many of them. I'd never seen such a congregation before. They raced along the riverbank, bellowing wordlessly as we rode farther away.

"I can't say I'll miss them," Les said.

An explosion of noise erupted behind us: cracks and booms. Both horses spooked and jumped. Only my quick reflexes prevented Butters from bolting out from under me.

We turned in our saddles to face where we'd come from. Across the river, the ghosts had found a large oak tree on the bank. They had combined their powers to topple it across the river, its trunk and branches creating another, straighter bridge.

The ghosts rushed toward us.

"The hells with this!" I gave Butters his head. He sprinted

for the city, Les and his mare close behind. The ghosts roared as they rushed to catch us before we lost them.

"They'll get inside the city!" Les shouted.

Before us, the old gates to Lilyan rested crookedly against the crumbling city walls, rusted off their hinges. The gates hadn't been closed since Costanzo Sapienza took the throne and declared Safraella patron to all of Lovero.

We dashed into the city, the horses' hooves clattering loudly on the flagstones. I pulled Butters to a halt. His legs collected beneath him as he slid across the flagstones. The streets were filled with people. They shouted and pressed themselves against the buildings, trying to avoid the stallion before he crashed into them.

Finally Butters halted and I twisted in my saddle, looking for Les. He and his mare stood quietly, watching the city gates.

The ghosts tried to enter, but just as at the monastery, an invisible barrier protected the city. All of Lovero behind the old, crumbled walls was holy ground to them. As long as the king and his subjects continued to worship Safraella, She continued to protect them from the angry ghosts.

A few of the common shrieked and ran away from the ghosts as they pressed against the barrier.

"How did they get across the river?" A man peered at the ghosts from a safe distance.

"They knocked down a tree." I slid off Butters. "They used it as a straight bridge."

The man faced me. He wore a garish mask, covered in

feathers and gems. I glanced at the others and they, too, wore masks and beads and bright-colored clothing. The scent of alcohol wafted off them.

"Good clipper." The man bowed courteously to me. "You grace us with your presence."

"In the morning," I said, "you will need to speak to your city officials and have someone remove the tree before more ghosts discover how to cross." The ghosts couldn't enter the cities, but they could certainly snare anyone too drunk to notice where the walls ended.

I led Butters out of the crowd. Les followed. We'd already attracted enough attention. Any chance of sneaking into Lovero had been destroyed.

My home. I took a deep breath. I'd returned. I was so close now, so close to avenging my Family.

My chest tightened in the familiar ache I'd grown accustomed to since my Family's death. Since my terrible mistakes.

Tears welled in my eyes. We weren't even in Ravenna and yet everything reminded me of them. A food vendor selling Jesep's favorite pastries dusted with sugar. A puppet troupe that would have made Emile squeal with laughter. The smell of the oil, the same kind we'd used to light our house. I could feel my Family in the laughter and joy of the common. I could feel them in the very air.

Les walked beside me, the horses trailing. He glanced at the people we passed. Everyone bowed to us. "The people aren't afraid of you."

I cleared my throat. "Oh, they're afraid. But their respect

is greater. Many of them dream of becoming favorable in the eyes of a Family, which would give them access to wealth and power and connections, not to mention an advantageous rebirth. Most of them will overlook their fear to take that chance."

"And the masks?" He stared at a particularly loud mask on a woman who laughed uproariously at the man whose arm she clutched.

"Susten Day," I said.

Susten Day was a holiday celebrating Safraella. It used to be my favorite holiday. The parties and food and dancing would last all night. And because everyone wore masks, I could be anyone I wanted. Now I knew that was the dream of a child. Safraella had offered me a chance to be someone else. I'd chosen to be me.

We broke out of the cramped street and reached an intersection, with a fountain and food vendors and entertainers. Fire breathers walked on stilts, their skin painted with gold and silver. Musicians played, their notes clashing with the songs people roared drunkenly off-key. The smells of the food vendors competed with the body odors of so many people. I wrinkled my nose. Had it always been like this? So boisterous and loud? It felt different, somehow. I'd always loved the noise and excitement, especially on Susten Day. Now it filled my senses, threatened to overwhelm me. It made me want to be somewhere else.

A group of children ran past, screaming and laughing behind their masks. A girl tripped and fell to the street before

Les. He helped her up.

"Thank you," she said, then spied his mask. She backed away. When she reached a wall, she bowed hastily, then scampered after her friends.

He watched her go. "I've never had children frightened of me before."

"That's only because the children of Yvain were in their beds when you were about your dark work. I promise you they would have run from you there had they seen you."

We made our way through the square, people parting around our horses, many shouting glad welcomes when they saw our masks. We broke through to the other side and found a quieter, less crowded street.

I sighed. "We're attracting too much attention. We need to find a stable to board the horses and get out of Lilyan before the Caffarellis find us."

A man in black leathers stepped out of an alley, clawed guards over his knuckles, the left side of his bone mask adorned with purple flames.

"Oh, Sister," he said. "We already have."

thirty-eight

†

PURPLE FLAMES. CAFFARELLI COLORS. THE MASK TICK-led my memory. I knew who this was, if I could only remember.

Three more clippers stepped from the shadows, each bone mask decorated with purple patterns that appeared almost black in the darkness.

Four of them. Fighting them would create a scene, and our only advantage lay in the fact that the Da Vias thought us dead.

"Brother." I inclined my head respectfully. "We apologize for the intrusion into your territory. If you let us pass, we will leave and pay any restitution you deem necessary."

We had to take this carefully. The Da Vias were the first Family now, and the other Families could easily be under their sway.

But my mother had been born a Caffarelli, so maybe that would be enough to buy us passage, if nothing more.

The clipper in front tapped his mask with the long metal claws of his left hand.

"What is it you're doing in Lilyan? Surely there are celebrations in your own territory?"

"We came from outside the walls."

He sighed. "Now you are lying."

"Brother," one hissed to the clipper in front. Their leader leaned away without taking his eyes off us. When the whispers stopped, the leader examined us anew.

"Come closer." He gestured with his claws. "Into the light."

Les glanced at me. Whether we were standing in the shadows made no difference if it came to a fight. I slid into the beam cast by a lantern hanging from a balcony above us.

Les followed and we stood beside each other, one hand holding the reins of our horses, the other concealing a weapon behind us.

The leader shifted his weight, some of his tension receding. "We'd heard a Saldana survived, but here stand two of you. And I do not recognize your masks."

I slid the mask to the top of my head. "The mask is new."

He searched my face. "Lea Saldana, then."

He pushed the hood of his cloak off, displaying messy, short, white-blond hair. He slid his own mask up.

He had a narrow face, with a nose that had been broken too many times. But he had laugh lines around his mouth, and his eyes looked relaxed and easy. He appeared to be a few years older than Les.

"Brando Caffarelli," I said.

He gestured at himself. "Brand, cousin. My father was . . . grieved to hear of the loss of your mother."

Traces of my mother showed in his appearance, especially in his hair color. I didn't know much about my mother's brother. I hardly knew anything about the Family she'd left behind when she married my father. She'd made it clear that the moment she became pregnant with Rafeo was the moment she gave up being a Caffarelli and became a Saldana.

Beside me Les pushed his mask to his head.

"Though," Brand continued, "now with you before me, perhaps I can bring him glad tidings?"

I shook my head. "We are all that are left."

He looked to Les. "I don't recognize you. You have the dark hair of some of the Saldanas but not much else. Certainly not their coloring or their stature." Brand gestured at my diminutive height, and then flashed me a smile to show he meant no insult. I'd been short my whole life. So had my brothers and my father. I was used to the teasing remarks.

"Alessio Saldana," Les introduced himself. A flush of pride spread across my cheeks and trailed down my throat.

Brand nodded and didn't question any further. If Les said he was a Saldana and had the mask to prove it, the other Families would take it as truth.

Brand spoke inaudibly to the three Caffarellis behind him. They disappeared into the shadows of the streets.

"So." He gestured for us to follow him into a quieter

square, with a garden and benches. He took a seat and we tied the horses to a pergola, letting them graze at the grasses of the garden, before sitting across from him. "Are you here to deal with the Da Vias?"

I folded my hands in my lap. "Yes. They've turned to another god. They're false worshippers."

Brand hissed between his teeth. "How do you know this? That is a grave accusation."

"Witnesses in Yvain. And I've seen some minor blasphemies from a few of them. I'd thought they were just being . . ."

"Cocky bastards?" Brand supplied.

"Yes. But they crossed the dead plains at night with the help of a priest of Daedara."

Brand frowned.

"You could help us," Les said.

I made a small noise in the back of my throat, and Les glanced at me. Help. Help killing the Da Vias. It was what I'd always needed, always wanted. It was why I had traveled to Yvain to find my uncle. I had thought the Caffarellis would refuse me, would side with the Da Vias, who had all the power now that the Saldanas were dead, but maybe I'd been wrong. Maybe they would have helped me all along, if I'd only put my pride aside and asked.

Brand leaned forward with his elbows on his knees, fingers interweaving together. "I can't see my father agreeing to that."

Les frowned. "Why not? The Da Vias are traitors to their

masks. They lessen the status of all clippers."

Brand waved a hand. "It's not that I don't believe you." He rubbed a knuckle down the bridge of his nose. "My father is a cautious man. He will not take a stance against the Da Vias, not with their numbers and their wealth."

"Not even as they worship another god?" Les asked.

Brand shrugged. "He would take a stand against that. I think many of the Families would, especially if it meant destroying the Da Vias once and for all. And certainly the Sapienzas would order us to if they discovered the truth about them. But no one, including my own Family, will take a step against the Da Vias without hard proof. Not with the power they wield. Your word is not enough, cousin."

My hopes deflated. He was right. Even Costanzo Sapienza, the king, for all that he loved my father, wouldn't take a stand against the Da Vias unless he had proof before him that they were traitors to our way of life.

What they'd done was so dangerous and stupid. All those people the Da Vias had clipped, supposedly in the name of Safraella, had been during their secret worship of Daedara. Many now probably wandered the dead plains as ghosts. And since the Da Vias had been hiding such treachery, it would be easy for the common to believe it of the rest of the Families. Or the king. The common would turn on us, believing us to be indiscriminate killers. It would create pandemonium.

The Da Vias played with fire and didn't seem to care if the whole country burned for it.

"If you could get the Bartolomeos and Accursos to agree

to an attack," Brand said, "I could probably convince my father then."

"There's no time to speak to anyone else," I said, "even if they agreed to meet with me. The Saldanas don't share blood with them."

"My father won't agree to just us, the fourth Family, alone."

"Fifth Family," I corrected.

Brand smiled sadly. "Fourth, cousin. We both know the Saldanas will never be the first Family again. At least, not in our lifetimes."

He was right, of course. But to be confronted so firmly with the loss of our status was to feel the pain of the loss of my Family again. Everything my Family had worked toward for generations, all the death and war faced by my father to put Costanzo Sapienza on the throne, ruined by the Da Vias.

"Maybe . . ." Brand hesitated. "Maybe you should let your Family go. You could join another Family. You could marry into the Caffarellis. We would be happy to have you. *I* would still be happy to have you."

Beside me, Les bent closer. He stared at Brand with hard eyes.

Brand leaned away, hands held before him. "I meant no disrespect. I didn't realize you had claims on each other. Adoption, then. My father would take both of you."

It would be so easy, to give it all up, to join Brand and his Family knowing that, truthfully, they were my blood family as well. To not have to be in charge, be the head of a Family, even though there were only two of us. Three if we saved Marcello.

But I'd stood before Safraella, felt the divine pain when She'd kissed me back to life. Whoever said death wouldn't hurt? She'd asked me. And truly, whoever said life was supposed to be free of suffering?

If I gave up now, it would be to turn my back on Her gift of resurrection. To turn my back on Her. I would be no better than the Da Vias.

I shook my head. "No. I'm sorry. The offer is gracious, but we cannot accept. We must do this thing."

From a dark alley, a Caffarelli clipper appeared. He leaned over and mumbled something to Brand before disappearing into the busy streets once more.

Brand stood. "My father says you are welcome to board your horses and to seek shelter in our territory through the end of Susten Day, tomorrow night. After that, he wants you gone."

Les scowled, but I nodded. We didn't need more time.

We'd make our move against the Da Vias tomorrow.

thirty-nine

†

BRAND SHOWED US TO AN INN LOYAL TO THE CAF-
farellis that would let us stay for free.

The simple room had two small beds, a wash table, and
a desk. We hadn't rested since the fight with the Da Vias,
and until I saw the beds, it hadn't occurred to me I should
be tired.

"We've been going without stop for over a full day." Les
dropped his pack to the floor. "And I just now realized I'm
exhausted."

"I think it was like with the food." I set my mask aside and
unbuckled my leathers. They stank. I could clean them before
we confronted the Da Vias. No. It didn't matter if my leathers
were soaked in blood and sweat. There was more to come.

"It was as though, for a moment, we were brand-new."
Les sat on his bed to pull off his boots and remove his own
leathers, stripping down to his linen pants. "I'm kind of sad
it's gone."

"Nothing lasts forever," I murmured, then dimmed the oil lamp on the table. The sun would be up in an hour or two, and I wanted some sleep before we left for Ravenna to find the Da Vias.

I climbed into the small bed, its wooden frame creaking loudly under my weight. The rushes in the mattress were lumpy, but they smelled clean, and the sheets felt smooth and soft against my skin. I lay on my side, facing the wall and its peeling plaster.

The last time I'd gotten any sleep had been in the jail cell in Yvain. Before that, the couch in Marcello and Les's home. And being dead, if that counted. I'd probably never again have a safe home or regular sleep. All I could do was count the beautiful things remaining in my life: the clean sheets on this rented bed, that the Caffarellis hadn't tried to kill us on sight, the cool night air on my skin.

The floor creaked. Chill air brushed across my back as Les lifted the covers and slid in behind me. I made room for him. He pulled me close, and the warmth from his skin soaked into me. Somehow, he'd read my mind, had understood my desire even though I hadn't spoken it aloud.

He brushed the hair from my face and kissed me on the neck beneath my ear. His mother's pendant pressed against my back.

"Les," I said. He kissed my neck again, his hands sliding around my ribs to my stomach. "My brother's still alive."

His hands paused. "Rafeo?"

I shook my head. "My other brother, Matteo. I heard

Claudia say it in the fight. After they . . . after Val killed you."

He breathed quietly behind me. "What does that mean?"

My throat tightened. I shrugged. "I don't know. I think it means he's a Da Via now. I think I'll have to kill him."

Les sucked in a breath.

"What is it?" I asked.

"It's . . . nothing."

He was keeping something from me, something he didn't want to discuss. But we were both in this together now, our fates intertwined when She'd resurrected us.

"He's not my brother anymore, anyway, if he's a Da Via."

"He's still your blood, Lea."

"No. The bonds of Family are stronger than the bonds of family. That's the way it's always been. That's why my mother turned her back on the Caffarellis when she married my father. It has to be that way, or no Family could ever trust another enough to arrange a marriage. And Matteo was always a stickler for rules and tradition."

"Hmm." Les trailed his lips to my shoulders, his hand slipping the strap of my camisole down my arm before he slid around to my stomach again. I placed my hand over his and guided him lower.

"Lea," he murmured against my flesh, "are we going to survive tomorrow?"

My skin fluttered beneath his fingers, and heat spread across my body before journeying higher to meet the heat of his lips.

"No," I answered, my voice breathy. "No."

He nodded, his loose hair stroking my shoulders. He trailed his other hand across my back. The whisper of my camisole as it slipped across my skin was loud in the still room. His fingers hesitated, brushing lightly below my shoulder blades. I shivered.

"Lea . . . ," he said, his voice no longer soft, but questioning. He removed his hands. "What is this?"

"What?" I twisted my neck.

He held me in place and ran his fingers over the same spot on my back. "You have a mark here." He pressed his fingers against my skin.

The warmth that had built in my body vanished. I shouldn't have a mark. . . .

"Was this where you were stabbed?" he asked.

I rolled over to face him. I moved his arm and pendant and examined his chest. There, where Val had driven his sword through Les's body, was a white mark.

"You have one too," I said.

I traced it. Shaped a bit like a starburst, it was smooth, completely unlike a scar. More like a discoloration of his skin.

He trembled, and I snatched my hand away. "Does it hurt?"

He captured my fingers and brought them to his lips. "No. Just a mark to remember that night by."

He leaned over and kissed my shoulder, my collarbone.

I ran my hands across the skin of his chest. "I don't

think I'll ever forget," I said.

His lips pushed against mine and he rolled on top of me, his weight pressing down as he continued to kiss me deeply, fervently. I returned the kisses, my hands sliding across his back, his muscles, his skin, imprinting the feel of him on my fingers.

If I died tomorrow, at least I had one last beautiful thing remaining in my life.

Fabricio's looked dull in the early evening light. The restaurant opened once the sun set, since most of their clientele were those who spent their daylight hours in bed.

The restaurant was as far north as the city allowed, pressed against the crumbled city walls. I imagined the ghosts pushed against Fabricio's after sunset, trying to reach me. Les and I hid in a shadowed alley, Les with the firebomb and extra materials in a satchel strapped to his back. I watched the front of the restaurant until he started to fidget.

"No one's come in or out," he said. "At some point we're just going to have to take a stab at it and see if it bleeds."

I tapped my mask and sighed. He was right, though I wished for more certainty about our task. My plan consisted of finding the Da Vias' home, saving Marcello, and killing them all. The how of it still eluded me other than *use the firebomb to set the place on fire.*

Whatever we decided, we needed to strike soon. It had taken more time than planned to make the firebombs this morning and the longer we took now, the less chance we'd find Marcello alive. Most of the Da Vias would be asleep until dark. Once the sun set, we would encounter more resistance.

I waited until a street sweeper passed by before I dashed out of the alley toward Fabricio's. Les followed quickly behind, and we tucked ourselves against the south side of the building.

Les whistled like a bird. He gestured at a window and mimed breaking it. I nodded and checked the street. No one had noticed us.

The clinking of shattered glass erupted behind me.

Les knocked the broken panes out of the sill, then climbed through. I followed, and we found ourselves in the dim dining room of Fabricio's.

The tables and chairs had been cleaned and perfectly arranged. The empty room seemed a dead place.

"Now what?" Les whispered.

"There can't be a secret entrance in the dining room," I whispered. "Too many witnesses to see them coming and going. Let's try the kitchen."

We walked through the maze of tables and chairs, careful to make as little noise as possible. Once we reached the kitchen, we searched the space, but there weren't any obvious trapdoors or signs pointing to where the Da Vias lived.

I tapped my mask, thinking.

"Over here." Les leaned across a barrel of wine.

I scurried over. Behind the barrel was a small door in the northern wall, hidden from sight.

Les rapped a knuckle on the barrel, and it echoed back. "I think it's fake."

Together we pushed on the wine barrel. It swung easily away from the wall, installed on hinges.

We stared at the hidden door. "It might be nothing," Les suggested.

"If it was nothing, they wouldn't hide it behind a fake barrel." I took a deep breath, then pushed the latch on the door. It swung outward, the hinges well-oiled and quiet.

I slipped through the door and found myself outside once more, in a tiny, hidden courtyard.

In front of me lay a crumbled section of the city wall, a gap open to the dead plains stretching behind it and the river glowing gold beneath the quickly setting sun.

To the right was the corner of Fabricio's, pressing up against the city wall, but to the left was another door. A door that led into the manor house next to Fabricio's. It was the only way to go, unless I wanted to cross the crumbled city wall and enter the dead plains, or go back into the restaurant. The courtyard led directly to the dead plains, the Da Vias' own secret entrance. They didn't even have to enter the city to get to their home from the dead plains.

Les squeezed himself out of Fabricio's. I stretched my neck and looked up at the four-story monstrosity of a house that towered over us. Everything about it spoke of the richest of inhabitants. I shook my head.

"What is it?" Les peered past the gap in the city wall to the dead plains.

"It's only . . . of course the Da Vias live in a giant mansion, displaying their riches for all to see. I don't know why I ever assumed they'd have tunnels like we did. They're too much in love with themselves to think of safety."

"To be fair, the tunnels didn't save your Family. Or my master."

I nodded. "You're right. Come on."

The door to the manor was unlocked, and I pushed it open quietly. Before us extended a hall bathed in darkness. Les pulled out his cutter and held it loosely beside him. I left my sword on my hip, but selected a stiletto. I was finally here to avenge my Family. To end my guilt and shame.

We slipped into the dark hallway, letting our eyes adjust. Les reached behind him to shut the door and I grabbed his arm.

"Leave it open," I said.

"Why? If someone comes across it, won't it make them suspicious?"

I glanced out the door and past the broken wall to the dead plains. "It's my backup plan."

We walked quietly down the carpeted hall. There were no rooms or doors, only a straight path that led to a set of stairs and another door.

The stairs were solidly built and didn't creak as we climbed them. At the door I glanced at Les. He tightened his grip on his cutter and gave a quick nod.

I slid Marcello's key into the lock and turned. It clicked. I pushed the door open, and light spilled over us.

We'd entered the Da Vias' home.

forty

†

THE INSIDE OF THEIR HOUSE WAS AS LAVISHLY DECO-
rated as I would have expected of the Da Vias. Rich tapestries
hung on the walls, as did painted portraits of Family members throughout the ages. Les and I walked across the thick
carpet. I should've been watching our path, listening for
people, but I couldn't help but stop and stare at a portrait of
Val. He looked so stern in the painting; the artist had failed
to capture his smirk of arrogance.

"Lea," Les hissed. I abandoned the portrait to follow him.

The hall opened to a large grand room, the floor tiled in
marble, columns supporting the ceiling that soared above
our heads. I'd been to balls at the palace that didn't have
rooms as decadent as this one.

There was another door across the room from us. I felt
exposed, stepping into the giant, open room, but we had to
keep going.

We scurried across the room, keeping our footfalls light

and searching the space around us. We reached the door and paused only a moment before we opened it and left the grand room behind.

Another hallway. This one had doors set in the walls. We stood before the first one, made of heavy oak.

The mark on my back twinged.

The door could have led anywhere, to a kitchen, a bedroom, another grand room. We could open the door and find it packed with Da Vias. But it was on the north side of the building, which was pressed up against the city wall outside.

"Do we open it?" Les asked.

We needed to stick with the plan. To find Marcello and then to burn the whole place down with the firebomb. Our time was limited, and if it ran out, I would have to make decisions I didn't want to make.

But there was something about this door. Even if it was simply a bedroom, maybe we could find someone still sleeping and convince them to tell us Marcello's location. It could be worth the delay.

I nodded. Les turned the door handle. My heart thudded in my chest and everything seemed too silent, too still. The door swung open.

It led to a bedroom, dark and empty.

There was no reason to explore it, to go inside and see what we could find. None. But my hand twitched. I crossed the threshold, slipping into the dim room.

There was nothing in it, only a canopied bed, unoccupied

and rumpled. I faced Les and shrugged. Maybe my instincts had been wrong.

A figure launched out of the shadows, tackling me before I could bring my stiletto up. I was slammed to the floor. Hands scrabbled for my neck. Fingers dug into my throat, choking me. I bucked, trying to break free of him. Another shadow raced into the room. Les.

My attacker rolled off, dodging the slice Les had aimed for his head. I rolled toward Les and got to my feet, coughing.

"Are you all right?" Les kept his eyes on the Da Via, who circled us in the shadows.

I nodded and unsheathed my sword. Sloppy of us, to think the room was vacant. But if my attacker was armed, he would have pulled a weapon by now. It was two against one, and we were prepared for a fight.

I nudged Les, and we sprang at him together. Les swung left. I dashed right.

The Da Via swiveled his head and made a quick decision. He lashed out at Les with a bare foot, connecting with his thigh. It wasn't enough to do more than bruise, but it caused Les to lose his footing. He stumbled, missed his swing.

The attacker turned toward me. I lunged, sword in my right hand, stiletto in my left. He dodged and grabbed my left wrist, squeezing my tendons. I jerked him forward, trying to free my hand. We stumbled into the light spilling from the hallway.

The Da Via was shirtless, dressed only in a pair of sleep

pants. His sandy blond hair lay disheveled about his head. I gasped. Matteo.

My hesitation cost me. He ripped the stiletto from my fingers, flipping it around and brandishing it before him.

Les circled back to me.

"Come on then!" Matteo snarled.

I stepped away, breathing heavily. I pushed my mask to the top of my head. Matteo stared at me for a moment, his expression of rage slowly replaced by astonishment.

"Lea." He lowered his weapon slightly.

"Surprised to see me?" My heart pounded in my chest, and not from the fight. I'd known he was alive. I'd *known* it. But I'd hoped I wouldn't have to face him. I'd thought Safraella had been urging me into this room, but maybe I'd been wrong. Maybe it had been a warning instead.

Matteo swallowed loudly. "You're supposed to be dead."

I pulled my mask down so he couldn't see my emotions flashing across my face. "You're supposed to be dead, too. In our house, burned like the rest of our Family."

He tightened his jaw. "Claudia told me you died in Yvain."

"She wasn't wrong. And which Da Via told you about the rest of our Family? Was it Nik? Or Val? Did they tell you how our mother died? Our father? Jesep?"

He narrowed his eyes and took a step back.

"You betrayed us!" I yelled. "Rafeo died in my arms because of you."

"Don't talk to me about Rafeo. I loved him, too."

"I loved him best! Where were you that night? Were you with them, or were you with us?" Beside me, Les dropped his free arm to his belt. I focused on Matteo.

"I was with them," Matteo answered. "I've loved Claudia for years in secret. Years. But Mother and Father wouldn't agree to any sort of union between us and the Da Vias. So I remained discreet. Much like you with Val." He sneered at me, and though there had never been much love lost between Matteo and me, his anger and bitterness poured through me like sour poison.

"When Claudia told me she was pregnant," he said, "and offered me a place beside her, I knew where I belonged. You damn well know Family comes before family, and I was a Da Via as of the night of the fire. It was a test for me. It was prove I was one of them or die. So I told them how to traverse the tunnel, and they used the key you so helpfully provided to get inside. It wasn't just me, dear sister, who betrayed our Family."

His words were another knife wound, this time in the heart. I couldn't catch my breath. My ribs pressed tightly against my lungs, and I struggled to make them obey, but they wouldn't. Ever since the night of the fire, I'd carried the blame of my Family's death. I'd given the Da Vias the means to reach my Family. But it hadn't been only me.

It had been Matteo who had killed us. My brother who had seen his Family murdered.

"You have a new mask," Matteo said. He glanced at Les. "And a new Saldana. Though judgment has yet to be made on whether he'll measure up to the reputation."

I raised my sword. A gust of cold flowed through me, as if my blood had been replaced by a chill wind. "He's more of a Saldana than you ever were."

Matteo snarled and twisted his wrist. I recognized the move. I pulled my sword back, prepared to defend myself, when something cut through the air, connecting with Matteo's neck.

A knife protruded from his throat. Blood poured down his chest as he stared at me in utter shock.

I looked at Les, his hand held before him from when he'd released the knife.

I couldn't move. I couldn't do anything but stare at my brother. Matteo gurgled and dropped the stiletto. He grasped the hilt of the knife, pulling it from his throat.

Blood poured everywhere. He took a step toward me. Another. He fell. I dropped beside him, pushing the mask from my face.

"Matteo." I pressed my hands to his throat, his warm blood spilling over my fingers. There was nowhere I could put them to stop the bleeding. I'd been here before. There was nothing I could do.

Matteo coughed up blood. He blinked once, twice, and then his eyes went dark.

I groaned, pulling my fingers away. I stared at them. The life's blood of both my brothers had coated my hands. I'd never be clean of it.

"Lea." Les spoke. I struggled to my feet, my hands leaving

bloody prints in the pale carpet beside Matteo's body.

"You killed my brother," I said to him.

He handed me a shirt that had been resting over a chair. I took it from him, but I wasn't sure what to do with it. Les stepped closer and clasped my hands in his. He used the shirt to clean the blood from me.

"I had to," Les said.

"Why?"

"Because She asked it of me. She told me that I couldn't let you kill your family, your blood. That I had to spare you that."

I blinked as he scrubbed at my hands. Safraella had granted me that mercy, even though Matteo was a Da Via now. And She'd sent me here to kill the Da Vias, when She'd told me to return them to Her.

"Lea?" Les asked quietly, pushing his mask up.

I sank against Les. He wrapped his arms around me, and I held tight to him as thoughts tumbled through my head.

"It's all right," Les said. "It'll be all right."

I nodded against him, my eyes jumping down to Matteo's body before they flicked away. Behind Les, tucked in a corner of the room, stood another door.

I pulled away. "There's a door. . . ."

He turned. I walked to it. The knob twisted easily in my hand.

Les dropped his hand to his belt. "We're running out of time, and we don't know what's in there."

I pushed the door open.

It was another bedroom. No, not a bedroom, a nursery. A crib stood to the side, and on another wall was a child's bed.

My arms shook. I clutched them to my chest. I stepped to the bed. A child lay in it, asleep. His cheeks were flushed with warmth, his black, curly hair resting against his face.

Emile.

forty-one

†

I FELL TO MY KNEES BESIDE HIS BED.

Les ran to me, but I focused on Emile. I brushed a lock of hair behind his ear, and he stirred in his sleep.

"Lea?" Les asked.

"It's Emile," I whispered. "My nephew. Rafeo's son. They didn't kill him. They took him."

I stood and watched him sleep, his breaths coming easily, his fist clenched beside his face.

"They took him," I said. "To make him a Da Via, to make sure he never remembered being a Saldana."

I approached the crib. Inside slept an infant girl, a blond thatch of hair crowning her head. Claudia and Matteo's child. I scanned my memory for her name. Allegra.

I should have hated her. She was a Da Via and the daughter of a brother who had betrayed us all. But I didn't. She was so beautiful.

"Lea . . . ," Les started. "What should we do?"

I stepped away. "We're wasting too much time. We need to keep going or we won't have time to set the firebombs."

"But surely this changes everything?"

"Does it?" I tugged on my hair.

"Wait." Les grabbed my shoulders and turned me to face him. "I know you say that Family comes before family, but I don't believe that. I think family"—he gestured to Emile on the bed—"should come first. And I also believe that family is what you make of it."

His words sank into me, twisting around my memory of what Safraella had said to me before the resurrection. She'd brought me back, allowed me to resurrect Les in order to kill the Da Vias. But She was a goddess of death. If She wanted them, did she really need me to deliver them?

"I don't know what to do," I whispered.

"Lea, you're the best thing in my life, and however long we have left here, I want to spend it with you. I will follow you no matter what you decide. But do you really want to give up what remains of your family just to make the Da Vias pay? If we only have time to save Marcello and the children or carry out your murders, which would your Family pick? Which would Rafeo pick?"

I sagged and Les wrapped his arms around me, pulling me close to him.

When Safraella had given me a resurrection, I'd thought about choosing Rafeo. I'd thought about bringing him back. But it would have been a shallow gift, to return him to a life where his son was dead. Nevertheless here slept Emile, alive and whole, and I couldn't leave him here, couldn't leave him in the hands of the people who'd murdered his father.

"His son," I answered.

Family over family, She'd said to me. But maybe She'd meant the opposite. Maybe sometimes murder *wasn't* the answer.

Maybe this time I could choose to save a life instead.

I pulled away from Les and wiped my eyes under my mask. I'd spent so long planning to kill the Da Vias for murdering my Family. But they hadn't killed all of us. This time I could choose family over Family. Vengeance didn't have to be everything.

And maybe vengeance wasn't as important as redemption.

"What should we do with that?" Les gestured to the bag that held the firebombs and extra supplies.

I sniffed. "Bring it, just in case. We'll find Marcello. Then we'll come here for Emile and we'll leave. Join the Caffarellis or leave Lovero, I don't care. As long as we're together."

Emile sat up in bed, rubbing his eyes with his fists. "Aunt Lea?"

"Oh." I rushed over, kneeling in front of him. "Yes, it's me."

He reached out for me and I grabbed him, holding him tight, his small arms wrapped around my neck.

He was so exquisite. I didn't want to ever stop looking at him. He let go of me.

"You went away," he scolded. "Did you bring my papa?"

My breath escaped me in a whoosh and I reached for him

again, but he saw Les over my shoulder and squirmed free of me.

"Papa!" He stumbled to Les. But when he got closer he slowed, perhaps seeing how tall Les was compared to Rafeo.

Les pushed his mask up and smiled at Emile, who stared at him suspiciously.

I scooped up Emile. He tucked his face against my neck, hiding.

"I don't have your papa." I rubbed his back. "This is Les."

"I want my papa." He pouted.

"Me too."

I walked him to the bed and set him down. "I want to you to listen to me carefully," I said. He nodded. "Les and I are going to leave you here—"

"No!" he shouted. I peeked at Allegra's crib, sure he would wake her. "I want to go with you!"

"You can come with us," I said. "But only if you're a big boy and can wait and be quiet." Before the attack Rafeo had been teaching Emile how to be patient, the first skill any clipper learned. "Can you do that?"

Emile picked at a scab on his arm while he kicked his legs. He nodded.

"Fine, then. You're going to *wait* and be *quiet* in your bed. And if you do a good job, Les and I will come back and find you and you can come with us."

Emile wrinkled his nose but nodded. I reached into my belt and pulled out the smallest knife I had, a push dagger designed to fit between my knuckles for a punch with a surprise. I handed it to Emile, and his eyes lit up.

"Be careful with it," I said. "You remember the rules?"

He nodded and held it in his pudgy palm. "Point out, not in."

I leaned over and kissed him on the forehead.

We left the room, and I watched him closely as we closed the door behind us.

"You just gave a weapon to a child," Les said.

"Yes."

"He's, what, four?"

"He's been handling weapons since he learned how to talk. He won't hurt himself."

Les shook his head. "Come on. Let's find my master and get out of here before we stumble on anyone else."

"This house is huge," I said as we stepped out into the hall. The sun was setting, I could feel it in my bones. "I'm not sure how we're going to find him."

"Nothing's beyond fixing yet. We can still save him. Save us."

I took a deep breath and nodded. Les was right. This wasn't the time or place to worry about it. We needed to find my uncle and get out as fast as possible.

From down the hall, a door creaked open and a man in his leathers stepped out of the room, stretching his arms above his head.

Les and I froze. He scratched the back of his head, his short blond hair messy from sleep, and glanced our way.

He did a double take. Tension filled the space between us

as he warred between running, attacking, or calling for help.

Les swore quietly beside me, dropping his hand to his cutter.

The spell broke.

The Da Via clipper took off, running down the hall as fast as he could. His footfalls made heavy thumps on the thickly carpeted floor.

Les and I sprang after him. The clipper had a head start on us and should have been able to escape. Yet somehow Les and I caught him easily. I tackled him, crashing into his back and forcing him onto the carpet. I sank my stiletto into his thigh and ripped it out, splashing the carpet with blood. He screamed, and I pressed the stiletto to the base of his skull.

"None of that now," I hissed.

He breathed heavily, his rising and falling body enough to lift me, but I didn't feel winded at all. I glanced at Les, who stood over us.

"Out of breath?" I asked Les.

He shook his head. "I feel amazing, like I could run for miles. And I can sense the sun's set."

"Me too," I said. Another gift from Safraella?

Below me, the Da Via clipper turned his head to look at me. His leg leaked blood at a steady rate. "I know you."

"If you don't shut up, you're going to get to know the point of my knife."

He looked at Les, then at me. He blinked. "You're dead. Both of you. I sank my knife into your back."

I examined him closer. I hadn't recognized him without

his mask, but his height and build were about right. As was his recently broken nose. "Nik," I spat. "I see you found your antidote."

"How are you here?" He squirmed under me, his eyes wide. "How can you be here?"

I jerked him to his feet. He wouldn't put weight on his injured leg, which bled heavily, and I was too short to keep a good hold of him. Les took my place and twisted Nik's arms behind him.

"We're here," I said, "because Safraella sent us."

He stared at my mask with wide, terrified eyes and didn't even try to struggle in Les's grip.

"Your Family has displeased Her," I continued. "She knows about Daedara, and She does not take kindly to treachery."

Nik swallowed. "I had nothing to do with that decision."

"Are you not a Da Via? Did you not use a priest of Daedara to cross the dead plains? You had a choice, and you sided with your Family over your god."

"Please," he choked, looking between the two of us. "Please . . ."

I held my finger to where my lips would have been on my mask. "Hush now. Here's what's going to happen. You're going to take me to my uncle, to Marcello Saldana. If he lives, we'll let you go to spend the rest of your life begging for Safraella's forgiveness. If he's dead, you'll die. Either way, I'd hurry before you bleed out."

I tapped his bloody leg with my stiletto, and he flinched.

"This way." He nodded down the hall.

Les marched him forward and Nik led us along the first hall, then another, until we reached a door that looked very much like all the other doors we'd passed.

"Through there," he said. "He's not dead. Estella wanted to deal with him tonight. He's not . . . in peak shape, though."

Les twisted Nik's arms until he grunted in pain.

I opened the door. It led to stone stairs, heading into darkness.

"My Family will find you," Nik said. I listened for voices or anything to tell me there was a person somewhere at the bottom of the stairs. "The sun's set, and if they're not up already, they soon will be. Even with Safraella on your side, you won't be able to stand up to all of us."

"Shut up." Les kneed him in his stab wound. Nik gasped, and his face paled.

I led the way down the stairs. Les pushed Nik before him, not caring if he stumbled or banged his leg.

Gone were the lush carpets and lavish wall hangings. The walls and floor were cold stone, damp from moisture and smelling of mold. There were four cells, reminiscent of the jail in Yvain, and the first on the right held my uncle.

"Master," Les breathed. He shoved Nik away from him. Nik stumbled and fell to the ground, crying out and cradling his injured leg.

Les pulled on the door to the cell. When it didn't give, he began to dig through his pouches for his lock picks.

Marcello sat on the floor in the corner of his cell, his head resting against his chest. His clothing was covered with filth, and even in the dim lantern light I could see the cuts that adorned his face and flesh and the blood and bruises painting his skin.

Marcello's eyes opened, and he blinked uncertainly before he lifted his head.

"Uncle," I called, and he focused on me. "We've come to save you."

He turned to Les, then slowly pulled himself to his unsteady feet.

Les popped the lock and rushed in to Marcello. Les tried to put my uncle's arms over his shoulder, but Marcello swatted him away before he grasped Les tightly in an embrace.

"Oh, my boy," Marcello mumbled as he patted Les's back and then examined his mask. "They'd told me they'd killed you. Both of you," he added as he pulled away. His lips were cracked, and his hair was tangled and matted.

"We did kill them!" Nik shouted from where he sat on the floor, using his leathers to tightly bind his thigh. "It wasn't even hard."

"You shut your fool mouth before I shove a knife down your throat," Les spat at him.

Marcello looked at me, questions racing through his eyes. I nodded.

"But how?" he asked.

"Have you forgotten that She is a god of resurrection as well?"

Marcello rubbed his face, wrinkled hands coated in dried and flaking blood.

"You're damn fools, both of you," he said quietly. "You shouldn't have come here. You shouldn't have come for me."

"But we did. I wasn't going to let them end us all."

"I've never seen such stupid, ignorant pride," he berated me. Les stepped between us and pushed his mask up.

"Master, shut up," he snapped.

Marcello glared at him, but Les put up a hand. "You don't have a say in it. Lea is the head of the Family, *our* Family. I side with her in this and all things from here on. Don't make me choose between you two, because all the love I have in my heart for you won't make me choose you. If you have a problem with that, you'll have to speak to Safraella on your own time, but right now we are saving you, saving the boy, and then getting out of here before any more Da Vias stumble upon us."

From the top of the stairs, the door creaked open.

Nik laughed. "Too late, Saldanas. Too late."

forty-two

†

THE THREE OF US RUSHED OUT OF THE CELL. FROM THE top of the steps a shadow tumbled down the stairs.

"Hello?" a voice called. The voice of a child, maybe no more than eleven or twelve. "Uncle Nik? Are you down here?"

"Raise the Family, boy!" Nik shouted. Les swore and swung toward him, his boot lashing out and connecting with Nik's temple. Nik slumped over, unconscious.

The boy's shadow vanished as he fled from the dungeon entrance, yelling as loud as he could.

"Well." Marcello brushed his hands on his pants. "That's done it."

"Let's move!" I said. We ran up the stairs and out of the dungeon.

The hallway was still blessedly empty, but I could hear the voices of Da Vias as the boy raised the alarm. I passed my sword to Marcello. We were in for a fight now. But if we could reach Emile quickly, we could flee the house and escape into the night, into the dead plains if we had to. Les and I could keep the ghosts away. I hoped . . .

We turned the corner. Two Da Via clippers raced at us, noiseless as they pulled out weapons, their faces hidden behind their masks.

Les swung left and I swung right, each of us focusing on a clipper, our communication silent yet completely understood.

I lunged at my adversary. He brought his sword up to block me. I dropped to my knees and stabbed him in the gut with my stiletto. He grunted. I hooked his ankle, pulling him off his feet so he crashed to his back.

Les swung his cutter at his adversary's mask. The Da Via pulled away. Les followed with a quick elbow to the face. The Da Via's bone mask cracked. A final swing with his cutter and the second Da Via lay on the ground beside the first.

Another entered the hallway. I jumped to my feet, ready to meet her. Marcello rushed between Les and me.

Once, for my birthday, Rafeo had taken me to see a show of traveling fire dancers. The women and men swung on ribbons and ropes that burned with flames. They ducked and weaved and spun through the air as it rained fire around them. None of them were burned.

Marcello fought like the fire dancers. All grace and silent movement as he danced around the clipper who wanted to kill him.

A moment later the Da Via was dead and Marcello turned

to face us, his chest heaving.

"Master . . . ," Les said.

"What?" he snapped. "Just because I'm old doesn't mean I'm feeble."

We ran down the hall once more, Marcello's breath wheezing in and out. I felt fresh. It had to be the resurrection, my stamina. Les's stamina. Perhaps She had given us this so we could do what needed to be done.

A figure stepped from a room, a tall cylindrical hat on his head, staff clutched in his grip. The priest of Daedara.

"Stop!" he commanded. He held the staff before him, and the crystal at the top flared white. Marcello covered his eyes and cried out, forced to step back from the light.

I felt nothing. The light was bright, I could see it in Marcello's reaction, but it didn't burn my eyes, didn't push me away. I stepped up to the priest and yanked the staff from his hands.

The priest stared at me, so shocked he didn't even fight me for his staff.

"But . . . ," he blubbered. "But I am the vessel for His holy light. . . ."

I snapped the staff over my knee and dropped the pieces to the ground. "You trespass onto Safraella's grounds. Your god has no power over me. Leave before you die."

The priest swallowed, his eyes wild and white, then he turned and fled swiftly down the hall.

"You could have killed him," Marcello said.

"He is a priest of his own god, worshipping in his own

way. Maybe I'm more favored than him and maybe not, but if he flees, perhaps he will warn other priests to stay away from Lovero. We belong to Safraella alone."

Three more Da Vias entered the hall. Had this not been a life-or-death situation, I would have rolled my eyes. They seemed to keep popping up.

The Da Vias charged and we took defensive stances. Three on three was manageable, especially with our skills. Still, the Da Vias were not easy. These three put the first ones to shame. They were older, well established in their abilities.

I darted left, dodging the daggers of my assailant. She was a lot taller than me, and I could practically hear her glee as she kept me on the defensive, pushing me against the wall.

To the right Les's assailant scored him across the back. But he carried the bag with the firebomb and extra materials, which shredded, protecting him. Two jars of acid fell out of his bag and thumped onto the thick carpet.

My attacker thrust at me. I used my lack of height to my advantage and dropped to the ground. I stabbed my stiletto into the meat of her thigh, then yanked it out. She gasped and her leg sprayed blood. I'd aimed for her artery and hit true.

She stumbled backward, pressing against her leg, then crumpled to the ground.

I snatched up a jar of acid. My uncle's assailant had pushed him against the wall, and I threw the jar as hard as I could.

It struck the Da Via in the back and shattered, the acid spraying over him and the carpet below. It hissed, eating into his leathers. He began to scream, sharp, panicked cries as he tried to rip off his leathers.

Marcello stabbed him in the throat, and his cries faded into wet burbles and moans.

Les finished off his assailant with a slash from his cutter, and we paused as Marcello caught his breath.

Les stared down at the dead Da Via with the acid-pocked leathers, which were smoking noiselessly. He slipped off his mangled pack. "Someday we should make some acid bombs."

I couldn't disagree with that suggestion.

We headed down the hall quickly. When we finally reached Matteo's bedroom, we slid inside, closing the door behind us.

Footsteps thundered outside the hall. More Da Vias. We were out of time.

"What are we doing?" Marcello coughed loudly.

I rushed to the nursery door, just off the bedroom. "Retrieving the rest of our family."

Marcello looked down at Matteo, dead on the ground. "Who is this? He has the appearance of a Saldana."

I opened the nursery door. "He's my brother."

"You killed your brother?"

"No," Les answered. "I did."

The nursery was just as dark as I'd left it. Emile lay on his bed, blinking with sleepy eyes, knife in hand.

I scurried over to him. "Time to go."

"Who is that?" Marcello asked.

"Emile Saldana," Les said. "Rafeo's son."

I pushed Emile toward Marcello and Les. Then I strode to the crib where Allegra slept. I gathered her into my arms, taking a blanket as well.

"Lea, what are you doing?" Les asked.

"We're taking her."

"Why?"

"Because she has Saldana blood in her too. She's family."

I handed her to Les, who held her still as she woke and began to fidget. I twisted the blanket around my leathers, tying it in the front as I'd seen Silva, our nursemaid, do when Emile was younger. I took Allegra from Les, and she cried until I tucked her into the blanket sling across my chest.

"You're going to fight in that?" Marcello pointed at me. "With an infant strapped across your chest?"

"If I have to." I grabbed Emile's hand in my left, leaving my right hand free for my stiletto. "Let's go."

In Matteo's bedroom, Les opened the door and peeked into the hallway. He opened it fully and gestured for us to follow him.

The hallway was deserted. I said a silent blessing of thanks to Safraella. Les scooped Emile up as we hurried down the hall, watching for more Da Vias.

One more corner. Then it was straight across the great room to the door and freedom.

We rushed into the great room and stopped.

In front of us stood more than twenty Da Vias, armed and waiting for us. In the center stood a women in her sixties.

Beside her stood Val.

I tucked Emile behind the three of us. The Da Vias blocked the exit from the house. We'd have to get through them to escape, but it didn't matter how good a clipper Marcello was, or how much divine energy coursed through Les and me, we couldn't handle so many Da Vias. Time for my backup plan.

"Marcello," the woman in the center said. She had a rich voice and gray hair that tumbled in waves around her shoulders. She wore no mask. Estella Da Via. "So quick to leave our hospitality, husband of mine."

He lifted his sword. "I've had better hospitality from sewer rats. And I see the years haven't been kind to you, Estella."

She glared at him, and a few of the Da Vias shifted in response.

"Let us pass," I said. "And no more of your blood need be spilled."

A few of the Da Vias laughed, but some of them looked to Estella.

"Lea?" Val asked, shocked. In the group of clippers, Blood Spatter and Grape Leaves turned to each other. Claudia, without her mask, pushed her way from the rear to stand beside Val.

"Val," I responded.

"I saw you die." He looked to Claudia and then to me. "How are you here? How did you survive?"

"These are secrets you would know if you hadn't turned your back on your god."

None of them laughed this time. Most of them shifted uncomfortably or glanced to Estella.

"Was it easy?" I asked. "Forsaking Her, who had given you so much?"

"So much?" Estella sneered. "So little, you mean. No children. Disrespected by the Saldanas and the Maiettas. Shamed among the Families. These are not gifts She gave us."

"Gave *you*, you mean," Marcello interrupted. "How much arrogance did it take to use your personal shame to convince your Family to turn away from Safraella?"

"Do you so quickly forget about Terzo's death? How you murdered him? My brother was loved."

"*You* murdered Terzo," Marcello countered. "You brought about his death when you set him upon Savio. *You* and your damned pride are to blame!"

She flicked her wrist, dismissing his words. "Savio was nothing. Terzo said he begged for mercy, like a common man."

Marcello moved to stride forward and only Les's arm blocking him held him in place. "And so instead you kill Dante and Bianca? Their children? All for what? To prove your point? To prove that your anger has festered inside you until it's all that's left?"

She shrugged. "A secondary benefit. But it was Dante's influence on the king that put my plan into motion."

"Marking your kills," I said. She faced me. "That's what this was about? You were afraid the king would make you mark your kills?"

"The Da Vias helped put Costanzo Sapienza on the throne, and this is how he repays us? Forcing us to spend our gold on the dead?"

"Oh, of course," I scoffed. "It must be extra hard, giving a coin to Safraella when you'd turned your back on Her! You killed my Family to keep your little secret safe, to keep it hidden that you'd turned to Daedara and were clipping people falsely. What about all those people who paid you? What about all those people who found the bodies of their friends and families at the cleaners and at least could take comfort that you had delivered them into Safraella's arms?"

"What about them?"

"All those people made angry ghosts." I shook my head. "Because one woman was spurned by a man she never even loved."

Behind the Da Vias, a flash of white appeared, then vanished. Les and Marcello shifted beside me. They'd seen it too.

Allegra stirred in her sling and whimpered.

Claudia pushed aside her brother and pointed at me. "Is that my daughter?"

I looked at Allegra, and she calmed. "No. She's a Saldana now."

Val grabbed Claudia's wrist as she rushed at me, holding her back. She swung her hand at Val, trying to strike him across the face. He ducked his head aside.

Another white flash appeared behind them. Closer this time. Then another.

"Claudia, don't," Val said. "She's been resurrected by a god."

"I don't care! She has my daughter!"

"I don't care either," said Estella. "Kill them. Kill all three of them."

The Da Vias moved toward us.

"You should care!" I yelled. They paused.

"And why is that, Oleander Saldana?" Estella snapped.

"The city wall outside your house is crumbled," I said.

"The entire city is surrounded by crumbling walls."

"But you've forsaken Safraella, which means you've given up Her protection. She's revoked it from your house."

Behind them, more flashes of light appeared, and a few of the Da Vias finally noticed them.

"And I brought the angry dead with us."

One of the Da Vias shouted. She shoved past her Family, trying to escape. More of them turned to see what had frightened her, and then the room filled with screams as they tried to run from the angry ghosts that poured their way inside the house, coming from the courtyard that led to the dead plains.

The Da Vias had turned from Safraella, and now She'd turned from them.

The ghosts, close to forty of them, screamed louder than the Da Vias as they chased after the living. Some of the Da Vias, in their mad fright, fought back, swinging their swords or daggers at the apparitions. The ghosts latched onto their flesh and peeled their souls from their bodies.

Chaos. Chaos everywhere. A ghost came too close to Les and was repelled. It crashed into a Da Via who'd almost made it out of the great room. Marcello snatched up Emile, then stayed as close to Les as he could. Cries bounced off the marble columns. Ghosts shrieked. Da Vias died.

Val, Claudia, and Estella stood together in the center of the room, trapped by the pandemonium surrounding them.

"Lea!" Val shouted, panic in his eyes as he dodged a ghost. "Help me!"

A ghost rushed at me but met Safraella's barrier. It recoiled, crashing into Estella. It knocked her soul completely out of her body. A ghostly version of the head of the Da Via Family floated in shock. Her body flopped about as the ghost tried to gain control of it.

Claudia shrieked. She and Val stumbled away as Estella's ghost tried to fight for ownership of her flesh.

"Just run!" I shouted at Val.

He glanced at me, then back at Estella. He grabbed Claudia's hand and took off, dragging her behind him.

I didn't wait to see if he made it out of the room. We walked toward the exit, the surviving Da Vias too busy trying to remain alive to pay us any mind.

Estella's body reared up as we passed. I placed my hand on its neck, ejecting the ghost from her body.

Estella tried to climb back into her body, but there were other ghosts willing to fight her for it. We continued on our way, out of the great hall, down the stairs and outside. A ghost tried to follow us, but Safraella's protection remained over the rest of the city. She had removed it only from the Da Vias' home.

Many of the Da Vias had been ripped from their bodies. Some would vanish, to meet Safraella and face Her judgment, but others might become angry ghosts, as Lefevre had.

It didn't really matter. I'd done what Safraella had asked of me. And I'd done what I knew in my heart was right. I'd saved Marcello and Emile and Allegra. I'd saved my family this time.

The ghosts could take the rest.

forty-three

†

I SLID OPEN THE SECRET ALCOVE AND STARED AT THE candles hidden inside. The candle with the black ribbon still stood tall. I picked it up. He'd left the Saldana candle among the others.

I lit the wick and slid the alcove shut before taking a seat. I didn't have to wait long.

The king walked into the room and sat across from me. I slipped off my mask and set it on the desk, rubbing my face.

"Are they all dead?" he asked, his voice emotionless.

"No. Surely some escaped. But Estella is. Perhaps a new head will steer them straight."

He blinked and took a deep breath. "I was told . . . Well. I was told a lot of things about what happened last night and I'm not sure which, if any, are true."

"What would you like to know?"

He picked up my mask, turning it in his hand. "You have a new mask."

"It was a gift from Her."

"And you truly used ghosts as weapons?"

I shrugged. "It wasn't as easy as all that."

He handed the mask back to me, and I placed it on the top of my head.

"How did the ghosts even get in? Surely my protection—"

"Was revoked from the Da Vias by Safraella. They were taking coin falsely from the people of Ravenna. She removed any protection on their home. The crumbled walls allowed the ghosts inside their house. You needn't worry about the rest of the country. Your protection will remain as long as your faith is strong, but I would make sure the people know not to use the Da Vias' services until they have once again proven themselves worthy of Her. The people of Ravenna can trust the Caffarellis. Or the Maiettas, if they must."

He nodded. I'd been so angry when he'd refused to help me. But he was the head of a Family too, the entire kingdom, and sometimes we had to give up what we wanted for the greater good of those we were responsible for.

Maybe it had taken me too long to realize this.

"You'll rebuild your home, then?" he asked. "Try to earn back your rank?"

I shook my head. "No. We won't be staying. There's no place for us here. Not now. Maybe never again."

He shifted in his seat before leaning forward. "Don't you think it would be best if you stayed in Lovero?"

"I'm the head of the Family now. I decide what's best." I stood.

"For what it's worth, Lea, I'm sorry. That it came to this."

"Me too," I said. "Me too."

I left the king in his secret room. Whether he kept the black candle in the alcove or removed it was up to him.

I didn't look back.

⸻

The sun had risen by the time I rode Butters back to Lilyan. I pulled off my mask and tied it to my belt. The last time I'd felt Loveran sun on my face had been after the fire. It was nice to feel it now, with my heart lighter.

I made my way to the inn where Les and Marcello were waiting for me with their horses.

Outside, a figure stood on a roof, his face covered by a mask of purple flames. He raised his hand. I nodded and he vanished.

"Friend of yours?" Marcello pulled himself into the saddle of the horse we'd found for him. Les lifted Emile to sit in front of my uncle.

I took Allegra from Les, tying her sling around my chest. "So it seems."

"Well." Les nudged his horse beside me. "Where to, then?"

"Yvain," I said. "At least for now. From there? Wherever we want. A traveler boy once told me that not everyone is lucky enough to get a fresh start."

"Ah." Les smiled. "And was this traveler boy dangerously handsome?"

"Definitely."

"And quick on his feet?"

"Not just his feet." I leaned closer to him.

"Maybe I should be jealous." Les reached for me, drawing me in for a kiss.

Allegra stirred in her sling, then opened her eyes and watched us. Les pulled away. "Was it worth it?" he asked.

"What?"

"Your family. Was it worth it?"

"Dying for?"

He nodded.

My family had been murdered, and it had been partially my fault. They'd left me alone to avenge them, to do right by them and by our Family. They could never be replaced.

But here I was, surrounded by a new family. The children of my brothers. An uncle who often seemed to despise me as much as care for me, and a fake clipper I'd found on the foreign streets of Yvain. But these descriptions didn't encompass who they were, what they'd come to mean to me. Emile had clutched that knife in his hands because he trusted me to take care of him. My uncle had rescued an orphaned boy from the streets before the ghosts could find him. And Les . . . Les had given me a reason to live again, in more than one way.

Trusting the wrong people had gotten my family killed. But trusting the right people had returned it to me again. Jewelry and dresses and feathered masks were beautiful things, but so were good food and sleep, family and friends, love and letting go. I would never again have the family

419

I'd lost, or the beautiful things that were taken from me. But maybe I could start again with this new family and see where it would lead. Maybe Les had been right. Maybe Family wasn't stronger than family. And maybe family was what we made of it.

Was that worth dying for?

"Yes," I answered. "A thousand times yes."

Les laughed, and I joined in. Marcello scowled at us as we made our way north.

Acknowledgments

And here we are with an actual, real book in hand. Ta-da! (Imagine some jazz hands here. Really good ones.)

But, as usual, there was no way this book would have happened on its own. I mean, obviously it had to be written, but I would have never gotten here without the help of some amazing and wonderful people. So begins the list of awesome.

Thanks to my agent, Mollie Glick, who did a fantastic job getting this book, and me, where I belonged. To my editor, Alexandra Cooper, who knew exactly how to make the story stronger without freaking me out, and Alyssa Miele and the rest of the wonderful team at HarperTeen. You are all amazing and it's a privilege working with you.

There were quite a few people who read previous drafts and helped shape the early stages of this book. Lola Sharp, Summer Poole, Brandon Stenger, Marieke Nijkamp, Matthew MacNish, and Tricia Conway, thank you for taking the time to read my pages. I owe you forever.

And thanks to cheerleaders Kristin Rae, Rena Rocford, Jennifer Kirkeby, Molly Beth Griffin, Megan Atwood, and my wonderful friends from the QueryTracker Forum. Most of you I've never met in real life and I hope we can rectify that one day.

To my UMWADS writing group: Hannah Oman, Austin Gorton, and Ryan Spires. Years of beer, bar food, and fake titles and look what happened. Who would have guessed?

High fives and hugs to the amazing faculty, students, and staff at Hamline University's MFA in Writing for Children and Young Adults. It was one of the best decisions in my life to apply and meet all you lovely writers. A special shout-out to my advisors Anne Ursu and Laura Ruby, who said the most wonderful things about my writing while telling me I needed to rewrite my essays. And especially to my classmates in The Front Row: Jessica Mattson, Brita Sandstrom, Josh Hammond, Zack Wilson, Jennifer Coates, Kate St. Vincent Vogl, Anna Dielschneider, and Gary Mansergh. I'm sincerely blessed to have met you. I can't wait to be friends for the rest of our lives.

Last, but never least, is my wonderful family. My parents, Joe and Sandy Ahiers, and my siblings, Anne Ahiers, Patrick Ahiers, and Cassie Ahiers. For never doubting, and for all the support and excitement. And, you know, the love.

31901059193096